Miss Mary Investigates
Book Two

Death in Highbury

An Emma Mystery

RIANA EVERLY

MISS MARY INVESTIGATES BOOK 2

DEATH IN HIGHBURY: AN EMMA MYSTERY

Copyright © *2021 Riana Everly*

All rights reserved.

Published by **Bay Crest Press 2021**

Toronto, Ontario, Canada

No parts of this publication may be reproduced, stored in a retrieval system, or transmitted in any form or by any means, electronic, mechanical, photocopying, recording, or otherwise, without the prior written permission of the copyright owner.

This book is sold subject to the condition that it shall not, by way of trade or otherwise, be lent, resold, hired out, or otherwise circulated without the publisher's prior consent in any form of binding or cover other than that in which it is published and without a similar condition including this condition being imposed on the subsequent purchaser. Under no circumstances may any part of this book be photocopied for resale.

This is a work of fiction. Any similarity between the characters and situations within its pages and places or persons, living or dead, is unintentional and co-incidental

Cover design by Mae Phillips at <u>coverfreshdesigns.com</u>

ISBN-13: 978-1-7771504-6-4

Dedication

For my husband, who promises he isn't bored when I start nattering about what Alexander and Mary did next.

Contents

Acknowledgements

There are always so many people to thank, because every book is really a community effort. The words might be mine, but they only came into existence because of the time, effort, and dedication of so many other people.
I wish to thank Mikael Swayze, who listened and suggested and guided and edited; my beta readers and ARC readers, especially Donna K and Laura M; also Maria A, Jo G, and Lori S for your comments and insight; and to my children who put up with yet another couple of months of their mother obsessing about people who don't exist when I should have been making them cookies and reading their essays.
Thanks also to Hadassah Swayze for her work on the silhouettes, and, as always, to Mae Phillips for her beautiful cover art. They say not to judge a book by its cover, but having something eye-catching and beautiful on the front never hurts, does it?
Cover design by Mae Phillips at coverfreshdesigns.com

Chapter One

An Unexpected Delay

Monday, May 11, 1812

This was most definitely not how the journey had been planned.

Mary Bennet let out a shattered breath as she stared once more at the letter that had fallen onto her lap. What was written within could not be true! Surely it was false! But she knew the writer. He would not lie. She read the letter again and took a deep breath as she strove to regain her equanimity.

"Miss?" A timid voice sounded from the doorway. "Would you like more tea, Miss? There is hot stew and bread as well, or biscuits whilst you wait."

"Tea and biscuits, thank you." Her voice sounded as ragged as her thoughts, but the young maid paid it no mind. She dropped a quick curtsey and dashed out of Mary's sight, presumably in the direction of the kitchens.

Tea would be good. It was normal, ordinary even, on this day when nothing was ordinary. Mary took another look around the room, as details she had previously missed made themselves known to her. The blue curtains, the worn wooden floor, the white cloth upon the table, the little jars and vases that sat upon the mantel. It was a somewhat tired but not unacceptable private salon in a village inn, almost certainly the best such place within miles. Similarly, the young maid had been polite and efficient, and the tea hot and strong. It was exactly the sort of place he would have selected for her to wait. If only he had known, when he made the arrangement, how long that wait might be!

As she waited for the maid to return with her tea, her mind drifted to the events that had led her here, to this inn in a small village in Surrey, alone but for her maid and with no thought as to when she might return home.

The events had all begun, she supposed, when Colonel Forster of the —shire militia had announced that the entire regiment would be removing to Brighton for the summer. It was hardly a wonder, Mary supposed, after the shocking events of last autumn, but the unit would be missed by many in Meryton. The shopkeepers and tavern owners would miss the custom of the officers and men, and the young ladies of the town would miss the sight of so many smartly dressed young men in their scarlet coats and tall hats. For the autumn and winter, there had at last been enough men present to equal the number of ladies at the town assemblies, and many an evening at cards or musical events had been enlivened by some of the officers.

Colonel Forster himself was a garrulous and friendly man when not on duty, and the young wife he had introduced to Meryton's society was even more so. What basis there had been for a friendship between Harriet Forster and Lydia, Mary would never know, for the former was a married lady of three and twenty, and the latter not quite sixteen and scarcely out of the schoolroom, but both were full of high spirits and rather silly. This, it appeared, was sufficient for the colonel's wife to request that Lydia accompany her to Brighton as her special friend.

Papa had agreed almost without a thought, and somehow it was decided that Mary would accompany the party to Brighton and remain for a week with her sister and Mrs. Forster before returning alone to Hertfordshire.

This was where Mr. Darcy's role in the events had begun.

He and her sister Elizabeth had been returning to London from their estate in Derbyshire and had broken their journey for some few days at Longbourn, the Bennets' estate. Lizzy was as radiant as any bride, having been married only a few short months, and Mr. Darcy was much improved in manner. He was as formal as ever he had been, but there was an ease in his movements and lilt in his voice that had not been present when first they had met, and he had become very pleasant company. That he had all but saved Lizzy's life last autumn was yet one more point in his favour. She could not have asked for a better brother.

Thus it was that after dinner on that day that the Darcys arrived, when Lydia had announced her invitation from Harriet Forster and Papa had acquiesced to squeals of glee from Mama and wails of woe and anger from Kitty, that Mr. Darcy had sat back in his chair and rested his chin in his hand, as he was wont to do.

"That is most interesting, Bennet!" the great man exclaimed. I have some business I wish to conduct in Surrey, part way between London and Brighton, near a small town called Highbury. There is an estate for sale in the area, and I promised to take a look at it for both Bingley," he mentioned Jane Bennet's future husband, "and my cousin, Colonel Fitzwilliam."

He turned his dark eyes to his wife and smiled a small secret smile just for her. "I had thought, at first, to ride down alone, but now I have an idea, if my wife will agree." Again he gave Lizzy his secret smile. Was that a flash of envy that Mary had felt upon seeing his face as he gazed upon his wife? What must it be like to be adored like that? She had little time to consider this, for he continued.

"If Mary will accompany Lydia on the journey to Brighton, I can assist her in returning home. Allow me to send my own carriage to meet you in Brighton, Mary. If it is acceptable, Elizabeth and I can drive down in my curricle if the weather is fine, and we can stay for some days in the area. I will then have more time to devote to examining the neighbourhood and the estate, and you and Elizabeth will be good company for each other whilst I am occupied. What think you, dearest?" He turned to his wife once more, as if seeking a reason to gaze upon her again.

"It is a splendid idea! Mary. Do you like it?"

How could she not? She had never travelled past London before, and the idea of seeing the sea was enthralling! She was nineteen years of age, more than old enough to manage the return journey in a private carriage with her maid. Furthermore, she found she longed to spend some time with her sister. She and Lizzy had always shared a sisterly love, but it was not until the events of the autumn that they had formed a bond as close as the one between Lizzy and their oldest sister, Jane.

"Yes," she replied at once. "I like it very much!"

And so the plan was formed and settled. Mary would travel with her maid from Brighton to Highbury, where she would meet her sister and new brother, and from there they would drive the additional short distance to the cottage he had planned to take for his short stay in Surrey. It was a simple and foolproof plan.

The countryside between Brighton and Highbury was beautiful, but the drive was long, and the small party took several long breaks along the way to allow the horses to rest. It was well past seven o'clock in the evening, therefore, when at last they turned from the turnpike road towards the town where they were all to meet. The sun was still up and the sky bright, but it would begin to grow dark before another hour was out, and she hoped it was not too far from the inn to the cottage.

But even as the carriage had drawn up to the inn, and as the footman had leapt from the box to announce their arrival and ask after the Darcys, Mary could see that something was amiss. A man who must have been the innkeeper rushed up to the footman and driver and conferred with them in hushed tones, after which Mary was hustled into this small but comfortable salon and presented with a pot of tea and a tray of small sandwiches and this letter. She knew the handwriting well, for Mr. Darcy had a distinctive hand. But the presence of the letter meant that the man himself, and her sister with him, were not here.

Without reading a word, she could see that something was wrong. The usually smooth and crisp handwriting was jagged and uneven, the result of hurry and distress, a portent of the dreadful matter mentioned within. She read the content, and then in shock, read it again.

Dear Sister Mary,

I must write quickly, and will dispense with pleasantries, for which you may castigate me when next we meet. All your family are well, never fear. But some dire events have occurred in London which prevent your sister and me from meeting you in Highbury as planned, and which must necessitate your remaining in that town for some amount of time.

I had considered caution in relating this to you out of concern for your sensibilities, but I know you to be a reasonable and intelligent young woman who will not swoon at the news. I will not insult you by refusing to impart it.

London is all in an uproar tonight, for only minutes ago, from the time that I write, the Right Honourable Spencer Perceval, our Prime Minister, was shot and killed in front of Parliament. I was in the neighbourhood when it occurred and heard the outcry but not the shot, and came right home to write to you.

I have sent Elizabeth back to Longbourn. She is not pleased with me, but her safety is paramount, and she may shout at me for all of her life should she wish. My only concern is her health and wellbeing. I will join her there as soon as I am able to conclude my affairs here, and we will remain there for several days until the City is brought back into order.

I must beg your forgiveness, Mary, for abandoning you in this way, and must entreat you not to return home, nor to travel anywhere near London, until such time as it is safe once more.

I will not forsake you altogether. I know a gentleman—as fine a man as I have met, and one of the few very sensible people of my acquaintance—who lives not far from Highbury. I have already written to him to request his assistance in providing for your security and comfort whilst we all await a return to order in our country. His name is George Knightley, of Donwell Abbey, and he will see you right.

I will send this message off at once with a fast rider, along with sufficient funds to see to your immediate comfort at the Crown Inn upon your arrival. (That explained the private salon and the tea and food.) Enclosed please find five pounds for any further needs you might incur, with a promise for more should it be required.

Your affectionate brother,
FD

The room seemed not quite in focus; the shock of the news and the surprise at being suddenly so completely alone and so far from home were making themselves known on her nerves, and for a moment, Mary dreaded becoming like her mother. Perhaps she ought to ask for some smelling salts. This was all rather troubling!

She was reading the letter for the third time, hoping it would impart different news on a subsequent perusal, when a tap at the door signalled the return of the maid. She carried with her a tray that held another pot of tea and a rather large plate of biscuits, which she set down on the table in the centre of the room.

"If you please, Miss, a gentleman is here to see you, asking after Miss Mary Bennet. May I show him in? It's Mr. Knightley, Miss. I knows him well, we all do in the town. I will sit with you."

He was here already? Mr. Darcy's messenger was very efficient! "Yes, yes, of course." She raised a hand to her hair to ensure it retained something of its morning style and straightened her skirts and fichu. Almost at once an unknown man strode into the room and made his bow. His appearance was of some surprise to Mary, for she had expected a different sort of man. This gentleman must be nearer to forty than to thirty, and his clothing was sensible country attire rather than the elegant garb worn by the dandies in Town. He seemed to be of average height, and whilst his brown hair held no trace of grey, light wrinkles were beginning to adorn the corners of his mild brown eyes. He was not so much handsome as appealing in looks, and he carried with him the impression of a sensible, intelligent, and decent sort of a man, and Mary liked him at once.

She rose to curtsey and waited as he introduced himself. "Forgive the impertinence, Miss Bennet. We must assume our mutual friend Darcy to have performed the honours through his missives. I normally would not presume, but these are strange times." His voice swam through the fog in her mind and she forced herself to focus upon him.

He seemed a straightforward person, not one to speak in circles around a topic, or to pad his meaning with extraneous verbiage as some dandies padded their thin legs and shoulders to better fit their clothing. She was a lady of simple meaning herself and appreciated his forthright manner.

"Yes, of course," she returned. Her voice sounded more normal in her ears now. "Please, I have a pot of tea, only now arrived. May I pour you a cup?" There was a second cup on the tray; the maid must have added it when Mr. Knightley asked after her.

He accepted the hot tea and asked briefly after her journey and general health before turning to matters of business. "I understand that the terrible events in London today will require you to stay with us for some time. I have taken the liberty of securing an invitation for you to stay with a friend of mine. He is a solid chap, leading family in town and all, and he has a daughter of about your own years. Emma Woodhouse is her name, and I hope you will become friends. Will that be satisfactory?"

Still half in a daze, Mary accepted. "Thank you indeed, sir. That would be most kind." She could not, after all, stay in the inn alone, even with her maid to accompany her. Although the Bennets were hardly of the circles that fed the daily gossip sheets, such an impropriety would nevertheless soon be known far and wide. It was much better to be the guest of a young woman of good standing.

Mr. Knightley proved as good as his word, and within half an hour, he stood with Mary at the front door to Hartfield, a large and elegant house just outside of the town. Miss Woodhouse herself answered the door and ushered the two inside.

"Oh, Miss Bennet! You poor dear! What an ordeal you have suffered. Come in, come in. Mr. Knightley, how kind of you to bring Miss Bennet to us. Of course we have a room for you. Do you prefer pink or pale green? The pink room is larger, but the green has a nicer view of the gardens. I would take the green, but I shall leave it to you. Come in. Have you dined? It is eight o'clock, so you must be hungry. I shall call cook for a tray; there is always something ready at Hartfield, for just such occasions. We are expecting company momentarily, and you are so welcome to join us and meet some of our society, unless you would rather rest. But really, I believe some cheerful conversation would do you good after all you have endured. My friends will be only too happy to meet you. Do come and join us at tea and cards, Miss Bennet, I implore you!"

The deluge of words was too forceful to deny, and once more, Mary found herself accepting. Despite not waiting to hear Mary's thoughts on the matter, Miss Woodhouse was correct: an evening of company would be better for her spirits than fretting alone in her room. It was part of her nature to dwell on matters too seriously, and with the unsettled thoughts brought about by Mr. Darcy's news, and her sudden predicament of being alone in a strange town, she knew her mind would turn her troubles into something far greater if left alone.

Within moments, Miss Woodhouse called to a footman to have Mary's trunks brought to her room, and then led Mary up the elegant staircase that graced the centre of the large entrance. As they walked, Miss Woodhouse a few steps ahead of her, Mary had an opportunity to observe her hostess.

Emma Woodhouse was, indeed, about her own age, perhaps a year or two older, and very pretty, with an open face and sparkling light eyes that seemed to promise mischief. She had an elegant sort of figure and an upright carriage, and Mary believed she thought rather well of herself.

Of course, Mary mused, if she were pretty and rich and the centre of everybody's attention, she might think rather well of herself too. But this had never been her lot. Instead, she was the plainest of five sisters, and the right in the middle in terms of age. She had enjoyed neither the adoration due to the precocious and witty older sisters, Jane and Lizzy, nor the doting poured upon the younger and more spirited two, Kitty and Lydia, and instead was mostly ignored by everybody around her. Perhaps it suited her nature to be so easily forgotten, for she always felt awkward when everybody's eyes were upon her. Mama pressed her constantly to exhibit her meagre skills upon the pianoforte, but whatever talent she felt she might possess always fell victim to the discomfort of performing for strangers.

No, she was far better suited for quiet contemplation and the company of one or two good friends of excellent understanding and depth of character. People like Lizzy or Mr. Darcy or that annoying man from London whom she had vowed to think on no more. No more! She had better attend to Miss Woodhouse, who was talking once more about the house and the tray of food and the company to whom Mary would soon be introduced.

Hartfield boasted an excellent staff, for the tray of hot beef pie and roasted potatoes was already waiting in the sitting room off the bedroom she had been offered. Miss Woodhouse quickly showed her the room, which was not large but very beautiful, in delicate shades of green and eggshell white, with pale yellow ornaments and decoration all done most tastefully. The wide canopied bed promised a comfortable sleep, and soft yellow draperies hung over the window that was said to enjoy so lovely a vista.

What caught Mary's attention, however, was the gown that had been laid out on the bed.

"When Mr. Knightley came earlier to explain your situation, I took the prerogative of setting out something for you, should you wish to change. We are not a particularly elegant party and your current gown will suit well, but I thought you might wish to refresh yourself."

"Yes, thank you." Mary picked up the dress. It was a pale blue, not her best colour, but it looked like it might fit her nicely.

"It is the most easy of my frocks to adapt to different figures," Miss Woodhouse explained, "owing to the lacing at each side. I did not know your size and thought this the most likely to fit. If I have overstepped, please excuse me." But her face and bearing suggested she had no real such concerns. Miss Emma Woodhouse seemed very much a young woman who enjoyed taking charge of people and situations, albeit with a happy and benevolent heart.

Too tired and overcome by the day to refuse, Mary thanked her for her kindness and sat down to enjoy her tray of food before venturing to the salon to brave the members of local society. The food was simple and excellent, and no sooner had she finished her meal when Alice, her maid, slipped in through a door in the sitting room to help her mistress dress.

The servants, Alice reported, were kind and helpful, and she had been offered as comfortable a bed to sleep in as she had enjoyed anywhere. If they had to be stranded anywhere, Highbury seemed almost ideal. Perhaps, after the turmoil of last autumn and the ceaseless roiling of her mind in the aftermath, and after the exciting but exhausting week with Lydia at Brighton, a few days of peace would be what she needed. Mama would not be calling on her every five minutes to do some task that Jane or Lizzy had been accustomed to performing; Kitty would not be pestering her constantly for help with her bonnets or embroidery, and Lydia would not be nagging her to cease her practice at the pianoforte. Perhaps there would be sufficient pleasant diversion that she could succeed in spending a day without thinking of... A man of no importance.

Alice helped her dress and redid her hair and then called for a footman to show Mary the way to the salon where the company were gathered for their pleasant evening of cards and friendship. Yes, this would be a most welcome respite indeed.

The tall footman bowed smartly and led her down the grand staircase again and then through a maze of hallways to a wide doorway that stood just ajar. He pushed the door open and took a breath to announce her, but before he could speak, a voice ran through the quiet conversation of the room.

"What? Can it be true? Yet another man has died?"

Chapter Two

A Friendly Welcome

Mary was both horrified and enthralled by these words. That somebody other than the poor Prime Minister had died was a sad matter. That this seemed to be one of several deaths was shocking. And yet Mary could not deny the thrill she had felt those several months past when she helped uncover the evidence to prove her sister innocent of a terrible crime. The accumulation of information, and the sifting through and examination of that information had been most stimulating. Despite the gravity of the situation, she would never forget the deep satisfaction of those discussions with ... that annoying man whom she had vowed to forget! And yet he, too, had played his vital role in saving her sister. No matter that he had offered his friendship and then withdrawn it. She would not cast all of her wrath upon him; only most of it.

"Come, Miss Bennet, you must meet our friends!" Emma Woodhouse was immediately at Mary's elbow, pulling her into the room. Her resolution not to think of *him* was to be reinforced by Miss Woodhouse's enthusiasm, so it seemed. Mary let out a sigh of resignation and prepared to be presented to all of Highbury's society, like some new exhibit at an exhibition.

"Of course you already know Mr. Knightley," her hostess explained as she steered Mary to two men sitting near the fire. The cosy room was warm from the candles and the several people who sat around in various configurations, but the hearth was ablaze, and a screen had been set up to direct the warmth and prevent a breeze. Mr. Knightley, her rescuer from earlier, rose from one chair.

"Miss Bennet, I am delighted you decided to join us. You are looking very well this evening." His bow was everything proper, but Mary noticed his eyes darted towards her companion as much as towards herself. How interesting! The gentleman must be fifteen years Miss Woodhouse's senior, if not more, but the heart knows no age, it seemed. Miss Woodhouse seemed quite unaware of the gentleman's attentions; indeed, he seemed unaware as well. It would be best, naturally, to remain quite silent on the matter!

The other man was much older still; he glanced up but remained seated. "Father, please meet our guest for the next several days, Miss Mary Bennet." There was a gentleness in Emma's voice that Mary had not heard before, and she was startled by this unaffected display of filial love and compassion. From her admittedly short acquaintance with the young lady, her impression was of a woman who placed herself at the centre of her world, doling out kindness and good deeds only as they reflected well upon herself.

That was unfair! Mary chided herself. She had made such rash determinations of people's characters before, only to be proven wrong, and she had thought herself warned against making such mistakes again. She must be more careful with her impressions in the future. Such prejudice was not kind, not what a good Christian woman ought to harbour in her heart.

For now, she turned her attention to Mr. Woodhouse. Although Emma was about her own age, the lady's father looked far older than her own Papa, almost as old as Grandmama who lived in London. His hair was all grey and his shoulders sloped from a frame that looked as if it had never been particularly hearty. Mary wondered if he were an invalid, and her eyes darted around in search of a Bath chair before she recalled herself to her host.

"A pleasure to have you as our guest, Miss Bennet." His voice was stronger than his looks suggested. He struggled to his feet but stood steadily once upright. "Forgive me, these old bones, don't you know." He dipped his head in lieu of a bow and settled himself once more upon his chair close to the fire. "Has Emma called for a meal for you? I do hope it was nothing too rich, for rich foods are not good after a trying day. I fear you will not sleep well. A bowl of nourishing gruel is better. Emma, dear, call Cook and insist that she send up some gruel for Miss Bennet. Is the fire laid in your room? It would not do to become chilled. There is a draught at the window—oh, she is in the green room? Better, for there is less of a draught there, but do take care to draw the curtains about the bed when you sleep, for the cold air will disturb your humours."

"Yes, Papa, Miss Bennet is very well settled in her room. I shall ensure she is comfortable before retiring for the night." Emma placed a gentle kiss upon the old man's forehead.

Additional pleasantries were exchanged, during which Mary received yet more advice about her health, before Emma took her by the elbow once more to introduce her to the other guests. This was a small party with only half a dozen or so guests, not including herself and Mr. Knightley, who looked as if he belonged in the room just as surely as the old-fashioned furniture or the heavy brocade draperies that hung over the (most certainly closed) windows.

A smart looking couple sat on a small sofa, talking in earnest with two ladies, one elderly and one of middle years.

Emma introduced the couple as Mr. and Mrs. Weston, who lived in Randalls, the house a half mile down the lane from Hartfield, and which Mary had noticed on the drive. Mr. Weston looked to be in his middle forties, his wife ten or more years younger, and clearly expecting a blessed event in two or three months. Emma's introduction explained their relationship. "Mrs. Weston was my governess, and as dear to me as a mother, until she married good Mr. Weston only last year! We were so pleased to have her remain in the neighbourhood, for I do not know what I would do without her!" The lady smiled kindly at her former charge and greeted Mary with sensible words and very pretty manners.

The two ladies sitting across from the Westons were introduced as Mrs. and Miss Bates. Mrs. Bates looked quite old and peered at Mary through thick spectacles, assessing her thoroughly but saying not a word. Her daughter, Miss Bates, made up for her mother's silence.

"Miss Bennet? A pleasure to meet you. Bennet, you say? I knew a family named Bennet once, back when Jane was young. Jane is my niece, sitting there by the pianoforte. Her mother was my sister, God rest her soul. She met a girl—Jane, that is, not my sister— whose family took Randalls before Mr. Weston bought it, and their name was Bennet, only now I think perhaps it was not Bennet after all, but something similar, like Barnett, or Benning or maybe Barrett, but the little girl and Jane became such good friends, and Miss Woodhouse too—do you remember them, Miss Woodhouse? No, I suppose you do not for that was the summer that Miss

Isabella—that is Mrs. Knightley now, for she married our Mr. Knightley's brother—was back at Hartfield with her baby and you spent the entire summer helping her with the child and had not time to enjoy with Jane and Miss Bennet, or was it Barnett? This is Miss Bennet, Mother," Miss Bates now shouted into the ear of the old lady beside her. "Bennet, like that family who took Randalls before Mr. Weston. Or was it Barnett? Do you remember, Mother?"

Mary considered Miss Bates as she continued her reminiscences of the Bennets—or was it Barnetts? —who had spent that summer here some years before. Miss Bates looked to be about seven or eight and forty, only a few years older than her own mother. But where Mama was pretty and animated in manner and of a pleasing plumpness and youthful expression, Miss Bates was very thin and plain, her movements more than her face adding unwelcome years to her appearance. Like the old lady at her side, Miss Bates was dressed in clothing that was clearly of good quality and fine fabric, but which was several years behind the fashion and somewhat worn at the seams and hems. The shawl that covered Mrs. Bates' shoulders looked to be Kashmiri and of a very beautiful pattern, but the ends were fraying and the colours of the weave fading here and there. Similarly, Miss Bates' hair held a simple style that would require no maid's assistance to do up every morning.

And yet, along with these signs of genteel poverty, the Bateses were clearly intimates of the first family in Highbury and were fully accepted as being of the finest society in the neighbourhood. They must, Mary reflected sadly, have once been quite grand, although now reduced in circumstances. This could have been her own lot, had Lizzy not married Mr. Darcy! She banished all thoughts of the entail upon Longbourn and her mother's constant moans of being banished to the hedgerows and returned her focus to Miss Bates and her tale.

Of greater interest to her than the matter of the recital, however, was that she recognised Miss Bates' voice. This was the lady who had commented, as Mary had followed the footman into the salon, that yet another man had died! Although she insisted to herself that she had little desire to embroil herself in another mystery, she must know more. Perhaps she would ask Miss Bates later, should she have time to speak further with the woman later on. She hoped the lady would be kind enough to answer her questions.

"…the summer that Jane went to live with Colonel and Mrs. Campbell—they were ever so kind to dear Jane, quite as generous as Miss Woodhouse here—but when she returned to visit her dear grandmama and poor aunt—that is me, Miss Bennet—they always sent some welcome token. But now Miss Campbell is wed and gone to Ireland, and Jane is returned to us. But come, Miss Bennet, you must meet my niece. Ma'am," she shouted again into Mrs. Bates' ear, "I said that Miss Bennet must meet Jane. Jane, Mother. Miss Bennet must meet Jane."

The old lady blinked but said nothing.

"Yes, indeed, Miss Bennet!" Emma seemed quite keen to escape Miss Bates' monologue, "Please let me introduce you to our other guests." She took her leave of the foursome and hustled Mary across to the pianoforte where a very elegant young lady sat at the keyboard, not playing but talking to a smart young man who stood sorting through a pile of music.

"Here, perhaps this one, Miss Fairfax," he spoke rather loudly as Mary and Emma approached, and handed the lady a selection he had pulled from the stack.

The lady herself blushed and took it to set upon the stand before turning her gaze to Mary. Emma made the introductions once more. Jane Fairfax was quite lovely in a very different way to Emma Woodhouse. Her beauty was of the classic and refined variety, where Emma's was broad and extravagant; and where Emma's eyes sparkled with ideas and emotions only just suppressed, Miss Fairfax's betrayed nothing.

"It is a pleasure to make your acquaintance, Miss Bennet." Jane Fairfax's manners were as quiet and elegant as her appearance. "Are you to be in the neighbourhood for long?"

Mary explained the situation as best she could in a few short sentences. "Only until it is safe to return to London, or until my sister and her husband decide to continue with their plans to visit the area."

"I will enjoy our acquaintance, then, as short as it might be. Please feel free to call whilst you are in Highbury." There was a coolness to her manner, but it bespoke a reserved nature rather than a disinclination towards the connection, and Mary replied that she would be pleased to accept. Out of the corner of her eye, she noticed a momentary wave of irritation pass across Emma's face, and she decided she had yet another mystery to solve, namely the cause of Emma's dislike of Miss Fairfax.

Could the answer to that be the young gentleman who was standing between the ladies? He had been introduced as Frank Churchill, Mr. Weston's son. He beamed broadly at Emma and flirted most shamefully with her, but his eyes, Mary noticed, flitted towards Miss Fairfax just as Mr. Knightley's had flitted constantly towards Emma. Oh my, this was quite a mare's nest she had landed in! How fortunate that all the parties seemed amicable, if not the closest of friends, lest it turn into a tragedy of Shakespearean proportions.

"I say, Miss Bennet," Mr. Churchill beamed at her, "I do hope you have a fine frock with you, or Miss Woodhouse may give you use of one of hers, for we are to have a ball the day after tomorrow, at the Crown!" He named the inn where Mary had sat as she read her brother Darcy's letter. "Its planning has quite consumed us for some time, and I would not enjoy it at all were you not to attend!

May I request a set of dances? My first is promised already, but I beg you to accept me for the second set."

Not one to put herself forward and happy enough to watch others at the activity, Mary seldom took to the dance floor, but such was Mr. Churchill's charm and easy appeal that she found she could not refuse him. He smiled as if she were the most interesting creature he had met in a long while and oozed flattery from every pore, albeit without encouraging anything other than an acceptance to a reel or polonaise.

Perhaps, for her short stay in Highbury, Mary could adopt a new persona, that of a social creature who enjoyed all the attentions of society. What good was there in being in an unexpected situation, after all, if one could not learn something from it. "Thank you, Mr. Churchill," she tried her own smile. "I would be honoured. I shall see if my trunks contain something suitable to wear."

Emma began to talk about what gowns she might own that Mary could borrow if need be, and once more, Mary felt herself secondary in the conversation to Emma's desire to be publicly useful.

As Emma accounted for each of her suitable frocks, Mary's eyes dropped to the sheet of music that Mr. Churchill had handed to Miss Fairfax. It was a short piece by Mr. Beethoven for voice and pianoforte, beyond her abilities but lovely. "That is a beautiful song," she offered with animation. "I have begun to learn it myself, although I cannot play and sing at the same time. Indeed, I believe I should never sing in public at all, for all that I enjoy the activity."

"You play, Miss Bennet? How delightful!" There was a spark of genuine interest in Miss Fairfax's guarded eyes. "When you come to visit—and we must set an engagement—perhaps you will oblige me by joining me in a set of duets I have only now acquired. There is no one else to play them with me, and I would dearly love to hear them in their entirety. Do say you will come! I have a sweet-toned instrument," her eyes dropped to her hands and a blush stole over her cheeks, "which is wanting for performers."

This was a welcome invitation. Miss Woodhouse was, to be honest, intimidating with her extravagant friendliness and her officious manner, no matter how kindly meant. Being so much more reserved herself, Mary felt herself more drawn to this quiet and subdued young woman with her interest in music and her promise of a beautiful instrument to play.

"Thank you, I would like that." Mary curtseyed and saw Emma force a smile.

"Tomorrow morning, then? I shall inform my aunt and grandmother. We will be most delighted to welcome you."

"Yes," Emma murmured. "Delighted."

Very shortly, cards were announced, and the gathering of friends divided itself along different lines best to suit the games and tables. There were two tables of four, and Mary excused herself from the activity, claiming fatigue and an inability to devote herself to the games, and asked if she would be rude to sit upon the sofa and read. Mr. Knightley also recused himself, but stood hovering at Mrs. Bates' side, whispering into her ear at intervals to assist her with her hands. The mood in the room was one of relaxed companionship, and the conversations turned from serious matters to those pertaining to Loo or Whist.

Mary sat with the book she had borrowed, alternately reading and allowing the murmur of conversation to wash over her. She had found a seat on a low divan positioned against one wall near the fireplace. It was not quite out of sight of the other seats, but the screen that Mr. Woodhouse had set up served to isolate it somewhat from general view. It was a good place to read, with ample light and good comfort, where she would not feel she was imposing upon the familiarity of the group.

The games continued for some time until it was time to break for some tea. Once more, the pairings shifted as the company selected their chairs and sofas for the light meal. Tired and not hungry after her late dinner, Mary elected to remain on the divan with her book, and was relieved when nobody came to encourage her to another seat. As the various guests took their tea and biscuits and settled themselves to talk, it so happened that Mr. Knightley and Mr. Weston took the two chairs by the fireplace, close enough that Mary could overhear their conversation.

Ought she to speak up, to make her presence known? The men must surely know she was there. Indeed, Mr. Knightley could see her very well from his chair, and surely no topic would be raised at a friendly evening of cards that would be improper for anyone present to hear. No, speaking would only occasion unwelcome attention and would embarrass the men. Better she turn her eyes to her book and leave them to their discussion.

"Sad business about old Mr. Abdy," Mr. Weston sighed. "It was unexpected."

Mary glanced up sharply, then, aware of the dangers of expressing too much interest, returned her eyes, if not her attention, to her book. They must be talking of the man who had died, the one that Miss Bates had mentioned when first she entered the room.

"Sad business indeed." Mr. Knightley's voice was low but reached her clearly. "Do you know much about it?"

She could see Mr. Weston shake his head. "He was right as rain on Saturday and nobody saw him at church yesterday morning. When his son went to look in on him this morning, he was cold in his bed. Shocking for John, of course, and sad for the grandchildren. His grandson Peter comes to help with my horses. I had it from him."

From above the top of her book, Mary could see Mr. Knightly shake his head and take a sip from a glass that did not seem to hold tea.

"How old was he? He had been around for a while." Mr. Weston continued. "I am rather new to these parts, but you have been here your entire life. Did you know the man when he was younger?"

"That I did," Mr. Knightley replied. "Poor old John Abdy, I had a great regard for him. Always kind and a hard worker. He was ninety if he was a day. He was clerk for twenty-seven years to the vicars; both to old Mr. Bates' predecessor, whom I do not remember at all, and then to Mrs. Bates' husband himself. Bates was a good man with no head for money, for all that Abdy tried to help. Kept the church going, but could not help Bates himself. When he passed, he left his wife and daughters with nothing; that was right after the older girl, Jane's mother, married. There was nothing for Henrietta, hardly a penny for his wife to live on, save the remains of her own settlement. We've always done our best to help them, but it's a sad business."

Mr. Knightley took another sip from his not-tea and went on. "Abdy was more careful, put aside whatever he could, kept a roof over his head and food on his table, even when he grew old and became bed-ridden with the rheumatic gout in his joints..." The man stopped half-way through his thought. "Pah! Listen to me! I am sounding like an old lady myself. Fact is, Abdy will be missed, but I suppose it was just his time."

"Ninety is past the age of God's calling. To pass at that age ought not to be a shock." Mr. Weston's head shook again. "Still, it did seem unexpected."

Mary settled back into her book. This seemed little more than the passing of an old man, sad but not tragic, and certainly no cause for alarm or concern, and most especially not in light of the dreadful public murder that had happened in London only that afternoon. But Mr. Knightley's next words shook her.

"It's the third unexpected death in a month: that is what bothers me. First there was Jack Smith, the wanderer. Fire burned out of control, it seemed. Sad, but it could happen to anybody. Then old Fred Watson died when that set of shelves in his smithy crashed down on him, with all the heavy iron and anvils and implements they held. Again, terrible accident, but accidents do happen. And now Abdy, of old age. Or so it seems. Any one of the three would pass as the hand of fate, with nothing but a tear in the eyes of those who loved them to mark their passing, but all together... Frankly, Weston, I admit that I am troubled."

Chapter Three

Meeting the Townsfolk

It was not long after this conversation ended that the soiree broke up. Mr. Woodhouse rose to his feet and gave an affected yawn, saying, "Oh my, look at the time. Ten o'clock already. I must entreat my dear friends to look to your health, for a good sleep is essential to your wellbeing. Mr. Perry advises at least eight hours a night, and nine if possible. It is not too cold for everybody to return home without taking a chill."

Emma offered a bedroom to Mr. Knightley, but that gentleman insisted on seeing the Bateses safely to their apartments before walking back to Donwell Abbey. To Mary's ears, these words and expressions were all well rehearsed and repeated often, all form and expectation, rather than from any real conviction from any party.

For her part, she was quite ready to accept Mr. Woodhouse's admonition to sleep, for this morning she had awakened in Brighton, a full forty miles distant! The long journey, the horror of the assassination, and the shock at finding herself at first alone and then amongst strangers, had all taken their toll upon her, and whilst she knew she had a great deal upon which to think, for the moment her body and mind craved the oblivion of slumber.

The fire in her room had been lit, and the room was warm, but the window also stood ajar to allow fresh air into the space, and within moments of changing into her nightgown and dismissing Alice, she was asleep in the soft blankets of her bed. Strange dreams troubled her, but she did not waken until she heard the quiet sounds of the morning maid tending once more to the fire.

She opened her eyes to the bright light that streamed through the open draperies of the window. She had opened them last night in hopes of seeing the promised view, and likewise had decided against drawing the curtains around her bed, for this welcome of morning was exactly what she had wished for.

The maid muttered something unintelligible, to which Mary replied likewise, and scuttled from the room, leaving Mary alone with her thoughts and the vista. It was, as Emma had promised, beautiful. The window opened upon the back of the house, treating its occupant to views not towards the lane and the town, but rather of the open countryside beyond. The house sat atop a gentle rise of land which opened up to a wide and verdant valley, limned with neat farms and lines of hedgerows, and shaded with patches of forest with the fresh dewy greenery of spring. A field some distance away promised the glories of assorted wildflowers, and the stream that ran through the farms and fields lent the bright spangle of reflected sunlight to further decorate the scenery.

She selected a simple dress from the clothing that Alice had unpacked for her last night and put her hair up in a simple twist before descending the grand staircase in search of the breakfast room. It was eight o'clock, not at all early for her own family to rise, but she was uncertain as to Emma's habits. She hoped there might be a cup of tea and somebody to guide her to a path where she might walk before her hosts descended from their rooms.

To her surprise, when she found the room she sought, Mr. Knightley was present. He must have arrived very early, especially so after his late return to his own home last night. He sat as if he belonged in the room, sipping from a cup of coffee and reading the newspaper.

"Miss Bennet!" he stood and bowed. "I hope you slept well. I had wondered if you were an early riser. Mr. Woodhouse is up with the sun, and Emma too, to walk with him before breakfast. Mr. Perry has advised him that exercise aids the digestion, and he is always an obedient servant to the good apothecary." He gave a warm grin and rose to help Mary with her tea and eggs. "I imagine they will return at any moment. Please, make yourself comfortable."

He engaged in some pleasant conversation whilst they ate, talking generally about the house and asking how she had enjoyed the evening. "Of course, the news about the Prime Minister is all over the town today. Sad business, that, quite shocking. I would not have mentioned it to you, but of course you know about it from Darcy's letter. I have not seen him in an age, Miss Bennet. Tell me, if you will, how he is. He is one of the few sensible men in London, and I enjoy our conversations."

Mary laughed and explained that Darcy had said almost exactly those words about Mr. Knightley, and the two entered into an easy conversation. Mary expressed her belief that Mr. Darcy was very happy with her sister, and her knowledge that her sister was very happy with Mr. Darcy, and then let slip how the gentleman had been of such help to the family. Of course, Mr. Knightley asked about the affair, and Mary responded, explaining the course of events that had nearly led to Elizabeth being brought to trial for murder.

"Had Mr. Darcy not heard of it and sent in that…" she sighed and resigned herself to mentioning the man she had sworn to forget, "that investigator, I hate to imagine what might have happened." She suppressed a huff. "He was of the greatest assistance in solving the problem. I could not have managed without his information and intelligent ideas."

"What ho, Miss Bennet? It was you who solved the problem?" Mr. Knightley sat back in his chair, one foot balanced on the opposite knee and a smirk upon his face. "I find I must believe you, for you do not seem the sort of lady taken by fancy. I long to hear your tale of it."

And once more, Mary found herself explaining how she and *that man* had sifted through the various clues and chance remarks to identify the real culprit. Mr. Knightley, to his credit, did not interrupt, other to ask clarifying questions, and nodded at appropriate moments.

"What can I say, but well done, Miss Bennet! I had assumed you to be a smart sort of young lady, but even then I had underestimated you. I… Ah, I believe I hear Emma and Mr. Woodhouse returning. Morning, morning," he greeted them, and of necessity dropped the subject on which they had been speaking.

After breakfast, during which Mary's previous impressions of her hosts were confirmed, she, Miss Woodhouse, and Mr. Knightley set off for the town to pay a call upon the Bateses and Miss Fairfax, and to indulge the latter's desire to play her duets on the pianoforte. The weather was fine and the walk easy and pleasurable, and for those welcome minutes, Mary was almost able to pretend that yesterday's events had not occurred, and all was as it ought to be.

She smiled at the farmers and villagers they passed along their way and replied prettily when her companions stopped for a moment's conversation with an acquaintance and to introduce her. Although Highbury was different in appearance from Meryton, it carried the same character: a comfortable village populated by people who knew and cared about each other's welfare.

All too soon their pleasant walk was at an end and they turned onto the high street where a smart row of shops lined the neat roadway. Emma pointed out the building where the Bateses and Miss Fairfax lived. The house belonged to a family in business, and Mrs. and Miss Bates occupied the drawing-room floor. They had, for their convenience, the use of a small kitchen area on the ground floor, next to which their one maid had her own room. It was not a large residence nor a fine one, but it was welcoming and open to company at all times, so Emma explained.

Before they could approach, however, an elegantly dressed couple exited the door that led to the apartments above. Emma snorted in disapproval, and Mr. Knightley scowled at her. "The Eltons," the young lady grimaced. "I suppose I had better introduce you."

"Emma!" Mr. Knightley warned, but Emma ignored him and took Mary by the elbow once more to lead her to the couple.

Mr. Elton was the vicar, a rather handsome man who bestowed upon Emma a smile that spoke nothing of friendship or amity. Here was yet another story to be learned or imagined, Mary was certain. He welcomed Mary to the neighbourhood and expressed all due shock and horror concerning the events in London that had forced her unexpected stay.

Mrs. Elton was very fine in her manner and appearance. Her dress was perhaps too elegant for a morning's visit in a country village, her demeanour a shade too superior, and her accent a shade too countrified, from some part of England Mary had not visited.

In contrast to Emma's unconscious understanding of her place at the centre of Highbury society, Mrs. Elton seemed very much aware both of where she ranked in the hierarchy and of where she believed she ought to rank. She reminded Mary of a self-satisfied Caroline Bingley, rather more pleased with herself than she ought to be.

"Forgive our need to hasten on our way," Mr. Elton squinted at Emma. "I must prepare for old Mr. Abdy's funeral. I stopped here only to condole with Mrs. Bates, for she knew him when they were younger. Excuse us." With hardly a bow or dip of the head, the Eltons slid their way down the road in the direction of the venerable church that loomed in the distance.

Their visit to the Bateses was further delayed when a young woman rushed from a small laneway. "Miss Woodhouse!" she called, "Mr. Knightley! Oh, Miss Woodhouse, how fine you look this morning! Oh, forgive me! I had not known you were visiting with a friend. I'll be off, not wishing to bother you then!"

By her dress and deferential manner, Mary took this young woman to be neither of the gentry nor of the working class, and from Emma's proprietary demeanour towards her, felt her to be a sort of protegee to the fine lady, one graced with the bestowal of Miss Woodhouse's beneficence and friendship. "No, do not leave on our account, Harriet. Miss Bennet, may I introduce my friend Harriet Smith? Harriet, Miss Bennet of Longbourn. We were about to visit Mrs. Bates and Miss Bates and Miss Fairfax. Is that your aim as well?"

Harriet carried with her a basket laden with a variety of pies and fruits and other such items. "Mrs. Goddard sent these over." ("Mrs. Goddard is mistress of the boarding school yonder—you must have heard mention of it, for it is a distinguished institution," Emma explained in a whisper.) "Cook made too much as usual, and we must find somebody to take the food before it goes off, and wondered if Miss Bates might help us."

They all approached the door together and began to walk up. "I always tell Mrs. Goddard that Mrs. Bates makes the best pies and tarts in the village, but Cook's are very fine too. I hope they will be able to use them."

They had arrived at the top of the stairs and Emma gave a sharp knock at the door, which was answered almost at once. The small party was invited in by the serving girl and led through a very small vestibule to a cosy sitting room, made even cosier by the presence of an imposing pianoforte that occupied much of the room. It was a beautiful instrument, quite incongruous in this small and unprepossessing space.

The room, to Mary's surprise, was quite full of company. Mrs. Bates sat at her knitting by the window, where the light was best, and Miss Bates and Miss Fairfax had risen from their seats at a small table near the quiet dark fireplace, in the company of none other than Frank Churchill! Once more, Mary observed the flitter of glances between Miss Woodhouse, Mr. Knightley, Miss Fairfax, and Mr. Churchill, that told of a tale far more complicated and involved than any of the parties to it seemed to acknowledge. In contrast, Harriet Smith's expression was wistful and innocent, and she seemed quite apart in so many ways from the subtle undercurrents that suffused the small parlour.

Sounding embarrassed to break the moment of silence that ensued, Harriet handed the basket to Miss Bates. "Mrs. Goddard had extra food, some pies and preserves, and hoped you might help us by taking them before they turn."

"How very kind, so obliging!" Miss Bates turned her nervous smile on the young visitor. "Yes, very kind indeed! Mother has been at her baking today, for all that she enjoys the activity so much, even if it is not what ladies ought to do, but it is a source of pleasure for her. Mr. and Mrs. Elton were by, so good of them to visit and talk of poor Mr. Abdy. I knew him when he worked for Father, of course, although that was many years ago and I had not spoken to him much after Father died and he went to live with his sons, but Mother was not able to go to the kitchens to bake. So kind of Mrs. Goddard to think of us. Let us see… oh, fruit tarts! Lovely. So lovely. Perhaps we can set them out with tea. Tea! Yes, please, let me see about calling for tea."

"Miss Bennet," Frank Churchill turned his smile upon her once more. "I could not keep myself away from the joy of hearing you at the keyboard. I do hope you do not mind. I have been helping Miss Fairfax sort through her music. Here is a set of marches by Mr. Beethoven, or this by Mr. Kozeluch, or look here, some sonatas by Mr. Mozart. Ladies, I rely on you to tell me which to set out."

The morning passed quickly; Mary enjoyed Miss Fairfax's quiet company and strove to match the other's considerable skill at the keyboard, and the musical results were not unpleasing. The clock chimed noon, and then one, and at last, having played many notes and consumed several pieces of fruitcake and lavender biscuits, Mary and the rest of the party from Hartfield took their leave.

"Thank you, Miss Bennet, for lending me your skills," Miss Fairfax said as they departed. "I would be very pleased should you wish to return tomorrow if you have time before the ball, or the day after."

This pleased Mary. "If I am still in town, the pleasure would be my own." She dropped a curtsey to her hosts and thanked Miss Bates and Mrs. Bates and followed her new friends down the stairs to the street.

The sun had brightened and grown hot, and the village was now quite busy, with shopkeepers calling from doorways and windows, children dashing from building to building, tradesmen and village folk scurrying about in their daily routines. A small group were clustered outside of the Crown, talking loudly of the news from London, and a larger crowd seemed to be gathered within, from the noise that spilled out onto the street. Behind the inn, which sat in a sort of island off the main square, Mary could see the stables and yard, where a carriage stood devoid of its horses. It must have arrived some time ago, the team that drew it even now being tended by the ostlers, its occupants taking nourishment in the inn and tending to their needs.

She had not thought Highbury to be a usual place for carriages to stop and take rest, since it was off the main roads and on the way to nowhere in particular, but people would travel where they must, and a respectable inn was not to be sneered at. Having spent her own time in its warmth last evening, she congratulated the travellers on their fine choice.

"Come, Miss Bennet, come with me," Emma dragged her towards a tea shop that sat to one side of the inn. "You must try Mrs. Latimer's ices. They are quite as fine as those in London, from what my sister tells me, and she has cakes and other treats as well. Do join us, Mr. Knightley. I shan't tell Papa, for he would be angry at you."

A sweet ice sounded the very thing, and Mary was happy to oblige. As Mr. Knightley trailed behind them, she allowed Emma to pull her past the crowd by the inn and towards the door, but as they passed the narrow lane that ran down the far end of the Crown, she heard a voice she never thought to hear again.

"Now, now, Mr. Cox, this is a very fine tale you've told me." She would know those deep tones and that broad Scots accent anywhere. "I admit it seems alarming, although such things are not unusual. I shall make some inquiries and will return to you as soon as I have something to relate. You're staying in the inn as well? Then I shall see you anon. And thank you again for the ride down. 'Twas much more comfortable a way to travel than by post."

It was him. Whatever was he doing here? He could hardly be seeking her, for he had not come to visit as he had promised before. What strange business could have drawn him to this village in the middle of Surrey, near no town or location of major importance? And moreover, could she possibly avoid him? She hurried her steps to move to Emma's side, the quicker to enter Mrs. Latimer's tea shop, but it was too late.

"Miss Bennet! Mary." He had seen her. There was no recourse but to halt her steps and turn to face him.

"Mr. Lyons." Her eyes were narrow and cold. She had not forgiven him, and she wished to let him know it.

"I say," Mr. Knightley exclaimed. "Lyons—I know that name. Darcy has mentioned you. Miss Bennet, this must be the very man you spoke of in your account of the incident last autumn. Can it be?"

With no good grace, Mary introduced the two men. "Mr. Knightley, may I present Mr. Alexander Lyons of London. Mr. Lyons, Mr. Knightley."

"We're back to Mr. and Miss, are we, Mary? Well, so be it." His voice was resigned, his expression sad, but Mary cared not. They had parted as friends, and then he had broken his promise. Now that the introductions were over, they might go their separate ways once more.

But Mr. Knightley shattered those thoughts. "We were about to take ice at the tea room. Do join us, sir. I would be pleased to know a friend of Mr. Darcy and of Miss Bennet too." And so the invitation was accepted, much to Mary's displeasure.

"What brings you here, Mr. Lyons?" Mr. Knightley sat back in the delicate chair in the tea room. The foursome had ordered their treats and were waiting for the serving girl to return with them.

"Two matters really," the red-headed Scotsman replied. "I had been engaged to look into a situation that pertains somewhat to these parts, and matters had progressed to the point where I felt I must come down to make my inquiries, but it was a commission from another source that brings me to Highbury itself." His eyes landed upon Mary and she forced herself to meet them coldly and then look away.

"Your business takes you to Surrey, sir?" Mr. Knightley balanced back on his chair.

"Aye, to Epsom Downs specifically, but enough of my business lies in the more general neighbourhood that it matters little where I lay my head at night. Highbury is as fine a place as any, and I may discharge my second duty here."

"That being, if I may so ask?"

"To look in on Miss Bennet. No, Mary, do not get yourself into a bother about this. Darcy was most concerned for your welfare, and to be honest, I was pleased to have a reason to leave London. The city is in an uproar, and little work was possible. He needed to return with your sister to Hertfordshire, but was most distressed knowing you were all alone. When he spoke to me about it, I accepted the task in a moment. I, too, was concerned for your welfare."

She refused to meet his gaze and was relieved when the serving girl brought the tray of biscuits and ices for the party.

All the time, Emma was sitting at the edge of her chair, her eyes wide with speculation. "And what is your business, Mr. Lyons, that brings you to our corner of Surrey? Do you race horses? You are far too tall to be a rider." Her eyes asked another question that Mary hoped she would not voice: *And how do you two know each other?*

"Not an owner, nor anybody with much interest in the races, Miss Woodhouse, other than a professional one. I am an investigator. I have been asked to inquire into irregularities pertaining to them. I cannot divulge more at the moment. I hope you understand."

Her eyes widened and a wide smile spread across her pretty face. "Oh, yes, indeed! I would not wish to interfere with your investigation at all, but... how fascinating!" She batted long lashes over bright eyes.

Was Emma flirting with him? Surely it could not be so. Emma was a fine lady; Alexander worked for his living. Certainly, he was an interesting man, and not at all unpleasant to look upon, especially if one fancied copper hair and those deep brown eyes, but Emma could not possibly turn her interest to such a one as he! It would never do!

Mr. Knightley's expression was quite unreadable. "How long do you imagine you will be in the village, Mr. Lyons?" he asked.

"That depends, sir, upon several details. I did promise my friend that I would not depart until completely satisfied that Miss Bennet is well and amongst friends, but as to my other inquiries, perhaps a few days will settle them, perhaps a week or longer. I've taken rooms at the Crown, and a fine establishment it is. I shall be more than content to remain here until I have my answers."

"The Crown? How wonderful!" Emma exclaimed. Then you will join us at the ball tomorrow night, of course. Mr. Churchill has already solicited Miss Bennet for a set of dances; perhaps once you see her happily engaged, you may decide to seek a partner for yourself." She grinned at him again, and Mary felt herself grow agitated. Emma Woodhouse was most definitely flirting with Alexander!

"Emma!" Mr. Knightley fairly growled his warning, but the young lady's smile remained bright upon her face. Seeing no respite from that quarter, Mr. Knightley tried to change the subject. "That was not your carriage we saw behind the inn, was it? It looks familiar somehow."

The Scotsman laughed, "No, no, not mine. I was kindly offered a ride with Mr. Cox, whom I know through my business affairs. He was conferring with me about a matter when Darcy came by and, hearing of my destination, offered me a seat with him. I am no fine gentleman, nor am I some wealthy merchant to have my own equipage, Sir." He spoke to Mr. Knightley but looked meaningfully at Emma. "Had he not been so kind, I would have travelled by stage or by mail."

"Mr. Cox, the attorney?" The curl at Emma's lip suggested disdain. Did she so dislike the man himself? Or was her quiet sneer directed at his need to work for a living? Certainly, even Mr. Darcy had disparaged Mary's own uncle Phillips, who was a village attorney at home in Meryton.

"Not your local man, Miss Woodhouse, but his brother Hugh. He also deals with legal matters through his business in London. As I said, it was a fortunate happenstance, and he has rooms at the Crown as well. His brother's house, he tells me, is very crowded and very noisy, although I do not know if the inn will be an improvement upon that!" He laughed again and Mary recalled other instances of hearing that hearty sound. She resented how much she had missed it. Missed him.

"Now, Emma," Mr. Knightley teased, "Our Mr. Cox is a fine man, and of great usefulness to so many here in the neighbourhood. His wife is a sensible woman; surely you know her."

"As you must know, I do not, by custom, associate with people from the merchant class, Mr. Knightley. Wealth cannot be equated with status or breeding. Why, one need only look at Mrs. Elton to see that. Likewise the Coles..."

"...are as elegant a family as ever you might meet, Emma, if only you would take the time to know them!"

Mary shifted back in her chair as this exchange rang between the two old friends, and she saw Alexander do likewise. What would Emma say if she knew that Mary's own dear aunt and uncle were merchants in London? Would she refuse to have anything more to do with her? Or would her status as the daughter of a minor country gentleman and—more likely—her new kinship with Mr. Darcy be sufficient to absolve her from such infamous connexions?

And how could she forget the presence of Alexander, with whom she had been flirting seconds before? He had admitted to his profession openly, and her rapt interest in it spoke of a wish to dally with a man's feelings that a lady ought not to possess. She glanced up and was relieved to see the look of unshuttered amusement upon her former friend's face. He would not be taken in by Miss Woodhouse! Or so she hoped. He had wronged her but did not deserve to be played with.

The heated words came to an abrupt stop as another lady entered the tea room and Emma cried, "Mrs. Weston! Do come and sit with us!"

The lady in question returned the greeting, and expressed pleasure at seeing Miss Bennet again and meeting Mr. Lyons, but refused the invitation. "Thank you, but no, Emma. I am merely here to talk to Mrs. Latimer for a moment about some of the cakes for the ball. But do come and talk with us, for you have such good taste in such matters."

Such an appeal seemed impossible to resist, and Emma excused herself from the table at once to join her friend.

"How many cakes are you getting, Emma? And what sort? Too many almond will not do... Excuse me for a moment, please." Mr. Knightley also rose and strode across to where the two ladies were waiting for Mrs. Latimer to take them into her office to discuss the cakes. Mary and Alexander now sat alone at the table, the empty plates and bowls the only witnesses to their words.

"I'm sorry, Mary."

"You have nothing for which to apologise, Mr. Lyons."

"We were friends. What happened?" Despite his strong brogue, his voice was as familiar to her as her own thoughts.

"Why did you not come? If not for me, for my sister, for your friend. You promised to be at their wedding, and then did not come, with no excuse or explanation."

He sighed and ran a hand through his too-long hair. "Darcy does not blame me. He knows I would not cry off the arrangement without a good reason, even if I am not at liberty to explain it. Can you not forgive me too?"

"But we were friends, confidants! It was when we acted together and revealed what we knew that we were able to save Lizzy. Could you not trust me, even with the simplest explanation?" Mary closed her eyes in frustration. From any other, she would have accepted this reasoning without a qualm. What was it about Alexander Lyons that made his unexplained absence so personal for her? She let out a snort. "I don't suppose that even the strange goings-on here would induce you to confer with me again. I am just a woman, and a silly one at that, I suppose, and you were pleased to see the end of me. Am I correct?"

He leaned forward, his voice dangerously low. "What on earth are you talking about, Mary? These are not words I ever said to you, nor thought to myself, or at least not after I learned what sort of first-rate brain you have in that head of yours. I would discuss all my cases with you if I could, but I am so often bound to confidence, just as a lawyer or one of your parsons might be—" He stopped and looked up at her sharply. "What strange goings-on? Anything to do with my horses, perchance?"

"I would not know, Mr. Lyons, for that would entail you telling me about them." She was being ridiculous, and well she knew it, but could not help herself. Annoying, vexatious, frustrating man!

"Mary, this case I may discuss. But not now. I will do what I can to arrange a time when we can talk. But now, tell me how you are managing? You seem to have found friendly faces rather quickly."

With another huff, she resigned herself to having to engage in conversation with him. She told him of her happy situation with the Woodhouses at Hartfield, and of the various people she had met during her few hours in the village. "The Eltons seem horrid, but I have quite taken to Miss Fairfax. She is rather reserved, but I know that one need not have an open manner to have a fine character, nor does one need to chatter all the time to be a friend. She has invited me to visit again and if I may, I shall do so."

"I would enjoy meeting her, I believe. Perhaps, if I am not otherwise busy with my case, Mr. Knightley might introduce us. I—"

His words were cut off when a frantic young man in the garb of a prosperous farmer rushed into the shop. "Mr. Knightley? Is Mr. Knightley here? Mr. Knightley! Oh, thank the heavens I've found you. There's been another one. Another accident. Now Harry Carnes is dead!"

Chapter Four

Meeting the Victims

Alexander swung his head around to look for Mr. Knightley. The man stepped out from the back room when he heard his name and was standing by the doorway as the farmer pronounced his dire news.

"Martin!" He nodded a greeting. "What has happened?"

The young man—he looked just a year or two younger than Alexander's own six-and-twenty years—scanned the tea shop. "Perhaps elsewhere?" Alexander silently agreed that the tea shop was no place to discuss a death. And from the man's frantic manner, he doubted this death was expected.

Mr. Knightley seemed to have reached the same conclusion. "Mr. Lyons, would you join us? I might be the magistrate, but I am not so proud as to ignore the providence of having an investigator on my doorstep. There have been too many accidents of late. Will you hear his tale with me?"

"Mmm, of course." Alexander narrowed his eyes in thought. "Most certainly. Carnes is one of the people I had hoped to talk to in respect to my own investigation. Perhaps these incidents are all connected somehow."

In response, Knightley had nodded once and said, "Martin, meet me at the Crown. Tell Mr. Stoller there that we need a private room with three chairs, good light, and a table. I will join you soon as I see the ladies safely off."

"Four." Alexander spoke without thinking.

"Excuse me, Mr. Lyons?"

"Four chairs." He glanced over to see Mary smiling at him. What he was doing was most unorthodox, but he had never been a man to fit nicely into other people's categories. "Miss Bennet might have some thoughts; I have learned to value her comments. If she would care to join us, of course."

Her face was grim, but her eyes smiled. "Thank you, Alexander, I would." He suppressed his own smile. She had called him by his name again. Perhaps this strange rift, of which he had had no notion, might be mended.

Knightley looked from Alexander to Martin, and then to Mary, seeming quite uncertain of whether to accept this strange request. "Without her, we might never have saved her sister from the gallows," Alexander added.

Emma stepped out of the back room. She had clearly heard some of the exchange. "Is that true, Miss Bennet? Why did you not tell me you were an investigator as well?" Her eyes were open wide and her mouth formed a small open smile. "How fascinating! Mr. Knightley, you must allow her to join you. You will tell me everything important, will you not, Miss Bennet? Or all the parts that will not shock me too terribly?"

Knightley gave a series of perfunctory arguments, but to Alexander's ears, they were purely for form. At last the magistrate agreed and turned back to Alexander. "If what you and Miss Bennet say of your joint investigation is true—and I have no reason to disbelieve you—I shall be thankful for any insight. Miss Bennet may come along as soon as I have seen Emma and Mrs. Weston home."

"Nonsense, Mr. Knightley!" Emma returned. "Do I not walk this path every day without assistance? Randalls is along my way, and I can accompany my friend when her business here is complete. Go and hear what Mr. Martin," her voice dropped at his name, "has to say. And Miss Bennet, I do expect a grand story when you return!"

Now, a few short minutes later, they were gathered in the private room at the Crown, waiting to hear what the young farmer had to say.

"Well now, Mr. Martin, please tell me everything you know." Mr. Knightley sat upright at the table, pencil and paper at hand, his eyes fixed upon the young farmer across from him. Alexander sat quietly at a smaller table at the side of the room in the Crown, his own notepad at the ready, keenly aware of the young woman who sat to his side. He ought not to have allowed Mary to join the men, but after her accusations he had agreed to her intrigued eyes.

"You know my farm, Mr. Knightley," the young man said at last.

"Robert Martin is one of my tenants," the magistrate explained quietly to Alexander and Mary. "Prosperous and innovative. Please go on, Martin."

"Thank you, sir. I was out in the far fields, where we've set up that new irrigation system we spoke about last year, to see how the planting is going. It's right near the edge of my farm, close to where Carnes has... had his paddock for the horses he trains. The big holding tank for the water for my irrigation pipes is set right against the old stone wall between our lands, being on the highest ground. The water wasn't flowing as it ought, and the pipes all seemed clear, so I went to check the tank. That's when I saw him, down in the bottom of the reservoir. He used to sit on that old stone wall to talk when I was there working, or to take his mid-day snack and drink, and something must have happened, and he fell from the wall into my reservoir and drowned. The remains of his meal were still on the wall. I've left it all as I found it and took my horse right to town to look for you."

Knightley was scratching on his paper as Martin spoke, but Alexander was watching the man's face. From the corner of his eye, he could see Mary doing likewise. Good girl! She, like him, was looking for any ticks or signs that the farmer was not telling all of the truth. From experience, he knew that one excellent way for a wrong-doer to divert attention was to deliver the news of the crime himself, but with only the details that would steer the inquiry away from him. To his eyes, Martin seemed guileless and innocent. Assuming, of course, that there was more to this than an accident. But what had Mary said, and Knightley too, about there being too many 'accidents' for comfort? He turned to his paper notepad and wrote:

Ask Knightley about other deaths
Commonalities amongst victims?

Now that Martin had finished his recital and answered the few questions posed to him, Knightley announced that he must see the scene for himself. "I shall summon my bailiffs to come with the wagon and some ropes to drag him out, and meet you out there. I know exactly the place. See me there, Lyons? Perhaps you might ride beside Martin. Miss Bennet, I really must insist on seeing you back to Hartfield. This will not be the scene for a woman, and especially not one as young as you."

Mary was on her feet at once. "Sir, I must protest." Her voice was steel, and Alexander was very proud of her for some reason. "I will not tell you what horrors I saw last autumn. I may seem a weak female in body, but my spirit is made of sterner stuff, and I shall not swoon or cause you trouble. And I may see something others might miss. I insist on coming along. I can ride, and if I may borrow a horse, I shall be of no trouble to anybody."

Once more Knightley tried to dissuade her and once more Mary triumphed. The magistrate was correct: this was, indeed, no place for a woman, but Mary had proven herself before, and Alexander had no fears for her. And, as she had suggested, perhaps a set of eyes accustomed to observing different things would be useful.

The ride took the small party through the streets and laneways of Highbury, and then across newly verdant undulating farmland. Despite his recent shock, Martin was a friendly and informative guide, pointing out interesting features of the landscape as well as other relevant details. "Donwell Abbey—that's Mr. Knightley's estate—lies there, just beyond that stand of trees. You can see the chimneys when we pass over the bridge. All this land is his, including my own farm. My sisters keep house for me, down yonder, across that meadow. Over there you can see the crest of land nearer to the road to Kingston, and there, yonder, you will see the stone wall that runs between the farm and the land that was let to Mr. Carnes, closer to Epsom. Carnes lets from Mr. Knightley, since that parcel is not as good for corn as for grazing. Have you heard of Ralph Hesselgrave? He's the one that's mad on horseflesh and the races hereabouts. There's lots of blunt in those pockets, and when Carnes proposed setting up the paddock and training grounds, Hesselgrave supported him in the matter.

"Hmmm, yes," Alexander murmured. "I've heard his name before. I might have some questions for him. Perhaps Mr. Knightley can perform the introductions."

Mary remained quiet on the ride, but Alexander could see her eyes absorbing all the information Martin was offering. She would know the exact route to take again, should she need to return to their destination, and she would be able to identify the key locations along the route. Smart girl!

Eventually the path the three took came to a break in an old stone wall, and here Martin urged his mount from the dirt laneway and onto the field, following the direction of the wall. The land dipped into a wide and shallow valley and then climbed again quite steeply, to what seemed to be the highest hill in the area. As they reached the very top, Alexander could see the collecting reservoir Martin used for his irrigation system. Three farm hands were milling around, waiting for Martin to return.

"I didn't want to leave anything unattended. John here was with me when we found... him. I sent the others to wait till I returned. They'll remain until Mr. Knightley arrives."

Here was a sensible man. Alexander had approved of his no-nonsense manner upon first meeting him, and took to him more now.

The three dismounted and tied their horses up at a stile further along the wall and walked to where the accident had happened. Now, as they approached on foot, Alexander could see more clearly the exact set up of the area. It was a still day and no breeze disturbed his hair as he scanned the area.

The wall, at the very top of the hill, was low and wide, more of a marker than any real barrier. The top was perhaps three feet across, and a man standing on it would see for miles across spectacular countryside. It would be a fine place to take some food or a drink on a pleasant day. This seemed to be what Carnes had done, for as Martin had mentioned, a small cloth still lay on the pale grey stones with the wrappings and crumbs of some bread, the rind of some country cheese, and the pastry from a pie or tart atop it. The entirety of it was weighted down by a flask of what smelled like strong ale. An apple core lay on the soil a few inches away from the base of the wall.

On the far side of the wall, a short way down a steep and sandy decline, there was a paddock with a stream running along one side of the wooden fence, and an elaborate set of buildings on the far end. The large one was a stable that appeared big enough for a half dozen or so beasts, and two smaller buildings on the side looked to be storage sheds or maybe a cottage for a man to sleep in if need be at night. A stand of trees cast shade on part of the enclosure, in which stood four magnificent looking steeds.

Immediately against the wall on Martin's side was a deep and wide trench filled with rainwater, at the bottom of which was a man's body. Had he fouled the water at all? There was enough dirt and sediment in the trench that Alexander could not see. Perhaps when the man's body was brought to the surface, he might examine it more closely. But for now, the story seemed straightforward: the deceased man had been taking his lunch, had somehow fallen into the tank immediately against the wall, and drowned.

"Any sign of a companion or visitor?" Alexander asked this of himself as much as of the men surrounding him, but then added, "No, leave the area clear for the magistrate and his men. We don't want to disturb anything before they see it."

Mary nodded. The three farm hands alternately gaped at her and squinted at her from the corners of their eyes, but she did not seem at all perturbed. Perhaps, in Hertfordshire whence she came, it was not uncommon for young ladies of quality to be seen tramping around scenes of unexpected death with an entourage of unrelated men.

Little was said as the gathering waited until at last Knightley's crew could be seen in the distance. He rode a large grey horse, and trailing behind him came a flat wagon drawn by a single brown beast with two men driving.

"My corn..." sighed Martin, looking sadly at his crops. The wagon would do no favours for his young plantings, but Knightley seemed the sort to damage as little as possible, and would ensure his bailiffs did likewise.

When the men arrived, Alexander let them attend to their business. Knightley surveyed the scene with a keen eye and scratched out notes on the paper he had brought with him. He walked the perimeter of the reservoir several times and tested the stones that made up the wall for anything loose or crumbling, although there was no indication of any such damage on the part they could see.

He spoke in a low voice to the farm hands and then leapt over the wall some distance from where the drowned man's meal had been set out and peered at the ground. He must be wondering what Alexander had wondered: was there any sign of another having been near?

"May I, sir?" Alexander's voice caused Knightley to startle, but he merely gave a terse nod and said, "Of course."

Alexander copied the older man's path and climbed over the wall at a good distance from the reservoir, then walked carefully to the top of the crest, his eyes on the ground as he did so.

"Rained recently? The ground is soft, but not wet."

"Two days ago. It was quite sodden, but yesterday was sunny and warm."

"I can see my own footprints on the soil. Yours as well, sir. Look there," Alexander pointed. "A single set of footprints leading from the shed and stables there towards the wall, then walking away a short distance," he peered at the pattern that moved back three or four feet from the wall, "and then back again. I reckon he climbed up here to sit and eat and enjoy the view. That his horse there?"

A fine-looking animal stood in the shade of the trees, drinking from the stream. It looked to be more of a gentleman's ride than a racing horse; the saddle and blanket that lay on a low table just in view substantiated that notion. "Must be so. The others are for racing. Look at those legs and those sleek forms."

There seemed nothing to see on the ground here. The man's horse had not approached the wall to accidentally knock its owner to his death, and there were no footprints suggesting any other person had been near.

Knightley must have been seeing the same things, for he murmured, "Can't imagine it being anything other than an accident, but mighty strange, all the same. Too damned many of them." Then he looked up at Mary and apologised profusely for his language.

"May I look?" Mary asked.

Knightley blinked. "Well, er…yes, of course, I suppose. Don't see why not, now that you are here. May I help you across the wall? Oh, yes, the stile. Just there. Much easier." It would never do for a lady to hoist herself up onto a wall, even a low one, in her morning dress. Alexander ran down on his side of the wall to assist her. Of course she was perfectly capable of climbing the stile without his help, but for some reason he wished to be of use to her.

She thanked him prettily but kept her eyes on the ground for the walk back to the top of the rise, just as he and Knightley had done.

"Nothing?" she asked.

"Nae, nothing."

Having achieved the crest and the site of Carnes' last meal, she surveyed the area and the ground once more and then turned her attention to the remains of the food, touching nothing but examining everything with her eyes.

"Do you have your notepad, Alexander?" she asked.

"Indeed. In my pocket." He retrieved it, along with the pencil he had used. "What must I write?"

She stared long at the evidence and then recited, "White cloth, old and discoloured, some food stains of grease and red fruit preserve. Wrapper with breadcrumbs, cheese rind, pastry crust, apple core," she pointed to where the core had fallen onto the soil at the very base of the wall, "and ale. Just what you observed earlier." She paused. "Any sign of food on the poor man's person? No, I suppose not. Pity."

She wandered about a while more, but added nothing to Alexander's list, and when Knightley asked if his men could form their nooses to try to capture the dead man's limbs to draw him up from his watery grave, she agreed and turned her back until the unpleasant deed was done.

From this point the men moved quickly. The two bailiffs, whom Knightley had introduced as Cowley and Tidwell, managed to hoist the dead man from the water-filled pit and place him onto the wagon to transport back to Highbury. Knightley surveyed the area once more before announcing he could see nothing else and asked Alexander if there was anything he had missed.

There seemed little else to do, other than find somebody to take care of Carnes' horse and the racing horses, which could best be done in the village, and the company soon returned to their mounts and rode back into town.

"I have questions, sir, and I am certain you have the same ones," Alexander ventured as they regained the path nearer to the village. "I would like to know when Carnes was last in the village, who saw him most recently, and when. Where does he live? Married? Children? Who will take care of his body?"

Knightley sighed. "As to the latter, he lived alone just outside of the village, since he didn't farm but only raised and trained the horses to race. He had a wife once, but the story is that she ran away, and he did not chase her. We all believed he was relieved to have her gone, so he could devote himself to his real loves, whom we met in the paddock. We will have to take his remains to the church, to the cold cellar there, until Elton can bury him properly.

"As to the former, I've already asked my men to set about the neighbourhood, asking exactly those questions. When was he last seen alive, and by whom? The answers to those might prove quite enlightening."

"And the others? The other dead men? I have my own questions, which I would like to ask if you have time to answer them. Perhaps over an ale…" he looked up and caught Mary's eye again as she rode beside him, "or a cup of tea? It is time to look at these deaths as more than one accident at a time."

Alexander took out his pocket knife and whittled the lead in his pencil to a sharp point, then opened his notebook and began a new entry labelled *Victims*. "Right," he nodded at Knightley, "Anything you have to tell me about these deceased men, I would be most appreciative to hear."

They were back in the private room at the Crown, all three seated at the large table in the middle of the room, two mugs of ale, a pot of tea, and a plate of thinly sliced spice cake between them. Knightley furrowed his brow in thought and brushed his hair off his forehead and then began to speak.

"Jack Smith was the first to die. It seemed like a terrible accident—they all did. He was not born in the area, but he had been part of this corner of Surrey for as long as I can recall. He had no occupation and often slept rough in the summers, or in a barn or loft in colder weather, trading some time in the fields for a bit of food or a place to lay his head when these couldn't be obtained otherwise."

"A tramp, then?" Mary asked.

"Of a sort. He worked hard when he needed something he couldn't come by otherwise, but he was happy to live without the conveniences most of us desire."

"Age? Family?" Alexander wrote these prompts on his sheet of paper as he asked the questions.

"His age was a bit of a mystery, as was his parentage. He never did say where he came from or who his parents were, but he was not a young man in my first recollections of him. He must have been seventy, perhaps more. Still a strong worker when he was called upon to do a job, as tough and wiry as an old rooster, and just as crotchety. No one even knew if Smith was his given name, or just one he chose for himself. To all intents and purposes, he was alone in the world, and he seemed happy with his lot."

"Did he always work for his food?" Mary asked the question, and Alexander poised his pencil to record the answer.

"He worked hard when it suited him, but it was not his chosen means of keeping body and soul together. He could more often be found knocking at the back door of one great house or another. He ate enough of my own soft fruits and day-old bread, and I had seen him at Hartfield, at Hesselgrave's house, at Riverton—that's Dolbeare's manor on the far side of Highbury—wherever there was a crumb to be taken and perhaps a soft pile of hay to sleep in. He even stopped by at the kitchen at the back of the house where the Bates ladies live. You will meet them soon, Lyons. They have fallen upon hard times, but old Mrs. Bates was the daughter of one vicar and the wife of another, and there is no poverty of Christian spirit in either woman. They might take gently offered charity from their friends, but they always manage to spare something for those more in need than they. Smith joked with me more than once about Mrs. Bates' pies and tarts being finer than anything he might get at Saint Jameses! Well, more's the pity for his loss."

"How did he die?" Alexander made another heading on his notepaper.

"It was back in early February, the seventh, I believe. The weather had been particularly cold and there was a coating of ice across the ground everywhere. I recall how difficult it was to ride to the field where he was found. It seemed he had taken refuge in a rough shack he had built out in the open area past Hartfield. He must have fallen asleep over the open fire he had built to keep warm. I knew that cabin—it was little more than a tent made of wood, scarcely large enough for one man, with no fireplace save the pit in the middle, more a buffer from the wind than any real protection from the elements, and in such weather one would have to be almost on top of the flames to get any warmth. We smelled the smoke and went to see what had transpired. It was a most unpleasant scene." He grimaced in the recollection of it.

"How did you know it was Smith? Was he not so badly burned?"

"His teeth," Knightley shook his head. "He had none in the front, and his skull... well, you can imagine." His eyes shifted to Mary before he could elaborate. Alexander silently thanked him for the consideration, no matter that Mary had seen as bad. "And his old dog was running around the woods, howling like something horrible. Poor creature was almost as old in its own way as poor Smith was, and no sooner had we finished our awful task when the animal just lay down and died. It was a sad, sad day, and seemed to everybody's eyes to be a dreadful, tragic accident."

Mary sniffed and dabbed at the corner of her eyes. Was she more upset about the man or the dog, Alexander wondered. It was not a pleasant tale.

"Was there anything left to examine?" Alexander's pencil hovered over the notepad again.

The magistrate shook his head. "Nothing but a pile of embers. Miss Bates was very upset when she heard the news. She had seen him only that morning when he had come by the back door, and she had urged him inside for a spot to warm by the fire, but he took the small package they had given him and insisted on heading off into the cold. She told me all that week and for the next month whenever we met that her mother begged the man to stay and then gave him an extra pie for his meal when he refused. Miss Bates has as kind a heart as you will ever meet, Lyons, and will always praise another's goodness, even if that other is her relation."

The men both fell silent and took another drink of their ales, whilst Mary refreshed her tea.

"Who was next?" Alexander asked at last.

"The next was Fred Watson, on the first of April. It was a Wednesday. One always recalls strange events on the first of April, for one never knows if a summons is genuine or in jest. On this day, it was very real."

"Tell me about Watson." The pencil scratched over the notepad.

"Watson was born in these parts. He was three and sixty when he died. His father was the village smith before him, and Fred took on the trade and assumed his father's smithy when the old man grew too old to work. He married old Abdy's daughter, and they had four sons, three of whom left the village to find work in London. The second had his father's skill and runs the smithy now. You can meet him if you wish."

Alexander nodded but let Knightley continue his tale.

"As I said, it was a Wednesday, around three o'clock in the afternoon. Andy—the son—was out at the forge, making shoes for Hesselgrave's racers, if I recall his tale. He said he heard a mighty din from the workshop at the back of the building where Fred was working on some task or another. He could not get through the door, for the entire rack of shelves that stood all the way up to the ceiling and which held the bulk of the steel and iron implements not used every day, had crashed down and barred entry. We had to open up the wall at the back by the window to get into the room. Poor Fred was at the bottom of the heap, quite dead. There was a dent in his skull the size and shape of the flat iron that fell right on him, but the weight of the shelves would have crushed him, regardless."

Mary spoke now. "Could anybody have pushed the shelves?"

Knightley sighed. "Not at all, from everything we could determine. They were precariously balanced, and a weight at the top might have brought the entire structure down, or a hard shove at the crucial place lower down, but anybody else in the room would have been crushed as surely as poor Fred. Further, if we could not enter, a second person could not have left. The window was large but barred to keep errant children out, and the door, as I said, was quite blocked by the shelves. It must have been that Fred stumbled back and set the entire set of shelves off balance. Just another terrible accident."

Alexander's pencil darted across his notepad, recording every detail he thought might be valuable. Then he sat up and took another sip from his mug of ale. "Sad business."

"Indeed." Knightley's expression was tragic. "We miss him. He was a good man. He really made something of that smithy. He came by some money about twenty years ago and used it all to buy the best and most modern equipment. People came from miles around to request special items and for his craftsmanship. Andy is skilled, but Fred was an artist."

"And what of the latest death, before Mr. Carnes?" Mary asked this question. "I heard mention that it was Mr. Abdy. Had he been ill?"

"Not ill, but very old, nigh on ninety years, and the very old tend to pass on suddenly, even when there is no immediate expectation of it. Mr. Perry attended him and said it looked to be a simple case of not waking up from a sleep."

"And then, just today, Harry Carnes. Another accident."

"So it appears." Knightley rubbed the bridge of his nose and scowled. "There are just too many accidents, and I cannot like it at all."

Chapter Five

Dinner at Harfield

What an odd set of tales Mr. Knightley had told. Mary had listened with her full concentration as the gentleman recounted the events around each death. He had, during her short acquaintance with him, seemed an intelligent and perceptive man, not given to flights of fancy or wild speculation, but attentive to detail. Whilst she would have found great interest in surveying each scene herself, his account seemed adequate. It would have to be so, for she could not travel backwards in time and make her own examinations. Nor would she really wish to do so. She had discovered she possessed a stronger constitution than a young lady of gentle breeding ought, and hearing of these deaths had been sad but not overly distressing to her nerves. Nevertheless, she could not wish to be a witness to a man's burned body, nor to whatever might remain after the soul was crushed out of a man by a massive weight of iron and steel. Even the glimpse she had had earlier, of the shape at the bottom of the reservoir, had been sufficient for a while. It was no worse than what she had seen last autumn, but it was not to be wished for again.

A tap at the door interrupted her thoughts. Mr. Knightley called for the person to enter, and Emma walked through the door. "Mr. Lyons!" She shone her dazzling smile at him, and Mary's eyes narrowed as he smiled back. "Miss Bennet, Mr. Knightley! I am so pleased to see you have all returned. Miss Bennet, I do hope it was not too terribly horrid. Are you well?"

Fixing a pleasant, and hopefully cheerful, expression upon her face, Mary replied, "Quite well, thank you, Miss Woodhouse. It is always distressing to witness something so tragic, and I cannot be unaffected by it, but I am in no danger of extreme distress. I must own that my dear mother has taught me enough about the state of her nerves that I am ever cautious about allowing my own too much licence!"

"What did you learn?" Emma asked the question of the group.

Mr. Knightley answered. "Very little, other than what we had been told. Mr. Carnes was taking his lunch on the wall at the top of the rise, and for some reason fell into the reservoir and drowned. Mr. Perry is examining his remains; if there is anything else to be learned, we must wait for him.

Emma rolled her eyes. "He will likely prescribe a course of light gruel and no sweets after dinner to aid the dead man's digestion."

"Now Emma!" Mr. Knightley's voice held the resignation of a long history of such scolding. "Mr. Perry will do no ill by your father, and if Mr. Woodhouse is happy to hear that his regimen best serves his health, what harm does it do for Mr. Perry to deny him? It soothes his mind, and excessive worry is perhaps your dear father's greatest concern." To Alexander, Mr. Knightley explained, "Perry is a diligent man, with more medical training than most of his sort have. He studied for a time at St. George's in London before becoming an apothecary instead of a physician, and I have full faith in him. If there is anything to be learned from Carnes' remains, he will find it."

"This is rather distasteful conversation, Mr. Knightley, and most especially so since I am charged with inviting you and Mr. Lyons," she smiled once more at Alexander, "to dine at Hartfield. Father has sent invitations to the Westons, and we shall all make a merry party!"

Alexander's eyes darted towards Mary in a silent question, to which she replied with a hidden smile and a shrug.

"Thank you, Miss Woodhouse," he answered her. "I am pleased to accept. But..." he looked down at his serviceable coat and simple waistcoat.

"We shall not be offended by your lack of evening dress, Mr. Lyons. Indeed, it will be refreshing to have company which recommends itself by interesting conversation rather than by sporting the latest from the pages of Ackerman's. Shall I send the carriage by in an hour?"

"Allow me, Lyons," Mr. Knightley interjected. "Perhaps I have something at Donwell that can supplement your wardrobe. After all, you did not travel expecting to dine anywhere other than the inn, I am certain. Good. You needn't bother with the carriage, Emma. I will talk to the ostler about taking some horses for the week, and then I may use my own coach. I imagine we will be out in the fields some fair amount of time before this affair is settled and the horses will be useful. Shall we, Lyons?"

Alexander smiled his acceptance, and the four parted ways to prepare for the evening, Alexander and Mr. Knightley to Donwell and Emma and Mary to Hartfield.

Once again, Emma presumed to offer Mary one of her own gowns. The two were not so different in shape that a suitable frock could not be altered to fit, and if Emma were the taller of the two, some tacking of the skirts by a skilled maid, and the application of a length of ribbon to hide the alteration, rendered the chosen gown quite suitable for Mary's height. As the maid wielded her needle, another maid took a brush and a set of pins and ornaments to Mary's hair. When Mr. Knightley's carriage rolled down the drive sometime later, therefore, Mary was looking quite as fine as ever she had looked.

Emma met the two gentlemen at the door. "This is coming as you should do," said she to her friend, "like a gentleman. I am quite glad to see you, and Mr. Lyons as well. How handsome you are in your evening dress!"

Stifling her annoyance at Emma's forwardness, Mary had to agree. She had never seen Alexander in anything other than simple working clothes. Even when he had paid calls to her family's home at Longbourn, he had retained his accustomed wardrobe. Whilst he dressed neatly, he did not aspire to the elegance of the town's dandies, favouring instead plain woollen garb that would wear well and wash easily. Now, in what must be Mr. Knightley's clothing, he caused her to stop and catch her breath.

He had not forsaken his habitual trousers for breeches and slippers of full dress, but the grey fabric contrasted beautifully with the dark blue silk of his waistcoat and the lighter blue of his coat. How the coat fit so well, Mary could not imagine, for Alexander was both taller and broader across the shoulder than Mr. Knightley. Perhaps the gentleman stored a selection of such coats for just these occasions. The entire outfit emphasised the red of his hair, but rather than making it seem foreign and garish, it turned the copper into an ornament in itself. From above a perfectly tied and blindingly white cravat, Alexander smiled at her.

"Miss Bennet, do you approve?"

"How could I not? I have never seen you dressed thus. It becomes you."

"I have never seen you dressed thus either," he cast his eyes down her pale green dress. "You do not know what a pretty picture you make. I am enchanted."

"Surely you cannot forget your hostess, Mr. Lyons!" Emma dropped a low curtsey before him. Her ivory gown set off her colouring perfectly, allowing her light blue eyes to shine like sapphires. The dress had been designed for her—as any wealthy lady's clothing must be—and it was cut perfectly to best display her lovely figure. Naturally, she looked beautiful. Had Mary been made for jealousy, her hostess' appearance would have ignited the green blaze of envy.

"Beautiful, Miss Woodhouse. A right bonnie lassie," he emphasised his strong Scots accent, and Emma laughed.

"How delightful, Mr. Lyons! And Mr. Knightley, also all dressed for the occasion! We shall all be put to shame here by your elegance. But do come in! Mr. and Mrs. Weston and Mr. Churchill have only recently arrived and are waiting for you before we go in to dine. Come, come!"

She gestured for Mr. Knightley to offer his arm to Mary, thereby leaving Emma herself to be led by Alexander. She beamed at him, and Mary felt that pinch of annoyance once more, before following her escort towards the parlour where the others had gathered.

As the group of newcomers entered the room, Emma made the introductions, and the requisite bows and curtseys were made all around. Suddenly Mary was proud of the fine figure Alexander cut in his borrowed clothing, and she was pleased to see the welcome he received from the others in the room. In the normal course of events, a working man of no famous family and with few connections would never be an honoured guest in the home of the leading family of an area, and she was equally proud of how naturally he took to the situation. He said the right words, affected the right manners, and generally behaved exactly as a gentleman ought. How different was this man from the one she had first met in Hertfordshire several months ago!

"Miss Bennet! Delightful to see you again so soon. You suffered no ill effects from your activity today, I hope?" Mrs. Weston remained seated but greeted Mary warmly. She really was a charming lady. Her voice held every suggestion of sincerity, and Mary was pleased to reply that she was very well indeed, despite the necessary sadness at the cause for the outing.

"I would caution you not to repeat such an activity, Miss Bennet," Mr. Woodhouse frowned sadly from his seat by the fire. "Emma told me what it was all about, and such distress can do your health no good, for it disrupts the digestion and leads to poor sleep. You had much better sit here with my Emma and join her in her painting, or perhaps in visiting Mrs. Weston, who will not allow you to overtax yourself. No, you had much better stay home."

"I thank you for your concern, sir," Mary dipped a deferential nod to her host, but declined to promise him to change her behaviour.

Mr. Weston, who had risen from his seat next to Mr. Woodhouse greeted her as warmly as had his wife, if with less of a maternal level of concern, and walked over to the newcomers to say some words to Alexander, leaving only one man standing in his place.

"Miss Bennet!" Frank Churchill now approached her from where he had been sitting across from his step-mother. "You are entirely charming! You look quite the image of perfection! And now what do I hear, but that your beauty is matched by a first-rate understanding and intelligence! You must come and sit by me, for I long to know more about you."

Such words Mary had never heard before. As the middle daughter of five, and—to hear her mother speak, at least—the plainest of the lot, an appeal to her beauty was quite unknown to her, and she found it both alarming and irresistibly appealing. Bemused by this attention, she allowed Mr. Churchill to guide her to a seat beside his own, where he began to flirt with her in quite a shocking manner. He praised her dress—"Not even the enviable Miss Woodhouse could wear it as you do!"—her hair, her eyes. "And I confess to being absolutely fascinated by the tales I hear of you, Miss Bennet! Did you really find the solution to save your sister last year? And all without leaving the first mark of a stain on her reputation? I am all amazement and would hear every word, should you wish to tell me. Please, I shall lay myself at your feet, so eager am I to hear it!"

The young man's clear interest in her was merely the first part of his charm, for he was also quite handsome, and by far the most elegant man ever to pay such attention to her. Alexander might look very well in his smart evening wear, but where he was elegant and formal, Mr. Churchill wore his fine clothes as if he had been born to them. Which, of course, he had. He was a dandy of the first cut: every hair upon his head was perfectly arranged, his sideburns were shaped to best accentuate his facial structure, and his buffed fingernails fairly gleamed. But most alluring were his eyes, which shone with the wonderment of having encountered something so new and unusual he could not name it. Mary was somewhat stunned and entirely flattered, for all that she felt like a new toy or shiny trinket.

She took the offered seat and, at Mr. Churchill's repeated request, began to recount the details from her adventure. He gratified her with occasional gasps of shock or surprise, and by asking a clarifying question or commenting on her ingenuity, and her vanity—what little of it there was—was greatly appeased. She felt admired for her looks and cherished for her mind and flattered for her character, and suddenly Emma's attention to Alexander did not vex her quite as much as it had before.

Mr. Churchill was a charmer and excellent company, with an amusing story to be told for every comment and sincere interest in her own tales of her family and home. When the gathering were called in to dinner, he offered his arm without a look to anybody else, and seated himself beside her at the table so they might continue their conversation.

The meal was excellent and the talk around the table most pleasant, and Mary decided that if she must be stranded in some unknown part of England, she could not have chosen better than Highbury. Only Emma's continued and doting attendance upon Alexander marred the perfection of the evening. She did not begrudge the young lady her interest in her friend, for he was an interesting and rather handsome man in his own right, but, well, he was her friend first, and she had hardly had a moment to talk in private with him!

She stifled the little voice inside her that protested that only this very morning, she had disavowed any further friendship with the man and refused even to think of him (never mind that he intruded upon her every thought). She had known him first and longest, and ought at least to merit some moments to discover how he had been keeping these last months. Better she should enjoy Mr. Churchill's attention and forget the tiny kernel of jealousy that settled in her heart.

After the meal was removed and the men joined the ladies after their port (for Mr. Woodhouse would never permit cigars in the house, as the smoke affected his respiration), Mrs. Weston asked Mary to play. "I could not help but hear of your visit with Miss Fairfax this morning. She praised your performance highly. She has such fine natural taste that her words can only be the greatest commendation of your skill, and we would be honoured to hear you."

What was Mary to do but agree? She settled at the very keyboard where Miss Fairfax had sat the previous evening and sorted through the music in search of something suitable to play. Mr. Churchill appeared at her side, making suggestions and offering to turn pages, and when, at last, they settled upon a set of Scotch airs, they were smiling and laughing together with the comfort of old friends. She set her fingers to the keyboard and began to play, and then, when she came upon a popular song, Mr. Churchill began to sing, and the time slipped away in a wonderful rush of notes and melodies and camaraderie.

She had almost forgotten about that miniscule germ of resentment over Emma's attentions to Alexander when, just as they were concluding their final song, she looked up to see him staring at her from across the room. He stood tall and regal against the lamplight that shone behind him, burnishing his red hair into something from an illuminated manuscript of old. He did not have Frank Churchill's easy comfort with his fine clothing and these splendid surroundings, but rather than seeming out of place, Alexander's stance spoke of elegance and of a deep and hidden power of personality. One seeing him would assume he was born to higher ranks than these, never imagining him to be the working-class son of a country doctor from some village near Glasgow. His bearing was that of a duke, or a prince.

Mary's gaze darted from Alexander to the music before her, and then to Frank Churchill's long fingers, and a great confusion grew up within her. Mr. Churchill whispered something about the company and Mary responded with a titter of laughter, and when she looked up again, Alexander's eyes were fixed directly upon her.

He was smiling, as he must do in such company, but the look in his eyes told not of mirth but of something else. Allowing her fingers to move of their own accord over the notes she knew well, she stared back at him. Then Emma Woodhouse walked up to his side and whispered into his ear, and he turned to her with a genuine grin, and Mary felt that tiny kernel in her heart turn to lead. All of a sudden, the question of the dead men took second place to the more troubling question that his expression sparked in her breast.

The next morning Mary rose early. She ought to stay in bed, for this was the night of the ball, but her habit was to rise with the sun, and she knew she would sleep no more. She dressed quickly and took a chocolate before setting off for a walk before breakfast. She would head towards the village, she told the footman who brought her bonnet and cape, should Miss Woodhouse be concerned about her whereabouts.

The sun was bright over the eastern horizon, but the air still cool, and she was glad for the warmth of her cape as she trod the now-familiar lane into Highbury. As she passed Randalls, she waved at Mrs. Weston through the window, and then smiled at the farmers and denizens of the village whom she passed along her way. As she approached the high street, she detected more activity than on the previous day, despite it being so much earlier, and she mused it must all be in preparation for the evening's ball.

"Oh, Miss Bennet! Good morning! I had not expected you to come this way, not so early." She turned about to locate the speaker and saw Miss Bates hurrying towards her. She called out her good morning and waited for the spinster to catch up. "Where are you walking, Miss Bennet? I am just now coming from taking some pies to Mrs. French—she just had her fourth babe and the next one is ill and she cannot work, and Mama always reminds me that as little as we have, there are those with less and we must look to their needs as surely as to our own—for when Mama bakes her pies there are always enough to share with those less fortunate. I was telling Jane just this morning—Did you like Jane? She is such a sweet girl, always has time for her dear aunt and grandmother, and even now is sitting with Mama so I might run out with the pies for Mrs. French—I was telling Jane that it is our duty as good Christians to be charitable in our every action, and as we have given, so have we received."

She stopped to draw breath, but before Mary could speak her agreement, Miss Bates continued. "We were ever so blessed when Colonel and Mrs. Campbell—that was our Jane's father's dearest friend—took her in and raised her so well, and with every advantage, with their own daughter, Miss Campbell, who is now Mrs. Dixon, which is why Jane has returned to us, for Mrs. and Mr. Dixon are gone to Ireland and Jane would not go with them. But our dear Jane has had benefit of a fine education, and she is so elegant and beautiful and refined, and she will make a marvellous governess, for that is what she means to so, nevermind that Mother and I would be pleased to have her live forever with us, although we have not so many rooms. But we are so fortunate, so very fortunate indeed, Miss Bennet, to have the apartments we do have, and enough to eat, although it is not so very grand and nothing like what we had when I was young and Father was alive and we had the parsonage, but rooms and possessions are nothing to friendship and in that matter, we are rich, so very rich. We are so fortunate in the Christian goodwill of our neighbours, so very fortunate."

"This sounds like a topic we have visited before. Good morning, Mary!" Alexander's voice cut through Miss Bates' monologue, and Mary felt a momentary pang of guilt at the relief this occasioned. She looked up to realise their steps had taken them to the square before the Crown, which now bustled with tradesmen and workers and all manner of people preparing for the ball.

"Alexander!" she called out, before correcting herself. "Mr. Lyons. Good morning. Of course, you are staying at the Crown. The noise of the preparations must have drawn you outside earlier than your wont." His smile rivalled the sun, and she felt her heart skip at the sight of his face. Gone were the beautiful deep blue waistcoat and the snow-white cravat, but having seen him so garbed once, Mary reckoned he looked just as fine in his plainer dress. She felt a blush spread across her face and looked down at the ground before her in the hopes that he would not see it.

Turning to her companion, she asked, "Miss Bates, may I have the honour of introducing to you my... my friend, Mr. Lyons? He has come down from London for some days on matters of business, and we are fortunate to find each other in the very same village. Alexander, Miss Bates."

Bows and curtseys and appropriate salutations were made before Alexander asked, "I had just now stepped out for a moment of air before finding a bite of something to start my day. May I offer you my company and a spot of tea? I have heard tell of you, Miss Bates, and am delighted to make your acquaintance. Please..." He gestured back at the inn and winked at Mary as Miss Bates beamed in gratitude.

"So kind, Mr. Lyons, so very kind. Yes, thank you, I would be delighted, most delighted. So very good of you. Perhaps if there is a little something left over, I might take it back for Mother and Jane. Very obliging, so very good of you."

Alexander stopped for a moment to have a word with the innkeeper and then led the two ladies into the same private parlour Mr. Knightley had used the day before. He spoke happily about the countryside and the weather and other such pleasant matters until, a few minutes later, the same young maid that Mary had seen before entered with a large tray laden with a tea pot and three cups and a plate of scones and biscuits that Mary knew the three of them could never eat. It seemed that Mr. Knightley had told her friend of the Bateses' unhappy situation, and the investigator was responding suitably. In their past interactions, he had denied her chastisement to be a good Christian, claiming rather not to be a Christian at all, but his behaviour, no matter the inspiration, reflected every good value that the church—which she held to with such devotion—could teach. No matter his personal beliefs, which he had yet to lay out for her, he had the soul of a good man.

There was no burden of conversation as they took their tea. Miss Bates seemed more than content to offer her thoughts on every such topic that took her fancy. She praised the warmth of the sun, the verdure of the landscape, the heat of the tea, the softness of the scones and the tang of the jam. "It is almost as fine as Mother's preserves," she offered, "although this is fine, very fine indeed, for never let it be said that Mrs. Williams does not make excellent fruit preserve, but Mother takes great enjoyment from her cooking, which she had need to learn before Father died for we could not always employ a cook, and Mother did become ever so proficient at it, and every year when the fruit harvest has come she enjoys setting up jars to last us through the winter. Last year Mr. Knightley sent us all his store apples, and had not a single one left, but Mother prepared for him several jars of the preserves in order that Mrs. Hodges might not be too angry. For all that we have taken our extra meat pies to Mrs. French, Mother and Jane will be ever so pleased if there is a scone or two to take back to them."

"She is ever a sweet lady," Mary breathed when at last Miss Bates looked upon her watch and took her leave for home with a basket full of scones and biscuits on her arm. "But I must admit to finding her a bit tiresome, and so very grateful and obliging. I shall visit with her tomorrow in order to improve my patience and forbearance, like the good Christians she admires so greatly."

His smile took on an ironic glint, which she ignored. This was a topic to be raised at a different time. Instead of teasing him further, she said, "You never did tell me what business exactly, other than being Mr. Darcy's set of eyes and ears, has brought you to this part of Surrey."

He raised his eyebrows at her and smirked, "I have scarcely had the opportunity to do so. All of your attention has been claimed by the elegant Mr. Churchill..."

"As yours has been claimed by the very pretty Miss Woodhouse." She faced him, hands on her hips as she stood by the doorway. She ought not to be alone with him—a single man to whom she was in no way related—but if Miss Bates' hasty departure had lent her this opportunity, she would take it. There was no one here to besmirch her reputation, and none who cared enough about her to make the effort worthwhile. "Now, please let me ask again: What is your assignment?"

He beckoned her to the table once more with a sweep of his head. She ensured the door to the parlour was closed and then joined him, sitting close so he could speak quietly.

"'Tis a simple matter, in many respects. As you might well be aware, many of the *ton* are besotted with horse racing, and some of these are becoming alarmed that the races are not completely equitable. That is..."

"They are concerned that somebody is interfering with the horses?"

He nodded. "That is something we must consider. A horse that so often wins or places well will suddenly lag the field, whilst a slower beast that never breaks the top five finds some burst of speed and wins. Depending on where one places one's bets, a great deal of money can be won or lost. If somebody has devised a way of depriving a steed of his vigour, or more incredibly, teaching it speed, I wish to discover it."

"And all of these unusual races have been at Epsom?"

"Aye." He grimaced, then puffed out a chestful of air. "The men who engaged me to look into this matter know some of the trainers and owners out this way, and have begun to wonder about their stable hands and grooms, if not the men themselves. It seems with the wagering that occurs, there is plenty of blunt to be made in betting against a favourite."

"Yes, I see." And she did. If the plushest pockets of Society put all their money on a favourite, the man who wagered against it would walk away with a tidy sum. And as Mary knew, some men would do terrible things for enough money. "Your clients wish you to investigate these individual cases to learn if there is anything, or anyone, shared in common between them?"

"Aye again."

"And have you discovered much?"

Alexander blew out another puff of air. "One name that arises in almost every instance is one we have heard before: Ralph Hesselgrave."

"The man who invested in the business of the one who died yesterday, Harry Carnes?"

"Exactly the same."

Chapter Six

The Ball

There had not been much time to converse. Alexander needed to call for the horse he had hired for the duration of his stay in the neighbourhood and begin his inquiries nearer to Epsom, and Mary replied that she needed to return to Hartfield before her hosts began to worry for her. They parted company with something less than absolute ease and went their separate ways.

Alexander watched her disappear down the street with a feeling of discontentment. He ought to have known she would be unhappy with him after he failed to appear at her sister's wedding, but had been unprepared for the depth of her ire. Amongst his friends, both in London and in the small village outside of Glasgow where he grew up, such a lapse would be met with a scowl and a disappointed sigh, and that would be the end of the matter. "Unavoidable affairs of business" were well understood to interfere with one's obligations to friends; Darcy himself had shrugged off the matter, saying only, "We shall miss you, but of course you must tend to your clients."

He would never understand Mary Bennet!

Taking one last moment to gaze after her as she disappeared around the corner where the street curved, he shook his head and went in search of the ostler to bring him his horse.

Yesterday's unexpected events had set his own work back by a day, but how could he deny Knightley's request? And, perhaps, this spate of supposedly accidental deaths might be related to his own mission here; some of the names were certainly familiar! Whilst Knightley was intelligent and a capable magistrate, he was not an investigator and might miss some subtle clue about both cases. As it was, the man had asked almost all of the questions that plagued Alexander, but now he must begin his own investigations in earnest.

He thanked the ostler for bringing his horse and swung up into the saddle. He had pored over maps of the region and had a fair sense of his direction and paused only for a moment to glance at the signposts at the side of the stable yard.

"Heading off towards Epsom, Lyons?" He glanced up to see Hugh Cox stroll out of the inn. "I'm heading that way myself, if you'd like the company. I know these parts and can set you down the right path."

"Much obliged, Cox. Were you not here to spend time with your brother and his family?"

The attorney laughed. "On the day of the first ball this village has seen in many a year? No indeed! I have just come from my brother's house. His wife, his daughter, even his maids, are scurrying about like frantic mice, calling about gowns and ribbons and stocking and shoes. Even my brother, who from Monday to Saturday cannot tell one of his coats from the next, is in a bother about which waistcoat will best suit the breeches he received from his tailor yesterday. If I spend the day there, I shall go quite mad, and so I am riding to Epsom to meet an associate there to go over matters for an unrelated case of a contested will. Ah, here is my fine beast. Shall we ride?"

The road was gentle and clear, and the two men conversed easily along the way. Cox related some details about his business in Epsom, a fairly simple case of a hithertofore unknown person claiming to be the deceased landowner's natural son and demanding a settlement, saying that his father had promised it to him.

"Can there be any truth in his claim?" Alexander asked as he watched the greening fields along their way.

"Unlikely. The estate is entailed, and the man left precious little else, being of a rather profligate nature and careless of passing on wealth to relatives he loved but little. There was, in short, almost nothing besides the estate to give, and that could not be promised away. There is also the detail of the claimant being a large and very fair man, whilst the deceased was small of stature and dark."

"It is well known that members of the same family need not share physical traits. My own hair," he indicated towards his red mop with his eyes, "is unique within my family, save for one aunt. Two of my sisters are blonde and the other dark brown."

"Very true," Cox admitted. "Looking at us, one would never believe me to be related to my brother, but my mother promises it is so and I would never disbelieve that good woman."

The two men enjoyed a laugh over this description before Cox continued. "But the veriest evidence against this claimant is the real nature of the former landowner. His lifestyle, as I said, was irregular. He never married, never wished to, but my sources suggest he was rather well known in certain establishments in Town where only men venture."

"Ah." Alexander had heard of such places. So too had he discovered that friends from university—fine, honest, and decent men—ran to such tastes. He could not believe it to be such a mortal sin if such good people were so inclined. He stifled a sound between a chuckle and a moan. How he would enjoy debating such a topic with Mary, with her fine mind and very different turn of thought, but how absurd, at the same time, to even contemplate raising such a topic with a young lady. But if he could, she would find her Bible and her book of sermons, and together they might tease out some threads of good and evil, of God-given nature and of free will. He regretted the impossibility of it. "And so you believe he could have no natural son because his inclinations did not run to women."

"Just so."

"But a youthful indiscretion, an attempt to correct his unnatural urges...?"

"I went to school with this man's younger brothers. He was known, from his youngest years, to be a molly. I cannot believe he could have approached any women for... well, for intimate matters."

"You yourself are not wed," Alexander raised his brows, but kept his voice light and teasing.

"Not for lack in interest, Lyons. I was engaged once. It lasted until the lady's father discovered a questionable ancestor and my profession. He had loftier aspirations for his daughter, and after that, I lost heart and devoted myself to my work rather than society. I still imagine I shall meet somebody whom I can like, who will not shun my rather un-illustrious forebears."

"I am sorry." There seemed little more to say, so he returned to Cox's case. "This claimant—you intend to confront him with this fact about the late landowner? You can hardly use it in court; you'll taint the entire family's reputation."

"We both know this, but he does not! I will merely assert that he cannot possibly be the old fellow's son and suggest I might cry rope on him, and wait for him to crawl off like the rat he is."

"I might have done just the same, had I set myself up in that line."

"Right," Cox inclined his head. "You've studied the law yourself. Glasgow degree, if I recall. Never could understand what you're doing investigating in London, but a man makes his own decisions."

"Aye." They rode in silence for a moment, and Alexander took the time to appreciate the beauty of the landscape. Then he asked, "You knew this fellow, if not well, then well enough to know a rather precious secret. Do you know many of the people in these parts?"

Cox pursed his lips. "That I do! My family weren't quite of the circles to associate with the likes of the Woodhouses, but we were well enough situated for most others, and not so high that we did not talk to the farmers and workers. What would you know?"

"I suppose I should like an accounting of the families in Highbury at some time, but for the moment, what can you tell me about Harry Carnes?"

"He's the one that died yesterday. Sad business. I knew him, but not well. We were townsfolk, wealthy, and of the middle class. Carnes' family were farmers, successful and well-to-do in their way, but wary of those of us who did not live off the land. Harry was three or four years older than me. I guess him to have been about eight- or nine-and-forty. He was not a farmer at heart, like his pa or brothers, but had a knack for the horses, always top-sawyer. I was not surprised when I heard he set himself up raising and training them for the races. He might not have trusted us town-dwellers, but he never minded making a penny off us."

This was interesting, but nothing that Alexander did not already know. Still, no information was without some value. "And as a younger man? Who were his friends? What did he do? Have you any knowledge of this?"

"Much the same as any lad, at least before we were sent off to school. I recall he worked for a time at the Crown as a stable hand, always wanting to be around his horses. Even as a youth he had in mind to raise and train thoroughbreds. I recall on one visit home for school holidays, sitting in the sun and hearing him go on to his mates about some grand scheme of his, and how he had convinced this lord and that squire and the other merchant to invest in his plans. Even the vicar was in, I recall, for we all joked about a man of God throwing his lot in with gamers and wagerers. Nothing came of that scheme, alas, and we all thought his plans were for nought, until he caught Hesselgrave's notice some ten or twelve years back. Then, suddenly, he had his blunt and his stables and his training grounds, and the money was starting to come in. He was finally a success at what he loved, and then to see him dead like that... well, more's the pity."

Cox slowed his horse as they came to a crossroads. "This is where we part ways, Lyons. I'm for Epsom town, straight ahead, but you want Hesselgrave's estate, down that lane and over the bridge past the woods. There's a large stone gate before his drive. You cannot miss it."

He waved goodbye, but then stopped and turned back for a moment.

"See you at the ball tonight, Lyons? Knightley lending you togs?"

Alexander clucked his tongue and grinned. "Correct to both! Until later, Cox. Thank you for the information."

And he turned his horse and rode down the lane to visit Ralph Hesselgrave.

❦

"Miss Bennet!" Mary heard her name called out for the third time that morning. She had just come into view of Randalls, and Frank Churchill was waving at her from the path leading through the well-tended gardens. She waved back and slowed her steps to allow him to approach.

"You are awake and out early, Miss Bennet, to be returning already. You have taken tea at the Crown, I see, for there is a spot of jam on your cloak. Aha, I have found you out! Is this your custom?"

"You have discovered my secrets indeed, Mr. Churchill," she laughed. "It is indeed my custom when I am at home. My sister always rose with the sun before she married, and as my bedroom was beside hers, the sound of her dressing and making her toilette awakened me, and I learned to enjoy the solitude of the early morning. Watching the world come to life is a quiet pleasure. I use the time to think of my blessings and make my morning prayers."

"You are of a particularly pious bent, Miss Bennet?" He offered her his arm and began to stroll towards Hartfield.

She frowned in thought. "No more religious than many, I imagine. I find comfort in the clear moral teachings of devotional texts, but I do not believe I have any greater or lesser faith than most of the good people I know." Except possibly one. This topic was one they had debated without resolution, and which now lay between them, not quite ignored, but neither dwelt upon. She was silent for a moment and added, "When the evil in the world becomes too great for me to contemplate, I take comfort in the words of those wiser and closer to God than I."

He did not respond, but tugged his arm ever-so-slightly towards his body, bringing her hand close enough to his elegant coat to feel his body's warmth. The sensation was unexpected and bewildering. They walked in silence for a few moments before he asked, "Is everything in readiness for the ball this evening? I must return soon to my aunt and uncle, near Richmond, but I begged their indulgence to stay with father last night, so as to be here to assist Miss Woodhouse with any final details. The ball was," he confessed in a theatrical whisper, "my very own idea!"

"Was it indeed, sir? Do tell me more!"

He began to talk and continued doing so until they arrived at the grand front door to Hartfield. Once inside the house, Emma swept down the stairs to confer with Mr. Churchill about those very details he had mentioned, and Mary begged to be excused to rest and begin to ready herself for the evening.

"Remember, Miss Bennet, I have claimed two dances, and am likely to claim two more. I beg you to wear your most comfortable shoes, for I should not like to be disappointed." He beamed at her and offered an elaborate bow and watched her take her leave. Mary did not miss the puzzled and not entirely satisfied frown upon Emma's face before she turned around. There was far too much going on beneath the civilised surface for her to make sense of!

Upstairs in her rooms she tried to read the novel she had borrowed from Mr. Woodhouse's library, but her mind would not be still. She had been so certain that Miss Woodhouse and Mr. Knightley held some unrecognised affection for each other, and even more certain about Mr. Churchill and Jane Fairfax. But now Emma was doting upon Alexander, and Frank Churchill was pouring all his charm upon her, and she began to doubt every inference she had ever made. Perhaps the evening's festivities would enlighten her somewhat as to where, exactly, matters lay between everybody.

At four o'clock a young maid appeared at Mary's door with yet another beautiful gown and proceeded to spend the next two hours stitching and lacing and brushing and pinning clothing and hair until Mary was dressed to the maid's satisfaction. "Are you pleased, Miss?" the girl asked, and when Mary looked at herself in the mirror, she could do nothing but gasp in agreement.

The gown which Emma had offered her had a persimmon-coloured skirt of rich silk, with a net overlay which boasted a thick border at the hem, embroidered in flowers the same colour as the skirt. The bodice was a very pale ivory, almost white, trimmed in short bands around the neck with the same silk as the skirt, and with short and full sleeves of the ivory silk, decorated with chevrons of the pink. A band of ivory ribbon was gathered below the bodice and tied into a bow at the back, trailing pretty ends as she moved, and flowers the colour of the persimmon-pink skirt adorned the careful twist of hair upon her head. Delicate tendrils of her hair, so carefully sugared and curled, floated around her face, and pearl ear-bobs and a matching necklace, generously lent by Miss Woodhouse, as well as long ivory gloves and a persimmon fan, completed the outfit.

If she had felt beautiful the previous evening, how much more so did she feel now, gowned like a princess. The curls of hair softened her features, which she so often marred with her serious expression, and the deep pink of her skirt and the trim of the bodice brought out a hidden glow in her complexion.

"It is... I am lovely! Thank you!" She beamed at the maid, who bobbed a curtsey and asked if Miss Bennet required anything else, before dashing out the door.

At six o'clock the Woodhouse party gathered to dine. Mary was quite afraid lest she spill something on the beautiful borrowed dress or somehow mar her perfect hair, but the meal was well planned with dishes that would not fall or stain, and she and her clothing survived the ordeal with no accidents. Emma, once again, was lovely in her white silk gown, decorated with pale blue ribbons and flowers, and with sapphires at her ears and her throat, her broad and open beauty radiant like the brightest of jewels.

"Will you not reconsider and join us?" Emma asked her father more than once before the carriage arrived.

"No, no, it is far too late, not at all healthy. You will ensure that there is a good fire so you do not get a chill? And that the hallway between the dancing room and the dining room is not too draughty. I am expecting Mrs. Bates to join me here this evening, to talk and play cards, and we will be quite happy together. I have sent the carriage for her, and we shall be most content indeed. We do not enjoy the noise and ado that you young people seem to like so much. No, do not eat too much rich food at supper, and be careful to avoid standing by the windows..."

The advice on maintaining their health continued until the carriage arrived and Mrs. Bates was helped out by a sturdy footman.

The two young ladies bid their elders a grand evening and set off, full of anticipation, for the ball.

At half past seven, the carriage arrived at the Crown, and Emma and Mary descended, careful not to soil their shoes or get mud on the woollen wraps they used to ward off the evening chill. Most of the guests were not expected until eight, but Emma wished to assure herself that every smallest matter had been taken care of and that no more of her advice was needed. She had, she explained to Mary in the carriage, planned each detail with Frank Churchill and with Mrs. Weston's advice, and she had employed only the very best people to carry out her plans exactly.

As they entered the inn, another carriage drew up and the party from Randalls waved through the carriage window at them. Mr. Weston alit first, the better to hand out his wife, and they greeted Mary very graciously and with the sound of genuine pleasure. The last out was Frank. He sent off the carriage and strode into the building with his accustomed nonchalance, but then stopped quite still when he spied Mary.

"Miss Bennet. How lovely. Every time I believe you cannot be more beautiful, you prove me wrong. How very well you look." He offered her his arm and led her up the stairs to the first storey where the ball was to be held.

The room for the ball, when they entered, was perfect, and Emma let out a small laugh of delight. "Well done, Miss Woodhouse," Frank applauded her. "It is exactly as I had hoped. You have worked wonders. Miss Bennet, shall we take a closer look? Do come with me, for I long to examine the ornaments and draperies in the corner, and the chalking on the floor. Do join me."

He had not allowed her to let go of his arm, and now he covered her hand in his as he led her to the aforementioned ornaments on their Grecian stands. They walked about together, so as to see that everything was as it should be. Every table, every chair, every candle sconce, every lamp, was deemed to be perfect.

"My only regret," Frank whispered so only Mary could hear him, "is that I promised my first two dances before I had the pleasure of your acquaintance.

"Really, sir! This is too much!" Mary chided him, but her eyes shone with the unfamiliar glow of openly receiving a handsome gentleman's admiration.

This tête-à-tête was interrupted by the sound of new voices from the doorway, and Mary turned to see Alexander standing at the threshold, with Emma gliding across the floor to greet him. "Mr. Lyons!" she cooed. "What a delight that you are able to join us this evening. My happiness would not have been complete without you."

Mary forced herself not to roll her eyes heavenward, but turned her attention back to her companion, who eyed Alexander from across the room and executed a cold and curt bow.

By now people were starting to arrive in larger and larger numbers, and Frank pointed out each family that he knew. The Coles came first, with their two daughters in the finest fashions from London and their son who looked to be attending his first ball. "The Coles made their wealth in trade," he murmured in Mary's ear, "and every year when they host their musical event, Miss Woodhouse insists she will not attend because she cannot be seen to notice them, but then is most vexed when the invitation does not arrive."

How interesting, then, that she should pay so very much attention to Alexander, who had not even wealth to recommend him. She must ponder this.

"Ah, there is Mr. Cox with his family. He is the village attorney, quite respectable, but some unpleasant gossip about a grandparent's origins. Italian, some say, and Papist! Quite shocking!"

More ado at the doors presaged the arrival of another couple whom Mary could not see at first, due to the crowds about them. The lady's location was known by a plume of white feathers that floated two feet or more above her head, and by an imperious voice that Mary had heard once before.

"Mrs. and Mr. Elton?"

Frank laughed aloud. "You have discovered the worst of us, Miss Bennet. Indeed, it is. I wonder that they did not... Oh, but I see they did. Please excuse me whilst I greet Miss Bates and Miss Fairfax. He bowed and walked off across the room.

Now that the Eltons had moved into the room and away from the door, Mary could see the newcomers. Hetty Bates looked about the space with wide eyes and a slight grin.

"...wonderful, Miss Woodhouse... magical... too very marvellous to believe...." Mary could hear her voluminous praises from across the room.

Behind her, Jane Fairfax stood in silence. As Mary watched, Frank greeted her with a perfunctory bow and a few words, to which Miss Fairfax replied equally shortly. First his, and then her, eyes darted across the crowds to where Mary was standing, and Mary had the very definite impression that the discussion related to herself in some significant way. From the expressions on their faces, she deemed the conversation not entirely pleasant. Although she knew the two only very little and had heard of no connexion between them, she had the sense nonetheless of a much longer and more intimate association than most people seemed to have guessed.

What, then, was Frank Churchill about with his outrageous flirtations and attentions to her? Did he truly admire her, or was he affecting some sort of masquerade to avert attention from Jane Fairfax?

The secrets in this small town were becoming more and more perplexing every moment.

Chapter Seven

Asking Questions

As the evening progressed, it seemed apparent that everybody had noticed Frank's attentions to Mary. He opened the ball with Emma, as was appropriate for the two people who had planned the entire event, and danced another set later on with Miss Fairfax, but danced two sets with Mary and floated about her for much of the rest of the evening.

Mrs. Weston, who was not dancing, raised speculative eyebrows whenever she walked past as they conversed. Mr. Knightley gave Frank more than one disapproving scowl, and Mr. Weston made a point to drop in a word in his son's ear not to neglect his duties as one of the organisers of the ball. Everywhere Mary turned people seemed to be staring and whispering and speculating, as can only happen in a ballroom.

If such had occurred in Meryton, Mary considered, if Mr. Bingley had behaved half as openly towards her sister Jane as Frank was behaving towards her, the entire town would be expecting an engagement to be announced that every evening. She could imagine Mama's strident voice, crowing about her good fortune at her daughter—her plain, uninteresting middle daughter, whom no one seemed to think of from one minute to the next—having captured the wealthy and most eligible Frank Churchill! No wonder every eye in the room seemed to be upon her.

Did Frank know what manner of expectations he was raising in the hearts of the denizens of Highbury, if not her own? She knew this was a passing flirtation, that she would soon be back in Mr. Darcy's fine carriage on the road to London and thence to Hertfordshire. Her lot was to forge whatever sort of life she could as the third and, to all intents and purposes, penniless daughter of a minor country squire; his was to live large on the wealth he was set to inherit from his doting aunt and uncle. In theory they were equals; in reality, he was as far above her as a lord was to a scullery maid. And yet, he hung upon her every word, praised her beauty, and lauded her achievements. If he continued his attentions, if he could sustain his charm and attractive manner past a few short days' duration, would she consider permitting him to call upon her at Longbourn?

Although with one sister so well married and another soon to enter that state, she need no longer worry about being cast into the hedgerows some unfortunate day. Still, she did wish for more for herself than to be the maiden aunt, reluctantly taken in by well-meaning relations, doomed to assist the governess and train unwilling fingers to play the pianoforte very ill. As much as she affected a demeanour of cool indifference to matters of the heart and devoted herself to her spiritual edification, her deepest desires were for a home and a family. For the sort of love her sisters had found. It was not her way to be jealous of their fortune, but the chance to experience something of what they had found was too tempting to be cast away without serious sober thought.

A new set of dances had begun, and Mary had begged leave to sit this one out and keep Miss Bates company. Frank had taken his father's hints and was now dancing with one of the Miss Coles, and Miss Bates required little input from her company to maintain the conversation, allowing Mary to contemplate the whirling scene before her. Patterns of dancers moved up and down the central space of the hall as the band played on, sprightly melodies springing from reeds and pipes and bows, leaping from agile fingers to nimble feet. There was Miss Harriet Smith, whom she had briefly met, dancing with Mr. Knightley, of all people! And there, Jane Fairfax was standing up with Mr. Cox's brother, the one from London whom Alexander had introduced, and Mr. Weston was leading Mrs. Cole through the quadrille. And there, laughing and smiling and paying far too much attention to each other, were Emma and Alexander himself!

Once again, a confusion of emotion swept over her. Why should Alexander not dance with Miss Woodhouse? She had no claims on him; indeed, an invitation to dance was more social obligation than declaration of affection. Many men were dancing with women not their wives. Why, Mrs. Weston was looking with great pride upon her husband as he handed Mrs. Cole through a set of the steps in the dance, and Mr. Cole seemed not at all perturbed at the sight of his wife so dancing.

If Emma wished to dance with Alexander, and if Alexander wished to dance with Emma, what possible reason could she find for distress? It was a dance, such as the ones she had shared with Frank Churchill, a pattern of steps and twirls upon the chalked floor, an exercise as much in rhythm and grace as in social interaction. Furthermore, it had not troubled her at all earlier when

Alexander had stood up with Jane Fairfax in the set of country dances, or when he had danced a reel with the youngest Miss Cox. Whyever should seeing him with Emma leave her so disturbed in spirit?

Could it be, she wondered, that of all the ladies in the room, he had not asked her to dance? He had hardly spoken a word to her, other than the obligatory greetings. After all, she had been kept so busy by Frank Churchill, and every time she had looked to find Alexander not dancing, he was talking to Emma. She and he might be complete strangers to each other, rather than the friends she thought they were!

And they were friends. Her chagrin at his absence from Lizzy and Darcy's wedding now seemed unreasonable. She had been disappointed, that was all. They had come to an agreement of sorts, and he had promised to see her again soon, and she had been anticipating some interesting and well-informed conversation. When he did not arrive as expected, her plans had been upset. Surely that was all.

And now that he was here, now that they had re-established their camaraderie, he was devoting all of his time to Emma! Emma could have no use for Alexander, other than enjoying his presence as she might that of an exotic pet. Some ladies had pugs, others pet squirrels, or colourful exotic birds; Emma had a pet investigator. She would parade him about the village whilst he remained, and then she would regale her entire acquaintance for months with tales of when she met him. It was unfair!

She must find a way to distance him from Emma. She must find a way to make him wish to spend time with her instead. And one way came immediately to mind. He was investigating suspicions of unscrupulous dealings in the horse races. As she had at Longbourn, she could ask questions here as well, and come to him with her answers.

Then, at last, they could meet and speak again as equals. As friends.

The room was awhirl with music and dancers. Even the most sedate country dance had taken on an uncommon energy. Not for the first time did somebody mention to Alexander that this was the first ball held in Highbury for many a year, and the entire neighbourhood had come out to glean every possible ounce of enjoyment from it.

He had been pleased to accept the invitation and had been quite prepared to wear the best suit in his trunk for the event, but Knightley had intervened once more and insisted upon seeing what might be lurking in his various closets and trunks at Donwell Abbey.

Consequently, his return trip from calling upon Hesselgrave—who had not been at home, more's the pity—had involved a detour past Donwell to call upon its master and to examine what might be available for him.

At any other time, Alexander would have thanked the man profusely and then refused the honour, preferring to dress as what he was: an unimportant son of a country doctor who made his way, with some success, in trade. That his stock in trade was his mind was irrelevant: he worked for his bread and made no pretensions to anything else.

This time, however, something compelled him to accept the offer, just as he had accepted the previous evening for dinner at Hartfield. He had elected to wear the same coat as before; it was plain luck that he had found the item amongst Knightley's offerings, and more so that the coat had fit so well. The valet had needed to perform only a very few alterations to make the item look as if it had been cut for him, for which he thanked the wizard of a man profusely.

"It was merely a tuck at the waist and at the sleeve, sir," Hodges had replied, but Alexander was duly awed, nonetheless. He was scarcely able to sew on a button himself.

To go with the mid-blue coat, he had selected a pair of ivory silk breeches and a dove-grey waistcoat with a thin blue stripe. He had, in his own wardrobe, suitable stockings and shoes, and Hodges had insisted upon travelling into Highbury with Mr. Knightley to attend to the final details of Alexander's appearance and tie his cravat. As he had discovered some months before when waited upon by Darcy's man, there was a selfish luxury in being so served, and he made certain to enjoy the novelty of it.

He was pleased with his decision. Highbury might not be London, where the first circles gathered to play and amuse themselves, but it had its share of elegance and wealth, and for a moment he was invited into those circles. Here, for tonight at least, he was not Alexander Lyons, country oaf and perennial stranger, but Mr. Lyons, honoured guest.

What he had not been quite so prepared for, however, was the attention paid to him by Miss Woodhouse. The previous evening at her home, he had been surprised but not alarmed, for he was a novelty amongst the familiar. Tonight, however, he had quite expected her to toss him a perfunctory 'Good evening,' and then dash off to tend to some matter that only she could fix and to fawn over and regale a hundred other men, all more wealthy, handsome, and important than he.

Imagine his shock, therefore, when all of her admirable charms were turned upon him and nobody else! She took his arm and showed him the hanging draperies, the flowers, the tables laden with food and drink, the special design of chalk on the floor for the dancing, and so many other details, asking his opinion on each one and looking at him as if his approbation were the most important thing in the world to her.

Although her assumed role as hostess carried with it some obligation on her time, every moment not otherwise claimed led her to his side. She danced with Churchill to open the ball, and then again with various well-placed members of the local society, but made a great showing of the empty slots on her dance card, which he most graciously offered to fill. They danced two sets together, and the look upon her face was one of triumph!

Mary was dancing as well, he noticed. He had noticed much of what she did, and with whom she spoke. For all that Emma was doting upon him, it seemed that Churchill was doting upon Mary. He ought to be pleased, for she had been very much the wallflower in Meryton, content to watch life from the wings. And how she had blossomed here, in this place where her accustomed ways were unknown and where she was welcomed as the season's brightest light, rather than as the quiet and oft-forgotten middle Bennet daughter.

Yes, he ought to be pleased indeed, to see her shine as she did in her beautiful gown and her elegant hairstyle. He was not, as a rule, a man to notice much about a woman's garb other than to assess it for evidence in a case, but he could not help but notice how the reddish pink of the skirt and trim brought out the soft glow of her blush and how the delicate tendrils of hair, usually swept back so harshly into a plain knot, drew attention to her eyes. He had heard her lament that she was the plain sister, the one who could never compare to the others in looks or personality, but this unplanned stay in Highbury had revealed a new side to Mary, one where she could step out of her usual role and become the beautiful young woman she had hidden for so long.

As he danced with the very lovely Emma Woodhouse, resplendent in her own white silken gown, he ought to be delighted that Mary was enjoying her evening so very much.

"A penny for your thoughts?" Emma gazed at him with her wide blue eyes. "Am I not enough to keep your attention?" She tittered at her joke. In her mind, she would always be more than enough.

"My apologies, Miss Woodhouse. I was overwhelmed by the splendour of the evening and my mind wandered. No man in your presence could ever wish for anything more." And how he forced himself to believe his words.

It was very late when Alexander took to his bed at last. The ball had been a success of the first waters. He had heard not a word of complaint, but a great deal of praise and appreciation, and he well imagined that much of the village would rise late in the morning. As it was, the sun was closer to rising than to setting; he must force himself to sleep for a short time at least, for his day could not wait until noon to begin. And yet, as so often occurs after a great celebration, his busy mind denied the needs of his exhausted body and insisted upon dwelling over such small details of the ball as he had noticed.

Mrs. Elton had paraded about the space as if she were queen of the hive, attempting at every moment to usurp Miss Woodhouse's place. She pretended to great elegance and social éclat, but from what Alexander had been able to learn about her, her money was plentiful but newly acquired and she had little else to recommend her. Her greatest claim to social pre-eminence was marrying the village parson. Indeed, in the quarter hour that he had been forced to abide her company, he had found her a vain woman, more satisfied with herself even than Miss Woodhouse, and overestimating her own importance. Her manners were inferior.

Emma, with her own understanding of herself as the centre of Highbury's society, had exquisite manners, but Mrs. Elton's were pert and overly familiar, and her notions insular and limited. She might consider herself quite grand, but her society would do her associates little good.

Mr. Elton was little better than his wife. There must be some story between Miss Harriet Smith and the parson, for when Emma suggested he dance with her friend, he immediately declared he had no thought of dancing at all. His excuse was clearly disingenuous; that he wished to slight the young woman was evident, and for a moment it seemed poor Miss Smith was doomed to be shunned for the remainder of the ball. But Alexander, who had been sitting to the side watching this interaction, had stepped up and requested her hand for a set, after which Mr. Knightley did likewise. The results had been a pleasant rescue for the pretty young woman, but it had left no kind feelings in Alexander's breast for the Eltons.

Alexander rolled over in his bed, hoping a new position would allow him the rest his body craved, but new images flooded through his mind. Now it was the memory of Miss Fairfax that interfered with his sleep. They were introduced only briefly and had had little time to converse, but her quiet and refined beauty was not lost on him, nor was her poise and elegance. She had seemed, at first, delighted with the ball, with the room, with the music. She had wandered the space with a distant look in her fine eyes, as if recalling pleasant times from the past. However, he could not but notice that when her eyes alit on Churchill and Mary, her face was suddenly drained of all animation. Did the lady have a fancy for Churchill? It hardly seemed possible, for their characters seemed so very different, one reserved and closed, the other exuberant and outgoing. It hardly seemed possible that Churchill might hold any affection for her, for all that he was dancing attendance upon Mary.

And now it was Mary's face which filled his thoughts. When had she become so beautiful? When had she become the belle of the ballroom? And why was she in another man's arms?

Sleep did eventually come, and the sun far too soon thereafter. With red and heavy eyes, Alexander washed and shaved and dressed for the day, and after taking more coffee than was his wont, called for his horse. Hugh Cox did not join him this morning; the attorney had been dancing and drinking well into the hours of the morning and had no need to rise before dinner. With the sun now well above the horizon, Alexander rode out of town in search, once more, of Mr. Hesselgrave.

Without the distraction of conversation, he rode fast, and the four miles of the journey passed in a moment. It was always a wonder, he reflected not for the first time, that familiar roads make distances shorten. What had seemed like a long journey only yesterday now seemed a mere nothing, a jaunt across the countryside. He slowed his horse to a walk and allowed his eye to rove across the scenery. Here, behind him, was Highbury, and there, around the curve of road, was the lane he must take to Hesselgrave's estate. The hill that rose unusually high, that must be the one with the stone wall, the one where Carnes had eaten his last meal and fallen to his death at the bottom of a reservoir of cold rain water. It was close, far closer than he had thought, and must be only a mile or two taken cross-country, rather than on the solid dirt lanes. What that might import, he knew not, but he reserved the fact to note down later on in his little book.

Once again, Hesselgrave was not at home. Yesterday he had merely inquired of the man's housekeeper as to his presence, and then had departed, leaving only his card but no mention of his purpose. Today he begged a moment of the good woman's time.

"'Tis not my place to discuss Mr. Hesselgrave's whereabouts."
She regarded him through narrow eyes and stared him up and
down, and for a very long time. He felt like a suspicious piece of
meat she was assessing at the butcher's. He straightened his back
and stared back.

"From London, are you?" She hardly glanced at his card, which
she held again in her hand.

"Aye."

"You don't sound like you are from London." Ah, so she had
noticed his broad Scots accent. One would have to be deaf to miss
it.

"I am not, not originally, but I've lived and worked there these
past three years."

"Come as an apprentice to a tradesman, then? I can hardly
believe that, for you are too well spoken. And tradesmen don't have
calling cards. Where were you before? What did you do?"

It seemed his only chance was in submitting to this
interrogation; she was speaking to him at least and not turning him
out on his ear.

"I come from a small village near Glasgow, Ma'am. Before
arriving in London, I was a student. At the university."

At this, her eyes flew open. She had not been expecting such an
admission. She took a longer look at his card. "Investigator, you
say? Is that taught now?"

"No, Ma'am. But the Law is. I took my degree there and then
read for the bar."

She peered at him again but did not speak for some time. At
length she gave a small scowl and nodded. "Very well. Your hair
puts me in mind of my Rabbie when first we married. He was a
handsome one then; still is to me. He's stable master here. Go one
around the back and ask for him. Tell him Mrs. Duncan allowed you
back. He might have a word or two to spare for you."

With a great smile and a clipped bow, Alexander did as he was bade and soon found the man. He looked to be somewhere between fifty and sixty, with a round belly and hair that still held echoes of its former fire. "Glasgow, eh lad? Closer to Falkirk meself!" And in a moment, he was Alexander's closest friend.

Rabbie Duncan was happy to answer Alexander's questions, and even more so to do it in Scots. It was not Alexander's first language, for the family spoke English in the house, as befitted the personal physician to a wealthy lord, but he knew the language well and was pleased to oblige.

The two men sat at a low table in the small office attached to the stables, and Alexander took out his notebook and wrote the date at the top of a clean page. Duncan held up a hand and disappeared for some minutes, then returned with two metal flagons of strong-smelling ale. He raised his cup in a silent toast, took a deep draught, and began to tell his own tale.

The Duncans had been at Riverton for six and thirty years. He had come as a lad, fresh from his father's farm in Scotland, begging for work in the stables or gardens. He was taken on and immediately fell in love with the pretty young lass in the kitchens. He had been one-and-twenty; she seventeen when they wed. Sally had been as smart as she was lovely, and Rabbie a hard worker, and in time both took on greater and greater responsibilities until she was the housekeeper and the head of the stables. They had four strapping sons and three grandchildren and were very pleased with their lot in life. Alexander smiled with appreciative respect as the older man told his tale and scratched down what details he deemed important for his investigation.

"My felicitations, Mr. Duncan! You have achieved what most men can only wish for: happiness." He saluted with his own sip of the quaff and settled into his hard wooden chair. "I had hoped to hear from Mr. Hesselgrave himself. When might he be back?"

The Scotsman pursed his lips. "The master is often away," he said as he cradled his cup in large, calloused hands. "Left day before yesterday, he did, and hasn't been back since. It's not unusual for him. He has dealings all over these parts, and sometimes stays where he's needed.

"Might you know where he is at the moment? Perhaps my own business will take me to him."

Duncan let out a harrumph. "Can't rightly say. He was off towards Dorking at first, but when he heard John Abdy died, he made some mention of passing by Highbury to see the old goat off."

This was interesting! "He knew Abdy, did he?" Alexander tried to make his tone nonchalant.

"Aye, from when they were younger. Hesselgrave is a mite younger than me, but his da, that is the former Mr. Hesselgrave, thought highly of the man, back when he was old Mr. Bates's clerk. Different stations in life, but they had some dealings in common, from what I recall. I was just a stable hand and gardener's assistant then, so had no notion of what their business might have been, but they was always loitering around the stables and I thought it might have to do with horse racing."

"Lots of that in these parts, I reckon," Alexander hoped he sounded nonchalant.

"Aye, there is. Lots of blunt to be made too, if you bet right." Duncan sniffed at his ale.

"Much fixing of the races? I imagine there's more than one toff who might wish to replenish his empty coffers with a crooked horse or rider." He pretended to look into the distance, but kept sharp attention on Duncan's face from the corner of his eye.

The man did not blink. "Aye, I dare say there is that. Nought that I know about for certain, though. More in the riding than in the beasts themselves, I'd wager. It's easier to convince a jockey to hold the horse back a nose than to spur him on hard. But there's also plenty of ways to give a runner extra speed. Some opium mixtures, down the gullet—that will make a horse think he has wings."

"Hmm… I had no notion. I'm not a betting man myself. I can't afford the habit!" He laughed at himself. "Tell me, if you wished to fix a horse like that—make him think he had wings to win a race—how would you do it?"

The older man wrinkled his nose. "I've no taste for that sort of thing. Bad for the animals. My lot is to care for them and see them do well, not burn them up like yesterday's kindling. Still, a handful of carrots with a wad of the stuff, right before a race. But not too much, else the creature will take off backwards or drop dead on you. That won't win no races. Elsewise, mess with the other racers. Something in their shoes, or something in their feed to slow them down. But that's mighty hard to do with a large field and not get caught at it."

"Is it worth the effort? The risk of being caught?"

Duncan laughed. "If you can win the right races, you need never want for a penny again in your life. Mind you, most who bet don't do it for the income, but for the thrill of it. It's more about the winning than the purse for some. There's a grand amount of blunt involved. A great many men with a great amount of cash are investing in the beasts and the races around these parts."

Alexander stirred in his seat. "This is some of what I wanted to speak with your master about. Mind if I take notes?". His pencil darted across the page in his notebook.

"Ain't got nothing to hide."

"Do you know anything about these investments? Have you any recollection at all of the particulars?"

Duncan shook his head, then took another drink. "It's many a year past, and I have no head for talk of numbers or percentages. I know horses, how to treat them and how to calm then and what they're wanting. I'm a good trainer and I keep the stables well running and organised, but their talk was more on business lines than the beasts themselves." He huffed again. "Like poor Carnes, I was. That was a man that knew horses. Dreadful news. You heard, of course."

Alexander made the appropriate noises and waited with his pencil hovering above the page. He was not disappointed.

"The present Mr. Hesselgrave was the purse behind Carnes' endeavour. He put up the blunt for the buildings and the training fields. I reckon if he went to bury Abdy before going on to Dorking, he may've come back to say his final words to Carnes. He'll also be wanting to make sure someone's tending those horses; they're fine beasts and the lads he hired on will do for a few days, but, to be truthful, there's a great lot of money tied up in those creatures. He'll be wanting someone with an eye for quality and a way with the animals to keep them in top racing form. Carnes was a top-sawyer trainer."

Alexander met the other man's eyes. "Have you any idea who that might be?"

"Not I, that's for certain. As I said, I've no interest in the races. But I guess he'll be wanting to talk to the other toff who's tossed some blunt into this venture. You must have met him; he lives in Highbury where you said you're staying. I oughtn't to know this, but I hear things when people speak. He's the parson there, name's Elton."

Alexander thanked Rabbie Duncan for his time and the ale and promised to return if at all possible for another conversation in the fellow's mother tongue. It had been good to speak Scots again, and brought back recollections of groups of rough-and-tumble boys roving through the village lanes on a summer's day, stopping off at one farmhouse or another for apples or biscuits or pies, laughing and joking and doing whatever young lads did when they weren't toiling in the fields. Those were good days, before the others learned that the Lyons family were different, not the sort to associate with, and forbade the children from playing any longer. The families might have respected his Pa's profound medical knowledge and paid him well for his services; the laird might have esteemed him and relied upon him for his every need as his physician. But trusting a man with your health was a far cry from trusting his family with your children's souls, and those nascent friendships with the village boys were soon put to an end.

He wiped the bittersweet recollections away as he rode back towards town and turned to more pressing matters. He had not learned what he set out to discover at Riverton, but he had discovered something else, and more than he expected. If Hesselgrave had some business dealings with both Abdy and Carnes, they must have been involved in some common projects. Had the other dead men been a part of it as well? The tramp's connection might be tenuous, but the second man who died—Fred Watson—had been a smith, and smiths worked with farriers, and farriers dealt with horses. There were too many connections for his liking, and the frisson of discomfort he had felt when Knightley first spoke of the succession of accidents began to fester into a sense of horror. He must find out what role, if any, Watson played in this enterprise. Suddenly the series of seemingly unrelated deaths took on a much more alarming aspect.

Chapter Eight

Unexpected Conversations

Mary opened her eyes to the sound of a dog barking in the yard outside. She had not drawn the draperies last night, and the sunlight that beamed into the room betrayed the rather late hour of the day more than she had hoped. She threw her feet off the side of the bed and reached for the small clock that stood on the bedside table. It was after noon already! How very unlike her to sleep so shamefully late!

It had also been very unlike her to be so popular at a ball. Having arrived at a course of action to take with respect to this strange spate of unexplained deaths and with the situation between Alexander and Emma, she had then allowed herself to enjoy the remainder of the evening. It was, she must confess, no difficulty to enjoy Frank Churchill's attentions, for what lady did not revel in being doted upon by a rich, charming, and handsome young man?

She had then danced and laughed through the rest of the evening and had returned to Hartfield very late indeed. She wondered who else in the house was awake. Emma must surely be, she mused, for Mr. Woodhouse seemed a creature of habit who would require his morning walk, and Emma, as his affectionate and solicitous daughter, would be awake and dressed to accompany him.

As imperious and pleased with herself as she was, Emma was not one to place her personal convenience over her father's needs, and this trait in itself redeemed her hostess from a multitude of other foibles in Mary's eyes. *Honour thy father and thy mother...* She herself had much to learn, and vowed to improve herself and moderate her pride at thinking herself as at all superior in moral tone to Miss Woodhouse.

Soon she was garbed in her walking dress and descended to the breakfast room. Miss Woodhouse was out with the master, she was informed. Expecting nothing less, Mary enjoyed a cup of chocolate and a slice of fruit bread with jam, and then set out herself for a walk towards the village.

Her object was the residence of Mrs. and Miss Bates. She wished, in part, to continue her association with Miss Fairfax, whose quiet and thoughtful manner appealed to her, and whose skill at the keyboard brought out the best in Mary's own meagre abilities. She also recognised something of herself in Miss Bates. For all that she found the spinster's monologues tedious and of limited interest, they were cut from the same cloth in many ways. Both were insignificant creatures in their respective worlds, with little to add to society by their own means and tolerated only because of familial obligation. Mary was the forgotten and plain middle daughter with great intellect and little heart, and with no conversation that anybody wished to hear; Miss Bates was the forgotten and plain spinster with little intellect and great heart, and with superfluous words that everybody ignored. Where Mary retreated into her books and music and sought solace in the words of God, becoming almost invisible to those around her, Miss Bates fought against this invisibility with her endless conversation, demanding that she not be completely forsaken.

The similarities were too striking to ignore, and Mary felt keenly that she must guard herself not to become a ridiculous figure like the older woman. With a rush of compassion, she had decided that it would do her no ill to pay a call upon the family and befriend Miss Bates, and if her unexpected and sudden fashionable reputation were to bring some small degree of consequence to the family, so much the better.

It was entirely secondary to her motives that if she did allow Miss Bates to speak at length, with some careful questions she might guide the lady into talking of the very subject she wished to hear! And if she happened to hear something that might capture the interest of Alexander Lyons, well, who was she to complain?

She hurried her feet along the way, and before long could see the first buildings of the village. Her path took her past the Crown, and she lingered for a moment to look at the site. The old Tudor timbers stood black against the white plaster of the original facade of the building, but the interior, as she now knew, was much expanded to the back and the sides, and was more modern, dating back only fifty years or so. The ball had been held in the halls on the first storey; the second and third housed the guest rooms, one of which Alexander occupied. Was he there now, still asleep after the previous night's festivities? Or had he not succumbed to bodily needs for excessive sleep and risen early, the better to discharge his duties?

She stared at the building and the activity that the aftermath of the ball had engendered. Three young lads were busy at the street before it with rakes and brooms, clearing the cobblestones of the dust and dirt of a hundred horses' hooves, and small armies of other servants wiped and carried and washed as the rest of the evidence of the party was packaged away. How much food had been prepared? How much eaten? Mary wondered what happened to the spoils and hoped that they would be distributed to the poor of the parish. Perhaps she might stop by the vicarage to visit Mrs. Elton and to inquire.

"Good morning, Miss Bennet!" She looked up with a smile upon her face. Only three days in Highbury, and everybody seemed to know who she was. That was Mr. Cox waving at her from the doorway. Of course, he was staying at the Crown as well. They had exchanged brief words last night, and she found his unpretentious company diverting and pleasant. "Off for a walk? Or do you have more serious business in mind?"

"Good morning, sir!" she waved back. "I have been taking a walk and thought to stop past the Bateses. I was fortunate enough to enjoy some pleasant conversation and music with Miss Fairfax recently and hoped to repeat the experience."

"May I join you on your walk?" the attorney asked. "Our friend Lyons seems not to be in his rooms, and I would not object to a moment or two in company. My brother's household, I fear, will all be asleep or repeating every moment of the ball. I enjoyed the experience once, but twice over would be excessive." He offered her a cheerful smile and she happily accepted his request.

Within a very short time they had arrived in front of the building where the Bates women had their apartments. Mr. Cox began to make his so-longs, but a voice from the upper windows stopped him.

"Miss Bennet! Have you come for a visit? How lovely? And you have brought a friend? Of course, Mr. Cox, we were introduced by Mr. Knightley at the ball. I did not know you from this direction. How kind of you to come, how very kind. Do come up! Mother is in the kitchens making her pies, and there is plenty to share. I hope you enjoy apple—Mr. Knightley sent us all his store apples, and they are so very good baked. Mother always says to me, 'Hetty,' she says, 'there is nothing so warming on a cool evening as a baked apple,' and when they begin to soften, they are ever so fine in pies. Jane is here, returned from her walk—I do not know where she goes, and so early in the morning as well—but we may enjoy some biscuits. Do come up!"

Mary and Mr. Cox looked at each other and smiled before approaching the door to the stairwell.

Unlike the last time Mary visited, now the small sitting room was devoid of other guests. Miss Fairfax was seated at the pianoforte, although there was no music before her, and it did not seem that she had recently been playing. It must be her accustomed place, Mary thought, the bench being one of only a few chairs in the room, and the aspect being as bright as must be possible, since the pianoforte sat in the light of a large window.

"Miss Bennet." Jane Fairfax stood and spoke politely, but her manner was cool.

"Jane, dear, did you meet Mr. Cox last night? You must meet Mr. Cox, for he has come down from London to stay with his brother until the dreadful affairs in the city are resolved, only he is not exactly staying with his brother, for Mr. Cox—that is, Mr. Cox's brother—has too busy a house for Mr. Cox's sensibilities—that is, this Mr. Cox—and... Oh bother! I have quite confused myself."

Miss Bates sat down in a pile of old fabric and confusion, and Mr. Cox laughed. "Oh, forgive me, Madam, I mean no disrespect, but I have wanted a good smile this morning."

"Oh, much obliged, Mr. Cox, I took no offence! Only, please, come and meet Jane. You really must meet Jane!"

Mrs. Bates was absent—presumably down in the kitchens baking the pies her daughter had spoken of—and Mary was able to sit quietly for a brief moment whilst Miss Bates made the introductions, relieved for a respite from having to make polite conversation. She affixed her smile of polite interest upon her face—the very one Lizzy had spent so much time teaching her—and let the conversation between the other three occupants of the room wash over her.

"…how do you do, Miss Fairfax?"

"…pleasure, sir…"

"…such an accomplished musician, such nimble fingers… most beautiful instrument… arrived without a note or any indication of who might have sent it… lovely weather… so fair for early May… no fresh eggs today… call down for some tea… might have coffee instead…"

Mr. Cox laughed again, a rich sound full of mirth and pleasure. "Thank you, Madam. I should very much enjoy a cup of coffee if such a thing is possible. How I do admire your home. It is not large, I can see, but my rooms in London are no larger, and a far sight less comfortable. Is the planning of it your work? How charming! You have found exactly the right place for the furniture to capture the best light, and the colours are just right to take best advantage of the angles of the walls."

As he talked, Mary could see that he was right. Miss Bates, if it were she who had arranged the sparse and worn furniture in this small space, had made the room as comfortable and elegant as it could be imagined. The lady beamed her appreciation and uttered the first sensible words Mary had heard emanate from her lips. "Thank you, sir. I have always found pleasure in colour and design, and I have done my best to make our rooms pleasing."

There ensued a perfectly agreeable and engaging conversation about furniture and the change in the fashions of decorating homes, and ideas of colour and placement of tables and chairs, a subject about which Mr. Cox seemed to have some interest and good opinions. Mary had never seen Miss Bates speak so intelligently on a topic. Could it be that the lady had the eye of an artist, but not the means to express her skill? Once more she found herself reassessing her initial impressions of a recent acquaintance: Miss Bates was not unintelligent at all, when speaking on a subject which lent itself to her innate skills. She sat a little straighter and listened with a keen ear, thinking that perhaps something of what Miss Bates was saying might well be applicable to her bedchamber back at Longbourn. Tea and coffee were brought and consumed, and the time passed more quickly and agreeably than ever Mary would have imagined.

In due time, Mr. Cox stood and made his bows. He had long overstayed his fifteen minutes, joking that the minute hand on his watch proclaimed his manners, but that the hour hand betrayed his lack thereof. "Do you walk, Miss Bates?" he asked as he took his leave. "I should enjoy your thoughts on the landscape and scenery of these parts. I have been so long in London that I have almost forgotten what beauty there is to be found in the sublime sight of a tree by a pond, or of patterned farmland against a blue sky." An arrangement was duly made, to the obvious satisfaction of both parties.

Mary also stood to depart, but Jane Fairfax spoke up before she could take her leave. "If you have no other obligations, Miss Bennet, I should enjoy your company at the keyboard. I find I have little else to occupy my time and your playing and company are good and welcome." The cool demeanour Mary had noticed upon first entering the room had softened, and Mary truly had hoped to spend some minutes exercising her fingers upon the soft ivory keys.

They spend some minutes searching for suitable music and then playing what they had found, never allowing the conversation to wander from this narrow path. Miss Fairfax must be unhappy about the attention Frank Churchill had been paying Mary, but this was not a topic that could be raised without encroaching into such intimate subjects that would be inappropriate for acquaintances of only a few days. Instead of words, therefore, they communicated with notes and tempi and the intricate conversation of the interwoven lines of melody, until at last they came to the end of the composition.

"Beautiful, so beautiful! What delightful music. How I wish I had the talent that you two possess—so much effort and skill—but I was never of the temperament to play, only to listen. What a delight to have such music in the house. How my dear father— that's Jane's grandfather, Miss Bennet, for she is my dear sister's daughter—would have enjoyed it, for he was very much a man to appreciate pretty music and good playing…"

Gone was the insightful and sensitive Miss Bates who had discussed her ideas of decorating so eloquently, and back in her place was the generous but simple woman whom Mary had first met. This one, however, was the woman she hoped might provide some thread of information she could feed to Alexander. She strove to find some manner to bring the conversation around to Mr. Abdy. The old man, whom she knew had been clerk to the lady's father, and who had been the second-to-last of these sad deaths, might have some other connection to the others which she could discover.

"Thank you, Miss Bates," she stood from the bench to stretch her arms and fingers. "I did not know you learned as a girl. Was your father very musical, then, to appreciate good music so? What sort of musical society was there in Highbury?"

Her attempt won success, for the older lady sat herself down upon the tired sofa and pressed her lips together in thought before starting to speak. "Father always loved music, and we had a fine fortepiano in our house when we lived in the parsonage, before we were forced to leave when Father died, for he was not wise in matters of finance and left us with very, very little, which of course we are obliged to make last as best we can under the circumstances. My sister was the proficient, not I, and as you have heard, her dear Jane received all of her talent, and I only wish we had not been forced to sell the fortepiano, for it was so dear to my sister's heart, and we can only be most grateful to my sweet Jane's secret friend who was so very kind to purchase her so thoughtful and generous a gift. But it was John Abdy, who has only now died, who suggested to Mother that after Jane—that was my sister's name as well as my niece's, who was her daughter—after Jane married Mr. Fairfax and left, we had no more need of the fortepiano for mother and I did not play, or not well enough to make the activity enjoyable at all."

She paused to take breath, and Mary did ask, "Was Mr. Abdy always so helpful to your family?"

"Oh, such a good man he was. He was my father's clerk for seven and twenty years, and always such a good and hard worker, and we had the greatest respect for old Mr. Abdy, although I suppose he was not so very old then, but as we were younger as well, he seemed old even if he was not really, but he was a most diligent assistant to my father, keeping records of the parish and who was born and who died, and who offered the tithes and other duties that a clerk does but of which I am ignorant, and he was most helpful in helping my father manage the accounts of the parish, for father was a man much devoted to his flock and to God, but he was, bless his eternal soul, not adept with his income, and without Mr. Abdy's assistance we might not have even the small amount that now sustains us."

"Rot and nonsense." Mrs. Bates spoke from the doorway at the back of the room. Behind her, Mary could see stairs that must lead down to the kitchens. Their single servant stood behind Mrs. Bates, steadying her after her ascent. "Abdy knew nothing. Your father, rest his soul, relied on the man for everything, but between them they could put two pounds together and make a shilling."

Mary looked up in surprise. Until now, Mrs. Bates' conversation had been limited to one or two words, and simple ones at that, and Mary had thought her diminished in her mental abilities due to her age. Miss Bates seemed the one to manage the small household, and was the one who led every conversation and offered their gentle hospitality, leaving her mother to sit at the periphery of the group at her knitting, or nodding off. Never had Mary seen even the first interest in the old woman in joining the discussion or making her thoughts known. Her only diversions that Mary had noticed seemed to be cards with Mr. Woodhouse, her endless knitting of large and shapeless objects, and her baking, all of which relied more on decades of repetition and the unconscious mind than on active intellectual concentration. This sudden voicing of the old lady's thoughts was quite foreign to what she had believed she understood.

Mary must ponder this more later. But for now, she had more questions. As soon as Mrs. Bates was seated and the servant had returned down to the kitchen to retrieve the promised apple pies, Mary began to probe. Subtlety and tact had never been her strengths, but a direct question might yield exactly the wrong results. She thought hard for a moment, and then commented, "Men often believe they are more capable than they are, and women less."

"Exactly!" the old lady sat up a little straighter and squared her sloped shoulders. "I understood far more than they, and offered my advice, but they would neither of them listen to the mutterings of a woman, no matter than I could see so clearly what they both missed. We might be wealthy had those foolish men heard my words and not fallen for the schemes."

"Mother, we were never wealthy!" Miss Bates hurried to make the correction. "We were comfortable, and never wanted for anything, but you must be careful not to misremember. My mother," she directed at Mary, "is of the age when memory begins to falter—of course we are all fallible in our recollections of things, for only the other day I had set myself the task of taking Mrs. Goddard the basket of toys for the younger children when I went to visit Mrs. Weston, and imagine my surprise when I returned home to find the basket sitting right here on the table—but, now what was I saying? Oh yes! Mother often has different recollections of matters than I do, and most especially so when--"

"Nonsense, Hetty!" the old lady interjected from her chair. "I remember the scheme as clearly as if it were yesterday. I... Ah, here is Bess with the pies. Some pie, my dear... Miss...?"

"Bennet, ma'am."

"Of course. Delighted to meet you."

"What Mother must be referring to," Miss Bates screwed her forehead in concentration, "was an arrangement for some of the local men to invest in some matters about horses, the details of which I never knew, for one did not discuss business in front of ladies. I do not know what came of it then, but Mr. Carnes became well-enough to do. Poor Mr. Carnes, having worked so hard, only to die like that—so very sad, most dreadfully unfortunate."

Affecting casual disinterest, Mary murmured, "Oh, was he involved in these schemes as well?"

"Oh yes, indeed!" Miss Bates stared at her with great insistence. "Mother always said it was his idea to begin with, his and Mr. Watson's. Something to do with the horses, I believe. So very many people here are interested in horses, for we are so very near Epsom

Downs where they race—have you heard of Epsom Downs, Miss Bennet? But of course, you must have done so! There were others involved in the scheme as well, but, well, we women were not included in these matters, so I know only a very little, and it is a very long time ago, nearly five-and-twenty years, or is it more? Or perhaps fewer? Would you like a slice of pie, Miss Bennet?"

From this point, there was very little else to be learned. The pie was duly sliced and served, and Mary praised Mrs. Bates excessively for it, as it was truly one of the best of its kind that ever she had tasted. Perhaps those years of mild want and meagre income had not been wasted, if such culinary skill was their result. She finished her slice and accepted a second with genuine appreciation before finally taking her leave.

"May I join you for a brief walk, Miss Bennet?" Miss Fairfax reached for her shawl as Mary took her bonnet.

"I would be pleased. I must return to Hartfield, but I should enjoy your company as far as you wish to walk."

It was not until the two young women had turned the corner and were out of hearing of anybody who might have been listening that Jane Fairfax cleared her throat. "I beg you to forgive my grandmother. She is sadly deteriorated from when last I visited, nearly two years ago. She means no harm, but often says things that are... that are not appropriate for the conversation."

Mary gave her friend a sad smile. "I understand, Miss Fairfax. I well recall my own friend Charlotte's grandmother as she grew older. Her recollections of times past were excellent, but she could not remember what she had been doing a moment before; she also sometimes spoke of inappropriate matters. None who loved her faulted her for it." She took a few more steps along the way and sought another subject for conversation.

"Have you been returned to Highbury for some time? Is it your intention to remain here? It is a very pretty village, with some fine neighbours."

Miss Fairfax allowed her eyes to wander to some place Mary could not see. "It is a lovely village indeed, although I am undecided about some in our society. You must have heard some of my story, Miss Bennet. Since the truth often suffers in the retelling, permit me to account for myself.

"I was not born here, although my mother was, as was Aunt Hetty. When my parents died, my father's dear friend Colonel Campbell took me in and raised me with his own daughter. He is the very kindest of men. He raised me as a lady and gave me an education to suit, which will allow me to make my own way in the world as a governess."

"A governess… that is… an admirable aspiration." Mary knew not what to say. She had known this from previous conversations, but no woman truly hoped for a life tending to other people's children and avoiding the inappropriate actions of cruel mistresses or lecherous masters.

"Say what you feel, Miss Bennet." Jane Fairfax uttered a harsh laugh. "It is not the life I might have wished, but it is far better than the life I might have had if not for the kindness and charity of the Campbells. Many a young lady with no other possibilities before her has descended far lower than this. And being a governess is not necessarily a dismal lot. Look to Mrs. Weston, who not long ago was governess to Miss Woodhouse. She was accepted, loved even, as part of the family and now is starting a family of her own. I have hopes… Ah, never mind my hopes. I am resigned to my future and do not dread it. My friend, now Mrs. Dixon, asked me to join her and her husband in Ireland, but I will not be a burden."

"I thank you for your candour, Miss Fairfax. I sometimes wish I had had a governess who might have given me the education I desired, rather than learning what I could from my mother and from what books I might pilfer from my father's library. I pray that your future holds much good and little ill."

As they wandered past the noisy street in front of the Crown, Mary thought she heard Miss Fairfax whisper to herself, "That, Miss Bennet, depends a lot upon you."

Chapter Nine

Talking to Elton

Jane accompanied Mary as far as Fords, where she stopped to inquire about mail for the family, whereupon Mary continued on her way alone. She had not gone more than a dozen steps when she noticed a horse and rider approaching. "Mr. Lyons," she waved to him, and was gratified to see his welcoming smile.

"Mary, you look very well today!" He pulled his mount to a stop and leapt down from the saddle to properly greet her. "I am only now returned from a partly unproductive interview. Are you expected somewhere, or have you a moment to accompany me as I return this fine fellow to the stables?" He gave her a cheeky grin and waited for her response. It was gratifying to learn that he seemed pleased to see her, for at the ball he had barely acknowledged her at all. Not that Miss Woodhouse had allowed him the time or liberty to do so....

"It would be my pleasure. I have come from the Bateses, and I may have learned something interesting."

"Interesting in what way?" He offered his arm, which she took, and he led her and his mount back towards the Crown.

"I discovered," she teased, "that Mrs. Bates is indeed capable of uttering more than three or four words in a row, and that she has rather firm thoughts on some matters. She seemed caught up in the notion that if not for Mr. Abdy and Mr. Carnes, she might have been a wealthy woman. Of course, her daughter denies the mother's claims, but perhaps..."

"Perhaps I might be in a position to discover more?" He beamed at her again. "Perhaps I might. You have taken tea? I slept little and was awake early and am in want of a strong cup of coffee. If your reputation can withstand it, I would appreciate your company. Perhaps the private parlour?"

She swatted at his arm. "Really, Alexander! We have spent enough time conferring in similar quarters without a chaperone that if my reputation were to be damaged by it, it should already be in tatters. I believe we are regarded here almost as relations, cousins, or perhaps brother and sister. Yes, thank you, I will gladly keep you company whilst you take your coffee."

"Brother and sister? No, indeed! I should not wish this hair upon another." He laughed again as he ran a hand through his glowing copper locks and Mary joined him. But, she reckoned, although his fiery red hair might not be at all fashionable, the ton preferring blond or dark tresses, it was a magnificent shade, and greatly appealing when paired with the right colour of coat.

He passed the horse over to the stable hands and led Mary into the Crown. He requested coffee and a lemonade for the lady, and was shown into the parlour. "I am being paid well for this investigation and my patrons have allowed me reasonable monies for costs incurred," he explained at her expression of concern. "I shan't be letting the empty manor house, but I may certainly take this room when I have need of it, and order food and drink as well."

The coffee arrived, and he poured himself a cup of the fragrant black liquid, adding neither sugar nor cream to his cup. "We learned, when I was a child, to take our tea without milk, and I enjoy my coffee likewise. Mmm," he took a deep sniff and then a tentative sip. "'Tis good remedy after the ale I had not so long ago. Shall I tell you of my morning?"

She nodded, and he did.

"I see," Mary frowned as he concluded. "So Mr. Hesselgrave and Mr. Elton are both investors in the enterprise that Mr. Carnes began, and now we know that Mr. Abdy and Mr. Carnes were a party to the scheme that Mrs. Bates mentioned from so long ago, and Mr. Watson as well. Could this scheme be at all connected to Mr. Carnes' horse-training operation? Could it have been started that long ago? There seem to be far too many coincidences for matters not to be connected in some way."

"Aye." She watched as Alexander reached into a large pocket in his coat and withdrew his notebook and pencil. He scratched down some notes and mumbled as he wrote.

"My business at hand is to investigate possible interference with the racing at Epsom. One of the dead men was a horse breeder and trainer, but seemed to have no direct connection with the races themselves. He was partly funded by two local gentlemen— Hesselgrave and Elton—who surely expect a good return on their investments. I must inquire as to the exact nature of their investment and as to whether they benefit or lose according to the outcome of the races.

"Furthermore, Carnes was involved in some scheme that Mrs. Bates mentioned, that was devised five-and-twenty or so years ago, in which, apparently, Mr. Bates was deprived either of his fortune or of the opportunity to make a fortune. That scheme involved the same Carnes, who is also sadly dead, as well as Abdy and Watson, also deceased under questionable circumstances."

Mary fixed unblinking eyes upon him. "Just so. There only remains to discover the connection with the other man who died, the tramp, Jack Smith. If he was at all a part of the scheme, it seems there is something else afoot, other than a series of tragic but unrelated deaths."

"My thoughts exactly. And there is one more matter which is beginning to bother me..."

"Where," asked Mary, "is the elusive Mr. Hesselgrave?"

Alexander's expression was most serious. "Exactly."

Mary remained for a short while to allow Alexander to finish his coffee, but then informed him she ought to return to Hartfield. The afternoon was well underway, and she must, she told him, inquire as to when to be ready for dinner. He offered to walk with her, but she insisted she was quite able to return the short distance alone.

What was it about her, he wondered as she walked down the street and around the curve of road that took her from his sight, that helped him to clarify his thoughts, that let those little details begin to slide into their rightful place? Did she ask the right questions? Did she goad him into a subtle battle of wits that forced his own thinking to become sharper? It mattered little, for the consequence was salutary.

He now had new tasks ahead of him, ones which would, were he fortunate, begin to provide answers to some of his questions.

First, he wished to speak with Mr. Elton. If he could not find Hesselgrave, who might well be continuing his business in Dorking, the other investor in Carnes' endeavour might do just as well. But he could not query the parson alone. He had no authority here, no rights to demand answers of anybody. For that he needed a local officer of the law. He needed Knightley.

He was ready to call once more for his poor horse when, to his pleasure, the very man himself walked into the inn. "Lyons!" the magistrate greeted him. "I was hoping to find you here. I've come from Randalls, where I have been charged with inviting you to dine."

"Thank you, I would be honoured. And I was about to set off to find you. Come, sir, let us talk."

He explained the situation as succinctly as he could. Knightley pressed his lips into a tight line as he nodded. "Indeed, I see. Elton would not answer one of your questions without some compulsion. Allow me to send a note to Mrs. Weston, and we may be right on our way to the parsonage."

He discharged his duty and the two men set off. "Have you heard any word of Hesselgrave?" Alexander asked as they walked. "His stable master seems to think nothing odd of the man disappearing for some days on business, but I cannot like it."

"I shall send a messenger to Dorking as soon as we return to the inn," Knightley asserted. "And perhaps our good vicar will have some notion of the man's whereabouts as well. Come, we are nearly arrived."

Their road to the detached cottage was down Vicarage-lane, which led at right angles from the broad main street of the place. A few inferior dwellings lined the road for about a quarter of a mile. There, at last, rose the vicarage, an old and not very good house, close to the road and with no advantage of situation, but which had been smartened up by its present proprietor and boasted some few trappings of ostentatious grandeur.

The entire place was newly painted and the few plants that were growing in the cracks between the road and the house were coaxed into elegant form and shape. The thatch of the roof was fresh and the old door had been painted a shiny black and now sported an excessively large brass knocker. Likewise, the windows were spotlessly clean and heavy draperies could be seen through them, obviously expensive even from the outside.

Mrs. Elton, when she arrived to greet them, was cool, and Alexander knew without a doubt that had he arrived alone, he would have been denied entry.

"You are the… investigator." She pronounced the word as if it tasted ill in her mouth. "From London. Not Mayfair, or Brunswick Square, I suppose, but from some other part of the city. Southwark? Or Cheapside?" She looked down her pert nose at him like he was a flea-ridden cur. Did she not know that she, with her coarse manners and trade-tainted riches, would have been less welcome in those esteemed parts of Town than he? For he, at least, enjoyed the friendship and patronage of men from the very first circles. Darcy would have a good laugh over this, when next they met for an evening of conversation. Alexander had little good opinion of the upper classes in general, but they paid his way, and some were—he grudgingly admitted—good company.

With the morning's conversation in Scots with Rabbie Duncan in mind, he replied in as broad an accent as he could manage, and watched Mrs. Elton's face grow white as Knightley's grew pink from suppressed laughter.

"Mrs. Elton," the latter uttered in his smoothest tones, "it matters little where my friend dwells. He is here in his capacity as an investigator and not as an arbiter of fashionable abodes, and moreover, at my request."

"Very well." She slid aside to allow them to enter, albeit with poor grace. "Jent, there will be a delay before dinner," she called to some unseen servant in the hallways. "You'd better wait in the salon. I'll summon Mr. E."

They sat for a very long time. No conversation passed between them. Alexander took the time to reread the notes he had already made in his book, and he withdrew a fresh pencil with a sharp point from his pocket. At last Elton entered. There had been no sound from the door. The man must have been in the house all the time, purposefully allowing his visitors to wait for him. If ever Alexander had entertained the notion that the parson was a decent sort of man, he now discarded them. *Caution*, he warned himself. *There are many rude men of poor character who are nonetheless neither murderers nor criminals.* It would do no good to pass judgment based on dislike without assessing evidence.

After an exhortation by Knightley for the clergyman to answer Alexander's questions, Alexander began.

"I am looking into some matters important to several men I know in London, and Mr. Hesselgrave's name has been mentioned on several occasions. I have no reason to suspect the gentleman of any wrongdoing, but he may have information that would assist me. However," he peered closely at Elton as he spoke, "I have been unable to locate him. He is not at home, nor can anybody tell me with certainty where he might be."

Elton sat as still as a rock in his chair. His eyes did not blink, his face did not twitch. Alexander continued. "I have discovered, through my investigations, that Mr. Hesselgrave had invested in the horse-rearing and training endeavour that Mr. Carnes ran—" still not a movement or flitter of an eyelash "—and that you were similarly involved."

Elton blinked and his face drained of blood.

"What can you tell me about this, Mr. Elton?" Alexander sat back in his chair with his notebook on one knee. Knightley sat straight in another chair, his face daring Elton to prevaricate.

"We thought... What I meant to say is... that is... It was a simple investment!" he blurted out at last. Then he sat, silent.

"Carry on if you please, sir," Knightley's words were polite, but his tone was very much that of a man who brooked no disobedience.

"Hesselgrave came to me last year, shortly after I arrived here, to speak of the venture. He said he did not wish to involve long-time residents of the area because of something that had occurred several years ago, something other than this particular idea. The two were not at all related, but bad feelings might remain. He asked that I listen to his story and make my own determinations."

He relapsed into silence.

"Go on, sir. Explain what he discussed with you. This can be discovered elsewhere, I am certain; it will be better for all if you are open."

"I have done nothing wrong!" Elton exploded. Alexander could see, once more, something small and nasty in the man and had to remind himself that the same was no admission of guilt.

"Very well." he let out something resembling a snort. "It was a simple matter of investing in a farm. A horse farm, that is, run by a tenant who raised race horses. As a clergyman I must not be seen to wager on the races, but a solid business venture... well, who is to judge me if others pay well for the product of the farm? There is no sin in this."

His eyes dared the two visitors to contradict him. When no opposition was heard, he settled back into his chair and spoke less defensively. "Hesselgrave had put some money into this project—Harry Carnes' farm, that is—some time before, about five or six years, he said. It had been successful and Carnes' had produced some good racers who often took the purse, and now he wished to expand operations. You know the deal, build a new set of stables, new training grounds, that sort of thing. There was nothing improper about any of it. A man is allowed to earn an income, after all."

"As a man who earns his own living, I can only agree, Mr. Elton. Please continue." Alexander twirled his pencil between his fingers.

"There is little to add, gentleman. I did not initially have the funds, but told Hesselgrave that I was interested. I tried... that is, I came into some money some months ago and called upon him and we came to an arrangement."

"With Cox as the attorney?" Knightley asked. Alexander scrawled notes on his paper.

"No. Fellow from Dorking. We did not wish to have anybody from the village involved. It was... unseemly."

"I see," Knightley nodded, and Alexander had the impression that the magistrate understood a lot more than what had been disclosed. "How did the investment progress?"

"It has only been a short time, sir!" Elton was incensed again, but quickly brought himself under better regulation. "The building had only just begun, but Carnes had received several inquiries from men well placed in the business of racing, and some monies had begun filtering in. It would have been a great success. Now with Carnes dead..." he turned his hands upright in supplication. There was no need to finish the thought. With Carnes dead, his investment might be lost.

This hardly seemed a reason to wish harm upon Carnes, and if Elton were involved with the interference with the horses before the races, it had preceded his investment in the project. But it was evident that the unpleasant man was involved somehow. However, there remained more questions.

"And Hesselgrave? I still need to speak to him. Where might he be?"

Elton shrugged, and his face resumed his stone-like aspect. "I cannot say. He was here on the afternoon of Abdy's funeral to talk about a new trainer. He departed before dinner, and I have not seen him since. I have nothing else to tell you."

"And Abdy himself?" Knightley threw out the question, pre-empting Alexander. "What was his involvement? We know he was in this somehow."

Elton narrowed his eyes and scowled. "He had no financial involvement at all."

"Sir!" Knightley barked and the vicar winced in his chair.

He snorted again. "It was Abdy's idea. I can only speak of what little I know, what I was told and picked up from hearing others. He began such a venture many years ago, when Hesselgrave's father was still alive. That initial attempt was not successful, but he had the original plans and knew the people who would be necessary to revive the plans. With enough investment, he believed it could make some people very wealthy, and Hesselgrave agreed."

"And what was his position, then, if not an investor?"

"In exchange for his contribution of plans and a list of racers and owners, he demanded ten percent of profits. Sadly, he did not live long enough to see a penny. Honestly, gentlemen, the man was ninety years old or more; I cannot imagine he expected to live long enough to profit."

"What happens to his share of the profits?" Alexander looked up from his notes.

"I do not know."

Knightley blew a puff of air that ruffled the hair settling on his forehead. "Do you expect us to believe this, Elton? You invested in a project without knowing how profits were to be shared?"

A sheen of perspiration had broken out upon the clergyman's brow and he shifted in his seat. "I truly do not know!" he whimpered. "I am a gentleman, with no head for business. Hesselgrave insisted everything would be equitable and... Believe me, I am not a fool! I did have my own attorney in London look at the agreement before committing a penny, but asked him only if the arrangement seemed fair. I did not need details. All I know about matters of finance is that I desire a comfortable income, and that a shrewd investment is a better means of procuring such an income than a country living. And that, sirs, is all I have to tell you."

"The Dorking lawyer's name, sir?" It was a command rather than a request, and Elton offered the information with a scowl.

Alexander wrote down on his notepad, *Find agreement, lawyer in Dorking.*

By now, Elton's voice had grown hard and he began to rise, but Alexander had one more question.

"What was Fred Watson's role in this arrangement?"

Elton blinked. "Watson? The smith? I buried him over a month ago. Dreadful accident. I only spoke to him when I needed shoes for my horse. If he had any part of this, it was not financial. You will have to speak to Hesselgrave. And now, gentleman, I must ask you to leave. It is time to prepare for dinner."

Alexander glanced over to Knightley, who gave a barely perceptible nod. They collected their hats and walked to the door. As they were about to depart, Alexander spun on his heel and asked in a casual voice, "By the by, Mr. Elton, where is Hesselgrave?"

The vicar stood as still as a stone again and recited, "I really could not tell you." Whereupon he closed the door with an audible noise.

They spoke not a word until they had returned to the main street that ran through Highbury. Knightley looked at his pocket watch. "It is after four o'clock. The Westons expect us at five. Shall I wait for you to ready yourself? Then we may walk to Randalls together. The Westons do not require full dress; I shall appear dressed as I am now."

Alexander took a quick look at his companion's garb: dark grey trousers above shiny black Hessians, an elegant but simple waistcoat with no adornments, and a cravat that any skilled man could tie without assistance of a valet, all beneath a well-cut coat of mid-blue. This was the comfortable wear of an evening amongst friends, much less fine than what he had worn to Hartfield. He had clothing that would suit.

"I am obliged, sir. I shan't be long in preparing myself."

"Very good." Knightley looked at his watch again. "Whilst you change, I shall send off a message to Dorking in search of our errant Mr. Hesselgrave and conduct one or two more matters of business. Meet you in the tavern in half an hour?"

Thus the plans were made, and thus they were executed, and before long the two men were walking down the road towards Randalls.

"What are your thoughts on Elton?" Mr. Knightley asked as they cleared the last house of the village.

"I believe his account of the investment he made, but he is not telling us everything."

"Mmm..." Knightley thought for a moment and then said, "This may well be nothing, but you ought to know it. I rely upon your discretion. When Elton arrived in Highbury, I sensed he was seeking to improve his lot in life. He offered for Miss Woodhouse last Christmas and..."

"And she refused him. Yes. He would have done better with her than with her replacement, but it is better for Miss Woodhouse this way."

"Indeed." Was that a sigh of relief from Mr. Knightley? Interesting!

After a few more steps, Knightley continued, "Emma had had him in mind for her friend Harriet Smith."

"The young lady from Mrs. Goddard's school? Pretty girl, and sweet natured. I danced with her last night. I must assume that Elton's reaction was not favourable."

"Indeed, it was not! He had an eye to money and social improvement, and marriage to a penniless girl of unknown parentage did not have a place in his plans. He was offended and angry with Emma, and most especially so in the light of her refusal. He absconded to Bath almost immediately upon discharging his Christmas duties and returned some weeks later with a wife."

"Not a love match."

"Between him and her money, I believe it was a love match indeed. And yet, strangely, they are very well suited and should do well together."

There were some more moments of pensive silence before Alexander spoke again. "Elton was approached about this investment, hoped to wed Miss Woodhouse for her dowry, and when that failed, married another wealthy woman and added his coin to Hesselgrave's pot."

"That is how it appears."

They were approaching the curve of road immediately before Randalls, and already Alexander could see the chimneys of the house above the trees that lined their path. He dared ask one final question, as much to observe its effect on his listener as to learn the answer. "If Miss Woodhouse had no interest in accepting Mr. Elton's proposal, has she then set her cap at another?"

Knightley's gait stiffened, but he answered easily enough. "She declares she has no wish to marry at all, being quite content in her life as it is. But I had thought, for a while, she was growing besotted with Frank Churchill. From the moment Mr. Weston took Randalls, she has been intrigued by the idea of Churchill, and since his arrival she has always been very pleased to be in his company. I had wondered... But no, these are private musings. To your question, the only person with whom I have seen Emma flirting, sir, is you!"

Alexander gave a hearty laugh and was relieved when Knightley followed suit.

Dinner was a comfortable and congenial affair. Frank Churchill had returned that morning to his aunt and uncle's abode. The distance of nine miles was but an easy ride for a healthy young man and a good horse, and his aunt, so Mr. Weston excused, needed him greatly. Alexander raised an eyebrow at the thought of a man like Churchill being needed by his aunt when his own father was so near, but said nothing. More than likely, the aunt desired his doting attendance and his willingness to accede to her every will. Still, men had done a lot more, and far greater evil for an inheritance, and if all Frank needed to do was be present and bring his aunt her tea and open her letters, he was a fortunate man.

The Westons were as pleasant in their own home as when dining out, and the conversation and food were both plentiful and excellent. It was evident to Alexander that Knightley was a frequent guest at Randalls, so much so that no formalities were observed, and the evening progressed with the ease of family. Alexander was gratified and honoured to be included in this intimate and friendly gathering.

They did not separate after the meal. Mrs. Weston excused herself briefly to retrieve her sewing, allowing the men to enter into whatever topics of conversation they desired. She would, her husband explained to Alexander, insert herself into the discussion if she felt so inclined, and that very little shocked or horrified her. "We may talk as if solely amongst men. My wife will not mind in the least."

Naturally, therefore, the topic quickly turned to that of the investigations. Alexander explained that neither he nor Cox had learned much of value about the possible interference in the horse races, although he had begun a new line into that inquiry. Then Weston asked about the recent deaths, just as Mrs. Weston returned to the room with her basket. Alexander wondered if she were making clothing for her baby and had a momentary pang when he wondered if he would ever have such an event to anticipate.

She settled herself on the sofa by the brightest window, far enough from the three men that they could talk freely but close enough that she could join the discussion if she wished. She gave Alexander a quick smile and turned to her sewing as Knightley began to explain in the broadest terms about what he and Alexander had discovered. Alexander raised his eyebrows and Knightley answered with an assuring nod. He knew these people; it must be safe to talk in their presence.

The gentleman finished his account and held his glass before his face, watching the amber port inside as he swirled it in the light. "We have been seeking, therefore, to discover any other connections between the dead men," he concluded. "It seems that Carnes and Abdy had dealings reaching back many years, but what of Watson? And that tramp who called himself Jack Smith? Could he possibly have been involved?"

"Watson?" Mrs. Weston interjected from her sofa. "That was a loss indeed. He was a kind man and an excellent craftsman. I met him when first I arrived in Highbury as Emma's governess, nearly seventeen years ago. We needed some specially made items for our lessons, and he was generous with his time and made us exactly what we needed. At the time, he had recently completed rebuilding his smithy. He said he had come into some money and he had used it to expand his operations and put in a separate forge and workshop for smaller and more specialised items. His son was apprenticing to man the main forge, and he was beginning to dedicate his time to the other aspects of his business. I recall this clearly, for he showed us around the new workshop with such great pride."

She pushed her needle into the white fabric and drew a long stitch. "I paid a call upon Mrs. Watson only a week before the accident." Her normally cheerful face was sad in the recollection. "She told me about some improvements she wished to do upon her house, and another expansion Mr. Watson hoped to effect at the smithy. He had such a great volume of work of late that he planned to add yet another forge." She sighed. "It is still possible that her son might undertake the new forge now that the business is his, but the new orders were all for the work that only her husband could do so well. Mark is a craftsman and a skilled smith, but Fred was an artist."

"Your words interest me, Madam," Alexander raised his crystal glass in a toast to her. "Have you any notion of the exact nature of the work Fred was undertaking?" He noticed Knightley looking on with great interest.

"I have no exact knowledge, Mr. Lyons, but I do believe it had to do with a rather particular alteration on a standard horseshoe."

Mrs. Weston had no other information to impart, but Knightley reminded him that the first expansion to the smithy had been completed about twenty years before, when the smith was only about thirty years of age and with a young and growing family. "That is regarded as either an excellent or terrible time to engage in such an endeavour, for if a man has the money to invest, it can increase his income greatly; however, if funds are short, he can deprive his family of their most basic needs and commit the entire family to poverty."

"In Mr. Watson's case, it was a successful gamble," Alexander sipped his port. "But of course, if I recall..."

"He had recently come into a great deal of blunt. Yes. The sort to allow a man to rebuild his forge."

"At about the same time that Mrs. Bates claimed her husband invested so poorly in the scheme suggested by Carnes and Abdy."

The conversation then turned to matters more pleasant until it was time to depart. Weston offered to call for his carriage to convey Alexander to the Crown and Knightley to Donwell Abbey, but both men demurred. The evening was fine and the sun not yet set.

They said their parting words and formed plans to meet again on the morrow when they were stopped by the sound of a rider approaching with great speed. The horse and rider came to a stop in the drive in front of the house and the messenger called from his saddle, "Mr. Knightley! I am right glad I did not miss you. There's a messenger just arrived from Dorking at the inn. Mr. Lutton said he thought you might be here and sent me right over with the message since I know the way. Mr. Hesselgrave seems to be missing. They found his horse at the inn where he stays when business keeps him in the town, but the man himself cannot be found anywhere!"

Chapter Ten

Mr Woodhouse Speaks

Mary had arrived back at Hartfield with plenty of time to change for dinner. She selected one of her own dresses to wear, rather than borrowing yet again from Miss Woodhouse, and hoped it would be acceptable. Harriet Smith had been invited for the meal as well, and if Emma thought meanly of Mary's best gown, she did not mention it.

Miss Smith was a very sweet girl, if not possessed of the greatest intellect. She was, perhaps, a year younger than Mary, but by her conversation and understanding, she seemed younger still. Or could it be, Mary pondered, that she herself pretended to be older than her years? She had always striven to distance herself from her younger sisters and situating herself with her elders rather than with those younger than her had been one effective means of success in this. She felt more comfortable conversing with Alexander, who was seven years older than her, with a university education, independence, and a career, than she was with Maria Lucas, who was older even than Kitty.

Nevertheless, Miss Smith was unobjectionable company, and Mary amused herself by watching Emma fuss about the girl, guiding her as to what her opinions ought to be on this matter, how best to conduct herself in that situation, and what her feelings must be when approached by some other person. Once more, Emma was happiest as the puppeteer, and Harriet Smith was her most recent puppet, all too willing to be guided from scene to scene by her benevolent mistress.

Once again, everything at Hartfield was perfect. The food was expertly prepared and was not dangerous to the digestion, according to Mr. Woodhouse. A small army of excellent maids and servants allowed for every eventuality, blending into the walls when not needed, present with whatever was required when the need arose. There was a footman waiting to serve each dish at the perfect temperature; there was another ready with a bottle of wine just when each glass was nearly empty. The table decorations were lovely without being excessive, and no detail was overlooked. Such was the level to which Mary's mother could only dream of her troublesome middle daughter to aspire.

And yet, for all the luxury, Mary wished for nothing else than to be back at the inn, in the comfortable and far less elegant company of Alexander, eating plain bread and a heavy stew while enjoying a deep conversation. Emma and Harriet might find great pleasure in debating the relative merits of a walk or a phaeton ride on a fine day, but Mary yearned to discuss God and literature and morality and the real nature of men's souls with the one person whom she believed understood her.

They did not always agree—rather, they disagreed more often than not—but Alexander held a key to her innermost thoughts, and when she expressed them, he knew of what she was speaking, and responded in language and thought and gesture that she knew. His arguments, his rebuttals, served more to build her sense of who she was than any amount of sweet pandering by Miss Woodhouse. How Harriet could bear it, Mary would never know, and yet the girl seemed in awe of her patroness and hung upon Emma's every word as if it were manna from heaven.

After dinner the company went through to the parlour, there to amuse each other until Mr. Woodhouse announced it was time to retire, for every body knew how important a good sleep was for one's health. Emma played a little on the pianoforte, and Harriet sang in a sweet but untrained voice, and Mary selected a set of sonatinas which she knew well. Afterwards, Emma and Harriet began reworking a bonnet that Harriet had brought, leaving Mary to converse with Mr. Woodhouse.

She complimented him on the house, on the meal, and thanked him again for his most welcome hospitality, which he accepted most graciously. "Think nothing of it, my dear, for what are we if we cannot help our brothers and sisters in their time. I think of poor Miss Taylor—that is, Mrs. Weston now—who was so loved and welcomed here. How sad she had to leave us. She would have been a great deal happier if she had spent all the rest of her life here at Hartfield. Oh, that Mr. Weston had never seen her."

Mary knew not how to reply to this and eventually offered her thoughts. "She seems very happy in her choice. Mr. Weston is a most gentlemanlike man, and it is not unnatural for a woman to want a house of her own."

"A house of her own? What need had she for that? She must have been far happier here. Ah, but it is done, and very sad too." He stared into the fire for a moment and then added. "John Abdy had a house of his own, with his wife when she was alive, and what little good it did him. Poor man." He paused again and returned his gaze to the flames that danced in the hearth.

"Did you know him well? It seems he will be missed."

"One knows most everybody in a village the size of Highbury," Mr. Woodhouse sighed. "We were from different circles, of course, and whilst one must not associate with people outside of one's rank, one may still be friendly and deal charitably with people. Abdy was Mr. Bates' clerk, of course, until Bates passed on to his reward. If he had eaten less fatty food, he might still be alive. Poor Mr. Bates. Mr. Perry warned him, but he would have his gristle and his pastries. Claimed fresh fruit in the winter was beyond his means, but most families have cold rooms for their produce. Ah, but I digress. Poor Mr. Abdy."

There was another long break before Mr. Woodhouse spoke again. "Abdy was a capable enough man, always polite, never spoke out of turn. He always had grand ideas, always spoke as if some reward were waiting for him tomorrow. Ah, he would have been better off living quietly in his station, but he always had some scheme he was so certain would be successful. Horses, canals, maize, even some strange idea about using steam to power machines that would run on rails to transport people. He never did become wealthy, lived out his last days in his small house, with his sons and grandchildren to take care of him. Poor John Abdy."

Mary did not think the man so poor if he were surrounded by and cared for by his family, but she waited to see if Mr. Woodhouse would speak further. He said nothing more. After a long silence, she ventured a sigh. "Did Mr. Abdy ever see success with his schemes?" It was most interesting that Mr. Woodhouse used the same word that Mrs. Bates had used.

The old gentleman thought for a very long time. "For some he did, for others not. I cannot believe he had a great head for selecting the best schemes, although he never seemed to lose more money than he invested. Or perhaps he was more adventurous in helping others part with their money than in risking his own. The very first, with the horses, seemed to do well enough, and I suppose a lot of people gained confidence in him after that. His later plans… I cannot say for certain. I had no need for his schemes. Hartfield has always provided enough income for my wants, and I have my dear wife's fortune in the four-percents for Emma. Poor Isabella, living so far away. She might have taken Randalls with her dowry, had not John preferred London. Poor Emma."

Mary had, by now, become sufficiently accustomed to Mr. Woodhouse's laments that she imagined "poor" Isabella to be quite well settled.

"Isabella?" Emma called from her seat. She must have heard the name. "I had a letter from her just today. The boys are all very well, and baby Emma is growing as you watch her! Isabella," she explained to Mary, "is my sister in London, and she is married to none other than Mr. Knightley's brother! Is that not amusing? We quite adore our shared nieces and nephews, and when he is very angry with me, Isabella's children are our path to reconcile. I was still in the schoolroom when they married, but Mrs. Weston will tell you how I foresaw they would do very well for each other. And so it has transpired!"

She gave a wide and self-satisfied smile before returning to her conversation with Harriet about the best sort of charades, and if poetry were superior to verse, or the opposite.

Mary listened to the discussion for a while with her accustomed detached boredom and believed that Mr. Woodhouse had dropped off to sleep, for he had not spoken in a while. Suddenly he raised his head and gave her a quizzical look. "We often played charades in my younger years. It was a great favourite in the neighbourhood on a summer evening, or in the winter if the roads did not become too covered in snow for the carriage. I was not the most adept at the game, but Mrs. Woodhouse—that is Emma's dear mother, now departed—was most proficient, and Mrs. Bates the cleverest of the lot of us. Though we might try and try, we never were able to catch her out, for she got all of them. She had a fine mind, better at figures and puzzles than many men I knew, always with an eye to the future. Pity she was not born a man, for she would then have been very smart indeed.

Mary's head snapped up and only with difficulty did she hold her tongue. Foolish old man, to believe that a woman could not be as intelligent as a man! One's sex had nothing to do with one's ability to think, to reason. What ridiculous and ancient ideas he had! Prudence triumphed, and she refrained from making a sound.

Her host stared into the flickering fire and continued, "Young Jane Fairfax promised to be as quick-witted as she. As a very young thing, all Mrs. Bates could do was boast about how Jane was counting to ten by a year of age and reading by four and playing the fortepiano at five. She seemed destined for such great things, a splendid match, no matter that her father left her with nothing but his name. Poor Miss Fairfax. Perhaps if her poor mother had eaten more gruel..."

He returned his eyes to the hearth, and in short time soft snores wafted to Mary's ears. She would learn nothing more from Mr. Woodhouse this evening. With a resigned sigh, she left her chair and moved to the sofa, asking if she might join Emma and Harriet at their contemplation of tableaux and parlour games.

The following morning there was a letter for Mary, brought to her as she took her morning chocolate and toast. She smiled at the sight of the familiar and well-loved handwriting on the envelope. Lizzy had written! She finished her chocolate and removed to a sunlit chair in the adjoining morning room and broke the seal. The letter was written on thick creamy paper, and from the generous space between letters and lines, such paper was plentiful in the Darcy household. Lizzy was fortunate indeed in her choice!

She looked at the top of the missive. It was dated the previous morning at Longbourn. It read:

Dearest Mary,

How I have been worried about you, my dear sister! When the dire news arrived at Darcy House on Monday last, my thoughts were not for my own welfare, but for yours, being stranded in a strange place with no one around whom you knew or who knew you, with only your wits for solace. But I know you, dear Mary, and I have come to admire you so greatly for your fortitude and strength, and yes, your bravery! I worried about you, but I did not fear for you, for if anybody of my acquaintance, with the exception of my most wonderful husband, would have the wherewithal to sustain such a happenstance with grace and composure, it must be you.

Therefore, I shall not ask after your health and comfort, for I know you are well and have made good of a terrible situation. I do hope you have encountered good people who have taken you into their hearts and homes for the interim, although Will assures me the inn at Highbury is a most excellent establishment and that you will want not in its lodgings.

Allow me to account for my own actions on that terrible day, Monday last. You shall hear it from my lips in due time, but such is my horror at what occurred that I must write of it, in the hopes of purging it from my soul.

We were all in preparation to depart London. Our travel trunks had been stowed on the second wagon, and my maid and Will's valet were set to alight. The curricle had been brought around, with the two fine steeds to draw it, and we were all in anticipation for a most pleasant journey, the weather being so fine and the sun up so late. We only awaited the return of my husband from his appointment near St. James', after which we expected to depart immediately.

Imagine my shock then, when he arrived at the house in such a flurry of agitation, with the dread news that the Prime Minister had been assassinated only minutes before! He was in the neighbourhood near Parliament, and saw not the vile event, but heard the ensuing noise and chaos.

Oh, Mary, the entire city seemed to dissolve into chaos, and Will insisted upon closing the house and ensuring all our staff were in places of safety. As much as I was determined to remain in Town with my husband as he dealt with necessary matters that could not be left, his determination was stronger still, and within moments he had set me into the coach with the trunks and Gert and Folsom and directed the driver towards Longbourn, as fast as the horses would manage. When I inquired as to his reason, he asserted that northward was the quickest way out of London.

He further insisted that he would do whatever he possibly could to assure you of our health and security and to secure acquaintances in Highbury to offer you hospitality and friendship. He insisted his messenger—a trusted servant from a village not far from Highbury—ride not through the city, but northward first and then around London in a half-circle so as to avoid the most dangerous roads, such is his care for those in his employ.

He, himself, rode to Longbourn that very evening in the curricle. I do believe that had he not expected the streets to become disorderly, he might have returned it to the carriage house, but in some ways he is still the proud man I first met last year, and he must take great care of his horses and carriages! Ah, such are men. It should not be necessary to add that both husband and conveyance arrived quite safely and in excellent time long before sunset, and here we have all remained since.

At last I come to the meaning of this letter.

Affairs in London are returning to normal, and Will believes travel is no longer perilous. Therefore, we propose to resume our previous plans on Monday next. The journey is not long—four and twenty miles to London, where we will ascertain that all is well with the house—and sixteen more to Highbury. Consequently, we expect to arrive in Highbury at around four o'clock in the afternoon of Monday, the eighteenth of May, whereupon we shall, weather permitting, remove to the cottage Will had initially let.

We do hope it will not be too much trouble for your new friends to tolerate your company until that time; should matters prove less than desirable, I am enclosing some bills of money, with which you may procure suitable accommodations for yourself and your maid; in addition, we request that you ensure that all costs incurred by the driver and footman and the housing of the horses and carriage be tended to. If this amount is insufficient, we shall remedy the situation on Monday.

I cannot wait to see you again, dear Mary, and hear of your sojourn in Highbury. I do hope it has been a pleasant and uneventful time.

Your loving sister,
Elizabeth Darcy

Mary folded up the letter and looked at the enclosed funds. Five ten-pound notes sat in her hand, enough to employ a butler for a year! In addition to the generous five pounds enclosed in Mr. Darcy's first letter, she would be able to take a room and see to the servants and the equipage with ease. Perhaps, then, after speaking to Miss Woodhouse of the content of the letter, her first duty ought to be to secure most of the bills and then walk into town to inquire at the stables and inn and attend to any amounts owing.

Should she happen to see Alexander whilst on her errand, she would not be averse!

It was not Alexander Lyons whom she met on the lane leading to Highbury, however, but rather, Frank Churchill. He stepped out of the front door at Randalls just as she was approaching the part of the lane where the short drive diverged from it, and she wondered if he had been watching from the window in anticipation of her arrival.

The thought was both troublesome and appealing.

"Walking towards the village, Miss Bennet?" he executed a deep and elaborate bow, twirling his hat not twice but three times before resetting it upon his perfectly coiffed head.

"As you see, Mr. Churchill." Her curtsey was simple and quick. Then, careful not to give offence, she added, "The weather is fine again today. Is it always so fair in Surrey? I have seen hardly a cloud in all the time I have been here."

"'Tis you who have brought the sunshine, Miss Bennet! For I cannot believe the clouds would dare show their faces when you are present." The man certainly was a master of flirtation! "But in all candour, I cannot speak much of the climate when you are absent, for I myself have been but little in Highbury. I was raised by my aunt, as you certainly know, and can be away only when she can spare me. How fortunate that she and my uncle have taken a house so near, that I may ride here almost every day." He gestured down the laneway in a silent supplication, and Mary accepted by taking the offered arm.

She strove to seek some topic safe and suitable for light chatter whilst they walked and quickly decided that the weather would serve as well as anything. "The clouds do not seem perturbed by my presence in Hertfordshire," she spoke lightly. "We very often will have a succession of four or five days of rain, with little interlude in which to take some air. It is less taxing in the cold of winter than in summer, for one may walk in the snow if one wears suitable boots, but to walk in the rain is seldom a pleasure."

"Ah, the snow! At Enscombe, where I was raised by my uncle and aunt, we saw a great deal of snow. Do you enjoy it, Miss Bennet? Do you, perhaps, skate upon the ice? I can picture you now, wrapped in a warm cape of the finest white cashmere, a pink winter bonnet upon your head... no, not pink." He peered closely at her until she felt herself growing as pink as the imagined hat. "You could never look anything but lovely, but green, rather, would better suit your colouring. Yes, a beautiful pine-green bonnet. But we may trim it with pink flowers, should you desire! I can see you gliding across the ice with a skill rarely seen, making figures and moving with grace and ease. And upon your feet, pretty fur-lined black boots made especially to keep you warm in the cold air, and over your hands, the largest ermine-fur muff that ever you have seen!"

Mary could not stop the bubble of laughter that this image occasioned.

"My dear lady? Do you object?" Frank's beam betrayed his jest.

"Only at the muff, sir! I have often seen ladies carrying such large ones that I believe they might crawl inside and fit their entire bodies within! A nice pair of gloves will do very well instead."

"As you command, Miss Bennet!"

She laughed again. He had not Alexander's depth of intellect and knowledge, but he was most excellent company, and she would never grow bored in his presence. She strove onward with her conversation.

"Does this region of Surrey receive much snow? We are not so very far from my home in Hertfordshire—not nearly as far as your own home at Enscombe, I am certain!—but climate does not always obey the map. I am curious about how Highbury looks in winter."

Frank looked thoughtful for a moment. "It does get cold here, as I can attest, for I was able to come to Highbury to congratulate my father and meet my new mother in February. It was the seventh of February, I believe, and whilst I have seen worse cold in Scotland, there was little doubt as to the season. There was a prodigious amount of snow as well, unusual for these parts, but not unheard of. I was pleased to be riding, for the exercise brought warmth to both me and my horse. I did not envy the driver of the wagon that brought my trunk."

Something about the date tickled Mary's memory. "Was that not the same day the tramp, Jack Smith, died?"

Frank's face stilled for a moment, but he answered in an easy enough manner. "I believe it was. I did not hear of it, of course, until several days after I arrived. Terrible accident, but these things do happen. Poor man took shelter where he could and sat too close to the flames. I've heard of similar tragedies back in Enscombe." He shook his head sadly. "It was most unfortunate that such a sad event should coincide so exactly with my arrival, a date which I had hoped to be remembered only in pleasure."

He uttered a sound rather like a cluck and then said, "Mrs. Bates seemed most alarmed when she heard the news the following morning. I was... I was paying a call, familial obligation of course, for the Bateses are not only dear to my father but also knew my mother, and one must maintain such precious connexions. I was there, asking after them all and relating news of common acquaintances, when Mr. Knightley came to pay a call and gave the sad news. The poor old woman looked up in quite a state of alarm, and I dare say near on spilled her tea. Jane—that is, Miss Fairfax— righted her cup, and a good thing too, for tea is expensive and stains terribly.

"I really was rather taken aback, for Mr. Knightley mentioned the event quite as an aside, more to excuse his late arrival than as an announcement. His duties as magistrate are not always pleasant, one must assume, and I shudder to think of some of the things he must have seen. Regardless, to hear of a tramp dying in the cold of winter is no rare event, sad though it may be, and Mrs. Bates' alarm struck me as notable."

"How odd for her to take such a shock," Mary mused. "Although perhaps it is not so very strange. If she has lived in the village all her life, she must know almost everybody to some degree."

"And even more so as the former vicar's wife. Her duties would have taken her into contact with people the likes of whom she never would otherwise meet or know."

"So I imagine. To hear of the death of one whom you knew, even a little, no matter how distantly or how expected the end, must always be cause for distress."

They were coming into the village now, and a wagon laden with trunks and boxes rumbled past them on the street, presumably heading towards the back doors to Ford's General Shop.

"I wonder what is in there! Frank deftly changed the subject to something more cheerful. "Perhaps it is a shipment of new bonnets from London, and perhaps there is one in pale pine-green, decorated with pale pink flowers!'

Mary giggled and bade Mr. Churchill come attend her whilst she went to browse once the crates were unpacked, but for all her affected mirth, she could not help but wonder how well, exactly, Mrs. Bates had known the tramp Jack Smith.

Chapter Eleven

Searching for Hesselgrave

Alexander and Knightley set off for Dorking at first light. If they were to spend the day searching for Hesselgrave, they wished for as much of that day to be available as possible, and to waste little in travel. It was not a long distance—less than ten miles—but the road wound through farmland and over rivers, and up and down hills and valleys, through woods and fields and some of the most beautiful countryside that Alexander had seen.

"We are not far from Box Hill," Knightley said as they crested a particularly impressive rise of land. It seemed about as high as the one atop of which Harry Carnes had eaten his last meal, but this one was thickly wooded, rather than carefully tended farmland. "Box Hill is a favourite place for picnics, well regarded as having a most spectacular vista of the surrounding countryside. Perhaps, once your task is completed to your satisfaction, you might take a half day to enjoy it."

"Thank you," Alexander replied as his eyes roved across the lovely land around him. "If it bests this in terms of beauty, it must be a wonder indeed."

As they descended the hillside, the sparse smattering of farmhouses and outbuildings began to grow denser, until they were in the outskirts of Dorking. It was a busy market town with an active main street and a large and impressive inn at the centre of the town, with stables behind it. Here Alexander and Knightley requested care for their horses whilst they took a quick breakfast at the public room of the inn and made some initial inquiries as to the state of Hesselgrave's room and the direction of the attorney who had drafted the investment agreement between Carnes, the missing squire, Elton, and whoever else might be involved.

The innkeeper, a small and wiry man with red hair to rival Alexander's and a blue apron, was at first reluctant to allow the newcomers information or a look into Hesselgrave's room. Only Knightley's superior manner and letters declaring his position, and Alexander's evidence of his occupation in London including a list of notables who might be called upon to vouch for him, proved adequate for the innkeeper to thaw his manner.

"May I see those names?" Knightley looked upon in awe. "You have half the peerage and some of the most influential men in the country. Is that really the Duke of York's own signature? I had no notion!"

Now the innkeeper seemed happier to speak. "We know Mr. Hesselgrave. He comes down three or four times a year for matters of business, stays for a week or so. He always pays in advance and never gives trouble. We hardly see the man, tell the truth. Other times, he comes down more briefly, perhaps overnight, or for a meal on a journey here and back in a day, if there are not so many matters requiring his attention." The innkeeper had no knowledge of what Hesselgrave's business dealings involved. Alexander would have been most surprised if he had.

At the mention of the Duke of York, the innkeeper agreed to unlock Hesselgrave's door. "No funny business, gentlemen!" he insisted. "I run a good and reliable establishment, and my guests pay well for the knowledge that their belongings will not grow legs." He insisted on staying at the door to watch the examination of the room, which suited Alexander well. There would be no accusations of wrongdoing or pilfering.

There was, in the end, little to see. Hesselgrave had brought with him a simple satchel, large enough for a change of shirt or two, his shaving kit, and a few other personal items. There was nothing indicating a prolonged stay, nor anything suggesting rapid flight. His boots and coat were missing; his slippers remained at the foot of his bed. There was a small pile of papers on the desk that proved to be bills that needed settling with local merchants, and a half-written letter to a sister, recounting an amusing incident he had witnessed between a farm girl and a runaway goose. In short, it looked as if the man had stepped out for a stroll and not returned.

Questions at the stables painted a similar picture. The man had arrived, committed his horse to their excellent care, paid for several days, and had not been seen since.

"Truth be told," the head groom told them, "I'd never have known had your man not arrived yesterday seeking him. When he comes to town, we seldom see him again until he leaves. His affairs seem to be mostly in the town, and those from too far to walk come to see him. We would never have known he was missing. Not at all." He ran a large red hand through greasy brown hair and frowned.

Having learned very little at the inn, Alexander followed Knightley down the High Street in search of the attorney. The offices were easy enough to find, as they occupied the ground floor of a rather smart new building just off the main road. The upper stories looked to provide the man's home, and the garden at the back, complete with wooden hobby horses and a collection of footballs, completed the picture of a young and healthy family.

The man himself opened the door. He was tall and rather prone to plumpness and very fair, with pink skin and bright blue eyes that looked all too innocent. The well-appointed space within, however, spoke of the success of a sharp man of law and a shrewd businessman, and Alexander reminded himself not to judge the man by his appearance.

Once again, it took a lengthy explanation before Mr. Newnam would agree to discuss matters at all. Alexander described the concerns about meddling in the races and presented his credentials once more, and Knightley, more to the attorney's liking, explained about the recent spate of unexpected deaths and the possible connection to the enterprise established by Mr. Carnes.

"Now Carnes is dead, Abdy is dead, and it seems that Mr. Hesselgrave has disappeared. We are concerned for his safety, and need to know who else is involved in this agreement, both to investigate those who might be behind the deaths, should they prove to be murder, and to warn those who might be innocent of wrongdoing, but are nevertheless in danger."

It was this final appeal to conscience that finally convinced Newnam to search for his copy of the agreement. He would summarise its content and allow the visitors to see the names of the interested parties; nothing else would he consider. But this was sufficient for the time being. If necessary, Alexander would find other means of getting to the information.

The basic terms of the agreement were as Mr. Elton had outlined: Each party invested a certain amount of money, with the exception of John Abdy, whose investment was deemed to be the idea and planning behind the scheme, and Harry Carnes, whose physical work and personal effort were counted along with a financial contribution. Abdy was to receive ten percent of the profits, and Carnes ten percent plus whatever was due based on the amount he had invested. The others were compensated from the remaining profits in proportion to their investment.

Other than the four parties to the agreement about whom Alexander and Knightley already knew, there was one additional gentleman, whose name was very well known in racing circles, but whose proportionate contribution was minimal, mere pennies to the others' pounds. "He was brought in solely for the power of his name, a reputational investor," Newnam explained. "He stands to gain very little should the venture succeed—other than knowing that he is wagering on some of the finest and best trained horses in the country—but he stands to lose almost nothing should the venture fail."

Alexander and Knightley looked at each other and came to a silent agreement.

"I do not believe this man is in danger," Knightley pursed his lips, "but I would beg you to send him warning to be on his guard, nonetheless. I have every suspicion that this entire affair revolves around money, not fame."

"I shall do so at once." The attorney scratched a note onto a pad on his desk. The innocent and guileless gaze had long since vanished, revealing the smart and capable man inside.

Alexander turned to Knightley and shook his head. "This answers a great many questions, but I can't help but wonder about Fred Watson and the tramp. Were they involved? If so, how?"

"Tramp?" Newnam furrowed his pink brow. "I certainly know nothing of a tramp, but the name Watson is familiar. He was not an investor, but the others did mention him more than once. He was the smith. He had dealings with them under a separate contract for the production of specially designed horseshoes, and whatever other special iron implements they required. I cannot see how his death would benefit anybody at all; rather, if his skill met but half of his reputation, his death would only harm them."

"And yet he was involved in some way." Alexander made a note in his booklet: *discover Watson's involvement.*

"So it seems," the attorney sighed. "I wish I could tell you who drafted that other agreement between them. It was not I."

"One more question, sir, which is quite pertinent to our investigations," Knightley asked. "What should happen should one of these investors die?"

"Yes..." Newnam stroked his chin. "I was unhappy with this clause, but the others insisted. I am paid for my advice and for preparing the legal documents; what the parties ultimately decide is not under my purview. In the event of the death or deportation of one of the parties, his initial monetary investment—should such funds remain intact—would be returned to his estate after three years. The profits, however, would be divided proportionately amongst the surviving parties to the agreement."

"And in the case of Abdy and Carnes?"

"Ten percent of the third year's profit would be paid to the estate on a onetime basis. After that, the estate would have no claim on further benefit."

Knightley sat in his chair, chewing his lips and nodding slowly. Alexander wrote down every detail in his notebook, asking for clarification and confirming what he had written before releasing a long sigh.

"Then," he said at last, "with each man's death, another becomes very much richer, should he have the patience to wait for the three years."

"That," replied Newnam with a very direct look, "is exactly what I did not like about it."

"We must find Hesselgrave," Knightley leapt up from his chair. "If he is still alive, I fear he is in great danger."

"You know what this has to mean," Alexander's breast was suddenly filled with dread. It seemed most unlikely, and yet every piece fit into place.

"Elton must be our man."

Newnam had not seen Hesselgrave since his arrival in Dorking some days before. He had come into the office on a very brief and uncomplicated matter of business and had been seen no more. Newnam had found nothing strange about the squire's manner and explained that a quick and singular visit was by no means unusual for Hesselgrave. The two did not visit socially, and once matters of business had been concluded, there was no need for a return visit.

When asked about Hesselgrave's other dealings in the area, the attorney was vague. He suggested some people with whom the squire was thought to deal with, and likewise provided the visitors with whatever directions he could, but was able or willing to confirm nothing.

Alexander and Knightley thanked their host and compensated him for his time and returned to the busy streets of the town.

They began their search within the town itself. The chandler happily confessed to providing Hesselgrave with specially crafted tapers for his household's use, but had not seen the man in several weeks; the orders were regular and were shipped by wagon, and accounts paid promptly upon receipt of an order, requiring very little in the way of interaction between the parties. Likewise, the tailor who made his clothing when he could not go to London had no knowledge of his whereabouts, nor the tobacconist nor the cobbler.

The woman at the bakery, who was known to create beautiful and realistic flowers from sugar paste, did suggest that Hesselgrave had often met with a local craftsman at the tea room attached to her bakery, there to discuss matters of hunting equipment, and provided the man's name. Francis Sheppard owned a workshop on the outskirts of the town and was often to be found at work. She knew of Mr. Sheppard's business because he was married to her sister. If either of the two gentlemen wished to purchase hunting guns, Francis would be able to provide them with the best available.

Alexander left with Sheppard's direction, a rich and fragrant spice cake to be enjoyed later that morning, and an order for an assortment of sugar flowers to be collected later. Mary would find them frivolous, he knew, but he hoped she would enjoy them, nonetheless. It was quite inappropriate to give a gift to an unrelated woman, but this being food and therefore ephemeral and comestible, he excused the matter to himself and his companion by asserting it was not a true gift in the usual manner of the word.

Knightley nodded his understanding and bought a similar amount to give to Emma. Then upon second thought, he bought two more boxes, one for the Bateses and one for Mrs. Weston, requesting them all to be held until the men returned later that day before riding back to Highbury.

Frank Sheppard's workshop was less easy to find than Newnam's rooms, but the man himself was affable and welcoming. His showroom held a rather impressive display of weaponry, including pistols, hunting rifles, longbows, and knives. Alexander had no liking for firearms and had no desire to increase his collection past the one pistol he occasionally carried when a case threatened danger. Knightley, on the other hand, looked upon the display cases with more interest, but limited himself to their task at hand, namely seeking information on Hesselgrave.

Sheppard was tall and heavily built, more muscle than fat from what Alexander could see, but with a gentle expression that belied the violent nature of his handiwork. His hands were clean but rough, and there were grease stains under his short fingernails.

"Sorry, gentlemen," he had been standing behind a workbench when Knightley explained their mission, but immediately led the men to a table at the far side of the room near a thick green door and pulled out three stools from the corner. "Hesselgrave, eh? Haven't seen him at all recently, but here, take a seat and have an ale, and I will search my mind for other men to ask."

He disappeared for a moment and returned with three glasses filled with fragrant yeasty beer. Some short minutes later, a rather pretty young woman appeared from behind the same door Sheppard had used, carrying a tray laden with bread and cheese and slices of cold meat. The woman looked similar enough to the one at the bakery that it could only be her sister. "Please," she gestured to the victuals and set a plate and napkin before each man, before disappearing back whence she had come. Alexander took bread and cheese and watched the others partake of the meat as well, then sipped at the hearty ale before him.

As they ate and drank, Sheppard began to list a series of names to try. Some they had already encountered, whilst others were new. Alexander wrote each down in his notepad, with whatever direction Sheppard could give.

"I wish you luck," he said at last. "Hesselgrave is a good customer, and moreover, a decent man. I should be very sad had anything happened to him."

Before parting, Knightley put in an order for a new hunting rifle, and Alexander purchased a rather cunning pocket knife that folded into a very small silver case. He might send it to his sister Deborah for her birthday, he told himself, but his mind's eye saw the knife in Mary Bennet's hand. He brushed that thought away and bid his farewells to the craftsman.

The remainder of the day was spent in one fruitless visit after another, some in town and some out in the countryside beyond, both on foot and on horseback. Alas, no sign of Hesselgrave could be found. No one had seen him for days, if at all, and no one had any knowledge to impart.

"There is some good news in this," Alexander sighed as they returned to the inn for a quick meal of bread and cheese before retrieving their boxes of sugar flowers and riding home.

Knightley raised his brows in sceptical question.

"We have not discovered his body. In every other case, there was no attempt to hide or delay discovery of the deceased's remains. If we have not yet found Hesselgrave's mortal coil, it may be that he breathes still."

"You are more sanguine than I," Knightley shook his head. "I find myself more and more convinced of a sad fate for the man. He was never one I counted as a friend, but he was not a bad sort and the neighbourhood shall be worse for his loss."

"What then, do we do about Mr. Elton? We may have every suspicion under the sun, but without proof that the other men were deliberately killed, we have nothing to hold against him. It is no crime to outlive one's partners."

"That is too true. We must, therefore, seek to learn more about these deaths. If we can find evidence that they were deliberately done, we may then find evidence of Elton's hand. 'Tis no easy task we have set, though. Watson died six weeks ago, and his forge and workroom have been repaired. There will be little, if anything, there to learn. We may return to Robert Martin's reservoir and speak to Abdy's children and grandchildren; perhaps there we will find something."

"And Smith, the tramp? Could he possibly be involved at all? I can hardly imagine it, and yet his death seems to be the one which began this unhappy succession."

"I cannot know. His may have been a true accident. But perhaps, along with seeking what we can about Carnes and Abdy, we ought also to find out as much as possible about the man who called himself Jack Smith."

They rode back to Highbury with little conversation. In light of their failure to discover anything about the plight of Ralph Hesselgrave, both men were sombre and the scenery, which earlier had been such a source of joy for Alexander, had lost some of its beauty. Even the treats which the man had stowed in the saddle bags had taken on an onerous aspect, now having become necessary burdens rather than the spontaneous and unexpected gifts they had been upon their purchase.

They descended the high hills and took the road leading to Highbury as the sun was nearing the horizon. It was still clear daylight, and would be for a while yet, but the long shadows to their sides reminded them that evening was fast approaching. It would be another night with no news of Hesselgrave, another night of being no further ahead in the investigation, and another night of no advancement in Alexander's own case concerning the races themselves.

Exactly what Knightley's sentiments were, he could only guess, but Alexander felt a deep sense of discontent.

As the sun began to bob and dip behind some of the tallest trees, the men approached the first houses of the village, and soon were on the main street nearing the Crown.

"What's this?" Knightley's call of concern brought Alexander from his dark musings. A small crowd had gathered in the street just past the inn, near the lane that marked the corner by the tea shop. Everybody was facing inward on some event, and the sound of loud weeping was heard over the accumulated noise of the gathering.

"That's Cox's house! Dear Lord, I hope he is not involved in this whole affair." Knightley pressed his horse forward, then brought it to a halt near the crowd and swung down from his saddle. Alexander followed, but held back a little way, not wishing to intrude on what might be somebody else's tragedy. He watched Knightley walk forward, his shoulders straight and his gait stiff, and the crowd parted for him as the Red Sea before Moses' outstretched arms.

He stood for a moment and spoke to some people, and then his shoulders eased. Alexander released a breath. Whatever dire event had occurred, it was no disaster, and he now began his own cautious approach, wishing to be of use but still very aware that he was an outsider in the community and that not all would welcome his presence.

The crying, he could now determine, was that of a young woman or a girl, and as he neared the scene, he could see a girl of about fourteen or fifteen sitting on the ground, cradling the head of a dog in her lap. The dog was not moving, and Alexander realised there had, indeed, been yet another death in Highbury.

Chapter Twelve

Evidence from the Dog

Mary's day had not been the most interesting since her arrival in Highbury. After walking into the village with Frank, she had turned one way to discharge her monetary obligations at the inn and Frank had bid her farewell, claiming he had an errand to run for his father.

Mr. Stoller, the innkeeper, had been quite happy to set aside a few minutes for her and wrote out a neat receipt for monies tendered for her to give to her brother when next they met. She spoke for a few minutes with the coach driver and footman, who both assured her of their comfort in their rooms and of the quality of the fare, and then went to the stables to complete similar arrangements for the care of the horses and storage of the carriage. The driver and footman had been visiting the horses every day and had taken them for exercise through the countryside, and neither had any concerns about the good health of the beasts.

Having completed her assigned tasks, she looked around for something to occupy her day. The Bateses and Miss Fairfax were not at home, and Mary could not quite look upon a visit to Mrs. Elton with anything resembling pleasure. Taking tea alone at the tea room seemed quite melancholy, and she had no other acquaintances in town. She stopped in at Ford's shop to look after some small gifts for Mama and Kitty, and then spent a rather longer time at the bookshop at the corner, where she spent a good amount of the remainder of Mr. Darcy's money. She did feel, perhaps, a moment's guilt over this, but soon smothered those thoughts when faced with a new imprint of a novel she had been longing to read.

When she returned to Hartfield, therefore, it was with a small parcel of three books in her hands, and upon greeting Emma and Mr. Woodhouse, she took herself to a sunny spot in the parlour, there to read. She took tea with her hosts at the appropriate time and then sat with Emma and Harriet Smith, who arrived later in the afternoon to help devise entertainments for a gathering the following week.

"Do you often read, Miss Bennet?" Harriet asked as Mary set aside her novel in favour of helping the others find ideas for Bouts-Rimés. It was an amusing diversion of poetry and rhyme, and Mary could not dislike it.

"I suppose I do, Miss Smith," she replied. "I often find myself alone and without company, but I am never lonely if I have something diverting to read."

"How sad that you want for companionship! At Mrs. Goddard's, there are always younger girls needing my assistance or wishing for my attention, and I do declare that I should go quite mad if I had to spend all day with only myself for company! I quite crave being around people."

"As do I!" Emma asserted. "Before Mrs. Weston married, she was my constant companion. How pleased I was to meet Harriet, for she has become quite indispensable to me!"

Harriet beamed with pride, and Emma cast upon her a look that was more suited for a proud owner looking upon a prized puppy.

"Do you read, Miss Woodhouse? Surely Miss Smith is often needed at Mrs. Goddard's school, leaving you with little occupation."

Emma gave a small pout. "I do read! That is, I try. I have been meaning to read more since I was twelve years old. I have set myself a list of books to read, and I do mean to read regularly, but there is always something more entertaining to do, for reading requires industry and patience, areas in which I must admit I am somewhat lacking."

"But together, we may read," Harriet volunteered. "Perhaps if we establish a routine, where we meet every week to read for an hour in silence, we may then reward ourselves with tea and cakes! Would that do at all, Miss Woodhouse?" Her eyes were eager and desperate for approval, much like the puppy Mary had envisioned, seeking a reward for sitting up or rolling over. Once more she was struck by how very young Harriet seemed, despite her years being so very nearly Mary's own.

Mary suppressed a chortle. "That may be an excellent idea for you." She hoped she sounded pleased and not as judgmental as she felt. "For me, reading is its own reward."

In such a manner, feeling very much a welcomed but incompletely understood member of the small party, she passed the afternoon. It was only after an early dinner, when Harriet declared she must be going, for she was expected back at the school, that Mary felt some glimmer of anticipation.

"If you would not object to the company, Miss Smith, I will walk with you to the village. I should be glad of some exercise."

Emma looked rather shocked. "But it will be dark before long! You cannot mean to be out in the dark!" Mary assured her she was quite capable of walking the short distance down the lane and back to Hartfield, for the moon was closer to full than half, and the lane well travelled. "My poor father would never be easy if I did such things! You must take a servant along with you on the walk. Thomas is tall and quite trustworthy. I shall summon him at once."

Mary had no choice but to agree. She did not, in truth, object to an escort, and would rather take her exercise in the silent company of a sturdy footman than not at all. But how very different life was here from what she was accustomed to at Longbourn. Her mother's nerves never quite seemed disarranged by her middle daughter's habits.

Mary and Harriet strolled down the lane towards the village, Thomas trailing them at a comfortable distance, far enough not to overhear private conversation, but close enough to provide immediate help in the unlikely event it was necessary. The Woodhouse servants were, from everything Mary had seen, excellent in every way.

The village was busy. Other than the evening of the ball, Mary had not seen it as night approached, and she was enchanted by the sight. Men, home from their days at their employment, were gathered by the front doors to the Crown, and from what her ears told her, a great many more were assembled inside, amusing themselves at drink and song and whatever such men did for entertainment. Women and children gathered in groups of four or five outside, exchanging news and enjoying each other's company, as their husbands and sons did inside.

Shopkeepers, craftsmen, merchants, prosperous farmers, all met and socialised under the dimming sky, until a great cry of distress split the air. "No! Help, please! My dog is ill!" A girl of about fourteen came running from a house, holding a small hound and crying. Several of the women dashed to her aid, but from what Mary could gather, it was too late to save the pet. The girl sank to the ground, still cradling her lost friend, and a woman who seemed to be her mother separated herself from her group to rush towards the weeping girl.

Mary knew the woman—this was Mrs. Cox, wife of the town's attorney and sister-by-marriage to the intelligent man whom Alexander had introduced as his friend from London, the very one who had enjoyed a sensible conversation with Miss Bates only yesterday. She had not seen the girl before; presumably she was too young to attend the ball. If only Mama had been so prudent with her own sisters!

"What has happened?" A familiar voice sounded behind her, and she turned on her heel to see Alexander dismount from his horse. Mr. Knightley had rushed past her already and was now standing at the side of the piteous pair, his shoulders slumped in shared sorrow.

"Her dog... I only saw it now, when she came from the house, carrying him. I cannot think he was alive even then." Unaccountably, her eyes filled with tears. This was not her dog, nor one she had known, and neither did she know the girl at all. But she understood sorrow and the pain of losing a beloved pet, and she sniffled in a most unladylike manner. Alexander wound an arm about her shoulder and held her close to him in sympathetic reassurance. It was very definitely improper, and most inappropriate, but at no time had Mary and Alexander's friendship been conventional, and it was not the first time they had held onto each other in times of distress.

Lyons, what do you make of this?" Mr. Knightley was walking back towards them through the gathered crowd. "Miss Bennet," he executed an elegant bow quite out of keeping with the circumstances. "I shall beg your leave to discuss unhappy matters before you. You have proven yourself to be a woman able to tolerate such things." She nodded in appreciation and he continued. "This is hardly a matter for a magistrate and professional investigator, but the girl's father is a friend of mine, and her uncle a friend of yours, I believe." He was looking towards Hugh Cox, and Alexander concurred. "Jonathan Cox, her father, said she might rest better if we looked into the matter; knowing we take her concerns seriously is important to the girl, and I am happy to oblige, if you are."

"Yes, yes, of course," Alexander agreed, as Mary nodded vigorously beside him. "If you would do the honour of introductions?"

The girl was Chloe Cox, the dog Latrax. Chloe looked at Mary with big red eyes and gave a half smile. She seemed genuinely grateful for the attention given to the seriousness of the situation, and equally so for the inclusion of another of her sex in the matter. If these men felt Mary worth including, then they would listen to Chloe with all due attention.

Gradually, between sobs, her story emerged. The family had dined earlier and had set out sweets and fruit to enjoy later after a visit with the neighbours and an ale for her father at the public rooms. She herself had been talking to a friend in the neighbouring house through the open windows when a horrible sound reached her and she discovered Latrax in great distress. By the time she reached him, he was frothing at the mouth, and in moments had stopped breathing. It was at this point that she had grabbed him and run outside in desperate search of her parents.

"May we see your house?" Mary had never heard Alexander's voice so soft and sympathetic, and she wondered if he was thinking of his own sisters. "Will you show us what he was doing when you heard him?"

The girl nodded and struggled to her feet. Her mother gave her agreement, and her father called to some friends to help take care of the dead dog. Mary followed Chloe, Alexander, Mr. Knightley, and Mrs. Cox into the house.

Chloe led them into the kitchens at the back of the house. In an alcove at the side, Mary could see the window seat by the open window through which the girl must have been talking to her friend. A large table sat in the middle of the room, on the other side of which was an open area which might be used for the family to dine and take their ease when not entertaining in the formal dining room. Behind the table, nearer to the wall with counters and cabinets and work tables and a large modern stove, there lay a large pile of detritus. Knightley stepped towards this mess to take a closer look, and Mary and Alexander followed.

The dog had been into the rubbish. A scattering of broken pottery, a dusting of flour, apple cores, pastry crumbs, empty vials, and similar objects had been strewn all over, leading to an open door in one cabinet and a tall bin that now lay on its side.

"My dishes!" Mrs. Cox moaned. "And our sweets. The poor creature has destroyed everything and paid the price."

"What could he have eaten?" Mary heard Alexander whisper to Mr. Knightley as he sniffed at some of the broken objects on the floor. "Cherry, almonds, cheese, what is that other odour, Knightley? Laudanum? Ale, bitter tea… What ho? Are those the remains of a houseplant? Could it be something toxic to dogs?"

The mess was sorted and categorised as well as possible, and in the end, the men accounted for several substances which might have brought about the end for poor Latrax. The plant, a type of lily, was listed as a possible source of whatever killed the animal, but there were also the remains of a jar of poison used to control rats, the remaining laudanum left by the apothecary for Mrs. Cox's elderly aunt who had lived with them for some time, the caustic cleaning powder the family's maid used, and a variety of other substances. All of these vied for the ignominious honour of dispatching the dog, along with the razor-sharp shards of the pottery plates he had pushed off the table and which had scattered across the floor.

"Dogs do eat anything," Mary hung her head and commiserated with Chloe, who had ceased her weeping and become really quite engaged in what the men were doing. Tomorrow the girl would become weepy again with the remembrance of this and with the guilt of having allowed her pet to get into the rubbish, but for now she would be well. Mary left her to the care of her mother and rejoined Alexander and Mr. Knightley.

"'Tis a pity not all cases can be solved so quickly," she sighed as they left the house once more.

"Not so, for we did not learn what substance it was that killed the beast. I would not consider this a success at all." Alexander's words were harsh, but his voice was sad.

"We helped a sweet girl overcome her immediate distress, Lyons," Mr. Knightley attempted to soothe him. "Knowing the exact source of the agent would have changed nothing. What matters is that she feels we have stepped in to help, that her concerns are worthy of our time. That will serve her better than knowing whether it was the lye or the plant."

Mary wished so very much to return the brief embrace he had given her earlier, but now, with Knightley's eyes upon them, it would not do. Before they had been lost in the crowd, amongst people overwhelmed with emotion. Now the immediate crisis was over, and good English sensibilities were expected to reign once more. 'Twas a pity, for Mary knew that Alexander could do well with a hug.

It was, by now, nearly dark. Mr. Knightley went to retrieve his horse from where he had thrown the reins to the hands of a villager whom he knew, and Alexander did likewise. "Let us take these fine fellows to the stables for a few minutes and see if that parlour in the inn is available," the magistrate rubbed at his brow between his eyes. I could do well with a drink. Lyons?" Alexander nodded. "Join us, Miss Bennet. I see Emma has sent Thomas to keep you safe. With your leave, I shall send him home and conduct you back to Hartfield myself. It is on my way back to Donwell Abbey, if you have no objection to me leading my horse."

This plan was deemed most suitable and so was set into motion. The room was indeed empty of other guests, and soon the three were seated therein. Alexander and Mr. Knightley each took an ale, and Mary requested a glass of wine, which she drank with as much need as enjoyment. Why this death affected her more than that of Carnes, she could not say. Perhaps it was because she was witness to the great distress the dog's sudden passing occasioned; perhaps it was because she knew that the poor animal was completely innocent of any crime. She regretted Carnes' death, felt great pity at the sight of his body, and prayed for his soul. No matter what he might or might not have done, he had not deserved to be killed— for despite the lack of any evidence, she was convinced his end was no accident—but she had not felt this wrenching and personal reaction that she felt watching Chloe Cox weeping over the furred body of her pet.

What sort of wretched creature was she, to weep more for a dog than for a man? Was her own soul so corrupt that she could conjure more tears for a beast than a person? She took rather too deep a gulp of her wine and settled back to ponder the condition of her deepest being as the men talked of their day. She finished her wine and poured herself another glass from the decanter, then took a deep draught of the heady liquid.

"Mary?" Alexander had reached over to touch her arm. She started at the contact and then settled her own hand upon his when he began to jerk back in mortification that he might have offended her. She did not object to his touch. She rather welcomed it, for he was comfortable and familiar and safe, and as much as she had argued with him in the past, and as much as they still had unresolved issues between them, he was safe. He was her friend. Now, at this moment, with the sight of the dead dog lurking behind her eyelids and waiting for every dark moment, she needed a friend.

Mr. Knightley looked down at Alexander's hand on her arm and gave a small smile. Then, without mention of what was under his eyes, he set about describing for her what he and Alexander had learned and seen that day. As he spoke, Mary finished her wine and then took another glass. She was growing warm and her thoughts were becoming unclear, but the suggestion that Mr. Elton might be the only surviving investor in Carnes' enterprise shook her back to a strange mental acuity.

"You believe the person behind the deaths is Mr. Elton?" Mary's shock was apparent. "But... but he is a clergyman, a churchman! You cannot really believe him guilty of murder!" Her mood shifted in an instant, from curious and eager for discussion to defensive and angry. The very mention of Mr. Elton had lit a spark under her, and her temper was the fuse. When the charge caught, Alexander Lyons would receive the damage. This she knew, and some part of her regretted it, but she could not douse the flame. This argument was too personal. Just like the dog, the poor dead dog, it was personal. She had no further reserves of will to buffer her moods. The incident with Chloe Cox had sapped them all. There was only her intimate sense of betrayal and loss at the death of the dog, her sudden questioning of her own goodness, and her damnable pride. How much wine had she consumed? She knew not, but poured another glass. Alexander moved the decanter to the far side of the table.

"The evidence does point to him, Miss Bennet. I wish it were otherwise, but..." Mr. Knightley shrugged.

"And you, Alexander, must be delighting in this." She knew she was being unfairly combative and accusatory. Her disagreements with Alexander in the past had revolved around issues of religion and faith, and she felt—quite unreasonably, she knew—that her unusual friend wished the guilt to fall on a minister of the Church of England in order to support his claims that the Church did not speak for him. The fuse was burning brighter now. It awaited only the charge.

"Now Mary…" Alexander's voice was low and filled with warning. "Let us not start on this again. My feelings have nothing to do with the matter, and you seem to take great pleasure in mistaking what they are."

"And yet how you must feel vindicated. For every drop of vice you can identify amongst these men, your own path, whatever it is, must feel stronger and stronger. First Mr. Collins, and now Mr. Elton: perhaps we may next examine the Archbishop of Canterbury for cheating his housekeeper of her earned wages."

"Mary!" It came out as a growl. "Let us please speak of the evidence and not your notions of what I do and do not believe. Please. Not now, not here."

Mr. Knightley shifted in his chair. It was clear he had no wish to be a part of this argument and would dearly love to find some way to leave. Mary opted to live up to her contrary nature and spoke directly to the older gentleman. "Mr. Lyons has declared to me in the past that he is no good Christian. In fact, he confesses to being no Christian at all. What think you of that, Mr. Knightley?"

If he had looked uncomfortable before, he seemed even more so now. He glanced at Alexander, who to his credit affected as calm an expression as Mary had seen, and then at Mary herself. "From my brief dealings with Mr. Lyons, Madam, I have no quarrels with his sense of right and wrong or with his morality. How he expresses this in his personal time is of little matter to me. I judge the actions of a man and not the words."

"Just so, Mary," Alexander spoke. "Have we not spoken enough that my meaning is clear to you? All of these matters—good and evil, sin and virtue—exist independently of specific belief. A man may espouse every value of his chosen church, may pray at the right times and bow his head and make his offerings, all in accordance with what is expected, and still be at heart a wicked person. One can say the right things, but unless one's actions reflect the true essence of those words, they are meaningless."

She glared at him. She had heard this argument before and was in no mood to hear it repeated. If he noticed her expression, he did not respond, but kept talking.

"Likewise, a good man with good in his heart will act well regardless of what he claims to believe, of whether or not he prays. There have been many such men and women in history. As our friend Knightley says, we do better to judge according to deed than to claim."

"But Mr. Elton is a clergyman, a vicar! This is more than a mere claim of faith. His entire world is centred around it. He studied for the church; he has made it his profession. Can one study the word of God, come to know it so intimately, and preach about it, and still take it so lightly that one can deprive a man of his life? I cannot believe it so! It is unthinkable!"

Now Mr. Knightley bestirred himself to speak. "I would like very much to agree with you, Miss Bennet, and we must all agree that in most cases, you are correct. I have known so many men of the cloth in my lifetime, as a child and as a grown man, here in Surrey and at school and in London, and most—nay, almost all—have been fine upstanding men, true paragons of what a godly person ought to be, models of virtue for the community. But sadly, regardless of occupation, a man is still a man, for good or ill. Such a person, if of an evil bent, will tend that way regardless of what means he uses to provide his living. If the character is weak, if the faith feigned, carrying the cross will not make a bad man good."

"Come now, Mary," Alexander pled. "Don't let this come between us. We were friends, I thought. We had discussed this and agreed to let it be. I have no quarrel with your Church, and none with your faith. If I find fault in a man, it is all to do with his actions and the proof I can find to bring against him. I take no particular pleasure in assigning guilt to Mr. Elton because of his vocation."

"You yourself, only moments ago, claimed to judge a man by action rather than by assertion. Well, Mr. Lyons, you may assert your fairness all you wish, but your actions declare you to seek to find evil in the Church, and that I cannot abide." She rose from her chair and looked wildly for her bonnet and spencer. Where could she have put them? Surely she recalled placing them on the chair...

"Miss Bennet?"

Mr. Knightley, ever the gentleman, was holding her spencer in his hands, and he helped her don the light garment. He likewise handed her the bonnet she now recalled she had set aside on the small table by the window and offered his arm.

"Allow me to walk you home. Let us stop to call for my horse, and then we may be off. I do believe the night air will help you feel more yourself."

Unable to speak, she nodded. As they left the room, she turned to cast one last gaze upon Alexander, who sat in his chair as if pinned there, a stunned expression upon his face. Then he turned his gaze away from her and stared steadfastly away.

Her stomach, which was not feeling too settled at the moment, plummeted with the weight of lead. What on earth had she done?

Chapter Thirteen

New Friends

When Mary woke the following morning, it was to the dull light of an overcast sky. She opened her eyes and then squeezed them shut immediately, sensitive even to the subdued light. Gradually and painfully, she made another attempt, trying to recall what had brought about the headache and malaise that overcame her. She brought herself to a sitting position in her bed and rubbed her temples, trying to think.

She recalled walking into the village and coming across poor Chloe and her dog, and then… Oh no! Alexander! She fell back down onto her pillows with an audible groan.

"Miss Bennet?" Her maid's voice sounded from somewhere near the wardrobe.

"Alice." She croaked out the name. How could she face her maid in this shameful condition? How could she face anybody? Miss Mary Bennet, speaker of chastisements, reciter of sermons, arbiter of all things moral, had come home drunk. She, who had held herself so superior to the masses who laid their good sense at the feet of physical indulgence, had succumbed. How could she ever look upon her family and friends again, knowing that she was as weak and pathetic as the worst inebriates of her acquaintance? Once more, she examined the depths of her being and was appalled. Pages from Fordyce's sermons swam before her eyes and phrases rang in her ears and the disorientation these occasioned caused the leaden weight in her stomach to roil and twist and...

Alice was there with a bowl as Mary rid herself of the contents of her unhappy stomach. Her maid stood silent and supportive until there was nothing left to come and then began to murmur quiet words of comfort as she wiped Mary's white and soiled face with a cool damp cloth.

"Mr. Knightley told us of the dog, poor devil. He said how it distressed you, how you needed a glass of wine. 'Twas no more than any sensitive lady would do, Miss Bennet. Poor pup, and the poor girl what loved it."

"Miss Woodhouse? Her father?"

"Both was in the parlour at cards when you came in. Mr. Knightley called for me right away, and I brought you right up here without seeing them. Mr. Knightley said he would say only that you were not feeling quite yourself because of the poor dog and had retired right away. I don't believe they know a thing. Nobody other than me and the gentleman knows, Miss. There's no one here blaming you, and I certainly shan't say a word."

Torn between relief at being understood and mortification at receiving her maid's absolution for her sins, Mary could find no words. She sat up in her foul-smelling bed and blinked at Alice, her mouth open, but without words. Once more Alice seemed to understand and disappeared for a few moments, returning with a fresh set of towels, both damp and dry, and a tray carrying some weak tea and dry bread. She washed Mary's face again and bade her take the tea and try to eat whilst the servants finished filling the bath in the adjoining bathing room.

"We'll have you changed and fresh, Miss, and you'll feel much better. If you can drink the tea with no ill effects, Mr. Knightley suggested a cup of coffee as well, if you don't mind the taste. He said it would soothe your head, should it ache."

"Yes. Thank you." She squeezed her eyes closed again. Ladies did not thank their maids. But Alice was acting more in the capacity of a helpful friend right now, and any suggestions that might ease the pain behind her eyes merited appreciation. Mary sipped her tea; it settled as it ought, and she requested the offered coffee to be brought, with an extra spoon of sugar. She had tasted her father's coffee on more than one occasion, and knew that suitably served, with ample cream and sugar, it was not unpleasant. The thought of rich cream was not a welcome one right now, so she would have to try the coffee sweetened, but black.

An hour later, washed and dressed, and with three cups of coffee inside her, Mary felt somewhat ready to step outside her room. The coffee had not been unpleasant at all, even without the cream, and her headache had subsided into something more akin to a bad memory than a gnawing ache. The clock on the mantel chimed eleven o'clock—terribly late for her—and she felt the need for some air, as much to clear the stench of vomit from her nose as for the benefit some exercise would surely bring her.

Emma was out with Harriet, and Mr. Woodhouse expressed his hopes that the room had not been too warm for her to sleep well last night, and an admonition to take an umbrella in case it should rain.

Mary thanked him for his concern and called for her boots and bonnet.

The sky was lightening—there would be no rain today, no matter Mr. Woodhouse's worries—but the sun still lay concealed behind a layer of clouds. This suited Mary admirably, for she was not so certain her improved headache would remain so improved in very bright light. Her feet turned naturally to the village, and she thought she might call in on young Chloe Cox to see how the poor girl fared.

As she walked, her mind strayed back to the horrible scene from the previous night. She did not recall every detail, but she remembered enough to be most ashamed of her behaviour. Had she really accused Alexander of rejoicing in the fact of Mr. Elton's supposed guilt? What had she been thinking? Or did she, at some deep level, really think that? Further, had she brought old grievances out before Mr. Knightley? No matter the investigator's apostasy, no matter the ultimate fate of his eternal soul, this was no subject to be raised before a man who was only one step closer than a stranger. And what did Alexander truly believe? They had never completed that conversation. She knew only that he did not subscribe to the articles of the Church of England, but not whether he held with a different tradition. He had told her he was neither a Presbyterian nor a Papist, as so many Scots were. What else could he be? He had once admitted she would not consider him to be Christian at all. Was he a disbeliever, an atheist? Could this be his secret?

She hoped she might find him very soon and grovel at his feet for his forgiveness. Then, perhaps, if he had such charity in his heart, she might ask him that final question and learn that one crucial fact about Alexander Lyons. She only hoped he would trust her after her dreadful accusations last night.

She had, by now, achieved the village, and she went immediately to the Cox's house, there to inquire after Miss Chloe. Mrs. Cox welcomed her in and offered tea, which Mary politely refused. Chloe was red-eyed and glum but composed, and she seemed quite touched by the visit. "I'm honoured, Miss Bennet," she wiped her eyes. "You do me such kindness, and you do not know me at all!" They talked of Latrax, of Chloe's favourite activities, of whether she preferred French to arithmetic, and of the poem she hoped to write in memory of her pet.

When her fifteen minutes were over and she stood to take her leave, Mrs. Cox walked her to the door. "Your kindness is noted, Miss Bennet," the woman curtseyed. "Both last night and today. Not every gentlewoman would take the time to condole with a mere country attorney's daughter." Mary knew she must be thinking of Emma. "You have made a fast friend in Chloe, and your good heart will not be forgotten."

Mary insisted on giving Mrs. Cox her direction at Longbourn, should Chloe wish to write to her to tell her of the poem and whether she decided to get another puppy. "Your actions speak volumes about your heart, Miss Bennet." Mrs. Cox dipped deeply and bade Mary a grand day as she continued along the street.

Something of Mrs. Cox's words gnawed at her conscience, but her mind was yet too unsettled to ponder over them, and she turned her thoughts to other matters, all of which fluttered away from her like autumn leaves in a gust of wind. Perhaps she might treat herself to a tea and piece of cake at the lovely tea room Emma had taken her to before.

There it was, just by the corner, near the inn. She waited for a farmer's wagon, heavy with its blanket-covered burden, to pass on the street, then crossed quickly before two young men on horseback cantered by. She was about to step up to the door of the teashop to let herself in, when through the window she noticed somebody who looked very much like Alexander. He was sitting facing mostly away from her, but that hair was unmistakable. She took another glance, and there, across the table from him, sat Emma Woodhouse! Emma was staring at him with stars in her eyes and laughing and... Mary's heart nearly stopped. Was Alexander holding Emma's hand? No, it could not be! The muted sunlight reflected on the tea shop window and the thin muslin sun curtains, which kept direct sunlight from melting the delicate edible ornaments on the cakes, obscured her perfect view of the table, but still, what she saw seemed quite inexplicable as anything else. He was holding her hand! And in a public space, a tea room, where anybody might see them! This was all but a declaration of an engagement. Tears came unbidden to her eyes.

How she had been betrayed. After all her words last night, which she had offered so hastily and regretted so completely, she had resolved to find him and apologise for her dreadful behaviour. But instead of listing with his serious gaze and assuring her of his continued friendship, here he was, courting another woman! How could he? In shock and disbelief, she stumbled backwards away from the window and fled back across the street, heedless of what might be coming down the thoroughfare, and achieved the far side, where the pavement opened before the inn, just before a curricle raced down the street. In her shock and distress, she stumbled on the uneven cobblestones and she flung her arm out to the nearby lamppost, thereby righting herself. Her ankle smarted, although it took her weight with no additional complaint.

"Miss Bennet!"

Frank Churchill was hurrying towards her with long, determined strides. He held his hat onto his head with one hand and reached out to her with the other. "Are you well? You nearly took a spill. Those stones must be looked at, for they are far too uneven. Here, allow me to help you to the bench by the shop. Can you walk?"

Mary tested her ankle again. It was tender, but nothing more. "Thank you, Mr. Churchill. I am quite well." She demonstrated by taking a few tentative steps, and then a few more with greater confidence.

"We cannot be too careful. I would never be easy again if I allowed you to go off with an ankle that might yet give you pain. Perhaps a spot of tea?"

The thought of returning to the tea shop brought the most acute discomfort, and Mary made an excuse. "Perhaps a lemonade? The bookshop has a room at the back where one may take a lemonade or an ice. Please, allow me." He looked so very handsome and so very hopeful that Mary could do nothing but accept with a smile. Alexander might be a cad, but Frank Churchill seemed everything a young man ought to be, and he was an excellent replacement for her erstwhile friend.

Alexander had not slept well. He had not expected to. Despite a tiring day spent in the saddle and searching a great part of Surrey for Ralph Hesselgrave, his mind would allow him no rest. Whatever had worked its way under Mary's skin for her to turn on him like that? That topic was part of a discussion they had had—and resolved, so he thought—so many months ago. For her to accuse him, then, of something she surely could not truly believe distressed him to the core of his being. And in front of Knightley, a man whom he respected greatly but did not really know! Did Mary really think him the sort to glory in the culpability of another person based solely on that man's occupation? Would she next accuse him of revelling in the downfall of a lord because he was not of noble blood, or of a pedantic gently born lady because he had to scramble for his own living? Could she really think that meanly of him?

He was enraged at the notion, and to his amazement, heartbroken as well.

After a fitful night, he rose early and made his personal devotions, and then with a portion of guilt attended to some correspondence, which he sent off to London by messenger, and then set off for a brisk ride through the countryside. He had many questions to ask and much to think about, but he needed to clear his head. He revisited the image of Mary, the night before, drinking one glass of wine after another, and groaned in sympathy for the ache her head would give her today, and then groaned again at his own pain in the light of her abuse.

He rode up to Robert Martin's farm, and up to the reservoir for the irrigation system at the top of the hill, knowing that the farmer would not object to his presence, and further knowing that the land in fact belonged to Knightley, who certainly would have no objection. He surveyed the area from horseback, and then after dismounting, on foot. He climbed over the low wall, took another detailed survey of everything around, filled another page in his pocket notebook with details he knew were meaningless, and then clambered up onto the wall where Carnes had taken his last meal. He sat there, looking over the landscape, imagining the sun somewhere behind the thick bank of pale grey cloud.

Where had Carnes seated himself? Alexander shifted about in his spot on the well. Sitting cross-legged in the very centre of the wall was possible, but uncomfortable, as the uneven stones pressed into his ankles and shins, even through his boots. If he twisted one way, with his feet hanging over the edge on Carnes' side of the fence, there was a pleasant, if limited, vista of the paddock, the stables and barn, and a thick growth of trees. If he moved the other direction, looking out over Martin's land, the panorama was glorious. At his feet, which hung over the edge of the wall, was the reservoir, the waters glinting even in the dull light of the overcast sky. But beyond it lay a patchwork of fields and rivers and lanes and hedgerows, Squares of various shades of greens and yellows and browns led down the hillside towards the village, punctuated every now and then by a herd of white cottony sheep or the brown and white mottling of cattle. The stream traced its own lazy path, and the village rose up in the distance like something from a picture book. This was certainly the lovelier of the two views, and Alexander was certain that had he been Carnes, this is where he would have sat to take his mid-day nourishment.

It would also explain why Carnes had fallen onto Martin's side of the wall, rather than his own. Had he leaned over too far to try to see something? Had somebody called his name? The reservoir that gaped just below his feet was not particularly large, but if a man were stunned and could not swim, it held more than enough water to drown in. The question was what, or who, had caused the man to lean so far forward that he fell?

Alexander settled himself onto the wall as Carnes must have sat, but no matter where he looked, or how far over he leant, he could see nothing that might have drawn the dead man's interest. Could it have had anything to do with his meal? Had he dropped something that he hoped to retrieve. Alexander tried to recall what the man had been eating. There had been evidence of bread, cheese, some pastry, a flask of ale, some fruit…Had he dropped a fork, or another piece of food? Or had a valuable button fallen from his coat? Alexander huffed out a breath of air and leaned backwards, resting on his hands as he contemplated what he knew. It was very little, but at least he felt certain of the reason why Carnes' body was found on Martin's side of the wall.

On a whim, he shifted back to Carnes' side and jumped down. A voice hailed him from the stable and he shouted back a greeting, explaining who he was and the reason for his trespass.

"Aye," the owner of the voice emerged. He was a short and wiry fellow of middle years with the look of a man who loved and understood horses. "Welcome then, ye are. 'Tis a sad, sad business. Harry Carnes were a good man, and if ye can find what did this to him, we'd all be grateful. He was not such a one for an accident to befall him, always careful he were. I'm Forbes. I help train." The words were friendly and welcoming, but there was a cautious look in the man's eye.

Appropriate greetings were exchanged, then Alexander began his questions.

"Who was here with him when he died?"

"No one. We've talked to Mr. Knightley's man, but none of us has anything of value to say. We wish we did, for we're wanting to help any way we can. There's another field for training for speed yonder past that wood there, and that's where Bobby and me was that day. When we got back, we saw nothing and thought he'd gone on home."

"Did you notice anything untoward with the horses in the paddock or in the stables? Any sign that somebody else had been here?"

The trainer narrowed his eyes slightly but shook his head. "No. Not a sight of anyone. There's no real way up here but past where we was, anyway. If someone had come, we'd 'ave seen him, 'less he come up from Mr. Martin's farm as you did."

With a vague flicker of hope, Alexander also asked Forbes about the suspected interference in the races. Forbes' eyes narrowed again. There was something the man knew and would not say. Still, the trainer supplied him with two or three names he had not yet heard. "Don't for one moment think they're messing things up, mind ye. More honest men I don't know. But they might 'ave heard something. Can't hurt to talk."

On a whim, Alexander asked, "Mind if I look about the stables and barn for a moment? I don't expect to find anything, but you never know…"

Forbes looked distinctly uncomfortable. "I don't know that's right, seeing it's not my property to invite another into…"

Now Alexander knew there was something to be seen. He shrugged as if in indifference. "Never mind, then. I cannot imagine what I would see. I know only enough of horses to tend to my own, and almost nothing about raising or racing them. The barn would tell me nothing." He turned as if to leave the area and climbed back over the wall. He retrieved his horse and rode off, but pulled the beast over to a copse of trees that would obscure the animal from sight, and when he was certain that Forbes no longer stood watching, he crept back to the wall. He waited for some time. Eventually another man ambled up to the stables where Forbes was at work and the two talked for a moment, before both disappearing down the hill, perhaps to the other training field the man had talked about.

There was no great amount of time to be wasted, and Alexander meant to make the most of the minutes he had. He crossed again and ran down to the stables and then slipped through the doorway. He was no great horseman, and what he saw looked, to his eyes, like what any other well-provisioned stable ought to be. The stalls were empty, for the beasts were out in the paddock or elsewhere, but they were a good size and with plenty of hay.

Only the last stall, more of a storage space than a place for horses, held anything unusual. There, upon the floor, sat an assortment of tubs and small vats, all stained about the top. He crept close. An unpleasant odour emanated from one vat, and he knelt to better sniff the contents. It smelled like some combination of horse urine and sulphur... that would make a sort of bleach! The others, by their own scents and the colours about the lids, seemed to contain henna of different shades. How interesting! Henna could be used medicinally, Alexander knew, to help with a variety of minor ailments. Perhaps Carnes used them with good effect when his horses were not quite right. Perhaps... another idea began to form in his mind.

He took his notes and then, after checking for the return of Forbes and the other man, crept to the barn.

This space was surprisingly well lit, and quite empty. Only the walls were of any interest, for they were covered with detailed pencil sketches and watercolour paintings of a bewildering number of horses. Whoever had drawn and painted them had an excellent eye and considerable skill.

The germ of his notion began to sprout. Perhaps Carnes was merely an artist with a single particular purpose and wished for a place to display his creations. But it was seeming less and less likely that this was an innocent diversion. He made his notes and then hurried back to the wall to cross over and disappear down the hill before Forbes returned.

Back in Highbury, there was a letter waiting for him at the inn from Darcy, thanking him for looking in on Mary and declaring his intention to come down to the area with his wife on Monday, to resume his original plans a week late.

Never had a case seemed so mired in the mud. There was no evidence any of the deaths was anything other than accidental, and the best clue they had was a man who could not be found. The same few pieces of information just came up again and again, revealing nothing new. And now Darcy was coming with Elizabeth, to look at an estate in an area where a murder might well be at work, and one so ingenious that he could not be discovered.

He would spend one more day in his quest and then would send an express to his friend urging caution.

He folded the letter and slid it into a pocket and then wandered out into the streets again. He must ask everybody he could think of about the tramp, Jack Smith. Perhaps Smith was the unexpected key to the puzzle. Smith, he had written in his notebook, had come to the area five-and-twenty or thirty years ago. That was where he must start. He must find the oldest villagers and see what they might recall.

"Mr. Lyons, good morning!" Emma Woodhouse's bright voice broke through his musing. "I have just now come from taking some baskets to some of our poorer villagers and could do with a cup of tea. Do come and join me. I would enjoy your company."

Alexander felt his brow crease between his eyes, and he opened his mouth to politely refuse her invitation. He had much to accomplish this day, many people to find and question in the hopes of learning something about Jack Smith. But, he realised, he knew not exactly where to begin. Knightley would surely provide him with some suggestions, and Mrs. Bates as well, but Knightley could be anywhere in the county conducting his own inquiries, and speaking with Mrs. Bates involved speaking with Miss Bates—or rather, being spoken to by Miss Bates. Perhaps Miss Woodhouse would have some notions of the best people to approach instead. He took a glance at his watch. It was nearly noon; he could well afford a half an hour in the company of this pretty and vivacious young woman if it would set him along the path he needed. Nor would he lament a moment of that time! Emma had not, perhaps, the depth of character he best admired, but she was charming and delightful and her admiration of him did little to detract from her appeal.

"Thank you," he replied to her, and he watched the lights flash in her pretty blue eyes. "I would enjoy a cup of tea, and if you do not mind, you may help me with my investigation."

At this, her eyes shone even brighter. "How very exciting! Yes, indeed! Let us go now." She stood waiting for his arm, but he had the notion that if he stood still, she would grab his hand and pull him behind her like a child with a toy on a string. Not stifling the chuckle that emerged, he offered the expected arm and led her to the nearby tea room.

They took a table far from the door, where they might enjoy quiet conversation whilst they took their tea. A tray was ordered, as well as some cake for each, and a pleasant conversation ensued. Of what they spoke, Alexander could not have said, but it was diverting and most enjoyable, and Emma laughed adorably at his meaningless jokes. The serving girl brought the tea and set the pot in the middle of the table. Emma reached to pick it up by the painted china handle, but as she poured some into her cup to check the colour, it slipped and she ended up pouring the hot liquid onto her other hand.

"Oh, how silly I am!" she laughed.

Alexander called the girl over immediately for some cold water, or ice if possible, but Emma brushed away his concern. "'Tis hot, but not boiling. I shall have a pink hand for an hour or so, and then shall think on it no more. Please, do not worry, Mr. Lyons." Her hand was most certainly turning pink, nevermind that she continued to laugh off her little mishap.

The girl came with the requested water and some chips of ice wrapped in a thick cloth. "Miss Woodhouse, please, allow me to look at your hand. My father was a physician, and I learned something of injuries and healing at his knee. If you will permit me?"

She giggled as he took her hand to examine the burn. It did not look serious, and her face betrayed no great pain or discomfort, but nevertheless he held the cloth with the chipped ice against the reddened skin. "If there is any injury, this is the best way to mitigate it."

"The touch of your hand, sir, is healing enough." Oh. She was most certainly flirting with him. Despite himself, he smiled. After last night's debacle with Mary, he could well use some pleasant flirtation and the attendant knowledge that he was not detestable to all women.

"La!" Emma exclaimed, mid-giggle. "Is that? No, I must be mistaken. I thought I saw Miss Bennet at the window, but now she is gone. It must have been a play of the light." And she returned to her lovely, lively, and utterly forgettable conversation.

Chapter Fourteen

Tea and Questions

Mary sat in the calm of the room at the Fords' shop and allowed her eyes to close in relaxation. The cold ice soothed her head as it slid from the spoon down her throat, and the tart lemon flavour was comfortable in her stomach as something richer might not be.

"Thank you," she smiled at Frank Churchill as he enjoyed his own treat. "This was an exceedingly good idea."

"Delighted to be of service, and most especially so to one as charming as you, Miss Bennet." He gazed at her. "May I order you another? I am loath to mention such a thing, but it seems this has medicinal properties for you today."

She allowed her head to nod. "Thank you, sir. Indeed, it does. I had an unsettled night... Did you hear about Miss Chloe Cox's poor dog?" He nodded. "I came upon her right after the poor thing died. She was most distressed, and it quite put me out of sorts for the evening." She omitted a few nasty details from the previous night and neglected to say a word about seeing Alexander and Emma at the tea shop. Instead, she added, "I awoke with a rather sore head, and the ice is restorative."

"And rather tasty too, I dare say. Another lemon?" He rose and went to the counter to place the order, then returned to his chair.

"I had indeed heard of the Cox dog. My father thinks rather highly of Mr. Cox, and the news was all over the village this morning. Of course, the sudden passing of a pet is not normally fodder for gossip, but it seems it was a rather public event."

Mary agreed and related as much as she could recall. "Ah, poor thing indeed," Frank sighed. "One can understand the girl's upset. Fourteen is an age where sensibility far outstrips soberness of mind. I hope Miss Chloe feels more the thing this morning. But come, Miss Bennet, let us talk of matters more cheerful than this. Perhaps you have discovered a new bonnet that you must gush over for at least half an hour. No? Then let us walk through the area of the shop where Mr. Ford keeps his bonnets so you may find one whilst we await our ices. Yes, come now!"

He grabbed her by the hand and pulled her from her seat towards that part of the shop of which he had spoken. Mary began to laugh at the inanity of it and followed her companion to examine bonnets and ribbons and lace and silk flowers. When they returned to their table some minutes later, they had all but redone every bonnet in their minds and had settled on the exact qualities that can make a bonnet perfect and those that can make it ugly. Laughter, a handsome and besotted beau, and another serving of the cool and tart lemon ice all served to render the remnants of Mary's headache negligible, and when they had finished their treats and left the shop some time later, it was with broad smiles and the easy companionship of old friends.

On her walk towards the village earlier in the day, Mary had formed some plans to visit the Bateses, and this she proposed to do now. She had expected Frank to offer to join her, for he had expressed both obligation and pleasure at previous visits, but he made a comment about needing to tend to some matter for his uncle at the silversmith. Her face must have fallen, for he stopped her in her steps and turned to her. "If the choice were all mine, Miss Bennet, I should like nothing more than to sit at your feet all the day. But alas, we are not the only two in the world, and we must take other people's preferences and desires into account. But perhaps we shall meet again soon. Tell me, how long do you stay in our little neighbourhood?"

"Of course, you are correct, Mr. Churchill, and I should not have allowed my feelings to intrude upon your obligations. My brother Darcy hopes to be here on Monday, and then I will stay with him and my sister at the cottage near Dolbeare for another week, perhaps two, as he concludes his affairs here."

"Then we shall certainly be in company again, and that pleases me greatly. Until we next meet, Miss Bennet." He took her hand and pressed a kiss upon the back of it, before bowing and turning down the street towards the silversmith.

Now she flushed for shame again. She had worn her feelings too openly upon her face. A lady ought never to betray her sentiments too openly; it would not do to solicit a gentleman's favour, but rather, one ought to affect a mien of pleasant detachment until assured of the man's affections. To do otherwise—to do as she had just now done—was to court gossip and innuendo, to be seen as a flirt like Lydia or worse, to damage her reputation!

But had not her sister Jane nearly lost Mr. Bingley when she did not allow him to see her sentiments toward him? Did Mr. Darcy not suspect that Jane's heart was untouched and then work to separate her sister from the man she loved? Perhaps there was error in both extremes. She sighed. Here was one more matter upon which she had much thinking to do. Being a gentlewoman was no easy task.

"Miss Bennet!" Mary looked up as her name was called. She must know more people here in Highbury, where she had been for less than a week, than in Meryton, where she had lived all her life! Or was it, rather, that at home she was invisible, the sister everybody ignored, whereas here she was a newcomer and therefore exciting and different and the object of everybody's interest and attention.

The voice that called to her belonged to Hugh Cox, Alexander's friend from London. She offered her greetings, and when she named her destination, he offered to accompany her. "I really must be back to London," he gave a grimace, "but I find I do not wish to leave the area quite yet. I have work I brought with me that I can accomplish at the inn, and it is only sixteen miles to my offices, where my assistant may send to me any important messages in the course of half a morning. Yes, I was planning indeed to remain for a few more days, or perhaps a week."

His speech, along with his enthusiasm at the notion of visiting the Bateses, left Mary wondering if Miss Bates was one of the inducements to stay longer in the neighbourhood. She had never heard the lady speak as sensibly as she had in the presence of Mr. Cox, and on the subject of design and natural beauty. Could there be a growing attachment? Stranger things had happened!

The walk to the house where the Bateses had their apartments was not long, and within moments they were ringing the bell. Miss Bates looked out of the upstairs window and called down, "Oh! How lovely! Visitors. Mother, we have visitors! Miss Bennet and Mr. Cox! Oh, how delightful. Please, wait just a minute. How lovely!"

She was downstairs in a moment to open the door and lead the visitors up to the small parlour where Mrs. Bates sat in the corner with her knitting, coughing every now and then. Jane Fairfax was present as well, sitting upon the low sofa by the other window, a book on the seat beside her. "I ought to have sent Dolly down to the door," Miss Bates let the words tumble out, "but she is busy in the kitchen at the back of the house and could not hear the door, and if I were to call her to come up only to go down again, it should take far too much time, and now here you are! Please sit," she offered as an afterthought. "Be comfortable. I shall call for tea."

Mary assured her hostess that she required no tea, but the servant was summoned, regardless. Miss Bates beamed her pleasure, and looked at Mr. Cox a lot, whilst Jane Fairfax sat very still and quiet upon her sofa. Mary could not help but think she was somehow the cause of the young lady's distress and resolved to be as kind and friendly towards her as her personality allowed.

Before she could think of a suitable overture, however, Miss Bates began to address Mr. Cox.

"I heard—indeed, how could we not, for it was so sad, so very sudden—of your niece's loss. Poor thing, to lose her dog in so horrible a manner. I trust you have seen her. How is the poor girl? Such a sweet thing she is—she always has a smile and some time for a silly old woman, always comes with something for Mother— such a darling girl, and so sad, so very sad. Please, Mr. Cox, pass along my deepest regrets to your dear niece."

He responded as he ought, and Miss Bates was silent for a moment before adding, "If the poor girl wishes to condole, you may invite her here to speak with me, for I shared her pain only last autumn—was it the twelfth or thirteenth November, Jane? I can hardly recall exactly, only I know it was shortly after Mother had her very bad cold—Mr. Wingfield said he had never known them more general or heavy—and it was immediately after we received your letter from the seventh, telling us that you had caught a bad cold, and of Mr. and Mrs. Dixon's wedding, which was blessed an event for them, even if it meant you needed to return to us here in Highbury, which of course is a great delight for Mother and myself, if disappointing for you, to have to come and live with two old ladies when you are so accustomed to much finer things and younger company, and... now what was I saying? Oh yes, the poor dog which Mother took in from the kind Christian goodness of her heart, a nameless mongrel from the streets it was, but a sweet-natured thing and so grateful to have a home, he must have been twelve or more years of age, when only last November—now I recall, it was the twelfth exactly—he just died. He was in the kitchens with Mother as she was preparing her pies, and from what Dolly told me, he was well when she went to find some parsnips in the larder, and dead when she got back, and poor Mother, just sitting at her pastry all the time did not even notice until it was too late. I had not known how much I loved that dog until he was dead, for he was always a comfort on a cool night and so doting as such animals can be. So sad. Poor Chloe."

Mary found herself gasping for air after Miss Bates' monologue, but Mr. Cox looked dotingly upon the lady, who was now dabbing tears from her eyes. Silly and prone to long-windedness she might be, but Miss Bates was assuredly as kind-hearted a person as ever Mary had known. If Mr. Cox could find pleasure in her words, he could do far worse for a wife, were that his intention.

And, indeed, he began now to speak of his own beloved dogs from his childhood. He and Miss Bates had been passing acquaintances in their younger days, both having grown up in Highbury, but their ages and stations different enough that they had not been in company together. The daughter of the town vicar was expected to be friendly to the son of the village attorney, even if he were two years younger than herself, but that was all. She knew nothing of his love of animals as a youth, nor he of hers, and at once they discovered another thing held in common.

"I should like a dog in London," he said with a sad shake of his head, "but my hours at the office preclude the ability to care properly for one. If I had a wife…"

He looked up rather in alarm at having said something far too personal, but Miss Bates merely gave him an understanding smile and replied, "Yes, I should like another dog as well, but it is hard to care for a pet now, and a young pup requires so much attention, which I have not the time to devote, looking after Mother as I do."

The old lady had been coughing all the while, and Miss Bates glanced over to her with a worried look. "I must ask Mr. Perry to come and visit again. Perhaps he has more of the remedy he gave her when she was ill last autumn. He also suggested not getting another dog, for the fur can cause problems in breathing for those so prone, and listen to poor Mother's coughs. I really ought to go…"

"I should be happy to find Mr. Perry before I return to Hartfield," Mary spoke up. She wished to be helpful, and she might learn something from the apothecary as well. "Is his shop on my way?" Miss Bates was very pleased with the offer and gave Mary the full direction, then turned her attention back to Mr. Cox.

Mary chose this as the opportunity to approach Miss Fairfax with words of friendship, and the two entered into a pleasant discussion of music, which in turn led to some more duets at the pianoforte. As they played, the others enjoyed their tea and cake, and when at last Mary rose to take her leave, she found she had been at the Bateses for nearly two hours and had rather enjoyed her visit.

Alexander looked at his fob watch. Four o'clock already. He pushed his hair off his forehead and huffed. The day, thus far, had been one futile or frustrating moment after another. His tea with Miss Woodhouse excepted, of course. Once he was satisfied her hand had suffered no damage from the hot tea, he settled into his chair and his most serious expression, asked her if she might know anybody with knowledge about Jack Smith. Her initial response had been another cascade of silver laughter, and a rather mischievous look in those light blue eyes. "Now, Mr. Lyons! How fierce you look. We are allies in this venture, are we not? Do not scowl at me so, and I shall tell you what little I know."

In and amongst her flirtations, she provided him with the names of some of the older denizens of the neighbourhood. Of course, she sighed with regret, John Abdy would have been the best man to ask, for he had known everybody and until his last breath had suffered no deterioration of mind or memory. But alas, he was now gone as well. "His son, also John, might have some information. He is not young himself, being five-and-sixty if he is a day, but of course he would have known Smith, who was about his age. Yes, I should most certainly start with him! When do we begin?"

We? Alexander discovered, to his chagrin, the tyranny of the pronoun. "I had thought," he began, then cleared his throat and tried again, "That is, I had rather expected to approach Mr. Abdy alone."

"Nonsense!" She smiled at him as guilelessly as if she had suggested he take an umbrella on a rainy day. "Of course, I shall accompany you. Somebody must introduce you, after all, and I know exactly where to find him!" She placed her bonnet atop her head and pulled on her gloves and strode to the door. "Send the account, Mrs. Latimer!" she called, "and it shall be paid promptly."

How different this world was than his own. Here, a rich young woman need carry no money on her person. Her very name and face were all that was needed to secure credit at every establishment. For one such as he, however, it was quite the opposite. No matter that he always paid his bills immediately and presently, no matter that his income was respectable and better than that of most in the teeming world of London's back roads and alleyways, there would be no credit for him. He, far less wealthy than Emma Woodhouse, must carry his purse with him and pay for every treat and necessity in solid coin.

Likewise did the young lady assume that her presence in his assignment would be both needed and welcome. He must find a way to disabuse her of this, for he far preferred to speak to his witnesses alone. He loped after her on the street, following her towards her destination, waiting to catch up before requesting that she give him the direction, but then allow him to approach Abdy *fils* without her. But there, across the street, something caught his eye. From the door to Ford's shop came the handsome and elegant Frank Churchill, followed by none other than Mary Bennet. She was smiling at him, now laughing, and looking up at him with admiration in her eyes. Or, so he assumed, for she was some distance away and her eyes were shaded by her bonnet. But her stance, her mien, how she turned to him and took his arm, all spoke of feelings deeper than a lady ought to have for one she had only met short days before. And after her abuse of him last night, what was he to think? Something burned angry and hot in his chest, and he did the first thing that came to mind.

He ran after Miss Woodhouse and told her how delighted he was that she would accompany him on his interviews.

John Abdy the younger was at his place of work. Like his father, he was a clerk, plying his trade at the offices of the village bank. When Emma charmed her way past the supervisor and was granted several minutes of the man's time away from his desk, Alexander saw the wisdom in allowing her to join him. That it also assuaged injured feelings was only a secondary benefit.

The man was hunched over his desk, poring over columns in a large ledger, pen in hand and pot of ink at the ready. A pencil lay on the desk by the lamp that illuminated his toil, and a pair of wire spectacles sat just within reach. Another pair were perched upon his long, thin nose. One pair for distance, another for close work, Alexander reckoned. His father had been likewise. Abdy was a thin man with long arms and fingers, his clothing neat but slightly worn, his plain cuffs stained with ink as they protruded from coat sleeves, his cravat limp after a morning at his desk.

Alexander walked over to introduce himself, and upon seeing Emma, the clerk stood up at once and bowed deeply. "Miss Woodhouse!" He then returned to Alexander and listened to his request.

"My condolences on the recent passing of your father," Alexander began. "I am sorry to intrude on you at such a time, but I am making inquiries into some affairs and hoped you might be of assistance." He went on to explain about his desire to learn about Jack Smith, and Abdy nodded with a sad, long face.

"Smith, the tramp. Yes, of course, I knew him. Not certain I can tell you much more, though." He looked at Emma and then back at Alexander. Was there something the man did not want to say in front of the lady? Regardless, he could take what information he could now, and return later if necessary.

"'Twas my Pa who knew him best, as much as any of us knew him," Abdy sat back in his chair. Alexander took a chair on the other side of the desk to write, whilst Emma was offered the ornate and heavily upholstered arm chair reserved for wealthy customers. "Nobody was quite certain when he arrived, for he was seen a little here and a little there before he wandered into the village to make some purchases with the few pennies he had. That was back when Pa was clerk to old Bates, the vicar at the time. I had the impression Smith was around the vicarage some before venturing further into the village. The vicarage is, you must know, nearer to the edge of town, and easier to get to from the woods where he made his bed." Alexander nodded. The vicarage was, to his recollection, a quarter mile down a side street, past some of the poorer cottages. A tramp would feel less exposed there than sitting in front of the Crown, at least until he had a sense of the friendliness of the locals.

"I was newly wed at the time, and working at the bank in Dorking, so I had little to do with the fellow, other than give him a 'good day' or a penny or two when I had to spare. Never really knew what he looked like, even, for his hair was long since grey and uncut and rather wild, and he wore a beard that covered much of his face. Had green eyes, though. I noticed, very similar to the vicar's. Unusual colour, so I noticed it. But that's about all I can tell you about when he arrived."

Alexander noted the man's words and made his notes in the book he always carried. "He never spoke to you? Never gave any indication of his origins?" Emma, who was sitting at the edge of her chair, gaped openly from one man to the next, as if the words they spoke were more exciting than any fantastical novel she had ever read.

"Did he wear any unusual clothing? Did he have any scars or mannerisms?" She spat out her questions as quickly as the man had finished his final syllable. "What of his manner of walking? Surely no man can be so absolutely lost!" Abdy looked to Alexander for permission to answer Emma's hurried questions.

"I saw nothing of any of this, Miss Woodhouse. I wish I had, to oblige you." He paused, having forgotten Alexander's own question, which he was forced to repeat.

The clerk shook his sad head. "No, the man hardly spoke to anybody, other than to ask for an apple or an old blanket or extra pint of ale. Not that he was a drunkard, mind. Never smelled anything on him, but a man always enjoys a drink now and again."

He paused for a moment. "One thing struck me as odd. When first I met him, he didn't sound like a down-at-heel at all. Not quite a posh accent, mind, but an educated one. I'd lay bets he knew how to read, and in Latin and Greek at that." Abdy looked as if he wished to say something else, but his eyes flickered towards Emma and he was silent.

What was the man not saying? He was so certain there was some other iota waiting to be learned. But he also knew when he would hear no more. Abdy did suggest another person to seek out, who had a farm near the woods where Smith had made his home when first he arrived, and who had allowed the tramp to sleep in his barn on the coldest or wettest nights.

Alexander thanked the clerk for his time, and then thanked the bank's supervisor, and led Emma back out onto the streets.

From here, matters followed the same pattern. Every man they spoke to had some small crumbs to offer, but with each, Alexander suspected they knew more than they were willing to say. Emma would often interject her own questions with the same glee as if she were solving a delightful charade, as often interrupting a useful response and thereby distracting the teller to the point of forgetting what he was about to say, as offering anything helpful. She was lovely and charming and everybody to whom they spoke wished greatly to please her, and Alexander rued the moment he ever first spoke to her. How he would prefer to have Mary beside him: quiet, thoughtful, calm Mary, who had the gift of melting into the background to the point that his witnesses forgot she was there. They would then speak easily, telling him what he needed to know, without deference to a woman's delicate sensibilities.

Instead, he heard only what the men believed Emma ought to hear, and when Alexander at last walked Emma back to the village where she was to meet Harriet, he had discovered precious little.

And now it was four o'clock, with nothing of value to show for the day, other than aching feet and a hole in his pocket from the phaeton he had let to drive around the area to make his fruitless visits. He handed Emma over to her friend with a good deal of guilt at the relief that ensued, and decided to pay one final visit, a return to the bank to speak with Mr. Abdy one more time.

The clerk did not look surprised when Alexander approached his desk once more. "I wondered if you'd be back," he shook his head.

"I wondered if, perhaps, you had some information to tell me that Miss Woodhouse ought not to hear."

"Not from me, that's to be sure. The man, Smith, was not unlike another named Smith you might know." Abdy raised his brows suggestively.

"Miss Harriet Smith?" The man nodded. "Can they be related? I had thought Miss Smith the natural daughter of... Ah!" He brought out his notebook and began to write. "Mr. Smith of no known parentage was exactly that, then? Of no known parentage?"

"Not exactly," Abdy dropped his voice. "It was not widely known, but, well, my father knew the man somewhat, and I was no child to be shocked by such things, and he confided in me once or twice. Smith's mother was unknown in these parts, but amongst a group, it was quite the well-known secret who his father was. Old Bates' was from these parts, from a small estate by a village near Dolbeare's. There was a much older brother, some sisters, and then Bates, the vicar, who was the youngest of those children. But then Smith arrived, and we knew old Bates' father had not been keeping to his wife. No, not indeed! One only had to look at those eyes, exactly the same as Mr. Bates, the vicar, who was only ten or twelve years younger. Those two were brothers, I'd lay money on it: one legitimate and born on the right side of the blanket, the other not. Jack Smith was almost certainly Jack Bates, and he relied as much on the vicar for keeping body and soul together as on the rest of us put together."

Chapter Fifteen

Letters from London

Whilst Alexander had been at these interviews, a messenger had arrived from London with a package of letters for him.

His sources in London had been quick! They must have begun work the moment they received his initial requests on Wednesday last, before he had begun to narrow down his list at all. He thanked the innkeeper and took the package up to his room, where he could examine the contents in privacy.

Whilst more detailed information could usually be found in the region where a person was born or dwelt, there was little that could not be discovered in London if one knew the proper people to ask, and his sources—his handsomely paid sources—knew the best.

Their reports had never been lacking, and he sat down with full confidence in the accuracy of what he was about to read.

The first several provided the curriculum vitae of several individuals he had since rejected as being involved in any nefarious way in his horse-racing task or the deaths.

Woodhouse, Henry (Hartfield)... the gentle old man had never been a suspect on his list at all. Mr. Woodhouse's concerns revolved around his digestion, the health of his children and associates, and the neglectful oversight of his estate. His wealth, which was impressive, came from his land and some few investments in highly secure vehicles in London, and a quick perusal of the report suggested that at no time had the gentleman ever dabbled in speculation or risky ventures, let alone gambling or wagering on horses. His was not a competitive nature; he would gain no joy or satisfaction from the thrill of such a game. No, Henry Woodhouse had always been deemed innocent of any wrongdoing.

Knightley, George (Donwell Abbey)... Likewise, Knightley's character and status seemed to absolve him *prima facie* from involvement. *Age 37, gentleman farmer, local magistrate, respected by all...* Alexander scanned through the report. Knightley was reputed not to be excessively wealthy, which might, in other men, place them upon the list of people to investigate. But Knightley's character was one of straightforwardness and honesty, and from everything Alexander had seen of the man, had he an increased income, he would almost certainly give some of it away and set the remainder aside for his nephew, who was the heir presumptive of his estate, should he himself not marry and sire his own son. Alexander would not quite scratch Knightley's name from his list, but he would also be most surprised were the man to be at all involved.

Similarly, he discarded Robert Martin, William Cole, Thomas Perry, and Charles Dolbeare, from the estate to the far side of

Highbury, as well as various of the merchants and servants he had met. For each he had made a comprehensive list of reasons to exclude, and he was satisfied with his decisions.

Next, he examined the reports concerning those whose innocence was less than completely assured.

Churchill (né Weston), Francis... Frank Churchill, age three-and-twenty, son of Mr. Weston by his first wife and no great friend to Alexander Lyons, Investigator. Alexander scolded himself for this admission. That he had no great liking for Churchill did not prove the man's guilt. Neither did the fact that Mary seemed to prefer Churchill's company for his own. Petty jealousy had no place in his investigation, however, and he reminded himself not for the first time to ensure that evidence and cold fact superseded spite. He had principles and he would adhere to them, no matter his secret and unflattering wishes.

He returned to the report on Churchill. *Left motherless at age two, raised by maternal uncle and aunt (Churchill), whose name he took in gratitude and as a condition of inheriting Enscombe estate in Yorkshire.* The report estimated his annual allowance from his uncle's purse, and Alexander whistled in surprise. No wonder the cad danced attendance upon his ailing aunt, if funds like those were at stake. For that much blunt a year, Alexander himself would gladly dote upon the health and happiness of an entire village of aunts. How fortunate for Churchill that his ailing relative had chosen to convalesce at Richmond, so very close to his father's home that he might visit every day. It was possible that this was pure coincidence, but equally possible that it was not and that Churchill had some say in the matter. If he did, for what purposes? Alexander made a mark in his notebook and continued reading.

Known in gaming houses, but not a regular patron at any one. Places reasonable wagers, wins and loses with equal equanimity, never bets more than he can afford, always pays debts on time. Has been known to forgive minor debts to himself. So the man was a gambler of sorts, Alexander noted with satisfaction. This was sufficient to earn him a mark of interest, but not enough to win him a conviction. Many men placed wagers now and again in a variety of circumstances. It was more notable that he was careful not to be so caught up in the excitement of it that he forgot himself and wagered more than he could lose. Further, that he seemed to lose as often as he won suggested that gaming was a diversion and nothing more to him. This was no hardened gambler, no dandy living from one throw of the dice to the next, and the fact that he paid his debts in a timely manner and was happy to forgive his friends' obligations to him suggested a man with a healthy flow of funds. His pockets were not to let, and he had no need for a few extra pounds, nor the desire to acquire as much as he might.

But Mary had mentioned that Churchill had arrived in the neighbourhood on exactly the day that Jack Smith had died. This, too, could be pure coincidence. Or it could be more nefarious.

Churchill was still a possibility in Alexander's mind, but not a likelihood. He went to the next report in the pile.

Weston, Francis (Randalls)… Formerly Captain Weston of the —shire Militia, the fellow had made his fortune in trade in London and had returned to Highbury, where he was born, to purchase the estate of Randalls some three years before. The previous autumn he had married Emma Woodhouse's governess, Anne Taylor, and the two seemed well matched and happy. *Not known in gaming houses, no outstanding debts in London, seen at the races but does not wager more than a shilling or two.* On the face of it, not a viable suspect for either the interference with the races or with the spate of deaths.

But there was more. Alexander read on and made his notes. Mr. Weston was a native of Highbury, and born of a respectable family, which for the last two or three generations had been rising into gentility and property, but had joined the militia as soon as he was out of school. He had met Miss Churchill of Enscombe whilst stationed in the north, and married her when he was two-and-twenty, and she one-and-twenty. Alexander looked at the dates. Weston had been out of Highbury when Smith first came to town and had not returned for more than a summer's visit until four years ago. It seemed unlikely that he was involved. However, Weston and his first wife had lived beyond their means during their short marriage, and Captain Weston had depleted his small independence. It had taken him nearly twenty years to regain his loss and build his fortune.

Were there still some debts outstanding somewhere, undiscoverable by Alexander's colleagues in Town? Some privately held loan, or some other obligation that had not made its way into official records anywhere? If so, the man might have cause to delve into matters less savoury than the respectable business he and his brothers operated in the city. A pleasant and friendly disposition and a gentle manner had disguised great evil before in Alexander's experience. He did not think the man culpable of the crimes, but neither did he remove him from the list.

Cox, William (Attorney)… There was little to link his friend's brother to the affairs under investigation, and Alexander regretted the need to consider the man, but his integrity required no less. Cox was of an age to have been practising in his trade at the time when Smith first arrived in the area, and to have been practising at his profession when the late Mr. Abdy had devised his initial scheme. He reviewed his notes from a discussion with Knightley about the dates. Yes, they corresponded well. Although he seemed not to be at all implicated in the current investment project, he might have been so involved in the past. And a man with a growing family was always in need of more income.

Hesselgrave, Ralph (Riverton)… As Carnes' primary investor, Hesselgrave was a person of great interest to Alexander. He had a vested interest in the outcome of the venture, and depending on the exact nature of the agreement, might win or lose by the man's death. If he had another trainer in mind, who would not take his ten percent of the profits, the gamble might well be worth the risk. And with each investor who died, Hesselgrave's portion of the profits would increase. He was definitely a man to consider, if not for two matters. One was that he seemed not to be a reckless gambler, but rather, a man who made carefully considered decisions in matters of business. Graft and murder seemed unlikely tools for such a man to employ. The second was that he could not be found. Alexander was loath to consider him dead without direct evidence, but considering what had happened to other investors in this venture, the possibility was becoming too great to ignore.

Elton, Philip (Vicar)... Born in London to a wealthy family, and related somewhat distantly to a viscount, Elton had assumed his obligations as the younger son in taking a position in the Church. At the age of seven-and-twenty, he was handsome, of some independent fortune, charming, and the most likely suspect on Alexander's list. With eager eyes and extra diligence, he settled in to read more of the report he had asked to be hurried along to him just this morning.

His sources were thorough, and Alexander had no idea how they found the information they did. The report listed the names of Elton's late father, his married older brother, who had inherited the house in London and a considerable fortune, his mother, and his two sisters. It provided the address, in a rather smart part of town, and gave a description of the house in such detail that Alexander thought he might know the colour of the cook's favourite towel. If Elton's income from his vicarage was moderate, his own independence and family fortune made up for any shortfall.

But once again, the story did not end there. Until he took orders at the age of five-and-twenty, Elton had been known in some of the finer and more expensive gaming houses in Town, and had amassed some debts, not so large as to be unpayable, but certainly more than he might spend on a pair of new shoes. His list of creditors was short but of rather impressive names, some of which belonged to highly placed members of the Ton, others of which were better known in more dangerous circles. Upon taking his orders two years past, however, Elton had satisfied all these debts; the discharge of which must have caused some pain to the family coffers.

Immediately after ordination, he had assumed the position in Highbury which he now held. At the same time, there had been a diminution of his accounts at the Bank of England to the amount of fifteen thousand pounds. This made Alexander whistle again. Such an amount was enormous, more than a tradesman could earn in five lifetimes. What had he done to lose that amount? Was this his repayment of his gaming debts? Although he still had a healthy balance in his accounts, the loss of that interest must certainly affect his lifestyle to the amount of 600 pounds a year. Was his investment in Carnes' venture an attempt to recover some of that loss? He had not put close to the amount of his loss into the scheme, however, and the investment was dated for long after the funds had been withdrawn from his account. It seemed that Mr. Elton was looking for some means to supplement his income by a rather large amount every year. That was most certainly reason for graft; it was also reason to kill.

Alexander read on, but his mind turned to something Knightley had told him. Elton, he recalled, had offered for Emma Woodhouse only last Christmas, presumably with her dowry of thirty thousand pounds in mind. Further, Emma had initially intended the vicar to marry Harriet Smith, but the man would desire a wealthy bride.

More pertinent to his task, however, was the man's insistence on marrying a fortune, regardless of the woman who came with it.

It was not love which prompted Elton to propose to Emma, for not six weeks after her refusal, he was married to a young woman he had only recently met in Bath. Her fortune of ten thousand pounds would not replace the entirety of the hole in his bank account, but it would fill a good portion of it. Elton needed money, and it seemed he was prepared to do a great many things to get it.

Alexander wrote the pertinent information and his thoughts thereupon in his notebook and leaned back in his chair with his eyes closed to think. His ideas were unfocused, however, and his position conducive to sleep, and it was with a start that he awoke some time later to a rap at his door.

"I say, Lyons, you in there?" Knightley's voice sounded from the other side of the door, and Alexander pulled himself upright to let the magistrate in. "Innkeeper said I might find you here. Any furtherer ahead? I was hoping to have a word about last night."

Alexander grimaced. He would rather forget the night had ever happened, but if he were working with Knightley, the man deserved to hear the worst of it. He struggled to his feet and opened the door. "Please sit." Alexander drew up the chair from near the fireplace for his guest. "Shall I call for some ale and a plate of bread and cheese?"

"Only if you had planned to take some for yourself. I had also called to invite you to join me for dinner at Donwell Abbey. It will be a simple meal, as I enjoy when not entertaining the neighbours, but I hope I might treat you as a brother for the evening."

The thought of a good simple meal with an intelligent friend was enough to put all ideas of another tavern meal amongst the noisy denizens of the village out of his head. "Thank you. I would be honoured and most pleased."

"I have requested that my cook prepare the meal without meat. I hope that is appropriate." Knightley eyed him with a curious look.

Alexander blinked. What did Knightley suspect? He opened his mouth to speak, then closed it again, and at last uttered a simple, "Thank you. It is appreciated." He kept his gaze level on his guest, wondering where the conversation would lead.

The magistrate seemed aware of his discomfort and spoke reassuringly. "I noticed that you partook only of the vegetable and cheese dishes when we all dined at Hartfield, and on our journey yesterday as well. It is uncommon, but not unknown, for people to abstain from meat for various reasons, personal and religious—but from Miss Bennet's unexpected comments, I started an idea..." He left his words hanging. "Fear not, Lyons. As I said, I judge a man solely by his actions and his character. You shall find no argument from me."

"I thank you for that, sir." He tried to keep his voice even, but he was nonetheless cautious. What exactly did Knightley think he knew? His was not the only reason a person might act as he did.

"Likewise, I must apologise for making you work on your day of rest." Yes, he knew. "It must be easier in London, where you may meet and worship with your people."

Alexander cleared his throat. Was what he was about to admit worse than what Knightley had deduced? Being a man of no faith was often seen as worse than being one of the wrong sort. "I am not a great diligent in my practice." He found the words, one at a time, and tested them before allowing them voice. "I am more absent than present in my community and often find that my work does not allow me the luxury of observance. Where there is a killer to be found, I cannot spare a day, even if God has commanded it. My tradition teaches the primacy of human life and insists that saving a life is the supreme commandment of them all. If I must ignore the Sabbath in favour of preventing another death, or even in the hopes thereof, I am prepared to answer for that sin."

Knightley smiled. "I am not your God, but I do not find you wanting."

Alexander allowed himself to relax for the first time since Knightley had entered his room.

"Does your friend Darcy know?"

"Of course! When he engaged me last summer for… well, for a very delicate matter, when we first met, he insisted on knowing everything about me. Considering the nature of his task, I would have done likewise. It mattered little to him. My integrity was his only concern." He took a deep breath. "But most of my acquaintance merely think me another Scotsman, and in that they are not entirely wrong."

Knightley stared at him for a long moment. Alexander felt the man was weighing whether or not to say something. Then, with a decisive shift of his shoulders, the magistrate opened his mouth. "It is not my place to speak of such things, but I find myself feeling rather like the older brother I mentioned in my invitation. You are what? Five-and-twenty?"

"Six."

"Then I am eleven years older and have seen much of the hearts of men… and women. Does Miss Bennet know?"

"She thinks me a heathen. I doubt she wishes to speak to me again. I cannot say what caused that… that embarrassing scene last night. I am sorry you were witness to it."

"You like her?" Knightley's eyes pinned him to his seat, demanding an answer.

Alexander allowed his head to drop. "I do. That is why her words hurt as they did. But it matters little. Even should she return my regard, there can be no future for us. The differences between us are too great."

His words hung in the air for a long time before Knightley responded. "Where there is love and willingness to compromise, little is impossible."

"Give up my faith in favour of hers? No, that I could not do. I might not observe it as diligently as I should, but my family, my traditions are too important to me."

"Which is why you work on the Sabbath but forego meat whose origins you do not know."

"Aye."

"Sometimes, Lyons, the solutions to our dilemmas are the ones that we never could have imagined. When the heart speaks, if we allow our minds to listen, who knows what simple answers might be found."

He fell silent once more. What was the impetus behind such personal questions? The man had met him only days before, and whilst they had fallen into an easy companionship and worked well together, such an intimate conversation was usually left to friends who had known each other for a much longer time. Unless... Ah! Knightley was not the only perceptive one in the room.

Miss Woodhouse! Perhaps he did not yet know it, but Knightley held a *tendre* for the lady. He surely had seen Emma's marked attentions to Alexander and wished to know his rival's sentiments. And behind her sudden fascination for himself, Alexander was rather certain that Miss Woodhouse was not unattached to Mr. Knightley. They would discover this in their own time, he imagined, once he and Mary were gone from the area and the excitement of their novelty vanished into the ether.

Instead of voicing his thoughts, he said, "Do you believe you would act in such a way? If matters were such that your heart and head were opposed, that you would listen to your heart and seek some unexpected solution?"

Knightley narrowed his eyes in thought and chewed at his lower lip. "Yes. I believe I would. There are few details so very important that we must throw away our chances for happiness on their account. There is almost always a way forward that satisfies everybody."

With another sigh, Alexander pushed his hair from his brow. "Regardless, in my case there is nothing for it. Mary seems to have made up her mind about me. I would be better to forget her."

"I would not give up all hope yet," the older man leaned forward in his chair. "She is young, very young, only eighteen or nineteen years, I believe. I know that many women are married at that age, and that she has the maturity and deportment of a woman some years older, but she is, in many ways, still a girl. Her thoughts, whilst clever and considered, are not all fully those of an adult, and she will change many of her opinions over the next two or three years. My advice, which I know you did not ask for, is to allow her to finish growing up. When she is settled into the woman she will be, then consider her thoughts and opinions. You challenge her, Lyons, you challenge everything she ever believed, and it will take her time to wrestle with ideas she has not before encountered and with questions she has never before asked. And in the meantime, be her friend. For she is not indifferent to you at all."

And once again, Alexander found he had no words to respond.

"Now, are those reports on the various people we have been asking about? I see my own name. I would have done likewise. Have you learned anything new about Elton? And then, whenever you are ready, I have hired a chaise and we can depart for dinner at my home."

Chapter Sixteen

Dinner at Randalls

After taking her leave of the Bateses and Miss Fairfax, Mary sought out Mr. Perry in his shop. The shop itself was easy to find, being situated on the high street at the corner of Broadway-lane, and very near to the tea shop. Forcing herself not to think of Alexander or Emma, or the vision of them sitting at the table with her hand in his, she walked past that establishment to the shop she sought and entered.

At the sound of the bell, Mr. Perry appeared from his workroom behind the long counter. Mary had seen him before, and had heard much of him from Emma, but had not been introduced. He was, from what Mary had been told, an intelligent, gentlemanlike man, whose frequent visits to Hartfield were one of the comforts of Mr. Woodhouse's life. He was somewhere around forty years of age, and he had a large family. Shockingly, according to Mr. Woodhouse, his children sometimes ate cake. Mary was quite disposed to like him.

She introduced herself and explained her mission, stating that she had left Miss Bates with a guest, and that she had offered to stop to make the request for a cough draught for Mrs. Bates on her return to Hartfield.

"Yes, the poor woman has weak lungs, I fear. She took quite ill last year, had a very bad cold. Not too many others were ill, and I fear her constitution is weakening with age. Was she coughing badly when you left her?"

"When I first arrived, we hardly noticed her coughs, although they were in fact somewhat frequent. By the time I left a few minutes ago, however, they sounded worse and were more frequent. She claimed not to feel ill, but I agreed with Miss Bates that she might have a draught or something to soothe her lungs."

"Ah, yes. She is somewhat set in her ways. I shall come by presently with the laurel water she always takes. I don't much like it myself, but she insists that it was useful in her younger days and is the only cure that will work for her. At least she knows to dilute it well. Mr. Woodhouse is much the same, relying on what he took when he was a young man, never interested in new advances. We modern men of science—for that is how I consider myself, Miss Bennet—are never satisfied with the old if something better is discovered. What a great time we live in, with our brilliant chemists discovering new things every day, it seems! Is Mr. Woodhouse well? I have not heard from him in a week, perhaps more! I only worry about the gentleman when he is not summoning me, for that is when I believe he might truly be ill."

He had been busy as he talked, bustling about his shelves, finding the right size vial and the proper bottles and jars from his cabinets. He then fell silent, concentrating exclusively on his task as he prepared the solution of laurel water. "Must be sure to get it right," he explained. "Every draught must be exact. Well, thanks for your visit, Miss Bennet. I shall summon my oldest lad to watch the shop and shall head right down to see Mrs. Bates."

Mary thanked him and bid him good-bye before starting back down the road to Hartfield. The apothecary had spoken more truth than he knew, and Mary found herself reflecting on custom and long-ingrained habits. Mrs. Bates might trust laurel water above more modern cures, dangerous though it may be, because it had soothed her in the past. Mr. Woodhouse put his faith likewise in old balms and medicaments, preferring the comfort of what he knew to the unknown of new concoctions. The thin gruel he recommended was clearly deemed superior to more modern ideas. Thinking about the gentleman's gentle obsession with his supposedly delicate health in the wake of changes, Mary was increasingly convinced that he would look quite askance at any innovation.

Was she the same? Despite her youth, had she fallen into that same way of thinking, so curated over the years, carefully shaped by her need to differentiate herself from her sisters, and matured into something impenetrable and resistant to change? She had decided this morning, before she witnessed Alexander's betrayal with Emma, to apologise to the man. But this was not enough, she now decided. An apology would be worthless unless she could free herself from whatever notions had taken such root in her to bring about such an outburst, and thereby assure both him and herself that it would not happen again.

Mrs. Bates relied on laurel water, Mr. Woodhouse on visits from the apothecary and thin gruel, and Mary, well, she relied on such deeply set notions of moral superiority that she could not accept the validity of anything different to her own view of the world.

The thought was beyond humbling. If she really wished Alexander's forgiveness, if she wished to extend her friendship—and maybe more?—to him again, she must do so from a new position, one where she would seek to understand his moral and spiritual foundations without casting judgement upon them. She needed to accept him as he was, and not as she thought he ought to be.

She must spend some time reckoning with herself, and then must swallow her pride and offer Alexander the apology he deserved.

She arrived at Hartfield to find Emma hurrying about at some undiscoverable task. It was difficult for Mary to greet her hostess with an honest smile, but charity, she reminded herself, must begin at home. She could not forgive Alexander for his dalliance with the pretty young heiress if she could not find it within herself to forgive the woman herself. Emma had no notion of Mary's innermost feelings. Indeed, Mary was only beginning to have a sense of her own feelings! Nor had Emma acted out of spite or with any intent to harm. This was Mary's first test of her new resolve.

"Good afternoon, Miss Woodhouse," she found her friendliest smile.

"Miss Bennet!" Emma's answering smile was everything warm and genuine. "I do hope you had a pleasant day. Mr. Knightley said you were unwell last night when he walked you home from the village. I trust you are much improved." The last came out partly as a question.

"Much improved, thank you. I required only some sleep and a long walk today, and I am quite myself again. Even better, perhaps!"

Emma stopped her bustling and cocked her head. She looked confused as to how to respond, but quickly flashed another great grin and said, "I am very glad to hear that." She shifted a small bunch of flowers from one hand to the other and added, "We have just this afternoon received an invitation to dine with the Westons at Randalls. I have accepted for my father and myself, and explained that I would let Mrs. Weston know of your availability when you returned. I did not wish to make plans on your behalf without asking you. We will take the carriage, though it is only a half a mile; the distance is not great, but Father grows anxious if he must walk home at night. Will that be satisfactory? I also took the liberty of finding you a gown and having it redone according to the alterations on the one you wore for the ball. I hope I have not been too presumptuous! You are not obliged to join us, but I would enjoy your company.

Mary could not decline such a generous and candid request, and she accepted the invitation and use of the gown with grace and pleasure.

"How delightful!" Emma set down her flowers and clasped her hands in front of her. "I shall send Thomas with the news to Randalls at once! Can you be ready to leave in an hour? Allow me to summon your maid!"

And thus it was that an hour later, Mary settled herself into the carriage beside her friend in anticipation of the short drive to Randalls.

The Woodhouses were not the only guests. Sometime after her departure from their apartments, a similar invitation must have arrived for the Bates family, for Miss Bates and Miss Fairfax were sitting in the front parlour talking to Mrs. Weston as they entered the room, and Mrs. Bates was ensconced in a comfortable armchair near the fire where the air was warm and the light good for her weak eyes. She held a skein of wool and some knitting upon her lap, but she seemed to be dozing rather than engaged in her activity.

Mary made the appropriate greetings and asked after Mrs. Bates' health. "Was Mr. Perry of use? He was preparing for his visit as I set back off to Hartfield."

"Oh yes, thank you, much obliged for your concern, Miss Bennet, yes indeed, Mr. Perry came past almost at once. Such a good man, always so kind, always with a moment to spare for dear Mother, that he is, and with his family so young and active, I cannot imagine how he always has time to spare, and never asks for more than the cost of the medicine, for all that he was talking of setting up his carriage, and that cannot come cheap, but yes, thank you, he did indeed come. He listened to Mother's cough and was prepared—so thoughtful of him, was it not?—with a vial of the treatment she favours, although I cannot think where the bottle she had when she was so sick with her cold last autumn might have gone, and he prepared her a draught as we waited and she took it, and listen, she is so very much improved already, hardly coughing at all, although Mr. Perry did recommend keeping out of draughty corners and not becoming chilled, and see how well settled she is now by the fire. The laurel water does make her somewhat sleepy, however, so we must forgive her if she is not the most attentive to conversation."

"Eh?" The old lady seemed to have roused from her doze.

"Conversation," Miss Bates fairly shouted at her. "We were talking of conversation, Mother."

"If Mrs. Bates is improved, then I am relieved to hear it," Mary offered before Miss Bates could begin another speech.

Mr. Woodhouse now took up the theme of the virtues of Mr. Perry, and he settled into a conversation with Miss Bates, leaving Mary to observe the others in the room. Emma had taken a seat beside Mrs. Weston, and Mr. Weston hovered protectively to his wife's side, periodically asking if she was well and if he might do anything for her. Her babe was yet two months or so from being born, and Mary believed she would never see as doting a father as Mr. Weston if his current behaviour was any signifier.

Jane Fairfax had found her customary seat by the pianoforte, and had begun to play some gentle and undemanding melodies that encourage conversation rather than demanded audience, and finding herself momentarily alone, Mary removed herself to sit by Mrs. Bates, where she might engage the old lady should she choose to speak, and where she might appreciate Jane's superior skill at the keyboard.

Mrs. Bates was awake but seemed uninterested in conversation, which suited Mary. She had been thrown into a great deal of company over the last several days, and whilst she was enjoying her sudden celebrity, it was also exhausting for her. She required that time alone, in solitude or absence of engagement with others, which her sisters seemed not to need. Jane was happy in her own company but preferred to be amongst others, and her younger sisters went quite mad when forced to be alone. Lizzy was, perhaps, the most like her, equally satisfied in solitary pursuits such as walking or reading as in a boisterous room of chattering family and friends.

What was Alexander's preference? The thought came upon her unbidden and she brushed it away. He would just as likely never deign to speak to her again after her shameful display last night. She must find him soon and beg his forgiveness for her sins. Yes, she, Mary Bennet, arbiter of righteousness and moral rectitude in all of Hertfordshire, had sinned before a man who claimed no faith.

She let out a deep sigh.

"You do not enjoy the music?" Mrs. Bates' question caught her quite by surprise.

"Please do not think that! I am enjoying it greatly. Miss Fairfax has a rare gift."

The old lady raised her head. There was a sharpness to her gaze, magnified through the lenses of her spectacles, that Mary had seen only once before, two or three days ago, when Mrs. Bates offered her first unsolicited comment on old John Abdy. Mary raced through her thoughts and memories in hope of discovering what it was that had prompted that first comment. She dearly wished to hear more.

Mrs. Bates obliged her with no need for an invitation. "Jane was always the brilliant one." Her voice was clear and focused. Mary sat closer, hoping to learn something, anything, of interest during this spell of lucidity. "She was our family's best hope. She was destined to make a brilliant match. Even as a child she was lovely and refined and blessed with everything a lady needs to capture a baronet, or even a viscount. Our family were not known in the finest circles, but the name was respected and unblemished, and our fortune fair. If she had a dowry, if she were not condemned to a lifetime of slavery to another woman's children, she could have been the salvation of us all.

"But no!" Mrs. Bates dropped her voice to menacing quietness. "My Jane, my beautiful granddaughter now has no hopes at all because of them!"

"Them?" Mary had to ask the question, praying that Mrs. Bates would not drift back to the vague character she first had met.

"Them." Her eyes were still sharp. "Why, Abdy and Smith, of course. I knew who he was, although he never told me. Not deemed suitable for a woman to know. Ha! They underestimated me, all of us, in so many ways. Why did he not listen to me? I could have saved us all. Those schemes! Pah!" She spat into the fire. "Got what they had coming, didn't they?"

Mrs. Bates narrowed her eyes as she stared into the fire. "Why do men not listen to their wives, Miss Bennet? We should all be so much better off were they to do so. Do listen to Jane play. Is she not gifted? Now where is my shawl, for I am cold." She coughed, and looked up to her granddaughter, her eyes once more lost in the mists of old age.

"Mother?" Miss Bates called from her seat on the sofa. "Mother, do you need more of your medicaments? Shall I ask Mrs. Weston to call for a glass?"

Miss Bates hurried over to see to her mother's comfort, and Mary excused herself to join Mr. Woodhouse, who was now speaking with Mr. Weston about the best sort of apples for baking. Here she could smile and feign interest whilst allowing her mind to work through what she had heard.

"Them." Mrs. Bates seemed quite fixed upon "them." What, exactly, had they done, and what had Mrs. Bates known that they felt she ought not to have known? I knew who he was... Had she learned something untoward about Mr. Abdy? That seemed unlikely, for he had been a respected denizen of Highbury for as long as anybody could remember. It must, therefore, be Jack Smith, the tramp of obscure origins whom Mrs. Bates had recognised, or somehow come to know.

Was this, then, rather than Mr. Carnes' investments plan for his horse-training venture, that was the key to understanding these strange events? Was it somehow wrapped up in the true identity of Smith? She must speak to Alexander, and as soon as possible! If he had learned anything about Smith, they might together work out what was happening in Highbury.

The conversation had now progressed to a dissertation of the best sort of apples for pies. "I do not hold with eating pie," Mr. Woodhouse proclaimed. "Perhaps only one very small slice, very thin, for the pastry is far too rich and will assuredly cause distress in the stomach before the hour is out. Perhaps only one very thin slice, and then with a bit of lemon, even on the sweetest pie, to aid the digestion. But really, one ought not eat pie at all." He shook his head quite sadly and dared Mr. Weston to object.

"I do enjoy a fine pie," Miss Bates had overheard this latter part of the dialogue and must have her say. "Mother was making pastry this morning—she makes a very fine pastry, Miss Bennet, quite the finest and lightest you will taste in a long time—and wished to bring one this evening, but it was not baked when your carriage arrived—so kind of you to send it, sir, really, we are so very much obliged to you, so grateful. She was rather sad it was not ready, and will send it over tomorrow, perhaps after services in the morning. Are you going to join us at church, Miss Bennet? Mr. Elton speaks exceedingly well. He makes such pretty sermons; you really must come to hear him. I am certain you may sit with Miss Woodhouse in her box, if you have no objection, of course, Mr. Woodhouse?"

The gentleman professed his complete approval of this plan, but said no more, for a footman entered at that moment to announce dinner, and the entire party rose as one to move into the dining room.

There was little more learned that evening. It being a very small group, conversation over the meal was general, and Mrs. Weston directed it perfectly, introducing such topics as to amuse everybody and overburden nobody. Afterwards, Mr. Woodhouse suggested cards, and the party divided itself into suitable groups. Mrs. Bates was alert once more and partnered with Mr. Woodhouse, allowing Mary no more conversation with her. The guests, led by Mr. Woodhouse, departed quite early, in order to take full advantage of the benefits of retiring before the clock struck too late.

The footman Thomas was waiting at the front door when the carriage returned to Hartfield. As he helped Mr. Woodhouse with his great coat and hat, and then performed similar duties for Emma with her cape, Emma turned to him and commented, "We had not expected to dine out this evening. Before you return home, tell Cook to prepare a basket for your mother and sisters. I would not have the food go to waste."

"Thank you, Miss Woodhouse." He bowed deeply.

"Do you not live at Hartfield, Thomas?" An idea emerged in Mary's head.

"No, Miss. Some do, but I live with my family in the village, near the vicarage. My wages allowed Mother to keep the house after Father died."

"May I ask you to perform a task for me? It should not take you out of your way."

"Of course, Miss."

Emma yawned. "I shall retire, Miss Bennet. Thomas, please give your good mother my regards. Until tomorrow, Miss Bennet." And she helped her father up the stairs, leaving Mary alone with the footman.

"I need to send a message to somebody at the Crown," she explained once Emma and her father had disappeared down the long hallway. "He is..." how could she explain writing a letter to an unrelated man? "He is in my brother's employ, and I have something I need him to do for me. Can you wait for me to write the note?"

"Of course, Miss. I'll be in the kitchens, asking Cook for the basket Miss Woodhouse suggested. She is a good mistress and always asks after my mam."

"Fine. Then I shall meet you there. I hope not to take too long."

She dashed upstairs and found some paper and a pencil in the desk allotted for her use. She sat down and wrote as quickly as she could.

Dear Alexander,

I have both information and questions. Please agree to meet me to discuss. I shall grovel for forgiveness afterwards.

Mary

That she had called him "dear" Alexander, she noticed after she had completed the note, and sat poised to rewrite her missive, but then let out a rush of air and instead, folded it and sealed it with the wax that sat in the inkstand on the desk. Let him make of it what he would.

She waved the paper in the air to let the wax set, and then ran downstairs to where she thought the kitchens were, to commit her missive to Thomas' helpful hands.

Her headache was starting to return, and she begged a cool compress from Cook before returning to her rooms to change for bed and retire for the night. Hopefully, the morrow would bring a response from Alexander, and the answers she needed.

Chapter Seventeen

Trouble at the Vicarage

Knightley had been true to his word, and the dinner which his cook had prepared was both simple and free of red meat and poultry. It was also very tasty. The cook at Donwell Abbey was creative and skilled, and Alexander enjoyed every bite. Knightley did not talk of the cases over dinner, asking instead after Alexander's life in Scotland, his family, and his work at the university in Glasgow.

"Father's patron, the local laird, was a generous man and saw to my education. I believe he would have been as happy had I followed my father into the field of medicine, but the law was more to my tastes, and after I achieved my degree, I read for the bar. He was exceedingly proud of me, almost as proud as my own parents. But when he died, his son became laird, and he was… less generous, both in purse and in spirit. He decided he did not need 'our kind' on his estate. When my father died, the villagers had no more use for us. Mother and my sisters went to live with relations in the city, and I made for London to make my way."

"But you are a jurist, a qualified barrister."

"I started off that way, aye, but I needed to do a spot of investigating for the man I was clerking for, and turned out to be good at it. Men came asking for my assistance, and I realised I could do better as an investigator than as yet another lawyer in the crowded city.".

Knightley thought upon that for a moment, then nodded, and turned to a new topic for the rest of the meal.

It was only after they had consumed the pudding that was set before them and sat with their brandies before the fire in the small parlour off the dining room, that Knightley reintroduced the matter at hand.

"I am quite eager to know what was in those reports you were reading when I found you." He was sitting back in his arm chair, one ankle resting atop the opposite knee, swirling the amber liquid around an elegant crystal glass. The effect was one of studied nonchalance, but there was an edge of curiosity in his voice that nothing could disguise.

Alexander chuckled over his own drink. "I had wondered which of us would raise them first." He took a sip, appreciating the hints of dried fruit and spice in the fine drink, but secretly longing for the leathery malt of his homeland's drink. "My colleagues in London are exceptional at what they do. I have learned some interesting things. You will forgive me for including your name in my requests. One never knows where a key piece of information might be found." He raised his eyebrows, and his companion raised his glass in return.

"No offence taken. I am curious, however, as to whether I was a serious suspect... or whether I still am."

Alexander laughed again. "Until I have all my evidence, the only person I do *not* suspect is myself, and even then, only if I have three witnesses as to my whereabouts at the time of the crime. But no, I did not believe you involved. Still..."

"Then I am curious as to what you have learned."

Alexander drew the wad of paper from his coat pocket, where he had placed it upon leaving his room, and read the reports, one by one, to the magistrate.

"Frank Churchill, eh?" Knightley snorted as Alexander concluded his recital of that report. "I cannot say I like the chap. He is playing at something, although I do not believe it to be murder. Did you know that he was long overdue to visit his father and new step-mother, always citing one excuse or another to avoid coming, after the wedding? When he did arrive, it happened to coincide exactly with Smith's death." Alexander looked up, but he said nothing and gestured for Knightley to continue. "Of course, we thought nothing of it at the time. A young man paid a visit to his father, and the old man died in a tragic fire. The two seemed quite unrelated. I still cannot quite manage to link them in my mind, and yet the coincidence is striking."

"Mmm..." Alexander took another sip of the fine brandy, still wishing it were whisky.

"Emma had decided she had a fancy for young Frank..." Knightley stared into the fire. He seemed about to engage in reminiscences and meandering musings, and Alexander was of no mind to stop him. He was an interesting man, and often the greatest insights were gained from seemingly innocuous comments. "Emma is a delightful creature, too smart and too bored for her own good, I believe, and always looking to meddle in other people's affairs, but I do not believe she always sees as clearly as she might. As I said, she had been fascinated with the idea of Frank before he arrived, and was quite ready to fall in love with him, until…"

"Until I arrived?"

"Yes. Indeed." Knightley stared at him.

Alexander asked the next question he had in mind. "And Churchill? Was he ready to be fallen in love with? Or did he have something—or someone—else in mind?"

Now Knightley chuckled. "You noticed that, did you? I can see why you are good at your occupation. He played the suitor to Emma nicely enough, but I suspect his affections are engaged elsewhere. Or rather, were engaged elsewhere. When your Miss Bennet arrived…"

"We have messed up your happy village quite thoroughly, have we not?" This was offered with a grimace. "Miss Woodhouse now pays all her attention to me, and Frank Churchill to Mary. This is a pretty kettle of fish." Alexander had not offered his other observation, that perhaps the man hoping to engage Emma's affections was sitting right before him. Knightley was a sharp enough man; he would discern it for himself when he was ready.

"If I may offer what seems a rather impolite comment Lyons, you have been good for Emma."

"That is hardly impolite, sir, although I do not quite take your meaning."

Knightley allowed his eyes to close as he leaned back in his chair. "Although it casts no aspersion upon you or your character, Miss Woodhouse has, until now, refused any social connexion with those of the middle class. Even Miss Smith, whom she has taken on as a project of sorts, she believes to be the natural daughter of an unnamed aristocrat. She will not like the truth when she hears it, I am certain. She would not associate with Mrs. Cox, although the lady is most pleasant and very sensible, nor with the Coles, for despite their considerable wealth, they are in trade. But then she met you."

Now Knightley opened his eyes to stare at his erstwhile rival, and Alexander gazed back through half-hooded eyes.

"If you will forgive me for saying so, Lyons, you are nothing of the sort she tends to favour. You are a stranger, a Scot, not at all from the sort of wealth she would expect, and even more mired in the middle class than the Coles, who at least employ agents to dirty their fingers on their behalf."

"I have never pretended otherwise. And—forgive me, sir—neither would I wish to be so. I had the opportunity to enter into a profession suited to the gentry and chose otherwise. I enjoy being useful."

"As a man ought to be, if he can." Knightley rose and poured himself another drink, then offered one to Alexander, who accepted gladly.

"And yet you say I am good for her?"

"Yes indeed, Lyons. You have cracked that seemingly impenetrable shell of pride she has. She has seen in you all that is admirable and has accepted you as her equal in the ways that matter."

"I am but a novelty, sir, of passing interest."

"Perhaps, but you have opened her eyes, and she will be a better person for it. I dare say I shall even see her at the Coles' next musical evening; she never has accepted before!" Knightley chuckled again, then sat straight in his chair. "As for the other reports?"

One by one, Alexander read them through, asking or answering a question as they arose to clarify matters. Knightley had known most, but not all, of Weston's dealings in London, and was surprised to hear the man had lost so great a sum of money during his short first marriage.

"I had known the first Mrs. Weston to be from a wealthy family, but had thought her more sensible than to spend through her husband's independence so quickly. They did not live in Highbury; I met her only twice before she died. I believe Weston is more fortunate in his second marriage, for the present Mrs. Weston is careful and prudent. But I digress. Please, Lyons, you have been thinking of this."

"Aye, that I have. After his wife died, after he allowed her brother and sister to take young Frank into their home to raise, Weston lived in London, working at the business his brothers had established." Knightley nodded and Alexander continued. "Whilst it is very possible to make a great fortune in business, and over a short time, for a man to go from empty pockets to the sort of wealth that allows him to buy as estate such as Randalls, it is not common."

"You are wondering whether the man owes a great deal of money to somebody in London? Or elsewhere?"

"Aye. Although if there were any record of such a debt, my associates would have discovered it. Are his brothers equally well-to-do?"

Knightley pondered this for a moment. "I believe I have heard Weston talk of townhouses in some of the finer parts of Town. I believe the business was, and remains, highly successful."

Alexander finished his drink. "I do not believe Weston is our man, but as I have said, I can excuse no one without evidence."

"Which brings us to the next report in your pile, if my eyes do not deceive me." Knightley sat forward in his chair and was staring at the sheet of paper in Alexander's lap. The name *Elton* was written clearly across the top.

"So it does." Alexander repeated his role of secretary for Mr. Knightley, reading the report in a slow and careful voice so as to omit no detail of what his associates had uncovered.

"Fifteen thousand pounds!" Knightley almost exploded when Alexander read out the sum of the withdrawal from Elton's accounts. "Thousand? My God, Lyons, that is a king's ransom! I do not know if I am more shocked as to the amount itself, or the fact that he had that much, and so very much more, to begin with. I understood that the man was a preening dandy, but had not the first notion of how wealthy the family must be. I wonder why he went into the church, rather than purchasing a small house and living off the interest."

"After buying a house, the interest would not allow him to live the way he wishes, I imagine. In the manse, he has access to his entire fortune."

"Hmmm. Yes, you are correct, undoubtedly. As to this withdrawal from his bank, you have no indication as to what these funds were to cover? No record of a debt?"

He shook his head. "Not that my colleagues have found. They are diligent in their reports. They ought to be, for what I pay them. I have yet to begrudge a penny of their fees."

"The man then needs to recoup six hundred pounds per annum to maintain his accustomed lifestyle. What was he to gain from this investment in Carnes' horse-training operation?"

"With his investment of five hundred pounds, not a great deal at first. But under the terms of the agreement, with everybody else's profits coming to him alone, it could be a thousand pounds a year or more, depending on the success of the venture."

Knightley pushed his chair back as he rose, then placed the crystal brandy glass on the small round table between the two chairs. Alexander did likewise. "Back to Highbury?" Alexander's question was almost a statement. Had Knightley not spoken, he would have suggested it himself.

"Hodges," Knightley called through the doorway, "Have the chaise brought around at once!" He turned to Alexander. "Although we have nothing specific to link him to the recent deaths, there are too many questions for my comfort. I believe we need another interview with our local vicar."

The ride to the village was accomplished in a few short minutes. Donwell Abbey was only a mile or so from the edges of the village, and a mile and a half from the vicarage. The last tinges of light had faded from the horizon and the sky was dark, but it was not so very late that the Eltons were likely to have retired for the evening.

Alexander jumped from the chaise as it stopped to help secure the horse, and Knightley strode to the front door to summon the vicar. Alexander could hear noise from inside the house, but it was a long time before somebody came to the door, and he had completed his task and was nearly at the doorstep when the housekeeper heeded the bell at last. In the crack of light that spilled from the house into the dark night, he could see the alarm on the lady's face.

"Mr. Knightley, sir," she bobbed just enough for propriety's sake. "Forgive me sir, Madam has taken ill, only a few moments ago..." She began to shift to return to her mistress, leaving the door open.

"Is it serious? May I be of assistance?" Alexander spoke on the doorstep. "I have some knowledge, gained from my father, who was a physician." He stepped into the light.

The housekeeper spun her head around. "I... I did not see you, sir. I don't know..."

"Lyons may be trusted, Mrs. Wright. Please, show us the way." Knightley's voice had the firm steel of authority, and Alexander felt the man switch from the concerned neighbour to the local magistrate in that heartbeat.

"Yes, yes, of course. Follow me." The housekeeper turned on her heel and walked back towards the room with the open door without ensuring that the newcomers had even entered the house. Her steps were rapid and her movements uneven. Despite the dispassionate mien she affected in her position, she was clearly much disturbed by something.

The room into which she hurried proved to be a small drawing room off the dining room. The house was not large, and Alexander believed that he had now seen much of the ground floor, for the salon which he had visited some days earlier could be seen through another doorway. A compact settee and two chairs were positioned around a low table which held a tea service and a small selection of half-eaten sweets and cheeses. Another bank of chairs lined the walls, ready for unexpected company.

The rest of the scene was somewhat less domestic and far less tranquil. Mrs. Elton lay on the floor beside the settee, her face red and her breaths coming in uneven gasps. Her eyes were closed; she seemed unconscious. Her husband knelt at her side, rubbing her wrists and looking far more panicked than a murderer ought to look.

"Augusta... Augusta, wake up, please, Augusta..." His eyes were red and wet, and he looked up at Alexander and Knightley in alarm and supplication. "Help her, please, do something! She fell ill, only now, only moments ago, I don't know what to do!"

Alexander pushed his way to the lady's side and without asking permission, took her wrist in his hand. He held his breath as he sought the spot he needed. The slightest thread of a pulse trembled through her veins. He looked up at the two men staring at him, both as still as stones, and blurted out. "She is breathing, but not easily, her pulse is weak but present..." As he took account of her symptoms, a great spasm ran through her body. He took a sharp sniff of the air. It was as he thought. There was no time to waste.

"Brandy. Elton, get her brandy, quickly." His voice was harsh, but it incited action. The vicar struggled up from his crouch on the floor and splashed some liquid into a glass. "Help me raise her head, Knightley." The magistrate was on one knee in a moment and pulled at the lady from behind until she was half propped against his body. Alexander took the glass of brandy and opened the ill woman's mouth, then poured some of the liquid down her throat. As much spilled as was swallowed, but he repeated his actions again and again until the glass was empty. The room was a mess and smelled horribly of spirits, but Mrs. Elton's face was less red and her breathing more regular.

Her husband continued to chafe her one wrist, whilst Alexander held a finger against the pulse at her other, and eventually he sat back on his heels and took a deep breath. "Mrs. Wright," he called, "Please lay a sheet upon the chaise longue in the salon. We shall carry Mrs. Elton there."

"Right away, sir!" She darted off to complete her task, and together, Alexander and Knightley carefully lifted the ill woman from the floor to move her to the adjoining room. By the time they had her settled upon the protected chaise, she was coughing and her eyelids were fluttering. Mr. Elton, as firmly fixed at her side as if he were attached with paste, maintained his anxious eyes upon her face.

"Here, let us make certain her head is raised, and if you have a throw to keep her warm... Excellent." Alexander accepted the blanket from the prescient Mrs. Wright. "I believe she is over the worst. More brandy, sir, if she can tolerate it, and then very sweet tea as soon as she is conscious. Mrs. Wright, might I bother you to put up some tea? Lots of sugar. Very good. Yes, I believe she will be well."

As he spoke, Mrs. Elton opened her eyes. She did not utter a sound but looked up at her husband with an expression half desperation, half relief. Then she opened her mouth to speak but could not, and fell back against the cushions behind her head.

"Rest, Mrs. Elton. You will be well. Can you breathe? Just nod. Very good. Take a deep breath... forgive me, madam." Alexander leaned his head close to the lady's chest, ignoring the vicious glare her husband cast upon him. "And again? Fine."

"All danger seems to have passed. When Mrs. Wright returns, sir," he addressed himself to the angry husband, "I should appreciate a moment of your time. We have some questions that require answers."

The vicar gaped at him as if uncomprehending, then slowly blinked his eyes and nodded. "Yes. Very well. Yes. But first I must see to Augusta..."

"We shall await you in the dining room." Elton blinked again, and Alexander dropped a short bow and pulled Knightley with him as he sought a place at the dining table to sit and make his notes.

"What was that?" Knightley asked as soon as the door was closed. "How did you know what to do?"

"I am a physician's son," Alexander breathed. "One does learn something. Even my sisters are more than adept at basic healing. Both even attended with him on occasion. As to what that was, did you not smell it?"

Knightley shook his head. "All I smelled with the bottle of brandy that you poured all over her. Good stuff too; bit of a waste, that."

"Before the brandy. There was the aroma of bitter almonds. Quite distinctive, if you know what to look for. It can become lost when combined with the smell of the fruits and pies and cheeses, but it was definitely present."

"Bitter almonds? But that is...." Knightley's head jerked up, his eyes wide and his mouth agape.

"Yes. Just so. Prussic acid.

Chapter Eighteen

Conferring

"How on earth did Mrs. Elton come to consume Prussic acid?" Knightley was pacing the perimeter of the dining room, the twitching of his fingers betraying the turmoil that must be raging in his thoughts. Alexander fought the urge to press the man into a chair to keep him still. "It must have been consumed, rather than coming in the air from some poison somewhere; otherwise Elton would have fallen ill as well."

"Aye." Alexander ran his hands through his hair and rubbed at the back of his neck. His agitation showed not in excessive motion, but in the tension that built up in his shoulders. This was threatening to become a very late night. "Once we have spoken to Elton, I will examine the food on that table. Prussic acid works quickly. It must have been something she ate from the table of afters."

"Would Elton have introduced it to her deliberately? I do not think well of the man, but this seems particularly cruel."

"Did you see his face? That desperation was genuine. On the one hand, he has little more use for his wife, for he has her dowry, but on the other, I do believe there is some genuine affection between them, or at least, as much as two such self-loving people can have for another. No, his distress at her illness seemed very real. An accident? Perhaps he had a sachet in a pocket that fell into her tea, or perhaps she took a powder or a pill for a headache or for her digestion, and found the wrong one, with almost tragic results. I do not think this particular event was deliberate on his part, but I am anticipating our interview with him with considerable interest."

"You said you do not believe this particular event to be deliberate. Does this mean you have suspicions about the nature of the others?"

There was no trace of mirth on Alexander's face as he replied. "Indeed. I am now convinced, if I had not been before, that these have been a string of murders. I wish I had been able to examine the other bodies. I might have seen something others with less suspicious natures might have missed."

"Others such as myself?" Knightley gave a wry grimace.

"With your forgiveness, yes. But why ought you to suspect something when each death looked to be pure happenstance, one more tragic accident? A fire, the collapse of heavy shelving, an old sick man dying of extreme age... none in and of itself would raise alarm. The only time when we might have learned something was with Carnes, but the water surely washed away any traces of poison. But now, with this evidence of Prussic acid, I am rethinking what you have told me about the others. I... Ah, here is

Elton. Shall I sit back and let you speak? I have my notebook at the ready. I shall be the scribe."

The vicar looked as if he had aged ten years in the last hour. His eyes were still red and his face white, with dark circles beneath those eyes that the ladies of the parish had considered so handsome. His hands shook, and he moved as if each step consumed all of his energy.

"Please sit, Mr. Elton." Knightley spoke to the man as a guest in his own home. "How is Mrs. Elton? Has she continued to recover?"

Elton nodded almost imperceptibly. "She is improved, but exhausted. Shall we call Perry, Mr. Lyons? I cannot thank you enough for saving her. I don't know what I would have done... what we would have done... It was so sudden, so unexpected. What happened?"

Alexander disliked the vicar a small degree less. Humility suited him, and it would do him good to wear it more often. "If I was of any good in helping your wife, her health is thanks enough. You may call Mr. Perry if you wish, but I do not know there is much more he can do. I would not recommend she take any sedative until she is completely recovered. Perhaps a mild camomile tea, but nothing else."

Elton bowed his head and was silent for a very long time. At last, he asked the question that Knightley had posed. "What caused it... whatever happened?"

Knightley spoke before Alexander had the chance to respond. "We believe your wife was poisoned, sir. With Prussic acid."

Now Elton's head jerked up like a puppet's. He gaped at Knightley like a fish, his mouth hanging open. Alexander had seen many an excellent performance at London's fine theatres, and had never seen a man act this well, this convincingly. He was ready to believe that Elton's surprise was real.

"P... Poison?" the vicar sputtered at last. "But what? How? Who?" His head shook, eyes darting from Knightley to Alexander and back again, blinking disbelievingly.

"We were hoping you might tell us, sir." Knightley took the lead again, and Alexander jotted down his observations in his notebook.

"I have not the first idea! Who would want to poison Augusta? And what is Prussic acid?"

Alexander spoke from the far side of the table where he was writing. "Prussic acid is a rather potent toxin. If the dose is strong enough, it can kill immediately. A lesser dose produces symptoms such as your wife suffered, which can lead to a worsening or death. It is very dangerous to have on hand."

"Is Augusta still in danger?"

"No, Mr. Elton. Unless she ingests more of the poison, she will recover well. I believe Mr. Knightley has some more questions."

Alexander turned his face to his notebook, glancing up often to take in any significant changes in Elton's expression. The man simply looked stunned as he answered, seeming to be too shocked to prevaricate.

No, he had never had cause to use Prussic acid. He had heard the word but had no notion of what it was or did. He had never met any of the deceased men before moving to Highbury to take up his position at the church. He had no idea where Hesselgrave might be found, nor was he at all concerned for the man, since he frequently travelled to Dorking or other locations on matters of business and remained there for a week or more. No, he had no knowledge of horse racing.

"I admit surprise, Mr. Elton, that you would invest a considerable amount of money—a thousand pounds, from what I have learned—in a venture about which you admit to knowing nothing." Knightley's tone was cajoling, and Elton's stunned gape turned to a malevolent glare. "Come now, sir. You are not a stupid man. You have spent enough time in the gaming halls and hells of London to learn that knowing your field is everything. You would not throw such a sum blindly. We shall find out in good time, Elton. You'd best tell us what we wish to know yourself."

The vicar sputtered. "You malign me, Mr. Knightley! I have done no wrong. This was a simple business matter, nothing more or less. One need not be a miner to invest in African gold, or know how to make sugar to own a plantation in the West Indies. It is no secret that I have some money from my family, and Hesselgrave approached me with an offer. He and Carnes are... were the experts, the ones who understood horses and racing and all that that entails. Through my family, I have some notion of managing funds, and all they wanted was some additional blunt to increase the scope of the operation. I exercised diligence and discovered they had been successful thus far. The plans to increase the stables and training grounds were moderate and careful, and as an investor, I saw little threat to my investment. That, gentlemen," he stared pointedly at Alexander, "is everything there is to say. If you are accusing me of something, I would suggest that Mr. Carnes' untimely death is likely to cause me a great deal of harm. His was the true skill in the venture. Hesselgrave will be hard pressed to find another with his way with the beasts. He could always produce a winner on the track, and the real betting men were pleased to look to his horses."

At that, Elton sat back in his chair, folded his arms across his chest, and sealed his mouth in a firm and tight line.

Knightley flashed a quick look at Alexander, who dipped his head a fraction of an inch in response. He could become accustomed to working with such intelligent and intuitive partners. Knightley was a very different character from Alexander's friend Darcy, but in these subtle ways—the deep intelligence, the quick understanding and cooperative nature—they were similar, and Alexander understood why Darcy had spoken so highly of Highbury's magistrate, even on a passing acquaintance.

Having received his answer in Alexander's half nod, Knightley asked the next question.

"I was hoping you might tell me, Mr. Elton, about the rather substantial withdrawal from your account at the Bank of England two-and-a-half years ago, immediately prior to taking up this living." Elton stared at him, unblinking. "This would be a difficult sum to forget, sir. And a difficult debt to ignore. Some fifteen thousand pounds." Knightley stressed the last word. "That is a vast deal more than most men earn in a lifetime. What was the purpose of the withdrawal?"

Knightley leaned back in his chair, arms loose by his sides, awaiting the response Alexander was certain he would not get. Alexander, in every way Knightley's opposite, leaned forward, hunched over his paper, arms and hands busy at his task.

For his part, Mr. Elton stood abruptly, sending his chair backwards with a scrape upon the wooden floor. Alexander felt the table shake with the violence of the man's push. "If you will excuse me, I must see to my wife," he spat out. And without another word or gesture of parting, Elton turned on his heel and fled the room.

The interview was most clearly at an end and there would be nothing more from Elton this evening. But the men could not leave before speaking to Mrs. Wright. Alexander inquired of her as to whether Mrs. Elton seemed to be breathing easily, and upon an affirmative response, he then requested a moment of the housekeeper's time.

"Mr. Elton was distracted," he padded the truth. "I would very much like to know what occurred before Mrs. Elton took ill. It seems to have been rather sudden." The housekeeper would likely learn soon enough that the mistress had been poisoned, but Alexander was not about to be the one to offer her that information.

Mrs. Wright led the men back into the dining room. "I cannot rightly say," she spoke slowly and deliberately, "for I was conferring with Cook about some matters of household management. About table linens, if you need to know, and how we might need to replace some." Alexander murmured an encouraging word, which the woman took as an invitation to speak further.

"They had finished dinner some time before, perhaps an hour, and had passed the evening in a manner they found pleasant. When I passed by on my way to the linen closet, Mrs. Elton was reading aloud from some book, but I did not linger to hear what it was. Is it important?"

Alexander regarded her in all seriousness. "I commend your attention to detail, but if the exact book becomes important, I am certain Mr. Elton can provide us with its title."

"Ah, yes. Very good. It was about an hour, as I mentioned, before Mrs. Elton called for tea and afters. Mr. Elton prefers cheese after a meal, in the French manner, whilst Mrs. Elton enjoys sweets, but we set out both, for the two will partake of both, in different proportions."

"Can you say who ate what this evening?"

"Do you think it was something in the afters?" Mrs. Wright looked offended. "In my house?" She stiffened in her chair.

"We must explore all possibilities, ma'am. No slight on your fine management is intended."

"Very well." Her exhale could be seen in her shoulders. "I cannot say who ate what. I did not enter the room again until the parson cried out, and that was only seconds before you rang at the door bell, Mr. Knightley. As you might have noticed, the plates were all in disarray. I cannot say which was taken by whom."

"And the tea itself?" Knightley asked this question. Alexander took advantage of the moment to scribble in his notebook.

"I prepared the pot of tea and set it out with two clean cups. Both take their tea with cream and sugar, which I set out as well. Do you now suspect the tea? Was the cream bad?"

"No, madam, I believe the tea is quite fine, as is the cream. Did Mrs. Elton take some of the tea, with the sugar, as I recommended?" Alexander laid down his pencil for a moment.

"Indeed, she did. And she seemed much improved for it."

"As I had hoped. One final question, I believe. What, exactly, did you set out for the Eltons for their afters? I would prefer as many particulars as you can recall."

The housekeeper pursed her lips as she thought. "'Twas cook who set out the tray, but I brought it to them. The maid already went home for the evening, for her mam lives just down the road in the cottages yonder. There was some bread in thin slices, already spread with butter, and cheese from Mr. Martin's dairy, which is some of the finest in these parts, let me tell you that! Although Farmer Mitchell's wife makes a fine cheese as well. There were the last two pieces of fruit cake that Cook made for Mrs. Elton's charity meeting yesterday morning, and some of the tart that Miss Bates brought over for that same meeting. She knows how Mrs. Elton loves her mother's cherry pie and insisted I leave the tart for the Eltons to consume and not serve it at tea. Then there was some of the berries that are just beginning to ripen in the garden, and two of the lemon-lavender biscuits that Mrs. Elton prefers. Oh! Might some of the wrong sort of leaf have been mixed in with the lavender? Some such herbs that can cause dreadful pains in the stomach? Oh, how terrible if I had been the one to make her ill! You will plead on my behalf, will you not, Mr. Knightley, if Mr. Elton decides to replace me as housekeeper?" She looked rather alarmed at this prospect.

Knightley smiled. "I cannot imagine it will come to that, Mrs. Wright, but I shall take your part, and at worst, shall do everything I can to find you suitable and equal employment."

She bobbed as close to a curtsey as she could manage in her chair. "Thank you, sir. Very much appreciated. Thank you."

There remained only to examine the tray of food itself, but when they entered the small drawing room where the near-disastrous event had occurred, it was to find the room completely returned to its pristine state. The tray had been cleared away, the carpet removed, presumably for cleaning, and the windows wide open to help clear the stench of the brandy. Alexander growled low in his throat.

"Who ordered this cleaned?" Knightley asked. "We needed to see if anything could be discovered."

"Terribly sorry sir," Mrs. Wright turned white, then red. "Mr. Elton insisted everything be taken away at once, before he went in to speak with you. My husband and the lad who lives in the attic cleaned it whilst you were speaking. I didn't know, else I would have said..." She seemed quite flustered, and rather upset. "He said to discard all the food, not even to allow the animals to eat it, to burn it if we must. I could not imagine why, but he is the master."

Alexander sighed. There was nothing to be done for it now. Any evidence had been destroyed. But there had been Prussic acid in something, even if he knew not exactly what. Finally, with a wish for Mrs. Elton's good health and after extracting a promise to summon Mr. Perry should the lady take even the slightest turn for the worse, he quit the house with Knightley in his shadow.

"That was a most interesting exhibition," Knightley breathed as they drove the chaise back to the stables behind the inn. "What do you make of Elton? Did you believe him?"

"I can hardly say. The man's reactions were quite unaccountable." Alexander thought back to the strange series of events. "His distress at his wife's illness seemed real, and his shock at learning she had taken poison seemed too genuine to be feigned. I was quite ready to absolve him of all guilt in that aspect of the affair, at least. But his belligerence at the mention of the fifteen thousand pounds, and his insistence that the drawing room be completely cleaned, obliterating all traces of evidence, seems to point in exactly the other direction. I hardly know what to say. What think you, Knightley?"

The older man tsked and shook his head. "I do not know how to account for it either. That he has some financial dealings he wishes no one to learn of, this I can comprehend. Most men have some secrets they would rather remain secret. I myself had a few incidents in my youth that are best forgotten—nothing illegal, Lyons, so you needn't smirk at me like that, nor immoral either. Merely foolish. But to order the room cleaned and the traces of the food destroyed so we could not examine them, this part is bothersome. Perhaps in the morning, assuming he sleeps and has some clarity of thought as a result, he will reconsider his actions. Shall we speak to him after services? In the church? He will not appreciate the location, but it might prompt him to offer us the truth."

"Yes. What time do services end? I shall not attend but can find you there afterwards."

They bid each other goodnight and went their separate ways, Knightley towards his chaise and then home, and Alexander to his rooms in the inn.

"Evening, Mr. Lyons," Mr. Stoller, the innkeeper stopped him as he made for the stairs. "Hoping you had a pleasant day, sir, but also, there's a message for you. Thomas from Hartfield brought it by on his way home for the night."

A note from Hartfield? Dear lord, he hoped Mary was well. After their argument, and after seeing her laughing and flirting with

Frank Churchill, he had doubts that she would speak to him again, let alone write to him. The note must be from somebody else at the grand house. A sudden image of Mary Bennet, pale and unbreathing upon the floor of some elaborate room at Hartfield, felled by the same poison and same poisoner as threatened Mrs. Elton, flashed through his mind and his heart thudded in his chest. Had she been asking too many questions, in that quiet and penetrating way of hers? Had she caused the wrong person to become afraid of discovery? The very idea of her being in danger was beyond distressing. It was devastating. He had admitted the truth to Knightley; he now needed to admit it to himself: He liked her far more than he ought. His heart was not only in danger. It was already lost. But what of the note? He both needed to read the message at once to learn what was wrong, and to throw it away for fear of learning something terrible, but neither option was his, for Mr. Stoller seemed to be waiting for some sort of response before retrieving the note.

"Er, yes, indeed, very fine, rather a bit of excitement just now, but I suppose you'll hear all about it tomorrow. Mrs. Elton took ill, but is recovered, it seems. You said something about a message?"

"Yessir, here it is, Mr. Lyons." He walked behind the counter that separated his office from the common area by the main doors and rifled through a drawer. "Yes, here it is, looks like a short one. I'll be bidding you goodnight, then, Mr. Lyons." He handed Alexander the slip of paper and turned back to whatever it was he had been doing before Alexander's arrival.

Alexander glanced at the paper and let out a shudder of relief. The writing on the front of the note was Mary's. She was at least well enough to write him a note, no matter how improper such an action might be. He took the stairs two at a time as he hurried to his rooms, and the moment the door was closed he broke the seal.

Dear Alexander,

I have both information and questions. Please agree to meet me to discuss. I shall grovel for forgiveness afterwards.

Mary

The rush of emotions that bombarded him was too intense and too varied to consider. She was alive, she was safe, she wished to talk to him, she wished to apologise to him... she was alive. He locked the door and fell onto the bed, and only then realised he was shaking.

The incident with Mrs. Elton had shaken him more than he had thought. Now that he had a moment to review the event in his mind, he could see how much he had been acting on instinct, and he thanked his late father for having spoken so much to him about his profession, and for having taken him along as an assistant on so many of his visits. The knowledge of poisons he had acquired through his father's books had come in useful on more than one occasion in the exercise of his occupation, but never had he depended on it to save a life before.

He was rather surprised that he had remembered the remedy for treating Prussic acid poisoning. It was quite amazing, really, what the mind could recall when needs must. For as he sat there, upon his bed in the Crown, he rather doubted that he could recall the name of his best friend from childhood at this particular moment, or how much jam he liked with his morning scones. The memory was a strange thing indeed; how often was that vital recollection missing, but how equally often did some flash of remembrance come at just the right time to solve a dire puzzle?

His mind was too uneasy to think properly: the hour too late and his body too exhausted. He read the note again. *Dear Alexander...* she did not hate him then! Had she thought of the meaning of her words as she wrote? Did she hold him in some affection as well? The notions swam in his head. *Information... questions... agree to meet....* How could he refuse? He wished to speak to her again, hear her apologies and try to understand the source of her frustration with him. He had something to tell her as well, when she might be ready to hear it. Knightley's warning sounded through his muddled and tired thoughts. *She is young... still a girl... allow her to finish growing up.* Yes, this he would.

But in the meantime, whilst he waited for her thoughts and ideals to mature into those of a more reasoned woman, he would still eagerly hear what she had to say. For her questions were profound, and her thoughts brilliant. Whatever she had to impart to him, he was certain, would help him more forward in this strange case.

Chapter Nineteen

Meeting Out of Church

Alexander awoke early on Sunday morning and did something he had never before done. He went to church.

He had walked past the building many times since his arrival in Highbury, not quite a week past, but had never stopped to consider the structure. Now he took the time to do so. The church itself reflected much of the architecture in this part of England, with its ancient foundations and more recent additions. The body of the building, he considered, seemed very old indeed, evoking images of Richard Lionheart and his returning Crusaders, with its heavy stone walls and pointed lancet windows, but the central tower seemed newer. Alexander knew little more than the average man about such details, but the angled buttresses that rose almost the entire height of the structure, along with the particular shapes of the arches and the intricate carvings above the door spoke to him of the early Tudors instead. Through that door, he caught a glimpse of a more modern aesthetic yet, with clean classical lines and light paint against dark wooden pews. The heavy sound of a large pipe organ rang through the air; it was likely a very fine instrument, but he had never been partial to the organ.

He had no intention of stepping inside for the service, however, or even to better contemplate the architecture. If the townsfolk were to think him a heathen, well, he had been called worse to his face. But he was quite certain that Mary Bennet would appear, and he must speak with her.

He was not disappointed. Exactly five minutes before the service was to begin, the Woodhouse carriage drew up before the ancient stone building, and three people were handed out by the footman. First Mr. Woodhouse emerged, testing the steps carefully before entrusting his weight to their support, followed by Miss Emma Woodhouse, dressed perfectly for the occasion, in her modest frock and matching cape. Last came Mary. She alit from the conveyance and stood still for a moment, looking all around her, and then up at the sun, which had deigned to show its face once more. Was she waiting for him? She must have known he could not refuse her plea.

"Miss Bennet!" She did not seem surprised to hear his voice, nor did she attempt to disguise the smile on her face.

"Alexander! I had not thought to find you here!" She turned to look at the stone edifice that loomed so large before them. "You are not going in? Or are you?" The momentary flash of excitement on her face almost made him consider the option.

"Alas, no. But I received your note. I wish to talk."

"And I wish to apologise." She looked directly at him, and unshed tears glistened in her serious eyes. "I have been doing much thinking, and I would not wish you to enter the church unless it is your own pure will. And even then, it might only be to find a quiet place to think, or to admire the windows, and I must learn to be content with that."

Was this her apology? It was not much in the way of words, but the sentiment and the expression on her face were eloquent and carried the ring of sincerity. She had clearly been examining her own deep thoughts and opinions, and he would not belittle what had been so honestly offered.

He returned her look and took her hand briefly as he said, "Thank you."

She bit her bottom lip and withdrew her hand, but he knew she understood him. "When shall we talk?" she asked. "There is a bench over there, by the graveyard, or perhaps we might walk... The weather is fine."

"You would not wish to miss your Sunday services, surely?"

"Perhaps," she looked at the ground, "we have matters to discuss that cannot wait. If we can share what we have learned, we might be able to prevent further disasters."

This sounded rather a lot like what Alexander had told to Knightley only last evening. He was willing to break a great many rules of his faith to save a life. Perhaps he and Mary had more in common than she believed. "I hope and believe this to be so," he kept his voice low.

Mary excused herself for a moment and ran ahead to inform Emma that she would not be joining the congregation this morning, much to her regret. Alexander did not hear all her words, or those of the reply, but Emma raised her head and looked his way, then turned back to Mary with a slow grin and a regretful glance. The young woman raised her voice so Alexander could hear her. "There is a small garden across the stream there," she indicated with her head, "that is part of Hartfield's estate, with a gazebo and some benches, should you wish to make use of it. I bid you a good morning, Mr. Lyons."

Alexander had the strange notion that this particular infatuation was over. Emma was beautiful and smart, but for all her joy of involvement in other people's affairs, she must know she could never compare in his eyes to Mary.

He bowed towards her and spoke of his gratitude for her consideration and then held out his arm for Mary. She took it, and as the last arriving members of the local congregation filed into the old stone church, he led Mary in the opposite direction towards the small footbridge and the path that lay beyond.

Whatever had come over her? Never before in her life had Mary chosen to miss Sunday services. They were expected, *de rigueur* for one of her social position, a necessary part of her existence, as essential as food and drink. As a child, she had been taken with her family, where she learned to sit still in her pew with her small leather-bound *Book of Common Prayer*, to sing with the community and listen in awe and respect to the words of the parson. Only when she had been ill had she stayed home, and this habit had remained with her until this very day. What had come over her, that she chose Alexander over the Lord?

No, she chastised herself. That was an unfair thought. God would be there, waiting for her prayers, which were always honestly and devotedly offered. She could make her own orisons later; indeed, she carried her book in her reticule. She could not take communion, it was true, but surely God would forgive her this once, just as she strove to forgive herself.

She wondered again what fed Alexander's soul. Was he an atheist? Is that why he visited no church? Or did he belong to the group which called themselves Friends, who had services called meetings, of which she knew so very little? She hoped that one day he might trust her enough to reveal to her this aspect of his life. Sadly, she had given him little cause of late to so confide in her. She would wait.

Alexander led her down to the stream where the bridge crossed over the burbling water, and then down the path that vanished into the thin woods. In a moment they were on the other side, in a large glade surrounded by artfully arranged trees that looked quite natural and were anything but, and carefully arranged shrubberies that gave the illusion of nature at its finest. Three stone benches flanked the open space, and a small belvedere graced one corner of the area, most particularly placed to take best advantage of the height of the trees and the gentle rise of land. Through the break in the trees past the structure, Mary could see the path continuing through more fields, and the distinctive roof and towers of Hartfield itself in the near distance. From the front doors of the estate, the road wandered for about a mile before reaching the centre of the village; through this silent path, the distance was perhaps a half of that. Mr. Woodhouse must be so concerned for his daughter's welfare that he required her to take the busier road, and she in turn must have forgotten that this path was even a possibility.

"Shall we sit?" Alexander gestured to one of the benches that faced away from the sun. Its heat would warm their backs, but not shine into their eyes, and she commended his thoughtfulness.

He saw to her comfort, ensured the stone was not too cold to sit upon, and then, placing himself at her side and turned to face her, he asked, "What did you wish to ask me?"

"I wish for you to tell me about Jack Smith."

His eyes went wide, and his face grew red. He knew something that he did not want her to know, but he would not spare her delicate sensibilities. He thought better of her than that, she knew, and would treat her as an intelligent and rational human being.

As if in response to her thoughts, he sputtered, "It is not something that ought to be spoken of in front of a lady, but you are made of sterner stuff than that. It seems that some around here knew a little more of Smith than what was commonly known."

"He was somebody's natural child? Someone from the village?"

Alexander cleared his throat. "Aye. In part. It seems that as well as being the son of a local man, whose mother was unknown, he was also old Mr. Bates' brother."

"Bates the vicar? Oh! I see why that would have been unsuitable. Whilst such men are hardly unknown, for the parson to be associated with such immorality is rather difficult. Some people knew this?"

"John Abdy's son did—I spoke to him yesterday. It was he who told me, although he was cautious to wait until Miss Woodhouse was not present."

Mary's shoulders stiffened at the mention of Emma's name, but Alexander did not seem to react as he spoke it. Instead, he uttered the syllables with cool dispassion. There would be time to sort out those thoughts later. She returned her thoughts to those of John Abdy, *fils*, and his knowledge about Jack Smith. "How did he learn of it? Through his late father?"

"Aye, so it would seem. And he was not the only one. He told me how much the two men looked similar, although the vicar was the younger of the two. If Smith came by asking for alms, I'd rather imagine Bates would have given him rather a lot to remain quiet about the connexion."

"Mrs. Bates knew."

Alexander sat up at these words, and he blinked before drawing out the notebook he always carried and writing something in it. "She did? How on earth did you discover that?"

"She told me. 'I knew who he was,' were her words, but she did not reveal the nature of her knowledge. I had thought it might be important, and now I feel it is, even more than I did before."

"What else did Mrs. Bates tell you?" Those warm eyes bored into hers now, and she shivered despite the warm sun at her back.

"She is a strange one; I believe she is suffering the first infirmities of mind that come with old age, for sometimes she is friendly enough, other times very vague, and rarely, most acute, especially so when recalling something from times long past. We were listening to Miss Fairfax play the pianoforte—she does play with such skill and excellent taste—and Mrs. Bates told me that she blames 'them,' Mr. Smith and Mr. Abdy, for her family's descent into poverty. She believes her granddaughter would not be destined for a life as a governess had 'they' not ruined the family, and she repeated her lament that she was not listened to, for she might have seen them better off. I wish she had spoken more, but she then drifted back to the vagueness of her current state.

"And what is it you are thinking, Mary? I know that mind, and it is never still."

"I cannot help but think that this entire series of events relates not to the investment in Mr. Carnes' horse-training venture, but that it began many, many years ago. Think of it, Alexander. Everybody was somehow involved in that scheme Mrs. Bates spoke of when first we arrived. Abdy was the one with the idea, Mr. Watson provided the specialised iron tools they needed and soon thereafter came upon enough money to expand his smithy, Mr. Carnes began his first stables, and now we know that Mr. Smith, who arrived at about that same time, was somehow connected as well."

Alexander frowned. "But what of Hesselgrave and Mrs. Elton?"

"Mrs. Elton?" This was unexpected! "What has Mrs. Elton to do with it all?"

"Have you not heard? No, of course you could not. She was poisoned last night. She might have died."

"What?" Mary leapt up from her seat. This was most alarming! She did not like Mrs. Elton at all, but the news was nonetheless horrific. She began to walk up and down in a circle before the stone bench, one hand rubbing at the other. "No, I had not heard a breath of this! What happened? How did you know of it?"

"Come, Mary, and sit, or else I shall walk with you." He stood and followed her as she paced around the glade. "I heard of it because I was there." She listened in stunned horror as he related what had occurred at the vicarage the previous night. He told her of the report he had received from London and his and Mr. Knightley's decision to beard Elton in his den. Then he told her of the commotion from inside the house as they arrived and of finding Mrs. Elton on the floor, struggling for breath. He told her of the brandy, of the conference they had had with Elton, and of the fifteen thousand pounds.

"And the lady? How does she do? Is she well?" The rest was of interest, but only Mrs. Elton's health really mattered right now. Had Alexander even thought to inquire?

"I stopped by on my way to the church this morning and spoke to Mrs. Wright. Mrs. Elton is tired and weak, but suffered no relapse and will be well soon enough. Elton was preparing to orate at the church, confident in his wife's recovery, and Mr. Perry was confident that we had done everything properly to rescue her."

"You, you alone, Alexander. From what you told me only now, it was your doing."

"'Twas only what I could recall from learning at my father's knee. He was a good man, and even after his passing, he is still saving lives." His eyes shone with moisture, and Mary felt a sudden chill go through her.

"But without you, she would have died. She would have been another victim. Oh, how awful! How simply awful." She collapsed inwards, arms wrapping about her body, and found herself being pulled against a warm and broad chest. Alexander's arms folded against her back, and he held her in a strong embrace. He shook... was he crying? Surely men did not cry!

"I had thought myself stronger than this," his voice rasped in her ear, "but when I think of her, lying on the floor, nearly dead of some vile poison, I find myself overcome by the shock of it. Last night it all seemed so distant, so clinical. But now, when I remember it... I... I ought to be a better man than this. I'm sorry, Mary."

She pulled back to look at his face. "Better? Being so affected by her suffering does not make you weak. You saved her life! How much better a man could you be? You are the very best of men!" She returned to his embrace and wrapped her own arms about him, and they stood there, leaning upon each other, until strength and composure returned. Thank heaven no one had seen them, for this was most untoward, but she and Alexander shared a unique sort of relationship, outside the realm of convention and expected propriety. This was not their first embrace borne of shock and emotional need. A deep part of her prayed that it would not be their last.

When they were recovered, they returned to the bench. Alexander drew out a handkerchief and wiped Mary's face clean of tears, then his own. Feeling more the thing, Mary asked the question she needed to know. "What was the poison? How did she take it?"

"The food—I smelled it in the food. That was how I knew what to do to counteract it. It was Prussic acid. It has a distinctive aroma, rather like almonds."

She furrowed her brow. The name was familiar, but she could not place it. "What is it, Alexander? Is it easy to come by? Something so dangerous ought not to be easy to find."

"It is found in many common substances, but one must often take a great dose for it to be lethal. It is in many fruit pits, or in some medicines like cherry laurel. It can be made by chemists in their laboratories, and the fumes are sometimes used to kill rats…"

"The dog!" She started again. "Could the dog, poor Chloe Cox's dog, have found his way into rat poison? If he got into the rubbish in the scullery, might there have been poison in there?"

"Hmmm, that is a thought! We had wondered what he might have found."

Something bothered Mary. Something gnawed at the back of her mind. Something important, something that would not leave her be.

"What was the food?" Could that be the important matter?

"We don't know. Elton insisted the remains be cleared before we could examine them. The tray, from what we saw when we entered, contained bread, cake, pie, fresh berries, cheese, tea with sugar and cream… I believe that was all. I am a poor investigator, but I confess my attention was on Mrs. Elton and not her tray of afters."

The gnawing grew more insistent, but the thought would not come. Perhaps if she concentrated on something else, the thought would reveal itself to her.

"Do you still believe Mr. Elton involved? Would he try to murder his own wife?"

Alexander sighed and rubbed his forehead. "I hardly know what to think. Everything suggests his involvement in the deaths as they relate to Carnes' venture with the horses, but there are only suggestions, no clear facts. And I would swear that his shock at Mrs. Elton's poisoning was real. He was terrified and quite stunned at the mention of poison. But still, other than Hesselgrave, he is the only surviving signatory to the agreement, and we fear for Hesselgrave's safety. There is also the matter of those fifteen thousand pounds. If he is, indeed, the last of the investors, his profits could well make up that missing money."

"Fifteen thousand... it is hard to imagine that sort of wealth. I am certain he would be most eager to recover that loss." The stone bench was growing cold on her back and uncomfortable. She rose to walk some more, and Alexander joined her. "And still, I cannot leave the feeling that this is all about something that happened long ago and not recently. I wish I knew..."

She began to walk down the path back towards the church. The service would still be underway, but the need to move was great. "Could the other deaths be due to Prussic acid as well?"

"It is possible, indeed. In each case, something else happened to obscure the effects of the poison, if that is what it was. But had Smith died whilst in his wooden hut, the fire would have been almost inevitable. Had Watson suffered a fit from the poison— which is one action it can have—that might have propelled him into the shelves, which then crashed down upon him. No one suspected anything other than old age for Abdy, for a man of ninety is no common thing. And Carnes, had he been sitting on the wall looking out over the scenery when he died, would have fallen exactly into Martin's reservoir."

"But how did they take the poison?"

"It has to have been in food or ale, something they had with them. That is why there was no sign of any other people around at the time of each man's death."

They were now back by the churchyard. Sounds of singing and organ music emanated from the building, and by unspoken agreement, the two wandered down to the high street.

"Miss Bennet, Lyons!" a hearty voice called to them from a short distance away.

"Mr. Cox, good morning," Mary bobbed to Alexander's friend from London, and Alexander shook the man's hand.

"Not a churchgoer?" Alexander asked with a wink.

"I rather overslept this morning," he replied with a rather large grin. "I was up a little later than is my wont, and it caught up with me. Fine day. We don't get ones like this in the city, what with the noise and smoke and all, wot? Out walking?"

"Discussing matters, rather," Alexander replied to him. "Miss Bennet has a fine mind, and her insights are often invaluable." He smiled at her, and Mary beamed brighter than the sun. She was unaccustomed to compliments and could not hide her pleasure."

"Any new thoughts, then?" Mr. Cox began, but he was interrupted by the sound of hoofbeats on the cobblestones behind him. He turned to see who was riding before moving out the way but stopped short.

Mary could see nothing unusual about the gentleman who approached. He was well enough dressed, no farmer this, with a florid face and a natural seat on his horse that made him seem almost one with the animal.

But Cox stood as still as stone and stared as if he had seen a ghost. Then, with a voice that might have carried as far as Dorking, he called out the man's name.

"Hesselgrave!" The horseman pulled to a stop. "My God, Hesselgrave, we have all given you up for dead! Wherever have you been? We've been hunting for you."

"Hunting? Me?" He guffawed and swung off his horse. He was a larger man than Mary had expected but moved with the grace of one much leaner and younger.

Mr. Cox made the introductions, and Alexander explained the urgency of their endeavour. At the mention of Mr. Carnes' death, the gentleman went white and staggered back a step.

"What? Harry dead? No!" He clearly had not heard this news. Mary wondered where he had been sequestered for the past week that he had no notion of it.

"Sadly, it is true." Mary watched the man's face carefully. His distress seemed genuine.

"But... Harry! He was my friend, my partner! His mother...I must take care of his family. She is my tenant! And, oh God, what of the horses? This is a disaster!"

Mr. Cox assured him that the horses were well tended. "Perhaps tomorrow we might discuss another matter concerning horses, you and Lyons and I. Our investigations may lead you to somebody who can take over Carnes' reins, if you'll excuse the expression."

"Yes... yes, of course. Come anytime. Carnes had a gift with the animals. He could coax a draught horse to grow wings. Why, when first I met him, I had a young thing, just grown to full size, that I thought to race. But the creature flew like a bird in my fields and lumbered like an ox on the track. Carnes asked for him for a month, told me to stay away to let the beast bond with his trainer. I came by the fields three days before the race, just to look in. I stayed far back—didn't want to interrupt the training—but what I saw amazed me. From a distance, I almost did not recognise him! Carnes had Septimus standing taller, looking stronger. When I crept a bit closer, I could see even his temperament was different. If I had not seen those markings on his side, where he's mottled a bit, and the star between his eyes, I'd have sworn it was not my Septimus at all, but a different animal entirely! Such was his skill!"

Beside her, Mary felt Alexander stop still. What had he heard? But Hesselgrave kept talking.

"Septimus won his race, and I poured a bucket of cash into Carnes' establishment. The horse never won again, but I could see what that man could accomplish. Mighty sad loss this is. Mighty sad. So yes, come tomorrow and we shall speak more."

Alexander's voice was tight, as if he were fighting to hold back something of great import. "Mr. Knightley will wish to be a part of this."

"Yes, yes. Of course. But Harry...? His poor mother. What will become of his mother?"

At this, Mary decided she liked the man. That his main concern was for the dead man's family over his own investment spoke well of his character, and she hoped he was not involved in either of Alexander's missions.

Now Alexander began to speak of their concerns and of the horse-training endeavour. "After Mr. Carnes died, we were most concerned that you might be in danger," he concluded. "Everybody, with the exception of Mr. Elton, was dead or missing. You cannot fault us for our worry, or for having established a search near Dorking."

Hesselgrave flushed red and sputtered. "I had no idea. So terribly sorry! If I'd known, but of course I didn't. I was... well, I was rather out of touch with everybody for the week."

"Would you mind, sir, telling us where you were?" Alexander's voice had taken on a conspiratorial tone rather than an accusatory one.

"Er, well, it's rather embarrassing, you know...." His eyes darted towards Mary and then back to the men. "Personal matters..."

Mary did not roll her eyes, but only by a great effort. Here was another man afraid to disturb her supposed delicate sensibilities. She found her most innocent and guileless smile and asked, "With a lady friend?" She batted her eyes.

Hesselgrave sputtered some more and turned an even deeper shade of red. Mary was afraid he might collapse of an apoplexy, but instead he gave her a look of respect and let out a deep sigh of resignation. "I must confess, the lady has the right of it. Mrs. Ewing, the tinsmith's widow, that is... she and I have an arrangement. I would marry her if she'd have me, but she insists she would never be happy at Riverton, and so we... we meet when I travel to Dorking for matters of business. I take the room at the inn, so no questions are asked, but, well... it seems I chose a rather unhappy time for our reunion. You will not spread this, please? She is a respectable lady and I would not have her the subject of gossip. We have taken great pains to be discrete. For her sake, if not mine...." He spread his hands in supplication.

Alexander reassured him. "We will need to confer briefly with the lady, but if her tale is yours, it seems to have no bearing on the case and there is no need for anybody else to know. You may rely on me... on us." Mary nodded earnestly, and Cox did likewise.

After a few more words of consolation, Alexander bid the stunned man a farewell. "Until tomorrow, then. I'll stop by to see you and also for a wee chat with your good stable master Duncan as well. 'Twas good to speak Scots again." Mary would have to ask him about this! "And a word of warning, sir: eat nothing you have not seen prepared yourself. I would hate to be proven correct in my concerns."

With a sombre nod of agreement, Mr. Hesselgrave swung back onto his waiting horse and continued along his way.

Alexander watched as the man and horse disappeared around the curve in the road. "We may need to reconsider Elton as our man."

"Hesselgrave's obvious good health undermines that theory, does it not?" Mr. Cox clucked his tongue and then straightened up. "I shall leave you to your walk and your discussions. Meet you at breakfast tomorrow, Lyons? Around eight? We can head off to interview Hesselgrave from there. Good day, Miss Bennet. I look forward to our next meeting. But I see the service is about to let out, and I would be present to walk somebody home. Excuse me." He gave a bow and a smirk and dashed off to the old stone building where the doors had just been flung open.

Chapter Twenty

The Proof of the Pudding

Mary looked over at the throngs who were emerging from the church. She ought to feel guilty for not being one of their number, but the only guilt she felt was for her lack of remorse at having missed the service. What was it about Alexander that always left her questioning, just a small bit, everything she had ever thought she knew about herself?

Her life had been so ordered before they met, so predictable and proper. With the word of God to inform her principles, and the word of Fordyce to guide them and give them shape, she had never had to think more about her spiritual inclinations than to decide which spencer would be most suitable for services the following week. But Alexander had disturbed all of that. He made her think, made her ponder her every choice, made her reconsider the unthinking and reflexive nature of her devotion. He challenged her every thought, and she liked it.

No, she had no wish today to be in that crowd of worshippers. She would still worship, of course, and would not leave off her weekly attendance, but now, today, she had made another choice and was satisfied with it.

She moved into the shade of a small stand of trees where she might observe those who had been doing their duty to God and His angels. Alexander moved with her, his long and easy strides matching her shorter hurried ones. There was Mr. Cox's brother, the local attorney, and there his wife and family, including his daughter Chloe. She wondered how the girl fared now, whether she had regained her joy after the traumatic death of her pet. There were Emma and Mr. Woodhouse, shuffling step by step to the waiting carriage, with Miss Harriet Smith at Emma's side, and Mr. Knightley talking patiently to her father. There were the Westons, preparing to walk the short half mile back to Randalls, though Mrs. Weston was beginning to look as if she would appreciate a carriage herself before long from the way she used her hands to lend support to her back.

There was Mr. Stoller, the innkeeper, and there Mr. and Mrs. Ford, and Mrs. Latimer from the tea shop. How many people she had come to know here in this village of Highbury! It could hardly have been only a week since her unexpected arrival here. Ah, there was Mr. Elton, looking pale and smaller than normal, but looking in no desperation to return home; his wife must be much improved indeed from what Alexander had told her of the previous night. What a horrible thing, to have been poisoned like that. And there were Miss Bates, Mrs. Bates, and Miss Fairfax, and oh! There was Mr. Cox from London, greeting his brother and nieces and nephews, but bowing low before Miss Bates and offering his arm to walk her home!

She had wondered about his intentions. They seemed so mismatched a couple in many ways—he an intelligent and educated man, a respected professional living in the bustle of London, and she a plain and unlearned woman of simpler thoughts and a tendency to silliness—but in other ways they might do well together. Miss Bates embodied kindness and would make Mr. Cox a good home, should he wish it. They shared more than Mary had expected as well. She recalled their conversations about art and design and natural beauty, during which Miss Bates had sounded anything but silly. Their home would be comfortable and very elegant, even on an attorney's moderate income. And Mary was certain they would soon find a dog to share their home, for both had spoken so fondly of their pets. How sad that Miss Bates should also have lost her dog so recently, and...

Oh God!

"Alexander!" She grasped at his arm. "We have to stop them."

Her heart beat in her breast as loud as the thunder of a hundred horses, and blood rushed in her ears. There was no time to waste.

He peered at her through confused eyes. "Who?" She hardly heard his words though the rush of panic that overwhelmed her.

"The Westons! We have to stop them now. Quick—they are only a few minutes ahead of us. We can catch up with them and stop them if we hurry. It's imperative." She had already begun moving towards the street and felt Alexander's strides as he matched her pace. Only her direct path was clear, in hard and bright focus that let the rest of the countryside melt into amorphous shadow and shapes.

"Mary? I'll come with you, of course, but can you explain what you mean?" He was there. Good. She prayed they would not be too late, that the Westons were not too far ahead, that he would succeed even if she could not.

"The poison... I know who did it and why. We have to stop them! I'll tell you as we walk, but we have to hurry, please!"

She increased her pace with Alexander at her side. Thank heavens for Mrs. Weston's delicate condition, for she would not be walking so fast that Mary and Alexander could not catch them. The distance was only a half a mile, but now, with their few minutes head start, it seemed both far too short and far too long. The road before them was busy, crowded with church-goers and their conveyances, horses and wagons and families on foot. They must get through, must hurry. At last, ahead of them, she could finally see her prey. They were not too far in front, only a few hundred years, near where the road curved by the trees.

As they rushed along, she told Alexander her thoughts, her breath short with her exertion, and as he listened, his eyes grew wide with alarm. "If you're right, Mary... Oh Lord, yes, we have to stop them!"

They caught up with Mr. and Mrs. Weston as they were about to turn off the road and onto the short drive that led to Randalls.

"Miss Bennet, Mr. Lyons!" Mr. Weston's greeting was as cheerful and good-natured as always. "Are you on your way to Hartfield? No? Please come in and take some refreshments. Mrs. Bates spoke to us at church and told us she sent over a cherry pie this morning with Dolly. She is always so clever to preserve the cherries when they are ripe on the tree, that we may enjoy them months later. We were looking forward to enjoying it with our tea. Have you tried Mrs. Bates' pies? She has such a delicate touch with pastry."

"No! Please, whatever you do, do not eat her pie! That is what we came to warn you about." Mary gasped. "I believe it is poisoned!"

Before long, Mary followed Alexander and Mr. Weston into the entrance hall at Hartfield. Alexander carried the pie in a small box. The butler had informed them that yes indeed, Mr. Knightley was present, and would attend them momentarily, if they would care to wait for but a minute.

They had scarcely had a chance to catch their breaths after the hurried walk from Randalls when the gentleman himself appeared at one of the doorways. "Mead said you needed to speak to me, that it was urgent." He took in all three visitors. "I see it must be so. Come into the morning room. Mr. Woodhouse will not mind. Emma is with him at tea."

Without preamble, Alexander spoke. "Mary thinks she has worked out who has been killing these men and how, and I believe she is correct. We only now prevented another disaster with the Westons. This pie will prove her right or wrong, but as magistrate, you ought to know all our thoughts. And—this can wait till a later conversation—I have uncovered the source of the racing irregularities! But now, the murders."

Knightley screwed up his eyes and stared at them all for a moment, then took in Mr. Weston's ashen face. "Yes. Yes, indeed. Is Mrs. Weston well?"

"In shock, I'd say, but physically unharmed. Miss Bennet and Mr. Lyons stopped us from tasting the pie. If it is true—"

"Recall Mrs. Elton, only last night!" Alexander interjected.

"—then we must act before anybody else is hurt."

Knightley sat perfectly still for two counts, then nodded decisively. "Yes. To the stables, or wherever we might find a rat. I am loath to do this, but it is imperative. Bring the pie, Lyons."

He led them out of the house through the kitchen entrance, and around the side to the stables. "Do you have rats or mice here?" he called to the young grooms who were sitting on a low wooden bench. "You will not be chastised; just the opposite. We must find such a pest."

The boys jumped from their low perch and assured Mr. Knightley that if there were a rat or mouse in the structure, they would find it forthwith, and within a very few minutes, one of the lads presented him with a large grey rat in a pail.

"Miss Bennet, you may wish not to watch," he offered, but Mary demurred. If she was correct, if she was to accuse somebody of murder, she must be strong enough to observe the evidence. Knightley found a twig and broke off a piece of the pie with it and dropped it into the pail. The rat did as rats do and began to sniff at it, then chew at it, and in a moment, stiffened and squealed and fell over.

Mary's stomach knotted as Knightley poked at it with his twig. "Dead."

Mr. Weston swayed on his feet and turned an unhealthy shade of white. "That... that was intended for us. For Anne. Oh heavens. The baby..." Mr. Knightley caught his arm and guided him to the bench.

As he did so, Alexander sniffed at the pie. "Cherry, and almond. Just like at the Cox's house. With the cherry, I could not smell the distinctive smell of the Prussic acid, but last night at the Eltons, the pie was apple, and the scent was more pronounced."

"Then it is true?" Mary asked. She glanced at the dead rodent and wondered if she ought to say a prayer for its soul... if rats even had souls. It was a pathetic creature now, a grey shadow at the bottom of the pail, never to move again. It was, in a strange way, her fault that the pest was dead. Then she thought that the creature might be Mrs. Elton, or Mrs. Weston, or—if matters were to go so far—Alexander or herself. She shivered at the thought. "I am sorry to be right."

"As am I," Mr. Knightley sighed as he stepped back towards them. "Lyons, see to the preparation of the chaise. I shall inform Mr. Woodhouse that we require its use for a short time. We shall take Weston back to his wife, and then it appears we must pay an unwelcome visit to the Bates ladies."

Mr. Weston was taken immediately to his home at Randalls, where he ran inside with scarcely a word, calling for his wife. The lady called back, and Mary had the impression of a tearful and desperate embrace in the vestibule as Mr. Knightley guided the horse back out of the drive and onto the street. The couple might have bad dreams for several nights, and may never eat pie again, but they were unharmed.

Alexander took the few moments they now had to tell Knightley and Mary of his discovery concerning his other case, regarding the strange results at the horse races.

"I still have much to discover," he said as the chaise rolled down the lane, "but this is what I believe. Carnes was playing an old game, switching a fast horse for a slower one, both to convince customers to purchase his animals, and to play the odds at the races."

Mary screwed up her forehead. Beside her, she saw Mr. Knightley's eyebrows rise. "How so?" she asked. "Surely each horse is different. Why, this one before us is a deep brown with white on his flanks, and ours at home is a dappled grey. I should know them apart in a moment."

"Ah, but Carnes was an artist. He had a way with horses, to be sure, and conducted much legitimate business in the way of breeding and training horses, but he also had a trick whereby he could disguise one horse as another. He painted them!"

"What?" Mr. Knightley all but shouted. "Painted them?"

"Aye. Just this morning, Hesselgrave said he would have thought his favourite horse was a different animal by its carriage and temperament, and so it was. I examined the stables yesterday, and found vats of bleach and henna, and a great exhibition of first-rate paintings of horses. Carnes had taken his own fine and fast beast and, with the bleach and dye, had recreated the likeness of Hesselgrave's horse. This is the animal that Hesselgrave saw in the training fields, and this is the animal that won the race. That is why the real Septimus never won again. Because he had never even won once!"

"Bravo, young man!" Knightley clapped Alexander on the back as he drove. "That is some fine thinking there! Yes, I shall join you on the morrow to talk with Hesselgrave and the others you believe implicit in this ruse. But now we have another issue to resolve, for we are nearly arrived."

No sooner had the chaise come within sight of the village and the street where the church stood its tireless watch over the area than Mr. Elton came hurrying onto the street. "Mr. Knightley, Mr. Lyons," he called out. He must have been watching the street in the hopes that one of them might pass by. "I have to talk to you. There is something you must know." Now he glanced at Mary and stepped back a pace.

Mr. Knightley raised his brows at Alexander, who shrugged. Their conversation, though silent, was clear to Mary. *Shall we stop and hear him out?* And the reply, *Our task at the Bateses can wait for a moment or two. Nothing more dire will happen today.* She envied the easy cooperation and understanding between the two men.

"Of course, Mr. Elton." Mr. Knightley pulled the chaise over to the verge by the churchyard and alit to set the brake and to tie up the horse. "Shall we speak here or somewhere more comfortable?"

Alexander leapt from the chaise and handed Mary down before extending his hand to Elton. The clergyman eyed it with some suspicion, but then took it in his to shake.

"How is Mrs. Elton today?" Mr. Knightley inquired. "Did she have a need to call Mr. Perry during the night?"

Mr. Elton exhaled heavily. "She is much improved, although tired. She slept well, even if I did not. I thank you again, Mr. Lyons, for your expert knowledge and care. And I must apologise for my own behaviour when we parted ways. I was rude. I was able to do much thinking as I watched over Augusta last night, counting her every breath, and I believe I owe you an explanation." He eyed Mary again and settled his mouth into a firm line.

"Whatever you wish to tell us, sir, Miss Bennet may hear." Alexander stepped up to her side and placed a hand on her back.

"It is hardly the subject for young ladies to hear..." the vicar countered.

"Please, sir!" Mary was growing tired of such treatment. "After what I have seen these past few months, there is little that has the power to render me insensible. I have learned more of the darkness and evil in men's souls that I can imagine they teach you at your seminaries. Imagine me as another man, then, and do not think to spare my delicate feelings." She pursed her lips and dared him with her glare.

"The lady has the right of it," Mr. Knightley added. "She is more than adequate to hear anything you have to say."

At length, the vicar relented with a sagging of his shoulders and led the three to the stone benches by the trees that surrounded the churchyard. "This is something which I would prefer not to mention within the church itself. I feel God will judge me all the more for alluding to my sin in His house."

Alexander raised his eyebrows. "Ah. I understand."

Mr. Elton began his story. "My family were wealthy and well connected in society, and although I knew myself destined for the Church, as I came of age, the reality of it seemed so far off. I acted as any other young man might, as almost all of my friends and companions did, and I took a mistress." He flushed a deep red, and Mary was reminded of a similar discussion with Mr. Hesselgrave only hours before. What was it with men, who seemed so incapable of living without their mistresses, but who felt such shame for it?

"With my personal fortune, it was no difficulty to maintain her in an apartment in the city, and I knew nothing other than this lifestyle. But," he paused to take a breath, "as I neared my twenty-fifth birthday and the time when I would take my orders and accept the living allotted to me, I began to reconsider my choice. I knew it was not something acceptable for a clergyman, and I resolved to give her up. This had always been our arrangement, in truth, and we were both satisfied with it. But events do not always live up to our expectations. About six months before our contract was to conclude, Imogen informed me she was with child. My child." He looked at Mary again and turned an even deeper shade of crimson. For her part, Mary simply raised her brows in what she hoped was an expression of the greatest nonchalance.

Mr. Elton swallowed and spoke on. "It was not uncommon to merely wish the lady a fond farewell and then think of her no more, but I could not do that. I never loved her, but I had been very fond of her, and, well, it was my child too! I am a selfish and petty man, sirs—and Miss Bennet—but I am not the sort to abandon a woman and infant to the cruelties of the world. As her time neared, and with her consent and approval, I purchased for her a small house in a village near Oxford, where her family lives. There she could present herself as a widow and live and raise our child with some respectability.

"The fifteen thousand pounds you were asking about—this is where the money went. I bought the house, deeded it to Imogen, and set up the rest in an account so she might live comfortably off the income and have the principal to settle on our daughter. I have severed all contact, as I know I must do, but receive some news from a friend in the village, and know that they are well and welcomed into society there.

"This is what I could not tell you last night. I had not thought anybody knew. The shock of hearing it, and most especially after the shock of nearly losing Augusta, was too great and I could not think. I can only hope you will understand my actions, and will not divulge my shameful secret to my congregation or to my wife."

Mr. Knightley looked down at him through narrowed lids.

"No, no, you misunderstand," Mr. Elton flustered again. "I will tell her myself. I know now I have to do this. But allow me the choosing of the time, when she is recovered."

The conversation was soon at an end. Mr. Elton wished to return to his wife, and Alexander and Mr. Knightley wished to continue to the Bates residence.

"It seems our suspicions of Mr. Elton were unfounded," Mr. Knightley mused as they drove away from the church. "Hesselgrave is alive and well, and Elton's great expenditure was for far more altruistic reasons than I'd have expected of him."

"Just so," Alexander replied. He spoke to Mr. Knightley, but his eyes suggested that his words were directed to Mary. "He is no worse than so many others of his age and class. He is a weak and puffed-up sort of a man, but not so very evil. He has done far more than most such men would do."

See? His eyes asked Mary. *I, too, am not so low as to accuse a man of sin based on his profession, nor do I seek to find evil where there is none.* And her eyes answered, *Yes, I see that now. I am truly sorry.* Perhaps she did know that secret language of men that she had so envied a short time ago.

Chapter Twenty-One

Accusation

"**M**other! We have guests. Guests, Mother! How lovely."

Alexander could hear Miss Bates' voice even before they had descended from the chaise. Knightley was the first out and got busy setting the brake and tying up the horse at a trough of water whilst Alexander assisted Mary in her descent from the vehicle. She did not need his help, this he knew full well, but he was pleased to offer his hand and she seemed pleased enough to take it.

He stood back with her, allowing Knightley to take the lead. This was his domain, his justice. Alexander and Mary had done their part and found the killer—or rather, Mary had done so, using only a small piece of the evidence he had uncovered. He was a strong enough man to give full credit to the lady. Now he would step back and allow Knightley to deal with these people, whom he considered not just acquaintances, but friends, as he saw best. The deaths, at least, would stop. There would be no more tainted pies.

Mary stood with her hand upon his forearm, his gloved hand atop hers. This felt all too comfortable and all too natural, and he warned himself not to allow the expectation of it. Instead, he focused his attention on the door. Knightley knocked and waited, as polite as ever he might be upon paying a social call. If this was how the magistrate wished to commence, Alexander would cooperate completely.

The maid appeared almost at once and bid them enter. One by one, they followed her up the stairs into the sitting room that formed the front part of the apartments. The room was quite full, and especially so considering its modest size. Mrs. Bates sat in a large and well-padded armchair by the cold fireplace, a shawl about her shoulders, her eyes half closed in the state between sleep and wakefulness. On one side of the room, near the pianoforte, Frank Churchill sat on a small sofa, in deep conversation with Miss Fairfax. Both rose gracefully to their feet as Alexander and his companions entered. Across the room, by the window that overlooked the laneway up which they had so recently driven the chaise, Miss Bates was already on her feet with Hugh Cox at her side. From the look on Cox's face, the newcomers had interrupted something. His eyes were bright and there was an expression of contentment—or was that subdued joy?—on his friend's face that Alexander had seldom seen before.

"Oh, how delightful! What a lovely surprise to see you, so very kind of you to come by to visit."

Alexander expected Miss Bates to continue on at some length on the degree of her delight and the exact nature of their kindness in bestowing their presence upon her humble home, but instead she dropped a gentle curtsey and turned to Cox with a great smile that made her seem almost pretty. His own face mirrored her grin, and Alexander felt his jaw drop open.

A titter to his side drew his attention to Mary and the smile on her face. To his amazement, there was no surprise in her expression, only pleasure. How long had she known of this quiet courtship that even he, having spoken to his friend at meals and drinks throughout the week, had not the first hint of? It was he who was the investigator, not she! She really was a remarkable young woman, and he felt very proud of her at that moment.

"What's this?" Alexander asked with smiling eyes. If he and his companions were about to bring the direst news to the room, there may as well be a glimmer of happiness too.

"You may wish us joy, Lyons! Hetty has agreed to marry me."

"I say! I am amazed, but very pleased for you, Cox. Very pleased indeed! My heartiest congratulations to both of you. Miss Bates, you have found a fine man in my friend."

Mary rushed forward to grab Miss Bates' hands and offer her such wishes that made both seem like giggling schoolgirls. For this moment, at least, the room was awash in mirth. Knightley smiled benevolently at them from his position in the centre of the room, and Miss Fairfax and Churchill looked on with happy incredulity on their faces. Only Mrs. Bates, in her half-slumber, seemed unmoved.

Knightley allowed the celebration and felicitations to continue for some moments before he cleared his throat and began to speak.

"I'm afraid that the news we bring will dampen this celebration," he intoned. At his words, the hum of chatter in the room died to stony silence. "Please sit. Mrs. Bates," he spoke loudly into the old lady's ear, "I need your attention, for I have some questions you may wish to answer." He sat himself down at her side and waited until her eyes opened. Alexander slid onto the bench at the back of the room and guided Mary down to sit at his side. They all waited with hardly a breath until Knightley began to speak again.

"We have all been saddened, recently, by an unexpected wave of deaths." Alexander noticed all eyes on Knightley and surreptitiously drew his notebook and pencil from his pocket to record his observations. Beside Knightley, the old lady coughed, but otherwise did not react.

"We had no notion, at first, that the deaths were at all related," he spoke in a calm and even voice. "Each seemed perfectly explicable, natural even, the case of dire accident but nothing else. When Harry Carnes died, however, there seemed to be too many accidents, and we broadened our investigations. We discovered a great many things, some of which have no bearing on this case. Other matters, however, became more and more important and central to what we learned."

He paused and looked around the room, meeting the eye of every person seated therein, before turning in a most gentle manner to Mrs. Bates. "Why did you do it?" He asked, his voice so low Alexander could hardly hear him.

She turned her head to him, eyes vague behind the lenses of her spectacles, but said nothing.

"We know it was poison in the pies. We know you gave them to people whom you knew from twenty years ago, when your husband was alive and was vicar here. We know who Jack Smith was, and that he often came around for alms, and we know about old John Abdy and his schemes. But I need you to tell us the rest. I wish to hear it in your own words." His voice was low and coaxing, the sort that would calm a fussy child or soothe a spooked horse.

Alexander could see Mrs. Bates' regard grow clearer as Knightley spoke. "It was their fault," she said at last. Her voice was as quiet as Knightley's, but the words clear and without hesitation. She coughed and continued. "We were never wealthy, but we had some small wealth; we looked forward to a genteel life of plentiful food and adequate comfort and no want. Then he came. Smith, he called himself, but we all knew who he was. He never troubled us, never threatened to disclose the connexion. I think he enjoyed his life free of the bounds of society. But we knew, and Mr. Bates felt forced by a guilt that was not his own to care for the wretch and gave him more money than he ought.

"That was when John Abdy came about. He had seen the coins my husband bestowed upon that bastard brother of his," she swung her head around to Jane Fairfax, who had gasped in horror, whether at the suggestion or at the word, Alexander knew not, "and offered up his scheme. 'You have funds,' he said, 'Invest in my plan, and it will make you a rich man.' Hah! I warned them. I warned them all, but they would not listen to me. Penny by penny, pound by pound, my father gave Abdy the principal of his entire fortune while we grew poor, and Abdy lost it, every farthing!"

"I'm sorry to hear that." He continued to speak in that low, calm voice that belied the severity of the issue at hand. "And what of Fred Watson, the smith, or Harry Carnes? Were they involved in Mr. Abdy's scheme?"

"Whilst we grew poor, they grew rich. For every penny Mr. Bates gave to his bastard brother and then handed to the thief Abdy, they somehow made two. Abdy used my family's money to build their wealth. Watson bought into Abdy's plans, and suddenly had enough to greatly expand his smithy and grow even more wealthy, and Carnes began purchasing horses to establish his operation. And us? We saw every penny disappear until we relied only upon the small income from the living. When my husband died then, so suddenly—and from an apoplexy at seeing his fortune stolen from him, I'd wager—we were left even without that. The small amount that was left allowed us enough to take this place and hire on Dolly, but even then, we had to use the principal as well as the interest.

And Abdy and Watson and Carnes grew richer and richer, all the while Hetty and Jane and I grew poorer and poorer."

She coughed again, then lifted her head to address the room. "They only got what they deserved!"

"Mother, no!" Miss Bates cried out. "You could not have done this!"

"Quiet, Hetty. You always did speak too much." The old lady's voice was cold and cruel. How much of this was her nature, and how much a cruel symptom of her dementia, Alexander did not know. Beside him, Mary drew in a shuddering breath, and he took her hand to offer her comfort. She blamed herself for revealing this side of Mrs. Bates, he knew.

Without breaking from his calm tones, Knightley asked yet another question. "Why now, Mrs. Bates? It has been twenty years. Why now?"

Her voice changed back to that of a sweet old lady. "Why? Because of Jane, of course." Her rheumy eyes found her granddaughter and blinked back tears. "Whilst Jane was happy, I was content to make do the best we could with what we had. But when her friend Miss Campbell married and she returned to us for some time before seeking a position as a governess, the deceit and unfairness of it all became too much, and I felt that I needed to take my revenge.

"Jane, my dear, smart, beautiful, talented Jane, who ought to have a dowry equal to her God-given attributes, who should have been able to marry a baron or viscount, or even an earl, is doomed to a life of servitude because of them. It's all their fault, and so I made them pay!"

Jane Fairfax had turned white as her grandmother spoke, and now she broke down in tears. "No! Please say I am not the cause of this. That I am responsible in some way for those men's deaths!"

"Hush, child," Mrs. Bates cajoled. "It is no less than they deserved." As Jane wept, Churchill drew an arm about her shoulders and pulled her into his chest. Alexander had suspected something like this to be the case. Mary was not the only one with such acuity!

"And the Eltons?" Knightley probed. "What about the Westons?"

"No!" Miss Bates cried out. "You did not injure the Westons! Miss Taylor—that is Mrs. Weston now—and her babe! Please tell me, Mother, please!"

"Mrs. and Mr. Weston are well, as is the child," Alexander spoke up. "Miss Bennet discovered your plan, and we stopped them before they ate the pie you sent them. But why? What harm did they do you?"

In the horrified silence of the room, Mrs. Bates laughed. "Elton! He is a fool, a self-important popinjay! That was our parish, our living! Every penny he earned ought to come to us!"

The veneer of sanity that had gilded the woman's earlier words began to crumble. Age had indeed caused her soundness of mind to slip, and the stain of insanity was leaching through. "And Weston—hah! Had Abdy not stolen Mr. Bates' fortunes, we might have bought Randalls ourselves, and lived there off the rents in comfort and elegance. There, my dear Jane might have had her own music room, might have entertained the Baron Fallbrook from near Epsom, or the son of the Marquess, but instead, all that ought to have been ours is now hers! That Mrs. Weston—she who was a governess and ought to have remained in her station—took the place of my Jane, who truly deserved it all. It should have been ours!"

With that, the room erupted into a cacophony of cries and shouts of disbelief and horror, and Mrs. Bates began to cough without cease.

"Mother!" Miss Bates leapt up in alarm and rushed to the old lady's side. "Let me get your tea. Dolly!" she called, "Dolly, Mother's tea."

"My draught, Hetty," Mrs. Bates gasped between coughs. "The vial Mr. Perry just sent—I put it in the drawer."

Miss Bates searched for the bottle as Dolly tripped up the stairs with a pot and glass. "Not too hot, Ma'am, so as you can drink it," she placed the tray on the table by Mrs. Bates' side, looking with alarm upon the woman as she succumbed to spasm after spasm.

Miss Bates poured a cup of the liquid as her mother grabbed the vial and poured a drop into the teacup. Then, taking the cup, she turned the vial upside down, allowing the entire contents to spill into the cup and drank deeply.

"No!" Alexander saw too late what Mrs. Bates was doing. He sprang from his seat on the bench in a desperate attempt to somehow stop her, to send the cup flying from her hands, but she had already consumed the tea and the contents of the bottle. She had already begun to fall as he reached her, the moment of his panicked dash across the room seeming to have taken an hour. Every movement seemed slowed down, as if somebody held the hands of a clock in place and by doing so, slowed time itself to a crawl. His hand reached out in front of him, neither fast enough nor far enough to prevent the inevitable. All he could do, then, was catch her as her eyes rolled back and she slid from her chair. She began to gasp, not from her cough now, but from the shortness of breath that can come with the poison. He was too late! It had happened under his very eyes and he was too late.

"Brandy! Any spirits, quick!" His voice rasped in his ears as he cast about for anything he might find to counteract the effects of the poison. Somebody thrust a flask into his hand. He looked up to see Knightley standing above him, his face grim. "There's not much in there, but it's brandy."

Alexander pulled off the cap and emptied it into the gasping woman's mouth, then tilted her head back to try to make her swallow it. It was something, but not enough. Not nearly enough.

At the edges of his vision, he saw Cox patting at his own coat pockets, and then reach into one to withdraw a similar container. It, too, held a mere trickle of brandy. Why could he not associate with sots and drunkards? Such sober men as Cox and Knightley were better company most of the time, and most certainly his companions of choice, but at the moment he would have appreciated an unshaven lout stinking of ale and shoving a flagon of sweet cider into his hands.

He spun his head around, hoping for more spirits, or for something sweet. "Is there more tea? Tea with sugar? Any wine?"

Miss Bates had been standing by in shock, unable to speak for the first time since Alexander had met her, but within moments regained her senses enough to scurry for the bottle of wine she soon presented to him. This too was offered to the stricken woman, and Alexander watched as an awful repetition of the previous night's events at the Eltons was played out before him.

With the ministration of the spirits, Mrs. Bate stopped her gasping, but did not open her eyes. Neither did she respond to Knightley shouting into her ear and hitting the back of her hand. "She is breathing, but it is very weak, and I can hardly feel her heartbeat. She is not young." He looked up at the others. "Call Perry at once, but I cannot say I like this. Lyons? This is more your area than mine."

Alexander knelt by the old lady's side as Knightley sent the maid to summon Mr. Perry as quickly as he might come. He pulled off one of her slippers, ignoring the shock he heard voiced above his head. He tapped at the bottom of her feet, then ran the tip of a fingernail up her sole. There was no reaction. Then his fingers felt for a pulse at her neck; there was some movement, but it fluttered under his fingertips, scarcely noticeable, and his ears detected only the faintest sense of breath as he listened at her mouth and nose. This was not good. He suspected there was little Perry or anybody could do. Mrs. Bates had baked her last pie.

He rose and murmured as much into Knightley's ear, then turned to observe the room. The momentary silence that had rushed through the space when Mrs. Bates had fallen was now broken by the quiet sounds of anguish. Miss Bates was weeping into a handkerchief that looked not to be hers, with Cox standing at her side, looking this way and that, his feet shuffling and his fingers twitching. He seemed desperate for something to do but knew not where he was needed. Jane Fairfax was staring dumbfounded at the scene, silent and still with her eyes fixed upon the unmoving shape of her grandmother and a tragic expression upon her face. Frank Churchill still held her tight against his side, and Miss Fairfax looked as if she were relying on him and not her own strength to remain standing.

There was a grim look of determination on Knightley's face. He had seen death before and would see it again, but he must now act the magistrate, no matter that these were his friends. Alexander felt the struggle within the man as he fought the need to betray his emotions in favour of remaining the one source of strength in the room.

And then there was Mary. She was still sitting on the bench where he had pulled her when they entered. She looked utterly heartbroken. He knew she was somehow blaming herself for this. She would be strong and insist that she was fine, but some part of her would cry out that had she but done something a little differently, she might have prevented this. He understood. He felt exactly the same way. He stepped towards her and opened his mouth to speak, although he had no words. His eye caught hers instead, and held it for a minute, and he felt all her sadness and self-recrimination flood through the space between them. He only hoped that in his eyes, she saw his respect and care and support. He wished for nothing so much as to crush her to him as Churchill was doing with Miss Fairfax, but whereas in the solitude of the glade near Hartfield he might do so, here such an action would be seen as a declaration. He could not afford that. Not yet. Theirs would have to remain a friendship alone for some time longer.

He might not be able to follow his heart, but he could still help his friend. With a gesture of his head, he summoned Hugh Cox to a corner of the room where they could speak without being overheard.

"Cox, you might not like this, but the alternative will be worse." He glanced over at Mrs. Bates, who now lay on the small sofa by the window, Knightley at her side. "I do not think she will last more than another day, perhaps two at most. If you wish to marry Miss Bates, you should do so at once, unless you are prepared to wait the six months or year of mourning, as is your lady's wish. Once her mother passes, it will be a very long wait. I can send a messenger to the bishop at once to request a licence and Elton can perform the ceremony the moment the messenger returns."

Cox shook his head in confusion. "I had not thought of this. A licence? Not banns? But that is at some considerable expense, not that I would begrudge a penny for Henrietta… And this is hardly the time to marry, with her mother an acknowledged murderer and at death's door… I do not know… But a year! Whatever shall Hetty do for a year? She has little enough to live on, and I can give her a good home. Miss Fairfax as well. With her mother gone, spending that year in mourning alone… Yes. You are right. I shall speak to her now. The choice must be hers. If she agrees, we will have a wedding before a funeral. Please, Lyons, you know what must be done. I trust you to prepare the letters and requests, and I shall sign them forthwith."

The next hours passed in a haze of activity. The Bates' apartments were not far from the Crown, and Alexander chose to return to his rooms to gather the paper and draft the letters which Hugh Cox could then sign before sending to the bishop for the marriage licence. He did not wish to further importune Miss Bates with a request for such precious and costly supplies, and he knew he would write more clearly and concisely in the silence of his private space than in the subdued bustle of the apartments.

He set out the details of the case, explaining the exact reason for this request and the necessity of haste, and with his legal training at the fore, asserted that neither party, whose full names he would set out later, had any impediments whatsoever preventing their legal marriage. He added whatever other details and relevant pieces of information he could think of, and then, with his papers in hand, rushed back to the Bates' residence.

He had left the small company in the capable hands of Knightley and Mary. The former would ensure that every observance of the law was adhered to and would perform whatever tasks were necessary when Mr. Perry arrived. Alexander had considered asking Mary to accompany him to his rooms as he executed his tasks, but discarded that thought as quite out of the bounds of propriety and asked her, instead, if she were well enough to remain and assist Mr. Knightley and the others as needed.

She had agreed without hesitation. There would be little enough to do; Cox was there to comfort Miss Bates, and Churchill seemed to have taken a similar role with respect to Miss Fairfax. There remained only the tasks of taking Mrs. Bates to her bed and attending to whatever Perry and Knightley discovered needed doing.

He returned, therefore, with a messenger in his wake, ready to set off to the bishop the moment the ink from Cox's pen was dry. This was accomplished in minimal time; Miss Bates had agreed with the plan, and the messenger was sent off with all haste. He would arrive in good time, with the letters and payment for the licence in hand. Perry had arrived in the interim, his sombre expression mirroring Alexander's less expert impressions.

There was nothing left to do. He and Mary bid their quiet goodbyes to Knightley and slipped down the stairs and back to the street. He would leave the gig for Knightley. He needed to walk, to expunge the horror of what had just occurred from his senses. Without a word, he offered a hand to Mary, who took it and clung to him, and they wandered down lanes and alleys and paths until they were far from the sight of anybody they knew, and then, at last, he opened his arms to her. She fell into his embrace and returned it, and they stood there for a very long time, half hidden under the shadow of a stand of trees, clinging to each other until the tears ran dry.

Chapter Twenty-Two

A Fitting Conclusion

"Now, Mary," Elizabeth Darcy laughed, "you must begin again from the beginning, for I have quite lost the thread of your tale."

Mary, Alexander, the Darcys, and Mr. Knightley were all gathered in a bright parlour at Donwell Abbey the following evening. With the late nightfall, the sun was still high in the sky at seven o'clock, and the five were sitting in conversation as they awaited the summons to dinner.

When the Darcys had arrived in Highbury two hours before, Mary had rushed through her account of the last week's unusual events, but she knew well that Lizzy would not be satisfied with so brief a tale and was expecting to repeat her account. Thank heavens Alexander was there beside her to add those details that she had not known or had forgotten. The entire solution had been a joint accomplishment, after all, each of them fitting in some pieces of the puzzle, as if each had half of the verses of a charade or riddle, requiring the other's half before being able to declare the solution.

"I will gladly tell my tale, with Alexander's assistance, of course, but I have not seen him all day and I would first hear his news." Indeed, it had been a pleasant surprise when she arrived at Donwell with her brother and sister in response to Mr. Knightley's invitation, to find her friend already there and waiting. She turned her eyes to him and waited for his recitation.

It was very comfortable, this gathering of friends. Although Alexander and Darcy had begun their association when Darcy engaged the investigator to search for his missing sister, they had since allowed the connection to deepen to that of a comfortable friendship, and Mary noticed that her brother-in-law smiled more in Alexander's calm company than in that of anybody else of her (albeit limited) acquaintance, save her sister of course. If someone had told her, only a few months ago, that the dour and arrogant Mr. Darcy would be joking over a tankard of ale with a Scottish working man, she would have thought them quite mad. Darcy's acquaintance with Mr. Knightley was more conventional, for both were of similar class and temperament, and would have had ample opportunity to meet at some club or another in London. As for Alexander and Mr. Knightley, she had seen how well they had worked together over the last week. The only new connexion was between Mr. Knightley and Lizzy, and both were so friendly and of such happy temperament that they were sure to become friends within moments of meeting.

Thus it was that Alexander could relate the events of his day with the ease and comfort of a man surrounded by friends.

"I met with Cox and Mr. Knightley here quite early, just after sunrise." he spoke to Mary, although Mr. Knightley would have interest in his account as well. "The messenger would not return with the marriage licence until ten or so in the morning, and we had much to do before then. We rode off to Riverton to speak with Hesselgrave, as we had arranged. He had some small amount of information for us on the agreement with Elton and the dead men, but it all seems quite respectable. He also had no further information himself on the horse painting affair and the irregular races, but he was able to give us some names of men who might have been involved.

"After Cox and Mr. Knightley returned to the church for the wedding, I went to pay some visits and learned a lot. It turns out that Hesselgrave was not the only person who saw what he thought was his own horse performing beyond expectations in Carnes' fields. Carnes also painted his very fast horse to look identical to slower horses in the regular races. He would substitute the horses under some guise, whether with the owners' knowledge or not, depending on each circumstance, and would place great bets on the supposedly slow horse. When that horse won, his friends would make a great fortune with the odds and Carnes would take a portion of that take. I shall discover more as I investigate further over the next few days."

Knightley looked genuinely interested; Lizzy and Darcy were feigning smiles. Alexander apologised for this diversion and asked Mr. Knightley to continue with his part of the tale. The magistrate cleared his throat and spoke. "Cox and I returned to the inn to find the messenger just returned. He had with him the requested licence for Miss Bates and Cox to marry, and we gathered them at the altar of Elton's church at once. They were safely wed before eleven o'clock, and all was pronounced proper as they signed the register."

"I am so pleased!" Mary could not hold in her pleasure despite the pall that hung over the wedding. "Poor Miss Bates... I mean Mrs.

Cox. But I am glad that she will have a husband to stand with her and comfort her over the coming difficult months."

"Indeed," Mr. Knightley added. "It will be impossible to keep the news quiet here that her mother was a murderer. But in London, where she will be known only as Mrs. Cox, that stain will not destroy her name, and she will be able to present herself as any good wife mourning the loss of a parent."

"And Miss Fairfax?" This was Alexander's question. Mary had some suspicions after her day with Emma, but looked to Mr. Knightley, who seemed to know much of what went on in Highbury.

"She will marry Frank Churchill." He looked at Mary, but she refused to react. She had never felt anything other than disinterested friendship for the man. He was smart and funny and handsome, to be sure, but he was not the one for her. She was pleased for Jane, although she considered the couple mismatched. "They had hoped to keep their engagement a secret, for his aunt would not approve of her genteel poverty, but it is unlikely that the news will not be spread about town before long. Perhaps his uncle will be kinder to him; or perhaps, if the rumours of Mrs. Churchill's health are true, it will not be an issue. Regardless, they will wait for a respectable time, perhaps six months or a year. In the interim, Jane will take up residence at Hartfield, so she may be near her betrothed when he visits his father and his wife."

He gave a twisted smile. "Emma is none too pleased, for Miss Fairfax is the only lady I know of whom she is jealous, but it will be for the good. Emma has begun to improve considerably of late. Many of her prejudices seem to have been removed from her eyes, and she has learned where she has been lacking. I quite like this new Emma."

Mary suspected that long before Jane and Frank Churchill stood at the altar, Emma and Mr. Knightley would be there. Her eyes drifted to Alexander, and from the half smile and expression on his face, he thought quite the same thing.

"What of Mrs. Bates?" Mary asked now. She had heard no news, good or bad, all day, for she had been sequestered at Hartfield with Emma and Harriet, and had only made her escape when news came that the Darcys had arrived at the inn.

"She is alive still, or rather, she was when last I heard," Mr. Knightley intoned. He would mourn the lady as well. She had been one of his circle, his friend. "I believe Cox will send a note the moment... the moment anything happens." It would not be long, perhaps hours, perhaps less.

There was silence for a few moments before Elizabeth spoke again. "Now, if you do not mind, Mary, I really must hear your story again. I shall listen very attentively and shan't interrupt once."

"Or perhaps twice," her husband interjected with a smile Mary had never thought to see on his face.

"Very well, twice. Three times at most." Elizabeth beamed at Darcy, who mumbled something about impertinent and headstrong women, whilst never taking his eyes—or smile—off her for a moment.

Mary now began to repeat her tale. She told them once more about the drowning of Harry Carnes, which had seemed to be one more in a series of unrelated and inexplicable deaths, and of the slow work involved in finding the connexion between the dead men.

"It seemed, at first, that the matter connecting them was this recent breeding and training business begun by Mr. Carnes and supported primarily by Mr. Hesselgrave's investments. Under the terms of the agreement, as presented by the attorney in Dorking, upon the death or deaths of any investors, the surviving party would gain their portion of profits, and for a long time, every evidence pointed to Mr. Elton as being that sole surviving signatory. He had also recently depleted his account at the Bank of England by the great sum of fifteen thousand pounds, which gave him great motivation for such a terrible spree." Even Mr. Darcy whistled at the mention of that enormous amount of money. She had not known the man could whistle.

"What turned your thoughts otherwise?" that gentleman asked.

It was Alexander who answered. "When Mrs. Elton nearly succumbed to the poison, his shock was palpable. He is a man of many failings, but I believe he loves his wife—and he deserves her—and would not seek to harm her, let alone kill her. He was either a better actor than any who has graced the stages in London, or his horror and dismay at her illness were genuine. When I mentioned the poison, I thought he might swoon. That set the first germs of doubt sprouting. When, the following morning, we encountered Mr. Hesselgrave, hale and hearty and very much alive, it further weakened our case. When Elton finally disclosed the purpose behind the withdrawal of the fifteen thousand pounds, we were satisfied that it was quite unrelated to our inquiries. Without knowledge of the poison and without a motive, Mr. Elton began to look guiltless in this matter."

"Was he the only one you suspected?" Elizabeth was sitting at the edge of her comfortable seat, her hands clasped and her face a picture of glee. She was enjoying this far too much; it had not been so long before that she had been the primary suspect in a gruesome murder. Perhaps, thought Mary, this was one way of recovering from her own ordeal.

"I considered everybody," Alexander replied, "although not all quite as seriously as others. Mr. Churchill loomed quite large in my suspicions for a time. His main crime was to arrive in the area exactly at the time of the first death, that of Jack Smith, the tramp."

"That would raise some eyebrows," Mr. Darcy commented.

"The events were indeed related," Mary now added, "but not quite as anybody thought. When Jane Fairfax returned to her family from her prolonged stay with the Campbells, Mrs. Bates, in the confusion of mind brought about by her age, settled on the plan of punishing those whom she saw as responsible for her granddaughter's sad plight of having to find a position. Thus, it was Jane's arrival that precipitated Mr. Smith's death. The tramp had never ceased coming to the Bates' kitchen and asking for food, and on that day, Mrs. Bates gave him a tart or pie to which she had added her poison. I now recall hearing of the kindness the Bateses showed him, giving him food when they themselves relied so much on the goodness of others. It seems that Mrs. Bates was, perhaps, not so very kind."

"And Mr. Churchill?" Darcy asked.

"His arrival, too, was all due to the presence of the beautiful Miss Fairfax. They were secretly engaged, and when she returned to the village, he finally found sufficient incentive to pay a long-due visit to his father and new mother. But Churchill had no quarrel whatsoever with Smith, not did he do the tramp any harm."

"However did you decide to look elsewhere?" Elizabeth asked. "If so much pointed towards this enterprise with the horses, what made you change your thinking?"

Mary felt herself puff up a bit. This had been her idea. She had only had to convince Alexander of the right of it, although, to his credit, he had listened and taken her comments right away. "It was Mrs. Bates herself who first put the idea into my mind. During some of her moments of lucidity, she complained about some scheme that was devised when her husband was alive and was vicar here. John Abdy, one of the victims, was the man who conceived of it, and it was he whom she most blamed for the loss of their fortune and her family's impoverishment. Every victim was somehow involved in that event twenty years ago, whether in reality, or in her mind. She blamed the Eltons because Mr. Elton holds the living Mr. Bates held, and therefore receives the income her addled brain told her ought to go to her granddaughter, and she blamed the Westons because she believed she ought to have enough money to have purchased Randalls herself. Their possession of it, therefore, was a sort of theft in her mind."

She glanced around at the others. They were all sitting rapt by her account. She might be most comfortable hidden behind a book, but she had learned, this past week, that there was pleasure to be gained from being the centre of somebody's attention, and she was most certainly enjoying that role right now. She sat up and straightened her shoulders and continued.

"It was at dinner at Randalls only two days ago, when Mrs. Bates told me once more about this scheme, and how the victims got what they had coming to them. I thought little of it then, but her words stayed in my mind.

"But what turned those words into knowledge was the dog. Or rather, the dogs."

Elizabeth cocked her head and a furrow formed between her pretty eyes. Darcy peered at her in confusion, and Mr. Knightley clucked his tongue. Only Alexander smiled. "Clever girl!" he whispered, and Mary felt he was proud of her.

"Mr. Cox, Alexander's friend from London, has a brother here in Highbury, and that man's daughter had a favourite dog. Three days ago, the poor dog died suddenly, and it seemed the animal had got into something in the rubbish that had killed it. But the very next day, Miss Bates told us about how she, too, had lost a dog only last autumn, at about the time that Mrs. Bates was recovering from a very bad cold. That pet, too, had died very suddenly whilst Mrs. Bates was baking her pies. It seemed a sad coincidence and nothing else, but when paired with Mrs. Bates' words, it became more ominous. Then I recalled that Mr. Cox, the local attorney, had lent a hand in old Mr. Abdy's scheme, and I realised that he, too, had played a part in the loss of the Bates' fortune. It seemed that Mrs. Bates had devised her murderous scheme several months ago and had tested her idea on her daughter's poor dog.

"The poison that killed Chloe Cox's pet was intended for the family. Latrax merely did what unsupervised dogs do, and helped himself to a treat, to his detriment and to the family's great distress. I hate to think what might have happened had the dog behaved himself."

Those looks of interest were now expressions of horror.

"Oh, how terrible!" Elizabeth breathed. Mary concurred. It was too awful to imagine.

"But what was the poison? An old lady like Mrs. Bates hardly has access to the sort of thing that killed four people and nearly killed several more. What did Mr. Lyons say it was? Prussic acid?"

"This, too, was something that kept me from alighting upon her for the longest time," Mary told her sister. "Mrs. Bates had had a bad cold last autumn, as I mentioned. She had asked for, and been given, laurel water for her cough by Mr. Perry, the apothecary. When she began to cough again this week, Miss Bates could not find the vial from some months ago, and she needed another. I offered to walk past Mr. Perry's shop on my way back to Hartfield to request some more. He is a friendly, talkative man, and he mentioned how Mrs. Bates relied on old medications, although they were not always the best or the safest, as well as how Mrs. Bates knew how to dilute it suitably to render it curative and not dangerous.

"When Alexander told me about the incident with Mrs. Elton, and how he had smelled the Prussic acid then, I asked where such a vile substance might be found. He explained that it is not at all uncommon and cited laurel water as one source. When I began to think about the dogs, and Mrs. Bates' cold, and the missing vial from the autumn, suddenly I knew exactly what had happened."

"Mrs. Bates used her medication to poison the pies." Darcy sighed and shook his head in distress.

Mr. Knightley turned to his guest. "Rest assured, my friend, there will be no pie at dinner tonight."

"I am glad to hear it!"

"The poison smells rather of almonds," Alexander added, "and as such, it was almost undetectable in the cherry pies, which often have almond in them. If I recall from my mother's kitchen, laurel water was sometimes used in miniscule amounts to add almond flavour. It is only in higher concentrations that it is so dangerous. In Mrs. Bates' pies, it was almost undetectable. Those poor men never knew what happened."

There was another moment when words seemed unfitting for the sombre mood.

The silence was broken by the sound of the door opening. A footman stepped through and announced in a clear voice, "Dinner is prepared."

Mr. Knightley rose. "Let us go in and make a toast to a happier time ahead."

The others concurred with great vigour.

"How long do you stay in the neighbourhood, Darcy?" he asked as they filed into the dining room. This was a small enough and comfortable enough group that there was no formality, no distinction of rank or fortune. They filtered through the doorway to take whichever seat pleased them at the table.

"A week, perhaps more should I find a reason to further examine the estate, or should my wife or sister enjoy the area."

"I hope you will like it very much," Mr. Knightley smiled. "I have found it some of the loveliest in England."

"And you, Lyons?" Darcy asked his friend.

Alexander looked over to Mary. "I have great hopes of completing my other investigation within a day or two, thanks to the information Hesselgrave offered us. At that time, I have nothing that calls me back to London immediately." His eyes were hopeful.

Darcy did not disappoint. "Then, I must insist that you spend some time with us at the house I have taken. There are rooms enough, and a small but adequate staff, and I am promised that there is an excellent cook as well."

Mary beamed. It would be quite acceptable to come to better know Alexander Lyons when there were no dead bodies to reckon with, or murders to solve.

Alexander beamed back at her. "I would be delighted, my friend. But I have one request. Please, no cherry pies!"

The End

Historical Notes

Horse Painting

As bizarre as it seems, horse painting was a thing! From the late nineteen-teens to the thirties, Peter Christian Barrie ran a lucrative, if covert, business painting horses, disguising one as another to confound the odds-makers at the races in a scam known as Ringing.

With a combination of bleach, hennas, expensive dyes, and a great deal of patience and talent, Barrow could paint thoroughbred horses so convincingly that even their jockeys and owners could not tell them apart. He would then run a fast horse in place of a slow horse, and everyone would think the slow horse was just having a particularly good day. And he and his investors would clean up at the betting tables.

He was unmatched in his painting skills, but not always in other aspects of the grift. Josh Nathan-Kazis explains in his article "History's Greatest Horse Racing Cheat and His Incredible Painting Trick" on Narratively.com"

In one baroque disaster in the fall of 1919, recounted in the turf writer David Ashforth's 2003 book Ringers & Rascals, which contains the definitive modern account of Barrie's life and works, Barrie dyed a 3-year-old named

Mexican Belle to look like a particular 2-year-old filly. Then he doped her with opium to slow her down for a race in South Yorkshire. Two days later he entered her again, thinking her poor previous showing would guarantee long odds. Hoping to goose her speed, he gave her twice the dosage of cocaine [which he used to give the horse an extra burst of speed] he usually administered to his starters. Mexican Belle, high as hell, chewed through her reins, ran free, and finished dead last.

Our fictional Harry Carnes, it seems, was in good company!

The Assassination of Spencer Perceval

O n May 11, at about 5:15 in the evening, British Prime Minister Spencer Perceval was fatally shot in the lobby of the House of Commons. He is the only prime minister to have met such a fate. His attacker was a businessman named John Bellingham.

Bellingham was born around 1770 in Huntingdonshire. His father died while he was still a child, and the family lived with assistance from his mother's brother-in-law, William Daw. When Bellingham grew up, Daw saw him first to the position of a junior officer on a British East India Company ship, and later as a tin plate manufacturer in London. Both ventures were failures, however, and Bellingham narrowly avoided debtor's prison. He now decided to change his ways and took a position as bookkeeper in a company that dealt with trade with Russia. He was successful enough at this that he was appointed the firm's representative in Archangel, Russia in 1800.

By 1804 he had returned to England and set up his own business in Liverpool. That year he travelled back to Archangel to oversee some dealings there. He had secured a pass for him, his wife, and infant son to travel to St. Petersburg, but his pass was rescinded by local authorities and he was arrested as being responsible for a supposed unpaid debt by a business associate. Despite an attempt at intervention by Lord Granville Leveson-Gower, the British ambassador in St. Petersburg, Bellingham was imprisoned from February to November of 1805. He sought redress with the Russian government, but only succeeded in angering them, and he was imprisoned again from mid-1806 to late 1809.

He finally returned home to England and set about demanding compensation for his ordeal from the British government, whom he considered to blame for ignoring his constant appeals for help. He petitioned the Foreign Office, the Treasury, the Privy Council, and Prime Minister Perceval himself, but all pleas were denied. In 1811 he returned to his wife in Liverpool, but he could not abandon his need for justice, and in February of 1812 he returned to London to renew his cause. He met with failure. Seeing no other means of redress, he decided to exact retribution through violence. On April 20, 1812, he purchased two pistols and had a tailor sew an inside pocket into one of his coats.

He carried out the killing in the early evening of May 11, just as parliament was preparing for its evening session. He could have escaped in the chaos that followed the shooting, but instead he sat quietly on a bench until he was seized by an official who had witnessed the event. He submitted without a struggle. When questioned as to why he had done it, he replied that he was rectifying a denial of justice on the part of the government.

Bellingham was detained and sent to trial for the murder of Spencer Perceval four days later. He was deemed to be insane and was convicted and sentenced to hang. He died on the gallows at Newgate Prison on May 18, 1812.

More from Mary and Alexander

You can read about Alexander Lyon's first case with Mr. Darcy in the prequel novella, **The Mystery of the Missing Heiress**, and Mary and Alexander's first case together in **Death of a Clergyman: A Pride and Prejudice Mystery**.

Turn the page for a taste of Mary and Alexander's next mystery, **Death of a Dandy: A Mansfield Park Mystery**.

from

Miss Mary Investigates 3:

Death of a Dandy: A Mansfield Park Mystery

Chapter 1 ~ Breaking the Journey

The house was quite fine, grand, even. Mary Bennet gazed around the drawing room, appreciating the clean, modern room with its elegant furnishings and accoutrements. It bespoke both wealth and taste, a combination most often distinguished by its absence. Pale butter-yellow wallpaper was broken into panels of pleasing proportions by mannerist columns in fresh white paint, which also covered the carved archway that led to the study beyond and the mouldings that flanked the high white ceiling. She closed her eyes and leaned back in her comfortable chair, ignoring for a moment the cup of tea and plate of biscuits that sat on the small round table to her side, and let out a long breath of relief.

"Is everything to your satisfaction, Miss Bennet?" Mrs. Meldola leaned forward in her own chair, keeping her voice low. She was a petite woman with dark hair and bright eyes, and possessed of a gentle manner. Her dress recommended her station as mistress of this beautiful house—elegant and modern and expensive, with none of the excess of the first circles of society. She was about thirty years of age, the wife of a successful businessman in Northampton, who was a particular friend of Alexander Lyons, Mary's friend and her escort on this journey.

"Yes, yes indeed, I thank you." Mary stifled a yawn. "I am merely fatigued by the journey. The tea and biscuits will certainly revive me."

Her hostess gave a sympathetic smile that promised understanding and turned to her husband and Alexander. This small, kind gesture was as welcome as diamonds to Mary, allowing her to enjoy the sweet nourishment without the necessity of providing sparkling conversation when she desired only quiet and a few moments alone, in mind if not in body. She sent a grateful smile back towards Mrs. Meldola for her consideration and sank further into her chair.

If one required sparkling conversation, Lizzy was the one to provide it. Mary had been parted from her dear sister, now Mrs. Darcy, for only two days, and already she missed her. But after more than a month at Pemberley with Lizzy and Darcy and the new baby, it had been time to return home to Longbourn. How fortunate that Alexander had been passing through Derbyshire exactly when Mary was preparing for her return journey. He had spent three days at Pemberley to visit his friend Darcy and bring a present for the tiny heir to the estate, and had offered to accompany Mary home.

It was a remarkable coincidence, Mary now considered, that Alexander had been called to Yorkshire as part of one of his investigations six weeks before. He had accompanied Mary northward then, when he had learned of her planned visit. The investigation, he informed her, was one driven more by a need for accuracy and attention, and less by the need for haste, and he was able, therefore, to time his own journey to coincide with hers. And now, just over a month later, he was returning from his home near Glasgow. It was rather too convenient, and she mentally chastised her brother Darcy for arranging matters thus. For she was certain it had been his fingers stirring this pudding. She let out a huff and hoped that none of her companions had heard her. They all seemed quite immersed in their conversation about Alexander's visit home and his sister's wedding.

Mr. Meldola pressed for details. "Tell me, Alex, of Sarah's husband. I can hardly imagine her as a married woman, for in my mind, she is still a girl of thirteen. Can it really have been so long since last I saw her?"

Mary sat back with her eyes half-closed and listened to Alexander relate what he knew of Abel Miller, the goldsmith, and aspects of the wedding. The details seemed strange to Mary's inattentive ears, but things might be different in Scotland, she presumed. Her eyes fluttered closed, and she allowed her thoughts to wander as the conversation washed over her like a warm blanket.

She had stayed in this house with the Meldolas on their journey northward and was happy to renew the acquaintance now. She had liked Mrs. Meldola, but had had little time to converse with the lady, for the night of their arrival had coincided with a gathering of local merchants in the house's large salon at the front of the house. The carriage which Alexander—or Darcy—had hired had arrived shortly before dark, and already some early comers for the gathering could be heard talking. With all due attention, Mrs. Meldola had shown her to a small but comfortable bedroom and had had extended an invitation to dine with her in her chambers whilst the gentleman convened below. Mary had demurred, citing a wish not to intrude on the lady's time and privacy, but Mrs.

Meldola had glanced around her and then whispered, "perhaps we may creep down the to kitchens then, and pretend to be children hoping for some of the extra tarts and treats from the cook's table!" She had emitted a giggle most unbecoming to the wife of an esteemed leader of the merchant class, but which had endeared her to Mary, and the two had followed through on this plan.

They took their meal of a tasty pie with bread and vegetables and a selection of fruits for afters and had talked of such inconsequential matters as the state of the roads and the comfort of the inn where they had stayed, and whether Mary's maid Alice, who also served as chaperone, was in need of anything.

This pleasant conversation was interrupted by Mr. Meldola, who burst in with all apologies, but, "Bertram is here once more, quite uninvited. He followed Framington to beg for the loan of more funds to repay somebody or another, and fell down quite drunk on the floor. Oh, dreadfully sorry, Miss Bennet!" Mary had been sitting on the side of the table furthest from the door, out of the direct line of vision of a newcomer, and Mr. Meldola only seemed now to notice that his wife was not alone. He executed a neat bow, but kept to his task. "Shouldn't discuss such matters before company, but..." his eyes wandered around the very informal environs of the kitchen and he shrugged.

"Again?" Mrs. Meldola huffed an errant curl of black hair from her high forehead, then tucked it into her cap. "I shall ask Mrs. Nicholls to set up the brown room for him. Can some of your companions help carry him upstairs when the room is ready?"

These were not the manners of the upper classes, but Mary did not mind them, finding them comfortable rather than forced and by no means disrespectful. Although she wished to leave the couple alone to discuss their unwelcome guest, the doorway to the stairs lay at the far end of the kitchen and she would have to pass by both master and mistress to achieve it. Instead of calling attention to herself by interrupting their hurried discussion, she willed herself to vanish into the walls. She had often considered herself nigh on invisible, knowing how her presence was so often ignored by those around her, and already once this evening Mr. Meldola had failed to notice her in the room. She shuffled backwards on the bench upon which she sat and fell into herself.

As if her wish had become reality, the couple continued their conversation as if she were not there, discussing whether to send for Bertram's valet, or whether to keep his whereabouts quiet for the evening. From what Mary gathered, it was not the first time the man had required a place to sleep off his drink, nor the first in which he was hoping to avoid a creditor or other such person. Who he was, Mary could not determine, but he seemed rather a wild and unsavoury sort and she wondered at the connexion with the respectable and amiable Meldolas.

At last, a decision having been reached, Mr. Meldola looked up once more and seeing Mary, blinked. "You must think us quite uncivilised, Miss Bennet..." he began, but Mary assured him she thought no such thing.

"Your civility is better demonstrated in your wish to help this man than in any display of outward polish, which is by no means lacking!" she hurried to add.

"Go on to your guests, Elijah," Mrs. Meldola squeezed her husband's hands. "I'll ready the room. Oh, Mrs. Nicholls..." she called through an open doorway on the far side of the hearth.

Mary took this as her opportunity to escape and bid both master and mistress a good evening before disappearing up the stairs to her own rooms as quickly as she could, wondering all the time about the unfortunate Bertram.

That had been the last of her conversation with Mrs. Meldola until her arrival once again this very evening. The journey back to Longbourn was five and sixty miles, too far to travel in one day, but very easy to complete in two, and there was no need for an early start in the morning. There would be plenty of time to converse at leisure before their carriage was called.

The hum of conversation pulled Mary out of her reveries. Of course... she was back in the comfortable yellow drawing room, her tea growing cool at her elbow, Alexander still telling his old friend Meldola about Sarah's wedding and his mother and sisters back in the village near Glasgow. Alexander glanced up at her and gave a quick smile. Had she fallen asleep? Had he noticed? They had their differences, she and he, but he was far too much of a gentleman to draw attention to her *faux pas*.

He now turned the subject to his days spent at Pemberley with Darcy and Elizabeth and the babe, allowing Mary to ease her way back into the conversation, and by the time she had told her new friends of the sweet young infant and her sister's glowing health and exultant joy, she was feeling very much back to full vigour. Those few moments of reverie had revived her completely.

Therefore she was quite alert when, a few minutes later, the housekeeper Mrs. Nicholls bustled into the room, leading a rather distraught-looking man of middle years and the mannerisms of a valet.

"Barnaby!" Mr. Meldola exclaimed.

"Most dreadfully sorry to disturb you in such a rude manner," the man's accent was impeccable, his gestures perfect. But his voice and face were laden with a panic which must surely explain his unbecoming intrusion into a man's private drawing room.

"Speak, please," Meldola rose from his seat.

"I have been seeking Mr. Bertram. He did not return to his rooms last night and has not been seen in any of the..." he cleared his throat and reddened. "In any of the usual places. I hoped he might have taken some refuge here, as I know he sometimes does." His eyes pled with the two Meldolas.

"I am afraid I cannot help you," Mr. Meldola spoke in a tight voice. "I have not seen him, nor heard word of him, in about six weeks, not since the last time he, er, requested a bed for the night."

Barnaby staggered to a chair and seemed about to collapse into it before remembering his status as a valet in the house of an esteemed merchant.

"Then I am most afraid," he choked, "that Tom Bertram has disappeared."

Watch out for Death in Highbury at your favourite bookseller soon!

About the Author

Riana Everly was born in South Africa, but has called Canada home since she was eight years old. She has a Master's degree in Medieval Studies and is trained as a classical musician, specialising in Baroque and early Classical music. She first encountered Jane Austen when her father handed her a copy of *Emma* at age 11, and has never looked back.

Riana now lives in Toronto with her family. When she is not writing, she can often be found playing string quartets with friends, biking around the beautiful province of Ontario with her husband, trying to improve her photography, thinking about what to make for dinner, and, of course, reading!

If you enjoyed this novel, please consider posting a review at your favourite bookseller's website.

Riana Everly loves connecting with readers on Facebook at facebook.com/RianaEverly/

Also, be sure to check out her website at rianaeverly.com for sneak peeks at coming works and links to works in progress!

Also by Riana Everly

Teaching Eliza: Pride and Prejudice Meets Pygmalion

The Assistant: Before Pride and Prejudice

Through a Different Lens: A Pride and Prejudice Variation

The Bennet Affair: A Pride and Prejudice Variation

The Mystery of the Missing Heiress

Death of a Clergyman: A Pride and Prejudice Mystery

www.ingramcontent.com/pod-product-compliance
Lightning Source LLC
Chambersburg PA
CBHW060235100726

47907CB00003B/642

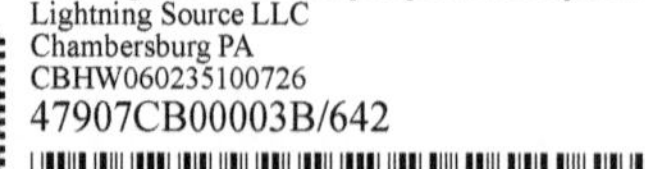